OVER THE RAIL

LYNN STEWART

UP WIND SYSTEMS, LLC

For Sweet Petunia

We're all a little weird. And life is a little weird. And when we find someone whose weirdness is compatible with ours, we join up with them and fall into mutually satisfying weirdness—and call it love—true love.

— ROBERT FULGHUM

1

Darlene saw them. She was not supposed to see them, but there they were, a little more than a hundred feet away, right where the waves were breaking. She pressed her back against the dune and brought her knees close to her chest. The wind had picked up, and the unseasonably mild November afternoon grew colder by the second, chilling her heart. She craned her neck to get a better look at the woman but could not make out her nuances. Darlene did not want to believe it, so she made up her own story about the couple frolicking near the waves. Maybe married, maybe not, escaping to the beach for a weekend. The man beaming as the woman swats his ass—private humor, a language known only to them. The scene was so absurd that a giggle shot out of Darlene's mouth. Her own husband of twenty-five years jogging (stopping mid-stride for a kiss and an ass swat) with 'the love of his life' as he'd described this woman seventy-two hours ago. The giggle morphed into a series of sobs. She had cried more in the past three days than she could remember crying in her entire life.

She lifted the bottom of her sweatshirt and wiped her nose. Screw it. She blew, right into the soft cotton. She held the shirt up with her teeth and grabbed a fistful of belly flesh. She could understand if

Denny had announced that he was leaving her for someone younger, thinner. But this? This woman who was now barely a spec on the horizon. From what Darlene had gleaned a few minutes ago, this woman was not much thinner than she was. More toned, yes, but not much thinner. And from what she could see, not that much younger either. Darlene raked her frizzy curls with her hand. Longer hair— that was another thing Denny's light-o'-love had. Longer hair.

The one-legged seagull that she had been feeding hopped toward her, positioning himself on a smaller sand dune, against the fence. In all her anguish, with the hours and days melding into a blob of heartache, she had enough forethought to grab a slice of bread on her way out the door. She tore a chunk off, tossed it to the bird, and scanned the horizon for Denny and his—what, exactly, was this woman to him? Girlfriend? Adulteress, obviously. But how does Denny introduce her? Partner? Lover? Soul mate? Pookie? Darlene did not even know the woman's name. Oh, sure, Denny had wanted to share everything—how long the affair had been going on, his girl-friend's name, her favorite food. No! She didn't want to hear any of it and plugged her ears with her fingers. Before she had a chance to escape into another room, he blurted out that they'd met at work— female quality control inspectors for commercial construction were apparently not very common. How did this woman end up capturing Denny's heart, and not one of his single colleagues?

Yeah, hindsight. Beautiful, marvelous hindsight. She should have known something was up when Denny, out of the blue, took up jogging last year. Right here at the beach, the week they spent with Shelly before sending her off to Colorado for veterinary school. Denny, with his paunch and love of the couch, suddenly jogging. In the months that followed, his work garb morphed from old Dickies and ratty golf shirts to new Dickies and crisp button-on down shirts in fun colors. She mentioned it once during an insecure moment when she wondered if he had been trying to impress someone else.

"I'm tired of walking around the job sites looking ratty," he'd said. No other explanation was given. Darlene wouldn't let it go. Every time he wore something new, she followed him around, grilling him.

"What do you want me to tell you? That I'm seeing someone?" He threw his hands up in frustration.

"Are you?"

"Of course not. God, Darlene, what's the matter with you?"

She'd been blind. That's what was the matter with her. She'd been blind. When she suggested counseling, he agreed, but not without a lot of grumbling. Several weeks in, she thought things were improving.

"Let's buy a beach condo," she'd said one night after what she thought had been a productive session with their counselor; Denny had gone the entire hour without complaining about her weight. They were sitting on opposite ends of the couch watching a house-hunting reality show on TV. "It would give us quality time together away from here. We could drive down once a month, even in the winter." She grew more excited by the second. "And we could spend a week or two in the summer."

Denny shrugged. "Sure. Why not?"

The thought of buying a weekend place gave her hope. It seemed like a perfectly sensible idea, especially since they rent a condo in Ocean City almost every summer. "Denny, look!" She pointed at the TV screen. "They're taking applications to be on the show!"

He smoothed his hair and smiled. "I'm pretty photogenic." He looked at Darlene, and his smile disappeared. "They'd never take us."

"Maybe I'll start running. I can sign up for one of those couch-to-5K programs." She moved to his side of the couch and put her hand on his thigh, no longer interested in the TV show.

"You hate running." He sat up and slid his leg out from under her hand. "Why don't you just stick with your yoga?" And that was the end of that.

Of course, she knew better now. Denny hadn't started jogging for jogging's sake—it was an opportunity to form a connection with that woman. The seagull bolted as she threw the last piece of bread.

"Birdie, I'm so sorry!" She'd been pelting him with bread for the past few minutes and didn't even realize it. "I really am sorry. Please come back." The seagull maintained his safe distance. *Poor, innocent creature.* She should be throwing bread at Denny. Nope. Not bread. Bricks. Cinderblocks. Concrete slabs.

Horrified at what she was apparently capable of thinking, she called Laurie, the realtor who had sold them their condo last year, her only friend at the beach. "I can't do the show."

"Nonsense. Of course, you can."

"Didn't you get my voicemail?" When had Darlene left the voicemail, anyway? Yesterday? The day before? She didn't know.

"Yes. You babbled a lot. I called you back, but you never answered." Laurie exhaled. "I figured I'd see you tonight for drinks like we talked about."

Darlene hadn't babbled. She knew she hadn't. She replayed the words she'd spoken into the phone: *Denny is leaving me. We're filming the show in three days. I don't know what to do.* What had she expected from Laurie? After all, she was not a close friend—just a situational one. Darlene didn't know who else to call. She didn't want to call the show's producers. And since Laurie was going to play realtor on the show, well, it made sense at the time. So, she'd called and left a voicemail. Now she regretted it.

"Look, Denny is here with his girlfriend. I can't do the show." She looked at her watch—the time matched the demise of the setting sun. She pictured Denny and his girlfriend in the shower, soaping each other up after their invigorating jog. She swallowed, unprepared for another cascade of tears. She took a deep breath and pinched the bridge of her nose.

"They're staying in the condo with you?"

"God, no." She stood, brushing sand off the back of her legs. "He still wants to do the show. I don't know why, but he does."

"So do the show."

Easier said than done. She simply did not know how she could go on camera with her face red, puffy and blotchy, looking like she was about to go into anaphylactic shock. Or standing next to Denny and having to suppress the urge to punch him. Or hang onto his leg like a toddler, begging him not to leave her.

"I want to sell the damned condo. I want no part of it. I want no part of the show." She shuffled up the beach access path, stopping in front of the steps leading to her balcony. She sat on the third step, slowly becoming aware of the smell of steak. She turned her head and saw the grill on the next-door neighbor's balcony, curls of smoke rising to the heavens. She felt nauseous.

"Of course, I'll help you sell the condo. But for now, you need to suck it up and do the show. The time to cancel would have been weeks ago, a month ago even. Not the day before. I'm sorry. Your hands are tied." Laurie paused. "So, I'll see you later for a glass of wine?"

"No. I can't do it," Darlene mumbled as she climbed the steps, her legs, leaden. "I'm not feeling well."

2

Perfect. Fran's briquettes teetered between flaming red and pinkish gray. He held his hands over the grill, enjoying the warmth. The woman sitting against the dunes, just beyond their row of condos, tossed something at a bedraggled-looking seagull. He stood on his balcony and watched, getting the distinct impression that she was either angry or distraught. Maybe a little of both. She continued pelting the bird with...rocks? Bread? Bread, he hoped. Earlier today, he watched her banging around on her balcony next door, right over the rail. She seemed so focused fluffing pillows on balcony chairs and sweeping up late autumn debris that she didn't notice him watching. Who puts out pillows this time of year, anyway? Strange.

"Yikes! My charcoal!" Fran opened the sliding glass door. Four, long-legged strides later, he was in the kitchen. He transferred the hunk of meat—swimming in a sea of soy sauce, brown sugar, mustard, garlic, pepper, and a few shakes of Worcestershire sauce— to a plate and carried it outside. He carefully laid the steak on the grill. Thankfully, the charcoals hadn't yet passed their prime. He closed his eyes as the meat sizzled.

"And the aroma pleased the Lord." Exodus, Leviticus, Genesis. So many references to smell in scripture. Fran remembered about twenty of them but knew there were more. "Then Aaron's sons shall burn it on the altar on top of the burnt offering, which is on the wood on the fire; it is a food offering with a pleasing aroma to the Lord. Leviticus 3:5." He recited the scripture out loud. For some reason, it was one of the few verses Fran remembered, word for word, from his short stint at seminary, nearly forty years ago.

He kept one eye on the steak and one eye on the woman sitting against the dune. The seagull, apparently frustrated with getting pelted, had moved away and was no longer beside her. He could hear the faint sound of her voice but couldn't make out the words. Talking to the waves? Or an invisible person sitting beside her. He curled his thumb and rubbed it along the smooth circle of his wedding ring. He promised to never take it off. Two years after his wife died, he still couldn't bring himself to remove his ring. Not even a silly little thing like death could make him take it off. Nope. Never.

He took a deep breath and flipped the steak, basting it with the reserved marinade. The woman yelled, pumping her fist into the air. He thought about what his sister, Laurie, had told him about the couple who bought the condo next door. *Bastard husband.* He felt sorry for the woman, truly. Laurie had warned him about the chaos that might erupt over the next few days. Tomorrow in particular. He honestly did not understand the appeal of those house-hunting reality shows. But what he really didn't understand was how this couple had owned the condo for a year, and he had never met them. For weekend people, they certainly did not spend a lot of weekends here.

He covered the grill and went into the house for a beer. Maybe he should walk down to the dune and introduce himself. Offer to throw a steak on the grill for her? No pressure, she could take it to her condo and eat it alone, if she wanted. But he only defrosted one, and dammit, he wasn't about to share his ribeye. It was big, fat, and juicy; he planned to eat the whole damned thing. The one upside to being alone—if there could possibly be an upside—was that he could eat steak whenever he wanted. Without eye rolls or reminders that his doctor wanted him off red meat. He patted his gut. Flat. Still. He hadn't biked in over two years and only exercised sporadically but continued to be a bottomless pit. He knew he had to be more circumspect now, especially given his kidney issues. But dammit, he only ate steak once in a blue moon. And when he did, by golly, he was going to enjoy it.

Stepping onto the balcony with his beer, he heard the slider next door slam shut. He set his beer on the rail and scanned the dunes for his neighbor. He must have just missed her. *Oh well. Maybe another time.* He opened the grill and eyed his steak. Perfect.

3

———

Someone might as well have died, she felt that badly. Darlene sat alone in their beach condo, their dream, the condo that was supposed to magically reignite their marital spark. She replayed the hours of that fateful day—three days ago—her last day of blissful ignorance: Denny had kissed her on the forehead, coffee mug in one hand, lunch tote in the other, before walking out the door to go to work. She left for work herself a half-hour later.

Watching the waves from their third-floor master bedroom, she combed the details of that day. She mined for clues, questioning every little decision, every move, every turn—as if one tiny alteration could have prevented the first domino from falling. It had been an ordinary day at the pharmacy, nothing special, a bit on the crowded side, a ton of people wanting influenza vaccines. Denny had even called mid-day to tell her not to worry about dinner—he would make minestrone.

"If I wanted to give people shots, I'd have gone to nursing school," Darlene announced as she walked into the kitchen a few hours later. Denny was at the stove and did not turn around. "I hate giving flu shots. Hate it." She noticed the smell of his minestrone the minute she opened the front door. She licked her lips, anticipating the soup.

She reached into the freezer and pulled out a baguette. It seemed like a good night to bring up the idea she'd been tossing around for the past few months—that they should sell their house and move to Ocean City permanently. He could telecommute some amount of time. Only a three-hour drive from their home in Northern Virginia. Easy for days when he would need to go into the office or to a construction site. And she could get a job in a hospital or maybe even a small-town pharmacy. She came up behind him and draped her arms around his shoulders. "Since when should pharmacists be expected to stick people with needles?" She said this mostly to herself, then kissed him on the back of his neck.

He slowly turned, stepping aside just enough for Darlene to see the glass of Johnnie Walker Blue on the counter, the ice mostly melted, the scotch primarily untouched. There were only three reasons Denny ever pulled out the Johnnie Walker Blue. One: when clients questioned his inspection reports. Two: after a particularly guilt-trip inducing phone call from his mother. And, three: when he wanted to discuss her weight. She could still hear his voice, disgusted, that she had not yet lost her pregnancy weight. *The baby is four*, he'd said. Every few years, the same conversation. *The baby is eight, twelve, seventeen.* How old was Shelly now? Twenty-three. Darlene patted her stomach, then sucked it in. Denny's mother died three years ago, so that crossed scotch reason number two off the list. She scanned her brain for anything Denny might have recently said about his construction sites but came up blank. She exhaled, letting her stomach relax.

"Dar." He turned off the burner, took her hand, and led her to the kitchen table. "Please sit down."

"I'm not fat, Denny. I'm curvy." She plopped in the chair. "You've got to stop ragging on me about my weight. I'm perfectly healthy."

"What the hell are you talking about?" He pulled out a chair and sat next to her, not at his usual seat on the other side of the table. He searched her eyes. "Who said anything about your weight?"

"Isn't that what you want to talk to me about?"

"No."

"Did something happen at work?"

"No." He folded his hands on the table and took a deep breath. "Yeah. Sort of."

AFTER DENNY'S PRONOUNCEMENT, Darlene ended up on the kitchen floor, curled into a tight ball, feeling like she had been hit by a train. *What about the show?* It was the last thing she remembered saying. They were supposed to be in Ocean City for the filming in three days. Her brain worked hard to hang onto something familiar, something to give her hope, even while feeling like she had been beaten to a pulp. Denny's face, red from crying, burned behind her closed eyelids. Was she supposed to feel empathy? Feel his pain? Feel compassion for the torment he said he'd been living with for the past six months? He'd been sitting at the kitchen table, watching her writhe in pain. At some point, she heard the chair scraping the floor. She didn't know how long he had been gone, but at some point, she listened to his footsteps on the wood floors in the hallway, getting louder and louder, approaching the kitchen. She wanted to move, wanted to get up, wanted to flee, but felt pinned to the floor by the weight of his confession.

"I'm a bastard." He crouched down beside her and helped her up to a sitting position. "My timing is lousy, I know."

"I don't want to talk to you." She shifted onto her hip and slowly, carefully, stood.

"Please, Dar. Just hear me out."

"Hear you out?" She turned away from him. "You just destroyed my life, and you want me to hear you out?" She turned back. "You couldn't have waited until next week? Until we were finished taping the show?" The fucking show. How many times had she done something impulsive after two glasses of red wine? Too many to count. But this one took the cake. Literally. The night after they decided to buy a beach condo, they found themselves semi-drunk, filling out an online application for their favorite house-hunting show. They even created an impromptu video with Denny's phone discussing their must-haves: *oceanfront or ocean view, easy beach access, two or three bedrooms, master with private bathroom, no projects.* Denny even pleaded into the phone's camera that the house had to have a tub. *No tub, no deal.* They uploaded the video, pressed the submit button, and that was the end of that. Life took over; they forgot about their submission and bought their beach condo. A few months later, the show's producer called. *Well, we already bought the house,* Darlene remembered saying, at that point, hoping to get out of it. *That's terrific,* the producer replied. *It makes the filming aspect much more manageable.* Darlene shrugged and agreed. Last month, when they called again to schedule the date for filming, well, she thought it might just be the spark she and Denny needed. If she were honest with herself, she would admit that their relationship had been flat for quite some time. Especially then, when Denny was likely plotting to leave her.

"I'll do the show, okay?" He put his arms on her shoulders. "Will that make you happy? I'll do the show."

Darlene backed away from him. "Make me happy? Never seeing you again is what will make me happy."

LATER THAT NIGHT, Darlene crawled into bed alone. She willed sleep but found herself staring at the ceiling, replaying random bits and pieces of their conversation, her hip on fire from laying on the kitchen floor for so long.

"I wanted to be in lockstep with her," Denny had said. Lockstep, as if this were some sort of military maneuver. Lockstep. "I didn't plan to do it today." He put his head in his hands and cried, coming up for air only to lay on more pain. "We made a pact."

"You made a pact?" Darlene could not believe what she was hearing. A pact? They made a pact? Things between her and Denny may not have been all unicorns and rainbows, but a pact? How blind had she been? Her husband, making a pact with another woman. Just yesterday, he sat on the couch with her feet in his lap, rubbing them after she'd complained that they hurt. Rubbing her feet after he had made a pact with another woman. A pact! It sounded more like a suicide pact. How did Denny even know that this woman would follow through with her end of the pact?

"She called just before you walked in the door." Had he read her mind? "She told her husband. The deed is done."

Darlene recoiled when he tried to take her hands. "What about the pact you made with me? The pact, sealed on our wedding day?" She glared at him. "The pact we made that we'd love each other 'till death?"

The clock on the nightstand taunted her. She turned it around, so she didn't have to watch the numbers morphing from one hour to the next. Staring at the ceiling fighting anxious thoughts, she made a mental list of everyone she needed to call. She'd wanted to tell Shelly, first and foremost, right amid the chaos. But Denny begged her to not call their daughter, holding onto the ridiculous notion of spending Thanksgiving at the beach and telling her then. For reasons she did not quite understand, she agreed. She also needed to call the pharmacy to let them know she would be starting her vacation two days early. She would go to Ocean City by herself tomorrow and try to get out of filming the stupid show.

She got out of bed and crept down the stairs, walking past Denny. He was laying face-up on the couch, snoring in the soft, rhythmic little puff-puffs that always drove her to distraction when he fell asleep first. The pot of minestrone was still on the stove, untouched. She poured herself a glass of wine and reached behind the cans of garbanzo beans in the pantry, grabbing a handful of chocolates out of her secret stash. Nothing like wine and chocolate to dull the pain— the throbbing, soul-crushing ache flaring up and emerging in places she didn't even know existed. She tiptoed back up the stairs and climbed into bed with her cure. Wine and chocolate—faithful to a fault, unlike Denny. She finally dozed, waking two hours later, just before dawn. For a joyous second, she gasped in relief. It was a dream. Until it wasn't.

4

———————

Bone-tired, Fran couldn't face loading the dishwasher. He left the remnants of his steak dinner on the counter and popped a K-Cup into his Keurig. Best advice his sister had ever given him. *Get a Keurig*, she'd said, not too long after his wife's funeral. He'd broken down in tears opening the bag of coffee beans they'd bought together just before learning she didn't meet the criteria to enroll in a promising clinical trial. Freshly ground coffee had been her thing. Give him a cup of any generic old coffee, and he was happy. The sight of the beans had sent him over the edge. As did the very act of putting grounds in the coffee maker, the sound of it gurgling and dripping. It was too much. It was all too much. So, he bought a Keurig. It took him a while to get used to it, but it served its purpose; it provided him with caffeine and didn't remind him of Sadie.

He took his cup and plodded up the stairs to the little nook he created off the master bedroom to use as his office. He and Sadie had hung a set of barn doors to separate the space from the sleeping area, for those times when he needed to work, and she needed to sleep. Later, he would leave the barn doors open and crawl into bed with her, and they would fall asleep to the rhythm of the waves.

Setting his cup down on the table beside his reading chair, he opened the sliding glass door and let the cold, salt-infused wind into the room. He picked up the document he printed earlier, sat down in his chair, and took a sip of his coffee. He was on a tight deadline to read through a proposal for a new, automated succession planning tool his client was considering. Fran had sold his management consulting firm four years ago, enabling him to buy the beach house and a little deli for Sadie. He missed the mental stimulation that work provided, so he offered himself as a consultant to the mid-sized firm who bought him out. He had no real hobbies; he reviewed and wrote proposals for fun. *Keeps the money flowing*, he frequently told himself. Twelve pages into the proposal, the steak began to assault him. Earlier, he had made a show of shoving the last forkful into his mouth, despite Sadie's aggravated look.

"You're destroying your kidneys." She'd been sitting on the countertop near the sink, her legs dangling over the edge. She let her bare feet bang against the dishwasher, a gentle percussion, watching as he ate his steak at the coffee table in the living room.

"It's worth it." He chased the hunk of meat with an endless gulp of beer, but by the time he said it, Sadie had vanished.

So, she was right, it was too much meat. His focus waning, he licked his index finger and flipped back three pages, re-reading the words until they all blended into one big, black blob. He should have eaten half the steak and saved the rest for tomorrow. He would still be killing his kidneys, but at least he wouldn't kill his stomach, too. He slunk down in the chair, tilting his head back until it was positioned comfortably on the top cushion. Closing his eyes, he thought about Sadie and how she snuck into the living room after he finished eating and put her arms around him. They held each other and clutch-danced, the waves being the only music they needed. Until he realized he was dancing alone.

5

———

Darlene stood in front of the sliding glass door and watched the sky transition from afternoon to evening. She let her mind drift to Denny on the beach; it should have been her frolicking with him, if not jogging. It should have been her swatting his ass. It should have been her laughing with him in anticipation of their upcoming half-hour of fame. She imagined fans of the house-hunting show watching, rooting for their favorite house, hoping Denny and Darlene would choose the same.

She shoved a piece of chocolate into her mouth and looked at the message printed inside the wrapper: *A smile is the quickest way to brighten a room.* She scowled and crumbled the wrapper, flicking the small blob, like a three-point basketball shot into the trash can at the other end of her dresser. She was celebrating a milestone. She had actually gone a half-hour without crying. Bravo. Her breath caught in her throat, and the sobs came rushing out. So much for milestones. She sat down on the edge of the bed and cried. Fighting it did not seem to work. How was she supposed to get this out of her system by tomorrow morning? Getting out of filming this show was apparently not an option.

She took a deep breath and unwrapped another piece of chocolate. Maybe this wrapper would have a practical message—life hacks for breathing, putting one foot in front of the other, living without Denny. She popped it into her mouth—half chewing, half sucking—and read the message: *Always time for love*. Right. Like it had eyes. She swallowed, using the back of her hand to wipe the chocolate residue off the corner of her mouth. She pinched the empty wrapper into a tight, tiny ball and flicked it across her dresser. Instead of pins, the catapulting miniature bowling ball knocked her two diamond stud earrings off the dresser. She crouched down, ignoring the clacking in her left knee and scanned the carpet around the dresser. She had wanted to rip this pathetic carpet up when they bought the condo last year, but Denny said it was in perfectly good condition. Brand new.

She should have ripped the damned carpet out the last time she was here by herself. When was that, anyway? Late winter? Early spring? She recalled the Jenga block inching its way out of the tower —the one she should have noticed, the one that might have made the past few days less of a shock. She should have known the minute Denny said he had to fly to New Orleans for a work emergency. *Problems at the construction site. My biggest client. I'm the building inspector, after all.* What could she say to that? Absolutely nothing, so she didn't even try. Never mind that they had planned to spend their twenty-fourth anniversary at the beach, just the two of them. New restaurants. Snuggles on the couch. Long walks on the beach. She even went as far as Googling traditional and modern anniversary gift ideas for year twenty-four. Traditional: opal, thought to inspire love, purity, and hope for the future. Modern: musical instruments, with all the passion and emotion that music signifies.

She crawled around on the carpet, feeling for her earrings. She reached under the dresser, patting the carpet in circles, feeling something sharp. *Ah yes. There you are.* She scooped them up and stood, wincing from the pain in her knee. A new pain. A fresh reminder of the impending doom of turning fifty. She was the last of her friends to hit this iconic milestone. Every one of them said their fifties were their best decade so far. Darlene found it hard to believe. If only she could go back to her thirties when Shelly was little, and she and Denny seemed to love each other.

She held the outfit she planned to wear for tomorrow's filming to her chest, letting the whole ensemble drape her from neck to toes and modeled it in front of the mirror. Denny helped her pick it out months ago. The Denny from before. The Denny she thought she knew so well. Slimming black slacks, a black tank top, and a multi-colored cardigan. She studied it against her complexion. Denny was right—black was one of her best looks. It made her fair skin look almost luminescent, and the colorful cardigan, well, it was just enough to keep things interesting. Just long enough to camouflage her jiggly bits. Of course. That's why Denny had picked it out. She would look better on camera that way. Why he wanted to continue with the charade of this show confounded her.

She pulled her hair away from her face, wishing it were long enough to put up. She released her hand, her curls springing back to life, silently cursing the genes in her father's lineage. She put the diamond stud earrings in and held her hair back again, studying her face in the mirror, then letting the curls spring back. It was no use. She was not photogenic. Never was, not even as a kid; in pigtails, she looked like she'd glued orange pompoms to the sides of her head. Even in her wedding photos, she seemed somewhat haphazardly put together. Her sister, Rachel, on the other hand, always looked gorgeous in pictures. She squinted into the mirror. What is that? Jowls? Where did they come from? Maybe she should just ask Rachel to hop on the red-eye and be her stand-in on the show tomorrow. Then Darlene could disappear and never come back.

Barbara Streisand said the mirror has two faces. Darlene wished it were so. If the mirror had two faces, there was a fifty-fifty chance that the other face would be better than the one staring back at her. Who was she kidding? The diamond earrings were supposed to make her look, what, twenty-five? Hell, she didn't want to look twenty-five. She would be happy with forty-five. Anything but the haggard almost fifty-year-old she saw staring back at her. *Mirror, mirror on the wall, who's the most matronly one of all? When did I get so old looking?* She pulled a sock out of the drawer and used it to wipe the mirror. Nope. The layer of dust was not the culprit. She craned her neck, jutting out her jaw to smooth her jowls. She leaned over the dresser to get a closer look at her cry-swollen eyes, and, big surprise, she started crying. Again.

Tears and snot running down her chin, she bent down and picked up the shiny red candy wrapper she flicked across her dresser. She dug her nail under a lip of loose foil, being careful to not tear it. She un-crumbled it and smoothed it out in the palm of her hand. *Always time for love.* Backing away from the dresser, she watched as her reflection in the mirror grew smaller and narrower, diminishing as she moved farther and farther away. She kept shuffling backward until she bumped into the bed, the sleigh bed she and Denny had bought from the previous owners. Not very beachy, but cute in its own way. She especially loved the patina, something she wanted to keep, while Denny wanted to sand and stain it. One of the few battles she had won. *Always time for love.*

She sat down and scooted across the bed until her back was pressed against the headboard, trying to quiet the what-ifs. What if she had been better about keeping her almost post-menopausal body in shape? She had never been particularly athletic. Okay, not particularly. She just wasn't. Period. Denny knew that from the get-go.

They had met in a college elective—Fitness Through Dance, of all things. Neither she nor Denny could dance; both were equally uncoordinated. The difference was Denny loved the movement, the sweat. Over coffee, they laughed about the instructor, who tried so hard to be like Jane Fonda. Richard Simmons would have been more entertaining. But the music was good, and she looked forward to what had become their thing—coffee after the class, joking about the instructor who berated herself for eating cannoli.

Maybe the Jane Fonda wannabe had been right all along—work off and sweat out the cannoli. The problem was, Darlene hated cannoli. Was she a bit soft in the middle after having Shelly? Sure. But now, she felt downright doughy. She grabbed her belly and squeezed, wondering if this was the real issue. Denny harangued her about it often. Maybe even more than she harangued him about sex.

"We do it more than once a month," Denny defended. "We do."

"That's not the point," Darlene countered. "The point is that you never want to. Yeah, you can close your eyes and get hard, but you don't want to, not really." Often, these conversations about his low sex drive ended up with her yelling, and in tears. "You're not normal, Denny. Normal men want to have sex with their wives."

"That's awfully presumptuous of you," Denny spat. "You have no way of knowing what I'm thinking and feeling." He lowered his voice. "Or what I want and need."

Darlene now wondered how much of her own jiggly flesh and aging skin played a role in Denny's lack of interest. She thought back. Had his drive always been on the low side? Or was it just in the last year, since he started jogging. Quick review in her head. When had he really started pulling away? After Shelly? A few years ago, when the numbers on the scale started inching toward the edge of one-sixty? Dammit, her weight did not excuse his affair. It was certainly no good reason to leave her.

She sat on the bed, replaying her entire marriage, wondering where and when things had begun to break. She looked down at her belly, wishing she could just disappear. She pulled the covers over her body and curled up into a ball, letting the sound of the rough November ocean soothe her soul. *Always time for love.* Easy for Denny. He found time for love with someone new.

She bolted upright, determined to find a way to cancel the film shoot, and go back home. She longed for the comfort of the pharmacy counter, the bottles of elixirs arranged, ordered, and ready to heal. She had tried getting out of work yesterday, tried starting her vacation early, but her boss needed her, at least for a half day. It had been a struggle getting herself out the door, but once there, counting out pills proved strangely calming. She pulled the covers over her head and willed herself to disappear.

~

THE THOUGHT of seeing Denny tomorrow felt like waiting for the result of a medical test. She knew she was in denial—seeing the two lovebirds on the beach wasn't evidence enough to support the diagnosis. Denny would burst through the door at any moment and tell her it had all been a mistake. Or a cruel April Fool's joke—in November. The results were in, and still, she couldn't believe it, the CT scan images contradicting her denial.

She poured herself a glass of chardonnay and sat on a barstool at the kitchen's small breakfast bar. Sight lines right to the ocean. She planned to be effusive on camera about the blue and white tile countertops. Early in the application process, the show's PR rep had explained that she and Denny needed to have strong opinions—both positive and negative—on camera. These tiles weren't like the cheesy tiles of the '80s. No, these were modern, newer, and a bit quirky. She suspected Denny would wax eloquently about every little flaw—real or perceived—that he could find. He would look hard to find the flaws, making them up even if they didn't exist. Knocking on every wood surface. Bouncing on a section of flooring and saying it squeaked. Conflict and drama. That was what made these shows enjoyable, captured viewers' interest. Conflict and drama. How about the story of the past few days? That would undoubtedly provide conflict and drama.

Sipping her wine, she was tempted to call Denny and tell him not to come tomorrow. The dread of seeing him felt like a rock in her gut. Seeing him on the beach had not been her imagination. Nor was it a cruel joke. The CT scan did not lie. The diagnosis was real. The image of Denny playfully jogging up and down the beach with her replacement was worse than if she had seen them making love. He looked so damned happy. She felt her eyes fill—damned tears.

The little cheese board that she'd built for herself sat untouched, staring expectantly at her as if wanting to shout, *go ahead and dig in. Enjoy. Bon Appetit. Mangiamo. L'Chaim.* Wiping her eyes, she wrapped the plate and put it away. Her cell phone buzzed, startling her.

"Dar." The sound of Denny's voice, incongruent with her sense of order in this new world. "What time tomorrow?"

"Where are you?" She guzzled the last of her wine. "I saw you on the beach today."

"None of that matters." He sounded hurried, and a tad annoyed. "I could be there Tuesday, maybe. But not tomorrow. Do you think they could film without me until I get there?"

"Denny, where are you?" Her heart raced, realizing she had been holding onto this charade of a show as maybe a way to what, win Denny back? She sighed, disgusted with herself. "You agreed to do this." Just a little while ago, she'd prayed for a pop-up, late-season hurricane that would cancel the filming, possibly forever. "Seriously, what's going on?" Muffled voices came into her ear space. Laughter, muffled, of course. More voices. More laughter.

"I'm with Remi."

"Remi?" So that was her name. Remi. Really? If she hadn't seen the woman with her own two eyes, she would have taken a 'Remi' to be young and willowy.

"Look, this whole thing is stupid," he said.

"What thing? The fact that you're leaving me for a woman named Remi?"

"The show. The show is stupid, Darlene." He exhaled loudly. "Look, just tell them I'm out of the country."

"Dammit, Denny. You're the one who said you still wanted to do the show." She could feel the pent-up rage burning her face. "You're the one who wants to play make-believe, have a Norman Rockwell Thanksgiving with our daughter, then yank off the tablecloth." She raised her voice. "Do you think the dishes would land on the table, intact?" When he didn't respond, she continued. "I'm done with you. Tell Remi to do the shoot with you." She got up and paced the length of the small living room. "The two of you can pretend to be the happily married couple." Out of breath, she let her body fall into the couch cushions.

"Now, isn't that a great idea?" His sarcasm was palpable. "Look, I'm sorry. When I told you I would still do the show, I wanted to do it for you, to make up for—"

"Make up for what, breaking my heart?"

"I'm sorry. I can't do this. I'm bowing out."

"Our contract says—"

"Fuck the contract." Denny raised his voice. "What are they going to do? Sue us? Withhold the $500 or whatever the hell they're paying us."

"A thousand. We're getting paid a thousand. Each. And they're coming here with the expectation of filming a happy couple on the hunt for a beach house." She pinched the bridge of her nose. Remi. He's with a woman named Remi. She took a deep, shaky breath, but said nothing.

"Dammit, Darlene."

She tilted her head back and stared at a cobweb dangling from the light fixture in the ceiling. "You're the one who wants to put on an act for Shelly. This is the ultimate act." She hung up, then stood and sat right back down, light-headed. She looked around the room. She still had to tidy up, hide personal things like pictures and tchotchkes, make the condo look generic like it was for sale. There was not much to hide. The show was sending a moving truck to empty the condo, make it look vacant. She didn't want anything touched and would insist they leave the condo intact. It could be part of the shtick—the buyer wants the seller to include the furniture in the sale price.

She collected the few family photos scattered about the condo: Shelly on the boardwalk, hair blowing in the wind, taken last summer. Darlene had already removed the one of her and Denny, taken that same day. There was also a picture with her sister at the beach when they were two and four years old. She picked it up and studied it, Rachel already a photogenic butterfly, posing like a balle-rina; Darlene sitting on the blanket like a lump. She shoved all the photos into the coffee table drawer.

Her phone buzzed. Denny again. She ignored it and poured herself another glass of wine. She climbed the stairs, leaving her phone behind.

❧

MORE POTENT NOW THAN a few hours ago, the buffeting wind howled —the precursor to a fall storm heading up the coast. The Weather Channel promised it would be gone before dawn, plenty of time for filming tomorrow. She had fallen asleep, her wine untouched, and now she feared she'd be up all night. She got up and stood in front of the mirror. Maybe it had two faces, after all. This time, she saw a reasonably cute woman staring back at her, still fleshy, but no longer dowdy. She tilted her head in different directions, hoping the camera would capture her good side tomorrow. The side that gave her nose a slightly smaller, more defined shape. The other side bore a striking resemblance to Buddy Hackett. Baring her teeth at the mirror, she examined them—her best feature by far—and made a mental note to thank her parents for all the orthodontic work they had paid for. Her hair had not yet sprung gray weeds, her red curls still as vivid as they'd been in her twenty's. The only problem now had to do with her outfit for tomorrow. It suddenly seemed all wrong. Who wears black dress pants and a drapey cardigan at the beach? Who goes on a house-hunting show with her philandering husband? She touched her chest, willing her heart to stop pounding. Taking several deep breaths, she sat back down on the bed, light-headed, on the verge of panic.

"Stop!" She threw her head back. "Just stop. Get a grip." Maybe she should call Shelly. God, she hated lying to her daughter. Denny was adamant about not ruining Thanksgiving. They stopped celebrating Hanukkah years ago and didn't celebrate Christmas. Thanksgiving was their thing. Their big thing. She put her head in her hands and sobbed, a string of future sad Thanksgivings running through her mind like movie trailers.

She peeled herself off the bed and shuffled to the closet, scanning its contents for something different to wear tomorrow. Something that would make her look more like herself and less like a woman trying too hard. She didn't keep much clothing here—two pairs of jeans, a green turtleneck, and four long-sleeved tee-shirts in varying colors. The items she brought with her for the week were not much better. Different, but still on the same plane as the items in the closet. Not TV worthy.

Frustrated, she stepped onto the small balcony outside the bedroom and let the blustery, ocean-laced wind extinguish the hot flash that was beginning to engulf her. She pictured a potato in the microwave, cooking from the inside and eventually exploding. That was precisely how she felt.

She placed her feet between the spindles on the balcony's railing and pressed her palms onto the top, hoisting herself up and holding herself in place with her thighs. The wind blew her hair back, off her face like a fashion model in front of a fan. She laughed at the image, the first time she'd laughed in days. A ship's light flashed in the distance, on the dark horizon, off to the left. She stared at the light until it became imperceptible. Leaning in to maintain her balance, she stretched her arms out and closed her eyes.

6

―――――

"What in the world?" Fran, following the sound of laughter, hoisted himself out of his chair. He turned off the light in his office to better see what was going on outside. He fully expected to see Sadie laughing and dancing around on the balcony—continuing where they had left off after dinner. He smiled and opened the door to join her outside, then stopped, frozen.

The crazy redhead next door. He squinted, then looked around for Sadie, confident the laughter was hers. Only it wasn't. He stood, breathless, as the crazy redhead tilted her head back, letting the wind swallow her whole. She lifted her head, then teetered a bit. Fran had the sudden urge to run outside and tell her to be careful, that it was dangerous, climbing on the rail, three stories above the beach. He flicked his office light on, in the hope she would see it and settle down. She didn't.

He stared at her as she posed on the rail like Rose in *Titanic*. Only there was no Jack standing behind her, holding her. He felt drawn into her laughter—hauntingly like Sadie's—intrigued at her ability to amuse herself. His mind drifted to a few hours before, when he watched her throwing bread at the seagull. Not laughing, but quite animated. And now here she was again, animated as if she were the only person on the planet, unaware of her dorky neighbor standing just over the rail.

Titanic Rose's short, curly hair blew wild in the wind. He imagined her face—he had only seen it in the distance—pale and freckled, her hair much redder than his hair had ever been before it started turning white. Blech, she would probably view him as an old man. A geezer. Still, he stared, her strong legs holding her in place, her arms spread wide, like an eagle's wings. He wondered what had gone wrong in her marriage, how anyone could walk away from someone so uninhibited and fancy-free.

"I'm the king of the world..." *Titanic* Rose's voice trailed off, the wind carrying it away, then bringing it back in the form of a song. "Near, far, wherever you are, I believe that the heart does go on."

Fran chuckled. The woman's laughter was like a song, but her song was like nothing he had ever heard. Slightly off-key with a passionate, reckless abandon. A bird singing for its life. He kept his mouth clamped shut until he couldn't hold it in any longer. He stepped outside, arms outstretched like *Titanic* Jack, joining her in song.

"You're, here, there's nothing..." Uh-oh. He walked right through the motion-sensor on his balcony, the night suddenly flooded in light. He let his arms fall to his sides. His neighbor whipped her head around, her eyes searching, finally landing smack-dab on him. Pale and freckled, as it was in his imagination, suddenly turning the color of...a red rose. Her green eyes caught the light, flashing like two beacons, cutting through the fog. Or slicing his head off. He suddenly saw the fire in her eyes and was worried that he had upset her. "Your name wouldn't happen to be Rose, would it?" It was all he could think to say. He stood motionless as she lowered one foot, then the other off the rail.

"No, my name is not Rose." She stomped across her balcony, muttering something indecipherable, slamming the door behind her.

∼

"Of course, I know your name isn't Rose," he said to the empty balcony, the sound of her sliding glass door slamming shut still ringing in his ears. He took a deep breath and went back into his condo. Sitting down in his chair, he picked up the proposal, flipped through it, and put it right back down. It was no use.

"Alexa, play '70s music."

"Here's a station you might like," came the device's soothing reply. "One Hundred Greatest '70s Rock Songs."

He leaned back in his chair and closed his eyes. The music was a nice distraction, or rather, a soundtrack, incongruent with his embarrassment. "Alexa, turn down the volume." He had been drawn to his neighbor, laughing and singing on the balcony, pulled into her orbit. Now he regretted flying into her space, interrupting her respite from what he guessed was a difficult time in her life. At least that was how his sister made it sound. He wished Laurie would mind her own business. He had no right to know this woman's baggage—it made him feel dirty, almost like a Peeping Tom. He shuddered at the thought. He could not un-know what Laurie had shared. Still, thinking this woman needed a friend was a waste of time. He wasn't even sure why he'd felt compelled to talk to her.

A simple, familiar piano introduction startled him. He sat straight up, then hung his head, massaging his temples as Jefferson Starship's *Count On Me* filled the room. It was Sadie's song, their wedding song, the song they selected for their first dance. He watched their small, intimate wedding unfold on the backs of his eyelids.

Fran realized with horror that he'd been so mesmerized by Rose or not Rose—he couldn't remember what Laurie had said her name was—that he hadn't given Sadie a thought. As if she didn't exist.

"God, Sadie. I'm sorry."

7

————

Darlene stood against the wall, her heart pounding. Her embarrassment knew no bounds. By the time she realized what was happening, she had only glimpsed the man next door, illuminated like a stage actor under a spotlight. In that split-second flash, she saw her best high-school friend, Eugene. They took summer jobs at the Pathmark just outside Philly after graduation. Stocking shelves and belting out show tunes, much to the store manager's chagrin. Eugene. She hadn't thought about him in forever. They drifted apart after that summer, but he was always her litmus test for men: would they sing with her, act silly with her, laugh with her? When she met Denny, he seemed like everything she wanted. Except that he never sang with her, never acted silly with her, and rarely laughed with her.

She did not know who the man on the balcony was, but she sure hoped he was just someone renting the place for the weekend and would soon be gone. She didn't need any intrusions this week. *Privacy*, she decided she would say on camera tomorrow. *The most important thing I want in a beach house is privacy.*

8

———

They never did it every day when she was alive. Even in summer, when the morning light poured in through the wall of glass, serving as a silent alarm clock, they only did it sporadically. But in the two years since Sadie's death, Fran met her on the balcony every morning to watch the sun come up. And when it rained or was too brutally cold outside, they sat side by side, just inside the sliding glass door, looking out. Together.

Fran carried the two cups of coffee up to the third-floor balcony and positioned them on a small table in front of a weather-worn double-Adirondack chair. He lifted his coffee to his mouth—still too hot to drink—and took Sadie's hand. They sat in silence, waiting for the first stroke of God's paintbrush, signaling the dawning day. As darkness began to lift over the ocean, the western sky behind the condo was still pitch black.

Fran blew on his coffee and took the first sip—always the best. He brought Sadie's quilt all the way up to his neck and pulled his stocking hat down around his ears. No doubt about it, autumn was here. In full force. Sleep never came last night. He was finally able to put *Titanic* Rose out of his mind and finish reviewing the proposal.

Now, he felt popeyed yet fuzzy in the brain and wondered how much longer he'd be able to function like this. He could easily do his consulting work during the day; it was his nights that needed occupying. The days were better. Little by little, they kept getting better; the nights were still so damned lonely. Sleep always seemed to elude him, even when he made a concerted effort. He even tried mindfulness training and meditation, but all it seemed to do was increase his mind's wanderings. He couldn't still his mind without it drifting to memories of life with Sadie.

The early mornings had their own rewards. Fran glanced at Sadie, the sky now a light periwinkle, the first hint of the orange ball peeking over the world's blanket. A handful of people dotted the beach, including a happy couple jogging along the hard-packed sand close to the water. The tide was out, and the wet sand stretched for miles to the left and right. By the time the sun came all the way up, his coffee mug was empty. He took a sip of Sadie's coffee; he always made it just the way she liked it, black with two teaspoons of sugar. She never drank it, but he brought it to her anyway. Dawn after dawn. Always.

Sweating under the quilt, Fran pushed it down and sat forward, catching a glimpse of the crazy redhead. There she was, sitting on the beach again, the same shabby seagull standing beside her. Last night, she seemed less than amused by his singing and irritated by his *Titanic* Rose comment. He glanced at Sadie out of the corner of his eye, feeling guilty for letting his mind drift to thoughts about his neighbor, the sound of her laughter, her awful singing. He squeezed Sadie's hand, hoping she hadn't seen what had gone on out here last night.

"Nothing," he said out loud. "Nothing went on out here." He looked at Sadie, but she had already retreated to wherever it was that she went when she disappeared. "Who am I trying to kid?" He took a deep breath. "Something did happen out here last night. I just wish I knew what, exactly, it was."

He folded the quilt and padded to the rail, watching a man

approach the crazy redhead. *Must be the bastard husband*, he thought as he picked up the two coffee mugs—careful not to spill Sadie's— and went inside.

9

———————

True to The Weather Channel's prediction, the storm blew out sometime in the middle of the night. Darlene stepped onto the balcony to stand by the rail and watch the sunrise. Last night's sleep had come in fits and starts, lasting a few precious minutes, followed by hours trying to quiet her mind.

She stared at the waves and yawned. Coffee. That was what she needed. She figured she had time to make a pot before the sun emerged over the horizon. She turned to go inside and froze at the sight of her neighbor sitting in an oversized chair, wrapped in a thick blanket, head tilted back, eyes closed. He held a coffee mug in both hands, its steam swirling around his face. How had she not noticed him when she first came out? He obviously had not seen her, thank God.

She tiptoed across the balcony, careful not to bump into anything. The last thing she wanted was to draw attention to herself; she did not want to engage with him. She opened the sliding glass door and was about to step in when she noticed a second coffee mug. So, he wasn't alone. He wasn't some weirdo hitting on her. Instead of this realization making her feel better, she felt the slightest bit of disappointment. Not that she wanted a weirdo (or anyone) hitting on her. It was just that for a moment last night, when he stepped onto his balcony singing, well, she didn't know. She just didn't know. The only thing she knew for sure was that she couldn't trust her own mind. Denny had screwed her head up to the point where she didn't know if she would ever recover. Now, all she had to do was get through this day. *Oy Vey*.

THE CLOCK on the microwave assured Darlene that she had fifteen minutes or so before sunrise. She pulled the coffee can out of the cupboard and felt gut-punched when she discovered only a thin layer of grounds covering the bottom of the can like a threadbare rug. She shoved it in the recycling bin and turned on the tea kettle, knocking on the wood column shooting up from the breakfast bar to the ceiling. Knock, knock, knock—something she did reflexively to ward off bad luck. Of course, she didn't believe in any of that crap. But she grew up with a Jewish grandmother who did it all the time. *Knock on wood. Kenahora. Poo-poo-poo.* None of it warded off the massive heart attack that killed her grandfather, nor did it ward off the cancer that took her grandmother six months later. It was an ingrained habit— Darlene simply did it without thinking.

She took her tea—a consolation prize at best—and opened the sliding glass door to the lower balcony. She stepped outside and set her tea down on the picnic table, tilting her head up enough to see if the man next door was still on his third-floor balcony. Yep. Still there, still alone, sitting in his chair. He appeared to be scanning the horizon, his hand stretched out beside him as if holding the other half of the chair for someone. She stood against the wall rather than risk being seen at the rail. The ocean looked glassy, the small waves breaking on the beach with precision and regularity.

In the distance, the horizon sported stripes of orange, white, and yellow—a gradient blur of candy corns. A bright spot rearing its head, sliding through the orange smudge, the reflection on the water like a searchlight pointing at the shore. Darlene stood hugging her body against the chill, her tea long forgotten, watching the beach wake up. An elderly woman trudged through the wet, packed sand, her arm linked with a younger man's, probably her son. A couple with two bundled toddlers sat in the sand, the toddlers running in circles around them. A woman in headphones power walking. And a couple, playful and robust, jogging. They stopped and looked toward the building. The man pointed, and they resumed jogging.

Be bold, she told herself. Even if her neighbor saw her, she doubted he would break into song or throw out more jokey comments. She shook her head. In another time, another circumstance, she might have enjoyed getting to know him—another Eugene in her life might be fun. But not now. Her life was a mess. The last thing she needed was a singing, jokey neighbor. She held onto the hope that he was a renter and would soon be gone.

She braced herself and walked quickly down the steps and through the access path until she was on the beach, staring at the jogging couple. She watched as their forms grew closer and came into focus. Denny? Could that be the red Patagonia half-zip that she gave him three birthdays ago? And the wool hat in the colors of the Maryland flag, the rim sitting above his ears, defeating the purpose of the hat? She squinted toward the horizon. Of course, it was Denny. Again. As if seeing the two of them yesterday had not been enough. Darlene turned away from their approach and tried to ignore Denny's laughter—a deep, from the gut type of laughter that he rarely shared with her. She turned back just in time to see the woman swat his ass. Just like yesterday. What was it with that woman and swatting Denny's ass? The woman giggled, piercingly high pitched.

Darlene plopped down in the sand and brought her knees as close to her chest as she could manage, hugging them with her arms. There was no wind, but the air and the sand were cold. Her seagull companion from yesterday hobbled nearby, inching toward her. Soon he was close enough to get her attention but far enough to escape quickly if need be. He apparently had forgotten about yesterday's violent bread-throwing.

"I'm sorry, little guy. I'm empty-handed today." She cocked her head toward him. "Maybe that's a good thing, right?"

Denny stopped a few hundred yards in front of the building and looked out toward the ocean. The woman—Remi—sidled up beside him. Darlene stopped breathing when she saw Denny put his arm around her and pull her close. The woman turned her head and looked at the building, then back at the ocean. In a split-second flash, Darlene sized her up in more precise detail than she'd been able to do yesterday; she didn't like what she saw. It was like looking into the window of a passing car. An image seen in a split-second, and you're making up stories about who that person is. The kind of house she lives in, her chosen profession, whether she is a cat, dog, or bird person, whether you could be friends with her, whether you'd want to be her. Nope, Darlene didn't like it at all. She swallowed the growing lump in her throat. Remi looked like an ordinary woman, neither pretty nor unattractive. Fun-loving and zestful. Real. Someone Darlene could have chatted with standing in a grocery store checkout line.

"Hey." Denny trudged through the thick sand and stood in front of Darlene. He was out of breath, his face rosy from the cold, rosy from his run, rosy from the glow of new love. His eyes twinkling like diamonds.

"Hey," Darlene said back, wiping her eyes with the cuff of her sweatshirt. She stood. "What are you doing here so early." She looked at the sky, sniffed, and took a deep breath, hoping Denny was too full of his own happiness to see the moistness in her eyes. "The crew won't be here for another couple of hours."

"I know. I was hoping to find you out here." He sat down next to her. "Did you get my voicemail?"

"What voicemail?"

"I called you again last night and left a voicemail."

She didn't remember hearing her phone. Oh, crap. Yes. Just before she went upstairs. "That's right. I deliberately ignored the call. Never listened to any voicemail."

"Dar, we need to talk."

"About Remi?" Her eyes scanned the beach. She took a deep breath and forced herself to sound brave and nonchalant. "Where is she? I'd like to meet her."

"She's jogging back to the hotel."

"Why is she even here?"

"Let's go inside, I'm freezing."

THEY WALKED UP THE STEPS, Denny leading, Darlene following, brushing sand off the back of her legs, trying not to notice how lean he looked, at least from behind. How had she not noticed this before? She grabbed her tea and opened the slider. Stepping inside, Denny took off his hat and tossed it on the coffee table.

"Holy shit, Denny. Did you dye your hair?" Darlene stood, wide-eyed, and stared at the dark brown all over his head, like someone had dipped it in a bucket of paint. Three days ago, he was completely gray. She never understood men who dye their hair. Not young men coloring their hair purple or green, like her younger brother, Liam, had done his senior year in high school. Or her young co-worker who highlighted his hair to give it—his words—a sun-kissed look. She remembered her own follies as a teenager, spraying Sun-In all over her head and sitting for hours on the beach, reapplying it after each dip in the ocean. Instead of a sun-kissed look, her red hair was covered in patches of school bus yellow. Her mother was furious. *I wanted to be blonde like Rachel*, was all Darlene could think to say to her mother, who ranted and scolded, bemoaning why anyone would want to destroy such pretty red hair. On the way to the drugstore to buy a kit to try and fix it, Darlene wondered why her mother never told her this before. She never remembered her mother telling her she had pretty hair; Rachel was always the pretty one.

"Is it that obvious?" Denny ran his fingers through his hair. The contrast between the dark brown and his pale complexion made him look sickly.

"Obvious?" She couldn't help the snicker that escaped her mouth.

She quickly covered it with her hand. "Oh, Denny. It's, um, it's not you." She shook her head. "What were you thinking?" Her mother's words.

"Of course, you would say something like that." He wrinkled his nose and brushed an imaginary fly away from his face. "What were you thinking, Denny, what were you thinking?" He tried to sound like a scolding wife. "I'm sick of it."

Darlene ignored him and refilled the tea kettle, wondering what it would be like to have a man so desperately want to impress her that he'd dye his hair. And why now? Why not six months ago?

"You said you wanted to talk." She sat at the counter. "You've got five minutes." She looked at the clock. "I need to shower and change."

He took a deep breath and sat down on the stool next to her. "I'm not doing the show, Dar."

"But you have to."

"I don't have to do anything." He ran his hand through his hair again, letting it linger, then grabbed a fistful of brown strands, opening his fingers and raking them all the way to the back of his neck.

"If it's about your hair, you could just wear a hat."

"It's not about my hair." He looked at his feet. "It's Remi. She doesn't want me to do the show. She doesn't like that we're pretending to still be married."

"We are still married." Darlene felt territorial. "It's been, what? Ninety-six hours since you upended my life. We've been married twenty-five years."

"Twenty-four and eight months." He searched her eyes. "You know it's over between us. Don't try to pretend we didn't have problems for the past few years. It's over. Has been for a long time."

"You're serious about this woman?" It would be so much easier if Remi looked like a bimbo. Or was half his age. So much easier.

"Yeah." He hesitated. "Yeah. I am."

"Then why did you do that to your hair?" She laughed; it was so much better than crying. God, she was tired of crying.

"I don't know." He hung his head, then looked back up at her. "I can't believe I'm telling you this, but I was feeling insecure. Now that she left her husband for me."

"So, you're worried that she'll see you in the cold light of day and suffer post purchase dissonance?"

"Something like that." He shook his head. "God, Dar, this is hard."

"Look, you had gray hair when she fell in love with you." Darlene burst into tears. "Why are we even talking about this?" She glared at him. "Dammit, Denny. What the hell are you doing here?"

"I'm sorry." He covered his face with his hands. "She hates it. Remi hates it." He took a deep breath. "It's supposed to last for eight shampoos. I wash my hair every day, so that's eight days."

"Go back to your hotel, jump in the shower, wash and rinse your hair eight times, then come back here ready to at least film the opening." She wiped her eyes. "We could tell them you had a work emergency and need to be on the next plane to Dubai. Or we could tell them the truth."

"My company doesn't have anything in Dubai, you know that."

"Denny, that's not the point. It's a lie. An excuse." She was incredulous. And frantic. She suddenly had more significant problems than what to wear today. "Look, I'm sorry we ever agreed to do this damned show." She wondered why she was sitting here with him.

"It will be months before this thing airs," he said, sounding desperate. "At the earliest. We'll be legally divorced by then. So, let's just be truthful about it. Then you can go on to do the house hunt alone."

Darlene dumped her cold tea in the sink, grabbed a fresh tea bag, and watched it expand like a blowfish when she poured fresh, boiling water over it. "You want a cup?" She stuck her hand in the jar and wrapped her fingers around a teabag for him, then released it when he shook his head. She sat down next to him and held her cup in both hands, relishing the warmth, letting the steam lick her face. She mentally went through the list of what-ifs, like she rattled off side-effects when discussing a new medication with a customer. Dizziness. Weakness. Drowsiness or fatigue. Cold hands and feet. Dry mouth, skin, or eyes. Headache. Upset stomach. Diarrhea or constipation. She slowly brought the cup to her mouth and sipped.

"What if we shoot the who are you and what are you looking for in a beach house segment?" She blew on her tea. "As soon as they get here, we'll tell them that you have a hard stop at whatever time; you figure it out. You can say you have to catch a flight because of a work emergency, blah, blah, blah." She sipped her tea. "I'll do the hunting alone, emphasizing that I'm going to send you pictures, blah, blah, blah. Then, when they shoot the update segment, it will be just me. I'll explain that we separated. I'll make something up about how we're splitting the house." She sighed. "By the time the show airs, everything will be out in the open."

Denny nodded. He looked, if not convinced of the merit of her proposal, at least like he would not dismiss it out of hand. "What do you want to do about the condo, anyway?"

"I don't know." She decided to be honest. "I want to sell the damned thing."

"Remi might like this place. I might want to keep it."

"You two can buy your own damned condo." She took her tea and fled upstairs, tears streaming down her cheeks, suddenly feeling possessive over the property that, just seconds before, she didn't want.

10

———

Darlene stood at the front door. It was really the back door, considering that the condo was beachfront; the back was the front. Or was it that the front was the back? She didn't know, and she didn't care. Still flustered and upset from her encounter with Denny, she watched as the production team pulled into the small parking lot. A tall woman emerged first, wearing a plastered-on smile. She balanced a Dunkin' Donuts box in the palm of one hand and carried a Box O' Joe in the other. Darlene held the door open and led her up a small set of stairs to the main living area.

"I'm Gloria," the woman said, dropping the donuts and coffee onto the breakfast bar. She extended her hand.

"Darlene, the homeowner." She heard the front door slam, followed by the sounds of men talking. The camera crew appeared at the top of the stairs.

"You can set up right over there." Gloria waved her arm at the corner of the living room. "Mind if I have a look around?" She was, apparently, having a look around with or without Darlene's blessing.

"Of course."

"We have a moving truck lined up," Gloria said as she walked up the second set of stairs to the bedrooms. "We'll empty most of the furniture out while you and Jesse—he's the cameraman who'll be following you and your husband around like the paparazzi—are at the restaurant filming with the realtor."

"No!" Darlene followed her up the stairs and didn't try to tone down her irritation. "No. I don't want anything moved. We bought the place furnished. I hid the family photos." She pointed to the empty walls. "As you can see, everything looks generic. Could be any beach condo anywhere." Gloria ignored Darlene's pleas and scribbled on a clipboard, hopping from bedroom to bedroom like a frog unable to decide which lily pad to land on. She paused in front of the bathroom and looked in.

"Very nice," she said. "You have a very nice house."

"So, we're on the same page?" Darlene stood, blocking the stairs. "No moving truck?"

"I have to pay for the movers. They're on contract."

"Pay them to do nothing."

"I can't do that."

"This is where I'm living for the next few days. I don't want my home disrupted."

Gloria's smile did not match the look of disdain in her eyes. She took a long slow breath through her nose; the air went in with a dull rattle indicative of someone either on the verge or the tail end of a cold.

"Have you had your flu shot yet?"

"What?" She looked at Darlene, confused.

"Your flu shot?" Darlene smoothed her cardigan. "I'm sorry. I'm overstepping."

"Are you a doctor?"

"Pharmacist."

"I hate to admit this," Gloria said, looking at the floor, "but I woke up with a sore throat this morning."

"Let's hit the kitchen. I'll give you some salt. Gargle with warm salt water three times a day. Should help keep whatever it is from taking hold." Gloria followed Darlene down the stairs. "And if you didn't get your flu shot yet, wait until this passes." She unscrewed the top of the saltshaker and poured a teaspoon or so into a mug and filled it with warm water, twirling it to dissolve the salt. "Here you go."

Darlene stood at the sliding glass door and looked out at the ocean, leaving Gloria alone to gargle at the sink. She heard the camera crew walking around downstairs. She saw a gray flash. Curious, she opened the door and stepped outside. Whatever she saw had disappeared. She was about to step back into the house when she felt something brush against her ankle. She bent down and scratched behind the interloper's ears.

"I'm happy to see your ship didn't sink," a male voice called out. Darlene whipped her head around and stared at the man next door, just over the rail. "Is this your cat?" He pointed at the gray ball of fur. She tried to think of a snarky comeback, but her mouth refused to cooperate. She shook her head.

"Sorry to interrupt," Gloria said, stepping onto the balcony, "but we need you inside." Darlene nodded and followed, leaving the man and the cat to fend for themselves. "So, we need to talk about your cardie." Gloria touched the bottom of Darlene's sweater and rubbed it between her fingers. She lifted it and held it to the light, shaking it. "It's too colorful. Too many colors. Too bright." She let go, and it floated down, falling back into position, draping and covering Darlene's hips. "Don't get me wrong, I love it. But on camera, it will hurt people's eyes." She looked at Darlene. "Didn't they send you a packet with instructions?"

"Probably." Darlene had a vague memory of a packet. But, like everything else she didn't want to deal with, it was likely stuck in the middle of the pile on her dining room table at home. "Look, I'm dealing with some personal things; I didn't read the packet." Why did she feel like she had to justify this? "This is the only decent outfit I have. Everything else is too schlumpy."

"Let's go have a peek."

Who did this woman think she was, traipsing around Darlene's condo, telling her what to wear, what not to wear, how her house should look? "That reminds me," Darlene said, looking at Gloria as she followed her up the stairs. "Where do we stand with the movers? I really don't want anything taken out of here."

"Trust me on this. Let us do what we do best." Gloria paused on the top step. "We'll film you looking at this house first. We'll have everything put back together and be out of here before dinnertime. Sound good?"

Darlene nodded and led Gloria into the master bedroom. She opened the closet. "This is it. This is the extent of my fall beach wardrobe."

Gloria scanned the meager offerings, pulling a scoop neck, three-quarter sleeve, chartreuse yellow shirt off its hanger. She held it next to Darlene's face. "There's nothing schlumpy about this at all." She handed the shirt to her. "I love this color. It's very fall. Put it on. I'll meet you back downstairs."

Darlene did what she was told, although she was internally fuming. She hated this shirt. Which was why it was here, at the condo, and not at home among her favorite pieces. She slipped it over her head and looked in the mirror. Blech. She looked like a bullfrog. She shuffled down the stairs, unsure of herself, unnerved by the sudden change.

"Ah, there you are." Gloria was holding a half-eaten donut. "Perfect. Much better for filming than what you had on before." She stood in front of Darlene, then walked around her and studied her backside. "The shirt is roomy enough to conceal the microphone battery pack. I love the neckline in the back, too. Sexy." Darlene curtsied and hoped the sarcasm of the gesture came through loud and clear. "Oh, and the little diamond earrings you have on are perfect."

11

They agreed to meet their realtor, Laurie, at a small diner five blocks from the condo. Darlene insisted on walking—demurring, then rejecting Gloria's suggestion that she ride with Jesse, the cameraman. Darlene wanted no part of that. None. Smalltalk was not her forte. Still, in the best of times, when she felt good about herself and wanted to be among other people, she accepted superficial chit-chat to be part of the gig. A small price to pay. Affected by the right gravitational pull and with the proper alignment of the planets, she even enjoyed the occasional small talk. But today, her world was off its axis and gravity pressed its thumb against her chest.

She tugged at the bottom of her shirt as she walked into the diner. She noticed Denny right away, chatting animatedly with Laurie. Jesse was at the counter talking to the manager. *And I'll need their consent,* she heard him say, pointing to the four people sitting in a booth against the wall. Laurie stood as Darlene approached the booth at the back of the diner.

"It's great to see you," she said, giving Darlene a perfunctory hug. "Denny and I have been discussing, um, the situation, and we both agree we'll make it look like everything is on the up and up. We're not going to say anything to the production crew. Just that he has a work emergency. Oh, and he took the liberty of ordering for you."

"Goody." Darlene glared at Denny. "I'm afraid to know." His hair was four or five shades lighter than it had been two hours ago. He must have taken her advice to heart and washed his hair eight times. She wondered what Remi thought of him washing it out, wondering now what she thought of his ridiculous dyed hair. Denny looked good in gray. Gray hair, gray shirts. He was aging well. Her heart sunk at the thought of him making a life with this new woman.

"I figured ordering for you would speed things up. I got you French toast with a side of eggs and bacon." He smiled. "You can get back on track tomorrow."

"On track for what?" The sadness threatening to choke her turned to anger. The tears she had been holding in came pouring out, despite her best efforts. Everything with him boiled down to her weight. Sure, she gained a few pounds during the past few years. Sure, her stomach sported a few rolls when she sat. But she didn't look fat. At least that was what she told herself. Curvy. Yes, she was curvy. She pressed a napkin into her eyes, thankful that she wore waterproof mascara.

"You okay?" Jesse sat down next to Darlene; he didn't wait for an answer "So, here's what we're going to do." He looked at her. "Are you sure you're okay?" She nodded. "I'm going to let the camer roll for a few seconds before your food comes out." He handed her a micro-phone tethered to a clip-on battery pack. She fed the wire down the back of her shirt and clipped the battery pack to her pants. Jesse helped her adjust the microphone and position it to her neckline. "There you go. Almost invisible." He sat back and looked at the rest of the group. "Any questions?"

"How will you know when the food is about to come out?" Denny, always looking to get the last word, or create a distraction, or conjure up a red herring.

"That's not the point, Denny," Darlene said.

"But he asked if we had any ques—"

"It doesn't matter how he knows when the food is about to come out." She scanned the room. "He probably asked the manager to alert him." She looked at Jesse. "Didn't you?"

"Exactly." He drummed his fingernails on the table. "Anyway, the camera will be rolling. Your food will come out. Once the plates are down and the waiter goes away, you'll 'ooh and aah' over your food. You'll take a few bites and say something about this being one of your favorite places to eat. Then Laurie will jump in and start asking questions about your must-haves for the beach house." He looked at Denny, then at Darlene, and finally at Laurie. "Everyone on board?"

"We watch these shows all the time," Denny said, holding his coffee cup in midair. "We know the format. We know the drill."

"Good." Jesse stood. "And that's my cue."

Darlene pressed the button on her phone's camera and switched it to selfie mode. Using it as a mirror, she scanned her face for post-cry puffiness, then smiled to check one last time that she didn't have lipstick on her teeth. She slid the phone back into her purse, ignoring Denny's disdain.

"Cameral rolling." Jesse waved his arm. "Cut. Cut." He motioned for the waiter to hold on, then turned to the happy home buyers. "I forgot to mention when I say, 'camera rolling,' that's your cue to act like you're deep in conversation. Don't actually talk. I'll edit in some cafe sounds. But look like you're talking." They all nodded. "Alright, then. Camera rolling."

The group did what they were told, Denny exaggerating hand motions like he was in the middle of telling a compelling story. Darlene threw her head back and pretended to laugh.

"Cut!" Jesse looked directly at Denny. "Your movements don't need to be so...big." He turned to Darlene. "You too. Tone it down a notch. Please."

"Can I have a minute to recheck my lipstick?"

"For God's sake, Darlene." Denny shook his head "Your lipstick is fine. Our food is getting cold."

"Camera rolling," Jesse said, ignoring her request.

The waiter sauntered to the table, carrying a metal tray with one hand and a folding tray-stand with the other. With a flick of the wrist, he opened the tray-stand and lowered the tray onto it. After passing out the plates, he quietly sauntered away, with a bit too much saunter, Darlene thought.

Denny reached across the table for the syrup. Darlene slid her plate away from his sleeve, which hovered dangerously close to her French toast. He held the pitcher over his Belgian waffle and let the syrup flow down—one long, amber thread—until each tiny square was filled. It looked like a neighborhood grid from an airplane window; instead of fresh, blue, chlorinated pools, the pools in Denny's waffle were filled with thick, sticky, golden deliciousness. Tiny swimmers frozen in liquid sugar, little sunbathers sitting in pool chairs. By the time Denny finished, the entire waffle was saturated, syrup pouring over the sides like a flash flood. He looked up at Darlene, who gave him a slow blink—a telltale sign of her annoyance.

"Here you go," he said, drizzling a thin swirl of syrup across the top of her plate. He put the pitcher down.

Darlene picked up the pitcher and let the syrup come rushing out and onto her French toast. She slammed the pitcher back down. "I'll have as much syrup as I damned well please." She cut a chunk of French toast with the side of her fork and shoved it in her mouth. "Yummy," she said, looking at Denny with wide eyes.

"Fine. Whatever." Denny shrugged and cut a dainty piece of his waffle. "It's your life."

"Cut! Cut! Cut!" Jesse stood in front of the booth, the camera on his shoulder, hand on his hip. "I'm not sure what's going on here, and yes, I can edit a lot of this out, but..." He looked at Denny and Darlene. "The tone here isn't exactly what our viewers want to see."

"Great," Denny said. He crumbled his napkin, slammed it next to his plate, and stood. "I'm outta here."

"Denny, sit down." Darlene demanded.

"Maybe we need to regroup." Laurie looked at Jesse. "Could we have a moment, please?"

Jess twirled in a graceful pirouette and sat down at the counter, setting his camera on the stool beside him. Darlene watched as he put his head in his hands. She braced herself for today being longer than she anticipated.

"I'm sorry," Darlene said to Laurie. "This isn't going to work."

"I agree. Not going to work." Denny looked relieved. "I'll just leave now."

"I'll tell you what." Laurie pushed a piece of egg around her plate. "Work with me here. We'll get through this diner scene quickly, then we'll go tour the first condo—your condo. Can you at least do that?"

"I don't know." He looked at Darlene.

"I can't be around him." Darlene blew her nose. "I just can't."

"I understand." She patted Darlene's hand. "We've come this far. If you do everything Jesse says, it will be quick. I promise." She slid out of the booth without waiting for a response and went to Jesse. "I think we're ready. Just keep rolling, please. We're really behind schedule."

Jesse collected his camera and shuffled back to the booth. "Could we get some natural light in here, please?" He looked at Darlene, who fiddled with the blinds, slowly adjusting them until he nodded in approval.

"Okay. Let's try this again. Do you remember what we talked about before? Take a few bites of your food, then follow Laurie's lead." He hoisted the camera onto his shoulder. "Camera rolling."

"Wow, they make the best French toast here." Darlene cut a small chunk, this time using her knife.

"Everything is good here," Denny said, taking a tentative sip. "And the coffee is the best in town."

"So, you two come to Ocean City often?"

"We do," Darlene chimed in. "In fact, we rent a condo here every summer." She took a deep breath. "We looked at each other one day and agreed that we should buy a place."

"So, here we are," Denny said. "I'm a quality control inspector for a large commercial construction company in the DC area." He shook his head. "The stress is twenty-four by seven. I hear the waves and I'm a new person."

"And what do you do?" Laurie looked at Darlene, who had a mouthful of French toast.

"I'm a pharmacist," she said, swallowing. She took a sip of coffee. Indeed, not the best coffee in town. Not by a long shot. "I love what I do. Not nearly as stressful as my husband's job, but I spend long hours on my feet." Hearing herself refer to Denny as her husband stung.

"Tell me what you're looking for. What are your must-haves?"

"Oceanfront, or at least ocean view." Denny took Darlene's hand and squeezed. "And a tub. I really don't care much about the inside. As long as it has a nice tub, I'll be happy."

"My biggest want is easy beach access," Darlene said. "I'd even give up square footage or the number of bedrooms for ocean-front." Denny's hand felt warm and familiar. She wanted to stay like this, frozen in time, and wondered if this exercise in decep-tion might rekindle something long lost. Remi swatting his ass on the beach flashed like a subliminal message. She yanked her hand away. "Really, that's the most important thing. Beach access."

"I'm going to need more than that if you want me to find you the perfect house." Laurie laughed, a cue, Darlene figured, for her and Denny to laugh too.

"At least a thousand square feet." Denny gestured for Darlene to chime in.

"Two to three bedrooms. And a master bedroom with a private bathroom."

"And a tub."

"How much are you willing to spend on this oceanfront, tub?"

"Our budget is $400,000 to $425,000, but absolutely no more than $450,000."

"I think we could stretch it to $475,000," Denny chimed in. "For the right tub." Everyone laughed, including Jesse.

"I have several places in mind," Laurie said. "One of them is just a few blocks from here."

"Let's go!" Darlene smiled.

"Cut!" Jesse exhaled. "It's a wrap. You people had me worried for a little while there."

"So, I'll, um, well, um, nice seeing you again, Laurie." Denny squeezed out of the booth. "And nice meeting you, Jesse." The two men shook hands. "Darlene, honey, I'll see you in about a week." He gave her a quick, perfunctory kiss on the lips. "Don't go making any decisions without me."

"Wait, you're not coming to the first house?"

"No, Darlene. I'm not. And it's already our house." He glanced at Laurie, who was talking to Jesse, then turned toward Darlene. He lowered his voice. "I'm done pretending that my house isn't my house. You're on your own."

"Can I at least catch a ride with you?" She flung her purse over her shoulder. "I walked here."

"You can walk back, then."

"I just think it will take too much time."

"Dammit, Darlene." He glanced behind him and lowered his voice. "I have an afternoon planned with Remi." He looked around the diner as if expecting her to walk in at any moment. "She's not happy about this, you know."

"Your girlfriend's happiness isn't exactly my problem."

"Lower your voice!"

"Why? You just said you're tired of pretending."

"Fine. I'll drop you off."

DARLENE SLID INTO THE CAR—DENNY'S car—a car at once so familiar and yet so strange. She had ridden with him in this car what seemed like a million times. It had been their preferred car to take on road trips, the one they always drove to the beach. His daily commuting car. A car she could no longer lay claim to, the passenger seat now occupied by another woman.

She mindlessly pressed the button to open the glove compartment, then closed it quickly when she caught a glimpse of a woman's fuzzy, red hat. Remi's, no doubt. She pressed the power button for the radio expecting to hear Denny's classic rock station but instead heard opera. Opera! She could not resist goading him and turned up the volume. He took his eyes off the road and glared at her, jamming his finger into the power button. Silence ensued.

"Come on, Denny. Since when do you listen to opera?" She laughed. Big, belly laughs. "Opera? Really?"

"It's better than the show tunes you listen to."

"You always liked my show tunes."

"I was pretending."

Pretending—they excelled at it. Now Darlene wondered if she and Denny had been pretending to be happy all these years. She had been happy, or at least she thought so. Her mind drifted to her neighbor on the balcony, stepping out to sing with her. What did that have to do with Denny? Nothing. Perhaps she and Denny were like oil and water. If she stared at the water long enough, the blobs of oil morphed and bent into interesting, sometimes beautiful shapes. Darlene had to look hard, though, to see the blobs forming a pattern of marital bliss. She never had romantic feelings for her high school friend Eugene, but she had fun with him. Being with Eugene had been easy. Much of the time, being with Denny felt like work. Now there was Remi. Not an affair. A relationship. She swallowed the lump in her throat. She never stopped to consider Denny trading her in for a jogging, laughing, ass swatting, red hat wearing Remi.

Denny pulled into the carport in front of their condo. Darlene was about to step out of the car when she saw the man from next door lifting a trash bag into the dumpster. She turned around and leaned against the window, the back of her head facing the street. Stalling, she searched for something, anything, to buy a few seconds. The last thing she needed was another encounter with him.

"It will mean a lot to me if you'd stay and just do this one shoot." She searched Denny's eyes. "Let's just do this one shoot together, then you're free to go." She sighed. "Please?"

Denny yanked his phone out of the center console and started texting. Darlene slowly turned her head to see if the coast was clear to exit the car without being seen. She looked back at Denny, who was still texting, and opened the door. The neighbor walked out of the trash corral and headed to the gaggle of production crew people in front of the moving truck. She lifted her leg back in and quietly closed the door.

"I can't believe I'm doing this." Denny looked up from his phone. He exhaled long and slow out of his nose. "Remi said to go ahead and do it."

"Oh, thank God," Darlene said, flaunting her sarcasm.

"I'll leave right now if you keep up with that attitude."

"Don't do me any favors." She got out and slammed the door, hurrying into the condo, not stopping to acknowledge the neighbor's cheery hello.

"Oh, good. You're both here." Gloria put her hand on the small of Darlene's back and ushered her into the living room. "We want to do a few shots of you and your husband on the beach."

Darlene whipped her head around to find Denny leaning against the kitchen counter, texting. Had they ever been that tethered to each other? Granted, the bulk of their marriage was in the dark ages before cell phones and texting. Now, it seemed that Denny couldn't fart without consulting Remi. He put his phone in his back pocket and joined them in the living room.

"Listen," Denny said, lifting his ball cap and scratching his head. "I didn't get your name."

"Gloria."

"Listen, Gloria." He repositioned the ball cap. "I'm on a tight schedule."

"He got called into work," Darlene chimed in.

"Emergency." He tapped his palm. "Big, work emergency. I can be here for this one house tour. That's it."

"The beach scene will only take a few minutes. Half-hour tops."

"What beach scene? I didn't agree to any beach scene."

Gloria opened the sliding glass door. "We really need to do this, Mr. Feldman. Jesse is out on the sand, waiting."

Denny brushed past Darlene as he stepped outside, mumbling *you owe me* through clenched teeth.

DARLENE TRIED to remember what it had been like when she and Denny saw this condo for the first time. She pictured herself a year ago, floating through the rooms, imagining the two of them growing close and growing old here. Weekends. Holidays. She imagined her parents driving down from Philly and spending time here. The possibilities bloomed like the first crocuses in spring. Of course, that was all before Denny shattered her dreams.

The beach scene took just ten minutes to shoot. Darlene stomped on the balcony, letting the sand fall off her shoes, before following Denny inside.

"I don't know, Dar," Denny said. "Where will we put a dining room table?" Jesse walked toward him with his camera. "How will we host Thanksgiving here?"

"We could set up a folding table, right here." Darlene stood in the center of the living room, drawing an imaginary rectangle in the air with her hand.

"I don't know. I suppose it could work."

"Look at the view," she said, moving toward the sliding glass door. "Definitely worth giving up a dining room for this view."

"I don't remember anything about a dining room being on your wish list." Laurie joined the discussion in her most commanding, yet jovial realtor-on-TV voice.

"That's because it isn't," Darlene said, trying to one-up Laurie with her own jocularity.

"Yeah, but it would be nice. Not a must-have, but nice." Denny stared into the camera and shrugged. "Just saying..."

They did end up having Thanksgiving here last year. It had been a joyful few days with Shelly. And it was the first Thanksgiving in nearly a decade that her parents didn't run to San Francisco to be with Rachel. She and Denny had been playful with each other, struggling to cook in the small kitchen, laughing and joking and deliberately bumping into each other to prove the point. They sat down to a mid-afternoon dinner at a folding table, decorated in a quasi-Martha Stewart kind of way. The sand, crashing waves, and endless ocean in the background, well, life didn't get much better than that.

"I hate these blue tiles." Denny rapped the countertop with his knuckles. "The grout would be a bear to keep clean."

"I like them. They're colorful and quirky." She laughed. "Like me."

Denny didn't react. Didn't laugh, didn't roll his eyes, didn't agree, didn't disagree. His non-reaction stung. Could she be still, even with the blatant flaunting of his new life, seeking his approval or acknowledgment? Wanting to stand out among the throngs as colorful and quirky? She suddenly could not wait for him to get out of here, for the crew to get out, to be done with this self-inflicted charade. What did she expect, anyway? Was there a part of her who thought this house hunting farce would make him love her again? Expectations. She hated them. Hated that she harbored them. Hated that she couldn't face exposing her complete and utter failure to the world.

She followed Denny up the stairs bemoaning the difficulty it might pose for her parents. "Maybe we should look at a one level condo."

"Yes! A bathtub!" Denny ignored her comments about the stairs and climbed into the soaker tub in the master bathroom. "Hon bring me a beer," he snickered.

"Big enough for two," Laurie said, winking.

Denny climbed out of the tub and wandered around the rest of the upstairs, bemoaning the paint color, admiring the view, observing that the balcony railing needed repair. "A hazard of being an inspector." He bent down and shook a loose spindle.

"These are all easy things to fix," Laurie said, leading them back downstairs. They stood in the living room and discussed the condo.

"Cut!" Jesse smiled. "That's all for today, folks."

Darlene watched Denny pull out his cell phone, this time making a call instead of texting. Probably letting Remi know he would be back soon and telling her to keep the bedsheets warm. Or better yet, she could draw him a nice, hot bath and bring him a beer. Denny didn't even like taking baths. At least not during their marriage.

12

Thunder in November, a fertile year to come. Darlene's father had hundreds of such sayings memorized from various sources, mainly from the series of farmer's almanac calendars that hung in her parents' kitchen during her childhood. *Fog in January brings a wet spring. A swarm of bees in May is worth a load of hay.* Darlene's grandmother—her bubbe—the queen of superstitions, hated these sayings. It was okay to knock on wood or kiss the mezuzah in the doorway each time she entered. Bubbe had a fit, though, whenever Darlene, Rachel, or Liam repeated their father.

The thunder abated, and Darlene yanked the strings of her hoodie, pulling the fabric tight against her neck. It felt as though the temperature had dropped ten degrees in the past ten minutes. The wind, calm this morning, had picked up and grown steadier since early this afternoon. Unseasonably warm all day, the weather pattern was ripe for a late-fall thunderstorm. She stood on the balcony, waiting for the movers to return the things they took away for the filming. It wasn't much. Just the bar stools, an extra recliner from the living room, the vintage couch on the first floor, a lopsided dresser from one of the guest rooms.

"Rose."

Darlene turned toward the condo next door. Clenching her teeth, she counted to ten. "Really?" Her tongue loosened, and her jaw pried itself open. "What is with you and this Rose obsession?" She was feeling defensive of her space, annoyed that he kept showing up when all she wanted was to be left alone.

"I'm sorry." He cringed.

She remembered his outstretched arms last night; breaking into song, opening the floodgates from her carefree youth. Summer days blocking and facing the cereal aisle, belting out tunes from *A Chorus Line* with Eugene. "You don't need to apologize." Or did he? After all, it was he who engaged her last night, interrupting her private thoughts. As he was doing now. "Actually, I take that back. Apology accepted." She walked over to where he stood and held her hand over the rail that separated their two decks. "I'm Darlene. I wish I looked like Kate Winslet, but alas, I don't."

"Nice to meet you, Rose." He laughed, his eyes crinkling into two tight slits. "Fran Wilkins." He took her hand, squeezed twice, then let go.

"Francis?" She had only known one male Fran in her life—her high school chemistry teacher.

"Francisco."

"Francisco...that's fun to say...Francisco..." Darlene studied him as she recited a line from *Elf*, her favorite holiday movie. His eyes were no longer slits but wide open. Brown. Light brown. Caramel. Or was it honey? She looked away. If he could reference a character in a movie, so could she.

"Buddy the Elf?" His eyes danced.

"The one and only." A clap of thunder. She winced, allowing her mouth to morph into the slightest smile. "Francisco...Francisco...Fran...cis...co-o-o-o." She shoved her hands in her pockets and turned to go inside, intrigued that he got the *Elf* reference. "We're even now."

"That's a nice purple hoodie," he called after her. "Very purply."

Another rumble of thunder. Another *Elf* reference. Very purply.

The orange and pink of sunset cast streaks through the western sky, over the top of their building. Or was it orange and purple? Or purple and pink? Or just purple? Very purply. Darlene suppressed a smile and waved without turning around. She opened the sliding glass door and went in, shaking her head, suddenly wanting to watch *Elf* on Netflix.

DARLENE CURLED up on the couch. She left the sliding glass door open despite the cold, the sound of the waves a soothing balm. The thunderstorm was now a distant memory, and the cold wind blowing off the ocean ushered in the briny scent of the sea. She pulled the fuzzy throw blanket around her shoulders until only her head was visible, then poked her hand out and grabbed the remote, firing at the TV like a target. She scrolled through Netflix and found *Elf*, happy to have a mindless distraction from what had proven to be a stressful day. Twenty minutes into the movie, she scrolled ahead—all the way forward to the part where Buddy accompanies his dad to work and meets a man named Francisco. Francisco-o-o-o. She closed Netflix after she'd watched that scene ten or eleven times, determined to put Francisco out of her mind.

The plate of cheese that she hadn't touched yesterday adorned the coffee table. Scrolling through the regular channel guide, she deliberately bypassed the house-hunting show that got her into this predicament in the first place. She scrolled down and, like a voyeur, scrolled back up and clicked. A young couple searching for their first home. A modest budget. An impossible wish list. Whatever happened to the concept of a starter home? The first house she and Denny bought had been a two-bedroom, one-bathroom bungalow on the outskirts of Washington, DC. It was built in the thirties but had undergone a renovation to modernize it in the sixties, complete with white Formica countertops with silver and gold speckles, and avocado green appliances. They eventually updated the kitchen, redid the hardwood floors, squirrel-proofed the attic, and sold the house for almost three times what they had paid. Dream house? Hardly.

"Your first house isn't your dream house!" She fought the urge to throw the remote at the TV. Instead, she flipped to the music channels and was surprised to find the Christmas music station already activated. Thanksgiving was still several weeks away. She clicked the station—*The Twelve Days of Christmas* already in progress—and tossed the blanket off. She closed the sliding glass door and looked at her watch—six-thirty, but it felt much, much later. A sound near her feet startled her. Ah, the cat, standing on his hind legs, paws against the glass. She crouched down and tapped on the glass, looking into the cat's emerald eyes. She didn't want to let him inside; she could give him a bowl of milk, though. And a blanket.

She climbed the stairs to the linen closet and scanned its contents, not seeing the old, pink blanket the previous owners had left. Except for a tear in the silky binding, it was in pretty good condition. She moved a pile of towels out of the way and spotted the blanket, haphazardly jammed in the back of the second shelf. She carried the blanket downstairs, filled a bowl with milk, and stepped out onto the balcony, creating a cozy nook for the cat. She glanced at the house next door. *Francisco...Francisco-o-o-o.*

DARLENE WAS ABOUT to step back into the house when she noticed her father standing in the kitchen. She closed her eyes and opened them again, wondering if she was hallucinating.

"You'll attract vermin if you do that." Sid Bloom tossed his keys on the counter and draped his coat across the back of a bar stool.

"Dad?" She stood on the precipice of the balcony and living room, frozen, unable to comprehend.

"You're feeding cats now? Since when are you a cat person? Didn't you get my voicemail?"

"Since never. I've never fed cats. Until today. What voicemail?" She looked at her father with knitted eyebrows. "Hello, Dad. It's nice to see you, too." She stepped into the house and hugged him, then took him by the hand and led him to the breakfast bar. He sat. She picked up his coat and hung it in the entryway closet, truly not remembering any voicemail. She picked up her phone and scanned her 'missed calls' list. Nothing from her parents' landline, nothing from her mother's cell phone. She opened the refrigerator and pulled out two beers and handed one to her father. Then she grabbed the cheese board from the coffee table and set it on the breakfast bar. "Now, what are you doing here, and where's Mom?"

"I'll get to that, but first, can you please turn off that music?" Frank Sinatra was belting out *Have Yourself a Merry Little Christmas*. "What is it with you and your husband with the Christmas music?"

Husband. The word pierced her heart and threatened to bring a fresh wave of tears. The night Denny dropped his bomb, one of her first instincts had been to call her parents. Now she felt resolved to not tell them. Because telling them would make it real. Because maybe, just maybe Denny would...come back to her?

"It's music, Dad. We happen to like it. It doesn't denounce us as Jews if we listen to *Frosty the Snowman*." She popped the lids off the two beers and didn't wait for her father to lift his bottle—she clinked it anyway and took a long, slow pull. She nodded, pleased with her latest homebrew—a hop-forward imperial IPA with enough malt backbone to keep things balanced. She would definitely use this recipe again.

"Rachel's hospital donated over $100,000 to the Squirrel Hill families in Pittsburgh. She organized the whole thing."

"I know that, Dad. You went on and on about it last Thanksgiving." Her stomach sank. She couldn't believe, at almost fifty years old, she still had to fight Rachel for their father's approval. Darlene fell short every time. Every stinking time. "Out with it. What are you doing here?" She didn't attempt to hide her frustration. "And for the last time, where is Mom?"

"She's at Rachel's."

Of course. Of course, her mother would be at Rachel's. In San Francisco. There was that damned name again...Francisco-o-o-o.

Why now, though, three weeks before Thanksgiving? And why wasn't her father in San Francisco too?

"What happened? Is someone sick?" Her father shook his head, clearly unwilling to level with her. "You know, I was just thinking about you earlier today. Believe it or not, we had a thunderstorm a few hours ago. It made me remember all your silly quotes." She pretended to look out the window but peered sideways at her father. Something was not right. He looked old. Incredibly old.

"Thunder in November, a fertile year to come." Finally, he raised his glass and clinked Darlene's. He took several gulps, leaving a trickle of beer running down his chin. "Where's that husband of yours?" He wiped his chin with the back of his hand.

"Not here." She put her beer down. "Traveling." She lied, although he could be traveling for all she knew. He never even said goodbye when he left after the shoot today. "For work. Dad, have you eaten dinner? We could order pizza."

"I'm not hungry," he said, slicing a chunk of sharp cheddar and shoving it into his mouth without a cracker. He chased it with a swig of beer. "This beer is good. One of yours?"

Darlene nodded, taking a swig of her beer. Denny hated bitter IPAs. Drinking this beer was like giving him the finger. She had four bottles left and intended to savor them.

"What is this song?" Sid spread a hunk of goat cheese on a cracker and took a small bite. "I never much liked goat cheese, but this one is nice."

"*I Want a Hippopotamus for Christmas*." And then: "I got the cheese at the market across the street, the one Mom went nuts over the last time you were here."

"Hippo for Christmas. How ridiculous." He got up and helped himself to another beer.

Darlene waited until he was back on his barstool before she slipped into the kitchen and hid two beers in the back of the fridge before grabbing one and carrying it to the bar. She refused to let her father guzzle her precious beer, her labor of love, now her *Fuck you, Denny* brew.

"Okay, Dad. It's time." She yanked the beer out of his hand. "No more beer until you tell me what's going on." She bore into his eyes. "You don't exactly live next door. When have you ever showed up, out of the blue on a Monday evening, all the way from Philly—without Mom, mind you—for no reason." In a fit of pique, he grabbed his beer bottle and guzzled it. Then he slammed it down. "Be careful! I reuse those bottles." She shook her head and braced herself for a long night. If there was one thing she knew about her father, there was no pushing him into talking before he was good and ready. "For someone who isn't hungry, you're sure eating a lot of cheese. Let me order fish tacos from that place you like."

"I don't want fish tacos."

"What do you want, then?"

"I want you to turn off that damned Christmas music."

Darlene found it odd that her father was making such a big deal about Christmas music. He never had in the past. She and Denny always enjoyed Christmas music—the cheesier and more annoying, the better. Sid Bloom had even been known to bob his head and— God forbid—sing. Throughout her childhood, he would go on kicks —bursts of convictions that he vehemently enforced for a few days or weeks. Eventually, time and the distractions of life would erode his resolve. In second grade, Darlene brought home a *Birth of Jesus* coloring book that a classmate had given her in their holiday gift exchange. Sid Bloom, ever the good Jew, made her give it back the next day. It was the one time in her life that she felt different—oddly different. And what second-grader wants to feel different? Why couldn't he just let her keep the damned coloring book? What harm would it have done? He could have used it as an opportunity to teach her about other beliefs. Darlene felt herself fuming over this long-buried memory.

She left him sitting at the breakfast bar and ignored his request that she turn off the music. She went straight out to the balcony, pleased to see the cat snuggled on the blanket. She folded part of it over him, surprised that he let her. The milk was gone. She would buy him some cat food tomorrow. She glanced through the sliding glass door and saw that her father was still sitting at the bar, oblivious to her whereabouts, distracted—at least temporarily—by the cheese. She texted her sister: What's going on with Mom and Dad?

Rachel: Can I get back to you? In the middle of something.

Darlene: Is Mom there with you?

Rachel: Not until the 22nd. Can't do this now. Text you later.

Darlene: K

Darlene dialed her mother's landline. No answer. She tried her cell phone next. Again, no response. She went back into the house, *Mary Did You Know* filling the room. She loved that song. She picked up the remote and turned the volume up, then sat down at the bar, next to her father, trying hard to conceal her concern.

"Can you please, please, turn off that Christmas music?"

"I like it, Dad. I'm not turning it off."

"I have never interfered in your life," he said, rubbing his forehead. "Your mother and I have never insisted that you follow a faith or attempted to force you or my grandchild to adhere to our faith."

"Dad!" She looked hard at him. "Denny and I practice the faith. You know this. Shelly grew up attending synagogue. She had a bat mitzvah, for crying out loud. We enjoy Christmas music. So what? I can't believe we're having this conversation." She noticed a layer of moistness around her father's eyes and squeezed his hand. The gesture opened the floodgates. He slid his hand out from under hers and covered his eyes. Darlene watched as his shoulders shook. Suddenly paralyzed with fear, she put her arms around him. "Dad. Dad? Dad. Look at me." He moved his hands, and she could see that the moistness around his eyes had turned into a soft, squishy bog. She jumped up and got him a handful of napkins. He blew his nose and looked at her.

"Your mother kicked me out." He sniffed and blew again.

"What do you mean, she kicked you out?"

"You know exactly what I mean."

"But why? Why?" She shook her head, exasperated. "Why?"

"I don't want to talk about it."

"Where's Mom?"

"I told you, she's at Rachel's."

"What makes you think she's in San Francisco?"

"That's where she said she was going."

"When did she leave?"

"Yesterday." He looked at her, distraught. "She said she needed to clear her head."

"So, she got on a plane and flew across the country to clear her head? That makes no sense." Darlene needed to broach this carefully. There had to be a logical explanation. Her rising concern threatened to choke her. Her phone rang, and she jumped.

"Mom!" Relief washed over her. Her father got up and stepped out onto the balcony. "Where are you? Oh, you're home...Okay...Dad is here...I don't know, he didn't say...Just this week, then I need to head home...Mom? What's going on? He's not talking...Yep...Okay...I will...Love you too."

"Come back in, Dad," she said, stepping outside, surprised to see her father crouched down, petting the cat. She did not know how she was going to deal with this. Dammit, she had to film another fake house-hunt tomorrow. God, she regretted getting involved with this show. "It's cold out here. Let's go inside." He stood slowly, his hand pressed into his lower back. She led him to the couch, helped him sit, and handed him the remote. "Put on whatever you want." She draped the throw blanket over his knees. He clicked away from the music channels and ended up on CNN.

"What did your mother say?" He looked straight ahead; his eyes glued to the TV.

"She was pretty vague, Dad." She patted his hand. "She's not in San Francisco." He turned from the TV and looked at her. "She's home." She took a deep breath. "Which is exactly where you should be."

"I'm not going back there."

"I'm going to bed. You can sleep on the couch, or in the guest room. We'll talk more tomorrow." She took her two beers and started to climb the stairs. "I have something tomorrow that I can't reschedule. I should be done by late afternoon. We'll grab some dinner, and you can tell me what's going on."

"I don't know what I'm doing. I might be gone by then."

"Dad, I can't tell you what to do. But you drove all the way here. How did you even know I was here? What if I wasn't?"

"Shelly told me."

"Did she tell you what I'm doing here?"

"Yeah, you're filming one of those ridiculous house-hunting shows. I always knew they were fake."

"They're not fake." She felt protective of her decision to do this, defending the very thing she just a second ago bemoaned.

"What would you call it, then?" He raised his eyebrow.

"Fake-ish?" She laughed and was happy to hear him laughing too. "Goodnight, Dad."

"Goodnight, bubbeleh."

13

The potato went around and around on the microwave carousel. Darlene watched from the comfort of her bed, imagining the microwave radiation spinning the water molecules in the potato, producing thermal energy. She moved closer to the microwave door, without even getting up, and felt at one with the potato, her own insides heating up in solidarity. Crap. She forgot to poke holes in the potato to allow steam to escape. She sat straight up in bed, frantically pressing an off button that didn't exist. She listened to the hissing steam, the pressure building, the potato hot enough on the inside to cause a severe burn.

She threw the covers off and jumped out of bed, then ran to the sliding glass door and stepped outside where the wind coming off the ocean doused the flames shooting out of her body. She fell into the chair, still not fully awake, drenched in sweat, her thin cotton pajamas plastered to her body. She closed her eyes and dozed, waking only when she couldn't stand the shivering. *Damned hot flashes.* She could see the red digital numbers of her bedside clock through the door—three-thirty. Absolutely no hope of going back to sleep. She stretched and shivered, then walked back into the bedroom. She put on her purple hoody (*very purply*) and tiptoed down the stairs. She paused on the second-floor landing and saw that the guest room door was closed—a sign that her father had not gotten on his horse and ridden away into the night.

Standing at the door, she was tempted to knock. Or, barge in, and demand to know what had happened between him and her mother. She could not imagine what sin he might have committed that resulted in her mother asking him to leave. She sat down on the top step and went through a litany of potential crimes: an affair; a secret gambling addiction; a violent outburst; spewing out intimate details of their relationship in the company of others. Darlene let her head flop between her knees. She had no idea. She simply could not imagine her eighty-year-old father involved in any of those things. She took a deep breath and stood. Holding tightly to the banister, she made her way down the rest of the stairs. Maybe, just maybe, her father had admitted to being in a long-term relationship with another woman. If Denny could do that, then why not her father, too?

She flicked the kitchen light on and opened the drawer next to the dishwasher. Her stash of chocolates lured like a siren. She pulled the bag out of the drawer and shook three candies out. Screw it. She shook another two. Five in all. A mere 210 calories, according to the nutrition facts on the back of the bag. The squares of chocolate, wrapped in red foil, sparkled in the fluorescent kitchen light like rubies. She tossed the bag back into the drawer and nearly squealed with glee. Shoved all the way in the back of the draw was a baggie filled with the coffee Shelly had brought back from Saint Lucia last year. She opened the bag and sniffed. Still smelled fresh. No matter. Because right now, stale coffee would be better than no coffee. She danced a little jig around the kitchen and loaded up the coffee maker.

Darlene turned on her laptop as the coffee sputtered and gurgled and dripped. The aroma quickly filled the small kitchen, filling her with delight amid the dark issues that had recently sprouted around her. At least for now, she could forget. Or for however long the scent coffee permeated the house. Or however long it would take her to drink the elixir. And for the few blissful minutes it would take to eat the chocolate, well, at least for that long, she wouldn't have to think about anything other than those fleshly pleasures. Manna from heaven.

"What are you doing up?" Her father's voice pierced the quiet.

"Dad?" Sid was sitting on the couch, his few strands of hair pointing hither and yon: *Key West-1,256 miles; Bar Harbor-722 miles; London-3,608 miles; Cancun-3,289 miles; San Francisco-2,949 miles.* The TV was on, muted, but on.

As she opened the cabinet and grabbed a couple of mugs, she noticed an unread text message on her phone, timestamped at around midnight: Your father thinks I'm fooling around with Jimmy Finch from across the street. I am not. Love, Mom. It cracked her up that her mother always ended her text messages with *Love, Mom.* As if there was any ambiguity about the identity of her texts. Oh well. At least, at age seventy-five, she was texting. She couldn't say the same for her father; he and technology did not mix. Like mixing bleach and ammonia—coughing, nausea, and shortness of breath all ensue. *I'm allergic to technology*, he would announce to anyone who dared suggest he get a cell phone. Darlene shuddered to think of him driving all the way here from Philly, alone, without one. She sighed and rubbed her forehead, trying hard to erase the mental image of her mother with that weaselly little man.

"Here you go." She handed him a mug of coffee. "Black, just the way you like it."

"What were you about to work on over there?" He pointed to her laptop.

"There's an article in a pharmaceutical journal about cannabis-based medicines." She winked, knowing full well how her father felt about medical marijuana. "It's the wave of the future."

"Well, a future I'm glad I won't be a part of." He slurped his coffee. "Thank God I retired before my patients started requesting prescriptions for weed."

She sat down beside him, her desire for chocolate suddenly gone. She would sit and sip her coffee for precisely five minutes before launching in on him about whatever was going on back in Philly. She watched as her father stared at the TV—an infomercial for Night

View glasses. She put her coffee down, her desire for chocolate back in full force. She left her father on the couch and sat down at the breakfast bar.

Opening her web browser, she bypassed the cannabis article and went straight to Facebook. Feeling bold and voyeuristic, she typed *Fran Wilkins* into the search bar, wondering if she spelled his last name correctly. She scanned the list of profiles that popped up, many of them women (she wondered if he had been teased as a child), until, yep, that's him. Silver-laced strawberry hair, high forehead, a crooked smile. And...and...his arm around a petit, pretty woman. She thought back to her two encounters with him—the night of the singing and just a few hours ago—and tried to recall if she had seen a ring on his finger. She never even looked. She did, however, remember the second coffee mug on his balcony. She sighed and closed Facebook, embarrassed she went there.

The chocolates sitting on the counter next to her laptop taunted, daring her to ignore them. She refused to be intimidated. She clicked on the link for the cannabis article and forced herself to focus, reading a sentence or two, then looking sideways at the five squares. She lifted her mug and let the last bit of coffee dribble into her mouth. Another sentence. Then another. One paragraph. Then another. Dammit. She struggled to recall what she had just read. She started at the top, then worked her way down, pausing to read the same sentence three times. It was no use. She slid the chocolates around on the counter, then stacked them, one on top of the other. By the time she placed the fourth one, her little tower of delight had tumbled. How about a pyramid then? Three on the bottom and two on top of that. Not exactly what she had in mind. Something was missing.

She got up, refilled her coffee mug, and pulled another chocolate out of the bag, carefully placing it on top, completing her pyramid. She smiled, pleased with herself, and unwrapped the top piece, shoving the whole thing into her mouth. Right now, she didn't care about the message written on the inside of the wrapper. All she cared about was the taste of chocolate. She popped the next piece into her mouth, half chewing, half sucking, barely tasting it. She repeated the process until all that remained was a sea of crumbled red balls.

"This is why you don't lose weight." Her father stood over her, hands on his hips. "Why are you doing this. You know diabetes runs rampant on your mother's side of the family."

"This is what I do." Darlene glanced at the clock; her mouth full of chocolate. "At four-fifteen in the morning when I can't sleep."

"A couple of hard-boiled eggs would be better."

"At four-fifteen?" She glared at him. "No, thank you."

Darlene was suddenly twelve years old again. Her father yanking away the money her grandfather had just given her for ice cream. Announcing, loudly, that Darlene was on a diet and did not need ice cream. *But I need ice cream*, skinny Rachel cried, eliciting a sympathetic *well, of course, you do* from their father. Darlene sat sipping a Tab while she watched Rachel making a show of savoring her cherry vanilla with a dollop of whipped cream. Rifling through a box of old photos recently, Darlene found a picture of her eight-year-old self in a pink dress, standing in line to ride a pony at her friend's birthday party. Darlene was cute. With curly, red hair. She must have stared at that photo for an hour, wondering why her parents thought she needed to lose weight. She looked like a normal, healthy kid. She found another photo from when she was twelve or thirteen. Shorter hair, longer legs, budding breasts. Still cute. Maybe a little fleshy, but she carried it well.

She regarded the candy wrappers scattered around her laptop, then looked down at her hoodie-clad body. Could she stand to lose a few pounds? Sure. But did she look horrible the way she was? She clicked the photo icon on her phone and scrolled until she found the picture that Denny snapped of her just a few months ago. Standing on the beach, hair blowing in the wind. Dressed in jeans and a tee-shirt. Same long legs. Bigger breasts. Still fleshy around the middle, but not significantly overweight. The way her father (and Denny) made her feel, she might as well weigh three hundred pounds. Most of the time, she had to remind herself that she didn't.

"What makes you so sure Mom is having an affair?"

"What?" He sat down on the stool next to her. "You talked to her again?"

"She sent me a text last night." She patted his hand. "Jimmy Finch? Really, Dad? Jimmy Finch?" She looked at him. "Jimmy Finch." She shook her head, unable to contain the laughter that erupted from deep in her gut. She laughed so hard she simultaneously snorted and leaked. Damned stress incontinence. She thought about the box of 'fashion' incontinence panties she'd brought with her. A free sample had come in the mail; two pairs, one blue, one pink, both adorned with butterflies. How had the marketeers known her size? The woman on the box had narrow hips and a flat stomach. Of course. The sad truth was, if they showed a fleshy woman on the box, no one would buy them.

She took a deep breath, trying to picture her mother having hot sex with this man. Her tall, elegant mother, and short, squatty Jimmy Finch, with his slicked-back combover, and chest hairs peeking out over his shirt collar. And the gold necklaces and pinky ring. Darlene gained control of herself. "I thought he had a girlfriend." She drew an invisible bouffant in the air above her head. "The one with the hair."

"I don't know what you're talking about." Her father looked dejected and hadn't joined her in laughter. "He always had eyes for your mother."

"Oh, Dad." The laughter threatened to choke her again. She swallowed. "Come on. What in the world would she see in him? Look at you. You're handsome and distinguished. A doctor. Wait a minute! You didn't catch them, you know, doing things, did you?" She could not bring herself to say the word sex in front of her father.

"No! God, no."

"Then what?" She stared at him. "What?"

"Let me see your laptop."

Darlene slid the laptop toward his side of the breakfast bar and watched him open Amazon. She stared, mouth agape, as her *allergic to technology* father hunted and pecked on the keyboard, clicking around on Amazon as if he owned it. He slid the laptop back in her direction.

"Why are you showing me this?" An ebook cover with a half-naked, older man stared out at her from the screen. *Beach Kiss*, by Belinda Moo.

"It's your mother."

"What do you mean?"

"She wrote it."

"Mom is Belinda Moo?"

"Would you believe it?"

"Actually, I'm quite confused. This book has more than two hundred reviews with a five-star average." She scrolled down in search of the publication date. This year. "When did Mom write a book?" She searched her father's eyes, trying, unsuccessfully, to decipher what was in them. "Dad, this is wonderful. What's the issue, why are you so upset about this."

"It's fifty times worse than the *Fifty Shades* books." He rubbed his chin.

"How do you know about those books."

"Your mother read them."

Darlene felt her face get hot, probably turning fifty shades of red. She hadn't read the series but had friends who did. She pictured her mother, huddled over a keyboard writing, and publishing a book. "This is wonderful, Dad." She smiled and patted his arm. "Seriously. It looks like she has quite a following."

"I fail to see anything wonderful about this."

"Come on, Dad. Why not? She wrote a book! How many people do that?"

"She wrote it behind my back after I asked her not to."

Darlene looked at the clock, suddenly worried that she would get trapped here and be late for today's filming. Wow, only four forty-five. Plenty of time. She refilled her father's coffee mug, wondering how this had anything to do with Jimmy Finch.

"I never even knew she wrote. When did all this come up? She never talked about it with Rachel or me."

"She wanted it to be a surprise. She planned to give each of you a copy for Hanukkah."

"What do you have against Mom writing a book? You're both retired. Did you want her to sit around knitting?"

"I don't care if she writes a book. I don't care if she writes a hundred books." He stabbed his finger at her laptop. "I just don't want her to write that kind of book." He shook his head. "Filthy."

"Did you even read it?" She could not imagine her mother writing a 'filthy' book.

"I read enough of it." He put his head in his hands. "That's not the point." He looked up. "I got upset when she told me what she wanted to write about. I didn't want any of my colleagues to associate my wife with that kind of trash."

"Dad, who cares. You're retired."

"I still serve on the hospital board and on various other committees."

"I just don't see how this is a problem, or how any of it implies Mom is having an affair with Jimmy Finch." Laughter bubbled up. Again. She must be high from all the chocolate and coffee. She brought her mug to her lips to take a sip, then thought better of it, as laughter threatened to expel anything she might ingest in the next few seconds. She couldn't help herself. She let the laughter rip.

"This isn't funny!"

"Yes, it is." She snorted. Crap. Leaked again. "Belinda Moo. Dad, she's calling herself Belinda Moo." More laughter, more snorting, more leaking. "Nobody is going to know it's her. I'm sorry, I have to pee." She disappeared into the bathroom, then reappeared a few minutes later, refreshed and a bit more subdued.

"Click right there." Darlene's father pointed at the *Look Inside* link for the book.

Darlene read the first few pages, unimpressed with the writing, yet wondering where her mother came up with the idea for *Beach Kiss*. Was she acting out some sort of latent fantasy about a male character who wasn't her husband? She flipped back to the shirtless hottie on the cover and then looked at her dad. Yes, Sid Bloom was a handsome man. But nothing like the guy on the cover.

"Did you notice what the male character's name is?" Her father looked at her, expectantly.

"Johnny Sparrow."

"Exactly." He slammed his fist on the countertop.

"Exactly what?" The chocolate and coffee spike had apparently peaked and was now on the way down. Darlene was rapidly growing weary of this conversation. "What, Dad? What."

"Johnny Sparrow. Jimmy Finch. She's writing about Jimmy Finch. Just changing the name."

"Dad, I'm done with this." She stood and gave him a little hug around his shoulders. "I'm glad you finally told me what's going on." She rolled her eyes at him. "I don't, for a second, believe that Mom is having an affair."

"I don't know. I don't like it. I don't like this book. I don't like your mother writing this kind of book."

"You don't have to like it." She winked. "Remember, it's not Mom who wrote it. Belinda Moo wrote it." She started climbing the stairs, then turned around. "Hey, you want to be on TV with me? You can be a stand-in for Denny. Help me find the perfect beach house."

14

―――――――

Darlene and Sid drove silently to the appointed condo, which was ten miles north, on Fenwick Island, Delaware. Not a place she or Denny had ever considered. She wondered if maybe they should have; the area seemed quaint and quiet. She rolled the window down a crack to let in some fresh air. Hot flash, she said when her father looked at her. He rolled down his window too.

"I don't see any condo buildings," her father said, sticking his head out the window and looking around.

"There won't be high-rises here, not like in Ocean City, anyway. I think the unit we're going to see today is in a carriage house."

"That's strange."

"Why is it strange."

"I don't know, it just is."

She regretted asking her father to tag along. It had been an impulsive invite, a way to get him out of his head and give him some-thing to think about other than Belinda Moo. She'd texted her mother before heading out, letting her know that Dad was okay and that she would try to talk some sense into him.

The GPS led them to a row of homes, just one block back from the beach. "I think it's this blue house on the left." Darlene slowed her Ford Explorer when she saw the van with the network logo, and the camera crew loitering in the driveway.

"I don't like the mold on the siding." Sid craned his neck to get a better look. "And there's no beach access. I don't like this one at all."

"Dad, it doesn't matter." She pulled up next to the curb and shut off the motor. "This is fake, remember?" She looked at him. "Actually, we need to pretend it's not fake. The things you just said would be great to say on camera."

"I'm a little bit nervous." He chuckled. "I've never had a camera follow me around."

"You'll do fine. Just be yourself." Darlene put the visor down and opened the mirror, crinkling her nose in disgust at the sight of her bloodshot eyes. She pulled a small vile of eyedrops out of her purse and put one drop in each eye, dabbing at fake tears as they slid down her cheeks. If only all her tears lately were fake. She swiped a stripe of lipstick over her bottom lip, pressed her top lip against it, and blended it with the tip of her finger. She studied her hair. The new gel she tried for the first time this morning had turned her curls into plastic-looking corkscrews. She rubbed her hands all over her head, the dried gel flaking in her fingers. *Wonderful. Now it will look like I have dandruff.* She let her eyes drift down to her shirt. It was similar to the one she wore yesterday, only this one was fuchsia and instead of chartreuse. Good enough, she thought. Good enough.

"Great, you're here," Gloria said, ushering Darlene up the walkway. "Who is he?" She pointed to Sid.

"I'm sorry, I should have let you know. I asked my father to come along and help me look at houses." She grabbed her father's hand. "Dad, this is the production manager, Gloria."

"Sid Bloom." He shook Gloria's hand. "I'm a retired physician. I'm here to help my daughter find her dream beach house." He leaned in closer and winked. "I know this is fake."

"Jesse! Over here!" Gloria waved her arms around, trying to get his attention. "Can we film Darlene and her father getting out of the car?"

"Dad, I guess we're getting back in the car." She pointed her key-fob toward it and pressed. "Where do you want me to pull in from?"

"Just go around the block and come in from over there," Jesse said. "I'll be waiting here with the camera."

"Is there any place special you want me to park?"

"Nope. Just pull up to the curb like you did before." He knitted his eyebrows. "Remember, the camera will already be rolling when you get out of the car." He turned toward Sid. "During editing, the narrator will say a bit about who you are and why you're here. No need to tell your life's story. Just get out of the car and walk up to the building. Look around while you walk. Maybe talk amongst yourselves about what you like, don't like." He looked at Darlene. "You know the drill."

"Tawk amongst yourselves," Darlene said, in her best Linda Richman accent. "I'll give you a topic—"

"Okay, okay," Jesse said, rolling his eyes. "I'll call *Saturday Night Live* and see if they would revive that skit, with you as its star." He shook his head.

"Now, I'm getting verklempt." She made the famous face from the skit, then pretended to cry.

"Any questions?" Jesse ignored her. "Oh, and Laurie's brother is filling in for her. He's not actually a realtor, but no one needs to know that. He'll be waiting for you at the front door."

"Is everything okay?" Darlene was disappointed. She'd wanted to ask Laurie about the neighbor.

"Some sort of emergency," he said. "A client making an offer on a house. Had to be now or never." Darlene nodded and opened the passenger side door for her father. She walked around to her side and climbed in.

"Aren't you going to put on your seatbelt," Sid said, buckling himself in.

"We're just going around the block. I'll be fine."

"No, put it on."

"Dad, we'll be fine."

"You never know. Some meshuggana might decide to pull out of one of those driveways."

Jesse rapped on the driver's side window with his knuckles. "What's going on in there?" He pinched the bridge of his nose. "We don't have all day. Let's get this show on the road."

"My daughter won't buckle up."

"It's the law," Jesse said. "Just buckle up and let's get on with it." Darlene rolled up the window and glared at her father. She put on her seatbelt and slowly backed away from the curb.

"Was that so hard?" He patted her hand.

"Yes, it was. We wasted five minutes sitting here, arguing, and being scolded by the cameraman."

"Are you in a hurry?"

"No, I'm not in a hurry. But I don't want to be here all day, either."

"What else do you have to do?"

"Nothing. I just don't want my whole day consumed with this."

"Then why did you sign up to do it?" He looked out the window. "This is illogical. The whole thing is a sham. You heard what he said. The realtor isn't even a realtor, for God's sake. What's the point? If you're not going to look at houses to buy and everyone's an actor, what's the point of this show?"

"We're not actors. The original realtor wasn't an actor. And I doubt today's realtor is an actor."

"Today's realtor isn't a realtor."

"I got that, Dad." She clenched her teeth, then slowly exhaled. "This isn't about the realtor. The realtor isn't the point."

"Then what is the point?" He looked at her. "Really, what is the point? I want to know."

"The people on these shows really are buying or have already bought a house. Maybe not in the same order or sequence as you see on the show." She pulled up to the curb. "Look, we're here. Just pretend you're an actor and behave yourself." They stepped out, as if their moves were choreographed. With Jesse's camera capturing them, she pointed at the building. "This must be it, Dad."

"What?"

"The condo. This must be the condo."

"Oh." He turned and pointed toward the Atlantic. "It's kind of far back from the beach. I thought you wanted beach access."

"I do want beach access. I also want to be in Maryland, not Delaware." She looked up toward the top of the house. "But I trust the realtor." She linked arms with her father. "Let's keep an open mind. I think Denny would like this area. It's much quieter than where we looked yesterday." She hesitated, unsure what to do next. Oh yes, walk toward the door.

"Still rolling," Jesse called out.

"Look at this," Sid said, stopping and pulling his arm out from under Darlene's. "An outdoor shower. I think every beach house should have an outdoor shower."

"That's a nice feature."

Halfway up the walkway, a man yelled and waved his arms. "Up here!" He pointed toward a staircase. "The unit is on the third floor."

"Hopefully, the view is good up there." Darlene gazed up at the man on the balcony, squinting, unsure of exactly who she was looking at.

"There are a lot of stairs," Sid said. "A place like this should have an elevator. It would be a haul with groceries."

Darlene ignored her father and kept walking, Jesse following close behind with his camera. At the top of the stairs, she turned and walked to what she thought was the front door of the unit. She rang the bell. "Francisco?"

"Rose."

"What the hell is going on here?" Sid pointed at the realtor. "You were supposed to meet us at the front door."

"I am at the front door."

"But we had to ring the doorbell."

"Laurie couldn't be here today." Fran, in full improv mode, ignored Sid. "I'm filling in for her."

"Nice to meet you. I'm Darlene." They shook hands, Fran squeezing ever so slightly, changing the atmospheric pressure. Looking at her hand encircled in his, she wondered when the thunder and lightning would start. "This is my father..." She stammered, unable remember his name. "Wait a minute. Laurie is your brother?"

Fran laughed, raising his eyebrows. "No, she's my sister. I'm her brother. Her one and only."

Darlene stood paralyzed, seeing him up close and in the full light. More silver in his hair than strawberry. His crooked smile more captivating than she had replayed half the night in her mind. She studied his eyes—so deep in his face that his brow bones cast a shadow. She squinted, trying to see beyond the shadow. Brown. His eyes were still brown. Light brown. Caramel. Or was it honey? She almost expected him to break out into song, again.

"Sid Bloom." Darlene's father extended his hand, relieving her of her thoughts. "I'm a retired physician. I'm helping my daughter find her dream beach house. You're not even a realtor."

"CUT!" Jesse pulled Sid aside. "Thank God, most of this is editable. Let's just keep the discussion about the house, shall we?" He softened. "I know he's not a realtor. We talked about this earlier. Let's just pretend he is."

"Are you really Laurie's brother?" Darlene stood up straight and smoothed her shirt, wondering why Laurie had never mentioned that her brother lived in the condo next door. She suddenly remembered the woman in his Facebook profile picture. She let her gaze glide down toward the ring of gold encircling the third finger on his left hand.

"I am."

"So, you're not a realtor?"

"Worst job in the world. You couldn't pay me enough money. I'd never do it. Never."

"But you'll play one on TV." She laughed, squeezing her pelvic muscles together, careful to take control of her bladder. Leaking now would be mortifying.

"Are you two finished?" Jesse stood, hands-on hips, tapping his foot.

"Where's my father?" Darlene turned around and found him at

the kitchen sink, turning the water on and off. "Dad, Jesse's ready to start rolling the camera."

Sid shuffled back into the tiny entryway. He stopped in front of Fran. "What did you say your name was, again?"

"Fran. Fran Wilkins."

"Are we ready?" Jesse hoisted his camera onto his shoulder. "Camera rolling," he said, without waiting for an answer.

"This property was built in 1987, has two master suites, plus a third, separate full bath." Fran stood in the middle of the open concept living area with outstretched arms. "The owners recently upgraded the flooring throughout."

"I like the color of the hardwood." Darlene regarded the lighter color, unlike the dark wood of her condo, which looked great, but now that she saw this, maybe someday she would change it. Nope. She wasn't even planning to keep the damned condo. A lump rose in her throat, thinking about Denny and his girlfriend. She took a deep breath. "How many square feet?"

"Eleven hundred."

"That's tiny. What about the price?"

"$369,900."

"That's well below our max budget." Darlene watched her father wander back into the kitchen. "Dad, now what are you doing?"

"I'm testing the water pressure." He held his hand under the faucet. "It's like a trickle. At this rate, a quick shower would turn into two hours." He turned the water off. "The kitchen is dated."

"We'd be getting a lot of house for the money. Especially this close to the beach."

"Close to what beach?" Sid ambled over to the sliding glass door and opened it. "I don't see any beach."

"Dad, we're one block from the beach. A quick walk. Or an even quicker golf cart ride." She looked at Fran. "Are golf carts allowed here?"

"You got me. I don't know. But I will find out."

"What kind of realtor are you?" Sid turned away from the sliders and sat down on the couch. "You should know these things."

"CUT!" Jesse lowered the camera from his shoulder and held it tight against his chest. "Mr. Bloom, we've been through this. Mr. Wilkins isn't a realtor. He's acting. For the show."

"So, you're an actor?" Sid stood, then sat down again. "I'm sorry, I didn't sleep well last night."

"Are you okay, Dad?"

"Just a little light-headed." He let his head fall between his legs. "My daughter couldn't be bothered making dinner last night. I didn't have any breakfast, either." Darlene ignored her father's accusations and rubbed his hand. She watched Fran open the refrigerator and pull out a carton of orange juice.

"It's not expired," Fran said, holding the orange juice above his head like a prize.

"What is he doing?" Sid leaned back against the couch pillow. "This is comfortable. Frank? Is the furniture included in the price?"

"As a matter of fact, it is." He handed Sid a tall glass of orange juice. "Drink up. It's Fran, by the way."

"Frances?"

"Francisco."

"You don't look like a Francisco."

"Dad!"

"It's okay. I get that all the time." Fran smiled. "I like to tell people that I was conceived in San Francisco, but that's not true." He looked at Darlene. "I was born there."

"My other daughter practices medicine in San Francisco. She's a neurologist."

"And what do you do?" He lowered his voice. "Rose."

"I'm just a lowly pharmacist," she said, overtly loud, to ensure her father could hear.

"She could have gone to medical school. She would have made a fine doctor."

Darlene walked away from her father and filled the empty juice glass with soapy water. She stood at the sink and let the warm water from the faucet soothe away her embarrassment. That her father couldn't imagine why any sane person wouldn't want to become a doctor was his issue, not hers. She hated the sight of blood, didn't like guts. It was Rachel, after all, who used to break her dolls' limbs and make casts for them out of masking tape. Rachel, who cried when she took the cast off a half-hour later, only to discover that the "bones" were still broken. No, Darlene never wanted any of that. She was happiest mixing things together to make other things. Anything that produced some sort of chemical reaction thrilled her. Even something as mundane as baking a cake. She supposed it was why she loved brewing beer.

Rummaging through the cabinet under the sink, she found a roll of paper towels. She tore one off and dried the glass, putting it back in the cupboard and turning, only to see Fran staring at her. She looked away.

"We really need to get back to work here." Jesse tapped his foot and looked at Sid. "You okay now? Because if you're not, I can film around you, then bring you back in at the end for a few frames."

"I'm okay. I'm fine." Sid stood and joined Darlene in the kitchen. "Go ahead. Turn the camera on. I'm fine."

"You're sure?" Jesse looked at Sid, who waved his hand and nodded. "Camera rolling!"

"I like the open concept." Darlene stood at the countertop, looking out into the living room. "I could be chopping vegetables and still talking to my guests."

"And I could sit here to eat my cereal in the morning and still talk to my daughter." Sid pantomimed eating a bowl of cereal. "The thing about cereal," he said between imaginary bites, "why not just call it soup?" He looked directly into the camera. "It really is soup, isn't it? Cold soup."

"Gazpacho." Fran sat down at the counter next to Sid. "I've always wondered that myself."

"CUT!" Jesse took a deep breath. "I honestly don't give a hoot if cereal is soup, gazpacho, or just cereal. Nor do I care if a hot dog is a sandwich or just a hot dog. Can we please stay focused here?"

Darlene felt the laughter well up before she had a chance to suppress it. She let it rip, cursing her bladder, suddenly not caring about the leakage, thankful she was wearing a pair of heavy jeans. She doubled over, laughing. Finally, she caught her breath and composed herself.

"Are you finished?" Jesse tapped his foot. "I'm not amused."

"I'm sorry." She giggled, pressing her cheeks together with her thumb and forefinger. "You should leave that in. It's hilarious. Seriously. You should."

"I don't think Gloria would be amused at all." He glared at her, then looked at his watch. "Speaking of Gloria—"

"Aye-aye," Sid said, saluting.

"Camera rolling!"

"The countertops are a bit dated." Darlene rubbed her hand across the beige laminate.

"An easy fix," Fran said, his eyes fixed on her hand. "The kitchen is on the small side. It wouldn't cost you very much to upgrade to granite."

"He has a point, bubbeleh. You're well under budget with this place."

"Look at this." Darlene opened the sliding glass door and stepped out. "It overlooks the lagoon."

"I'm glad the porch is screened." Sid joined Darlene outside. "Mosquitos."

"If you stand right here, you can catch a glimpse of the bay." Fran stood next to Darlene and pointed.

"That's just it." Darlene inched herself away, feeling flustered and tongue-tied. "My husband and I really wanted a beach view." She emphasized the word husband, as if Denny were not, at this very moment, with another woman. Her eyes filled. She turned and quickly stepped back inside.

"Sometimes, you can't have everything, Rose." Fran followed her into the condo.

"CUT!" Jesse looked befuddled. "Rose? Who the hell is Rose?"

"I'm sorry." Fran made a fist and knocked on the side of his head. "Senior moment. Won't happen again."

"Camera rolling!"

"You can't beat the perks, though." Fran counted on his fingers. "Extensive landscaping. You also have a large outside storage closet for bikes, chairs, and umbrellas. And a pool."

"I didn't see a pool," Sid said.

"It's behind the green building."

"Green building?" Darlene did not remember seeing a green building.

"There are six of these carriage-type houses that make up the community. Oh, and there's a tennis court."

"What are the HOA fees?" Sid rubbed his hands together.

"$350 a month."

"Ouch." Darlene didn't find that amount unreasonable, but hey, this was TV, and she needed to not be so agreeable all the time.

"Remember, bubbeleh, you're getting a lot of perks with this place." Sid led the way down the hall and into the first master suite. Darlene and Fran followed him, with Jesse and his camera trailing behind.

"These floors are squeaky." Sid shifted his weight from one foot to the other. He jumped in place, then banged on the wood with the heel of his shoe. "Are you sure they're new."

"They were upgraded a year ago."

"This would drive me crazy," Sid said, looking at Darlene.

"Good sized bathroom." She ignored him. "Double vanity. And a tub for Denny."

"Your husband likes to take baths?" Fran looked wistful.

"Yes." She lied. Denny started this thing with the tub yesterday, but in reality, he hated taking baths. She shook her head, suddenly hating him, suddenly wondering if he takes baths with Remi. "He likes to sit in the tub with a beer."

"Sounds heavenly." He looked at his left hand. "My wife loved taking long baths."

"Loved?"

"She died." He looked at the floor. "Two years ago."

Darlene gasped, surprised at the tears that suddenly sprang from her eyes. She turned her head and quickly wiped them away.

"It's okay. I'm okay. Mostly. Until something hits me. Like this." He waved his arm at the tub.

~

DARLENE WONDERED how she could have been so insensitive. Loved? How could she have said that? It was none of her damned business. Maybe it was the faraway look in Fran's eyes when he said that his wife loved taking long baths. Darlene hadn't stopped to consider that she had died. God, she could be so stupid. She needed to learn how to keep her mouth shut. Poor impulse control, as her mother always said. When the urge to make a point struck, Darlene often felt physical pain if she couldn't expel a word or phrase buzzing around inside her mouth like a trapped bee. It would be better, oh so much better, to just swallow the damned bee.

"I hope we're almost done here." Sid rubbed his belly. "I could sure use a sandwich."

"We are." Fran stood in the doorway. "Jesse wants to film us looking at the other bedroom, then we'll head outside."

"I didn't mean to upset you." Darlene looked at Fran, as her father brushed past in search of Jesse and getting this day over with.

"You didn't upset me." He smacked his lips together in a half-hearted attempt at a smile. "You had no way of knowing."

"But, you were upset." Darlene couldn't help herself. There was another bee in her mouth, and it needed to escape. "I know I had no way of knowing. But I upset you. I am so sorry!"

"Let's just drop it," he said.

"Just please accept my apology." His nonchalance bothered her; she needed closure, for what reason, she wasn't entirely sure.

"There's no need to apologize." He gestured toward the door with his hand. "Let's not keep Jesse waiting." He looked at his watch. "I need to get out of here myself. My sister owes me. Big time."

"Okay. But I am sorry."

They walked out of the room together. Fran looked at Darlene and put his finger up to his mouth. "Shhh!" He took a few steps toward the second master suite and stopped in the doorway, gesturing for Darlene to come to look. He leaned toward her and whispered. "It looks like they're filming."

Darlene suppressed a laugh. Her father was sitting on the bed, leaning his head against the headboard. He climbed off the bed and pressed his hands on the mattress.

"Nice and firm," he said to the camera. "This will be our room when my wife and I come to visit."

"Not so fast, Dad." Darlene stepped into the room, smiling. She nodded at Jesse, who let the camera capture the moment as she walked to the window. "Of course, you want the room with the view." She turned around and stood by the bed. "I think you and Mom can have the other room. This one will be for Denny and me." She angled her head slightly to look at Fran, but he had disappeared from the doorway. A tiny bit disappointed, she wandered into the bathroom. "Well, Dad, the other bathroom is much nicer. But this one will certainly do."

"CUT!" Jesse stopped the camera. "Perfect. Perfect. Let's go do a few shots outside, then we'll call it a day."

15

———

The ocean under the high noon sun dazzled with shimmering light all the way to the horizon. Fran stood against the fence and watched as Darlene plopped down in the sand and took her shoes off, leaving them unattended in her haste to get to the water. He had walked the one block with Darlene's father, ensuring he got safely across the street while Jesse ran after her with the camera. Good fodder for TV, he supposed.

He watched her stop just shy of the demarcation between wet and dry sand. She bent down to roll her jeans up above her ankles. He could see her feet sinking into the wet sand as she walked gingerly into the water. He could almost feel the cold as he watched the waves breaking over her feet. She threw her head back in laughter as she jumped and shimmied through the small waves. God, her laughter reminded him of Sadie's, yet Darlene's was different, more explosive.

As the waves receded, she scooped up handfuls of shells, examining them in her hand before tossing them back. She walked a few hundred feet along the beach, hopping over waves as they hit. She turned around and froze when she realized Jesse was filming her. Fran was glad it wasn't him being filmed. He feared he would feel like he'd been caught naked in the Garden of Eden, frantically searching for a fig leaf. But Darlene, or Rose, seemed to drink it all in. She smiled into the camera; all Fran could see was the light in her eyes.

"I love the beach. It's absolutely life-giving. Even this time of year," Darlene said, milking her two minutes of fame.

"CUT!"

"I didn't know you were filming," she said, out of breath.

"I wanted to capture your joy." Jesse looked at his watch. "Viewers love stuff like this. It makes good filler right after a commercial break. But now I really need to go. I guess I'll see you tomorrow."

Darlene nodded and walked back to where she had left her shoes. She sat down and lifted her face to the sun. Fran watched her, only half paying attention to Sid, who was standing beside him and rattling on about something Fran couldn't keep straight in his mind. He felt giddy with delight as the crisp, sunny afternoon filled him like a drug. Darlene's eyes were on him as she made her way through the sand. His fight or flight response kicked in—all he wanted to do was go back to his condo and look for Sadie. Darlene stepped off to the side and held a signpost for support while she put her shoes back on.

"Frank says he knows a good sandwich place." Sid took hold of his daughter's arm to pull her away and move the day along.

"Fran. It's Fran." He looked at Darlene when he said it, ignoring Sid.

"So, where is this place?" She looked at her feet.

"You can follow me there." He said it fast, suddenly not wanting to go home—wanting to go anywhere but home.

"I'm familiar with the area. Just tell me what it's called."

"Would you rather I not join you?" His heart sank.

"I'm sure you have lots of important things to do."

"I'm hungry," he said, laughing. "I can do the rest of my mundane tasks later." His eyes pleaded. "Let me buy you lunch. It's the least I could do for the unexpected stand-in."

"It's okay. Really, it is." she said. "My father and I will be fine."

"Darlene. What are you doing? Let's go already. I'm about to pass out." Sid walked away, back toward the street.

"You'd better go after him." Fran tried to keep the disappointment out of his voice. "Sadie's. It's a deli called Sadie's." Darlene nodded and went after her father, leaving Fran with a hard-to-identify feeling in the pit of his stomach.

16

———————

Everyone, it seemed, craved a sandwich. It was strange that a beach town deli would be this crowded on a Tuesday afternoon in early November. Darlene had never heard of this place, probably because it sat outside her circle of existence. Plus, she typically did not eat big lunches, and when she went out to dinner, it was someplace she could walk easily or take Uber. This place would be an awfully long walk from her condo. Plus, she didn't see any alcohol; no bar, no beer taps, no shelves lined with red and white wines.

She scanned the menu—typical deli fare—and wondered why, of all the places he could have suggested, Fran suggested this place. Their last conversation played on a continuous loop in her mind. The sound of her own voice ringing in her ears made her cringe. She didn't mean to sound so cold and dismissive. Her uneasiness at having turned him down sat like a piece of lettuce lodged against the back of her throat. She couldn't cough it up, couldn't swallow it down. It was stuck there until it was ready to let go and slide down her throat on a wave of water. She wasn't sure why she didn't want Fran to join them for lunch. Was she still embarrassed that she had triggered his sad memories? Or did talking about the death of a loved one hit too close to home? Her brother Liam's death still sometimes felt raw—given the right trigger—even though he has been gone for almost twelve years. Still, she could not imagine the grief of having your soul mate ripped from you, taken too soon. She had never thought of Denny as her soul mate. A painful realization after twenty-five years. She wondered what had caused Fran's wife's death. Was it a battle with an extended illness? An accident, like Liam? What if it had been a suicide? She shook the thoughts from her mind and concentrated on the menu.

"They don't have knish." Sid flipped his menu on the tabletop. "What kind of deli doesn't have knish?"

"Dad, this is Maryland's Eastern Shore. They specialize in crab, not knish." She shook her head, exasperated. "I thought you wanted a sandwich."

"I did until I came in here and smelled the pickles." He turned to watch a waiter bring a plate to the table in front of them. "Look at the size of that thing." He craned his neck, just as their server approached. "What do you recommend?"

"Oh, easy," the server said. "The pulled pork on flatbread. We put the coleslaw right on the bread. Gives it a nice crunch. It's one of our specialties."

"I don't eat pork." Sid ran his finger down the choices on the menu. "It's not kosher."

"Dad!"

"And you don't have knish."

"What's knish?" The server looked puzzled.

"Please, excuse my father." Darlene was horrified, but not surprised by her father's behavior. He was not kosher. Except for that one time when her grandmother gave her father a hard time about letting his kids eat bacon. Thus, began one of his kicks. *We're going to start keeping a kosher home,* he announced. It lasted two weeks, maybe three. "It's been a long day already. He's tired."

"I'm not tired." He opened his menu and pointed. "I'll have turkey on rye."

"Me too. With bacon and fries, please."

"You don't need fries." He raised his eyebrow. "Did you order bacon just to upset me?"

"I ordered fries because I want fries. And I ordered bacon because I like bacon." She handed her menu to the server. "Fries. Bacon. And a large Diet Coke."

"I'll take a coffee. Black." He turned to Darlene. "That stuff will kill you."

"The fries or the bacon?"

"The Diet Coke. The fries will just make you fat. And the bacon. Don't get me started on the bacon."

"Trust me, I won't."

They sat in silence. Darlene looked around at the people, listened to the clanking of utensils, the murmur of voices, the occasional chuckle, or burst of laughter. She had taken a couple of drama classes in college. One of her professors said that in restaurant scenes, the extras are told to say "rhubarb and custard" with varying vocal inflections, accents, and speeds. For years she couldn't walk into a crowded restaurant without thinking about this. She learned firsthand, a few years later, that extras say rhubarb and custard silently, pantomiming gestures, acting like they're rooted in conversation. The sound is added in later. She was an actual extra in *Collateral Damage*. A long, frustrating day, tiny compensation, and a new appreciation for what goes into making movies. She wondered anew, why she agreed to be on this stupid house hunting show.

"Dad, we need to talk about the elephant in the room." The server returned with their drinks.

"What elephant?" Sid gripped his coffee cup with two hands and held it up to his mouth. "The fact that they don't have knish here?" He put the cup down without having taken a sip and looked at Darlene with knitted brows. "Or the fact that you ordered bacon right under my nose."

"Oh, come on, Dad." She sipped her Diet Coke. "Since when, other than that time Bubbe shamed you, do you care about bacon?" She waited, and when he didn't respond, she continued. "You eat bacon. Mom eats bacon. Rachel, who can do no wrong, eats bacon."

"Rachel does not."

Darlene was not going to let Rachel push her out of the way and come between her and her father, not this time. She whipped out her cell phone and texted her sister: Do you eat bacon?

"What are you doing?"

She showed her father the text. "We'll see who's right."

"Why does there need to be a right or a wrong?"

"It's the principle of the thing, Dad."

"What principle? What's all this about?"

Darlene sighed. She did not quite know how to answer, because she didn't truly understand the question. Didn't know how to unpack fifty years of baggage. Every time she attempted to unpack, she'd get some of her clothes out of the bag, then she'd get frustrated and walk away, often adding to the bag as she went along. The next time she unzipped the bag there would be twice as much inside—items she never remembered adding. She took a deep breath. "In yours and Mom's eyes, Rachel could do no wrong." She looked at her left hand, at the ring encircling her finger. Why was she still wearing it? "At least I gave you a grandchild."

"That was a low blow." Sid looked away.

"She never married. Wasn't that your dream for both of us? That we'd each marry a nice Jewish boy?" She glared at him. "Oh, wait. She went to medical school and became a doctor, like you. I guess she gets a pass for that." She didn't want to go there, but she couldn't help herself. "And don't get me started on Liam. You never forgave him for not following in your footsteps."

"Enough!" He put his head in his hands. "I don't want to talk about Liam."

"Why not?" She felt tears stream down her cheeks. "You and Mom never talk about what happened. It's like Liam never existed. He was my baby brother." She pressed her napkin into her eyes. "I miss him."

"And he was my only son! You don't think I miss him too?" Her father stood, then sat back down. "I wish I never came here. I should have—"

"Gone to Rachel's?"

"No." He looked up. "I should have stayed home. I should have stood up to your mother when she asked me to leave."

With the arrival of their sandwiches came the unspoken understanding that the difficult topics would be set aside, brushed under the rug, once again. Darlene salted her fries, waiting for her father to issue a warning about salt. But he didn't. He sat, staring as if he had never seen a sandwich before and didn't quite know what to do with it. She suddenly regretted her comment about Liam and hoped it would soon be forgotten. It always was. Because if it didn't get discussed, it didn't happen.

"These look delicious." She needed to break the spell and get them back to some sort of baseline. "They're huge. I'll probably only eat half. We could heat up the other halves for dinner, like a panini. They'd be great with beer." Her father didn't respond, he just stared.

"She would sit there, tapping away at the keyboard, with a smile on her face." Sid picked up the sandwich and took a small bite off the corner. "A dreamy smile." He shook his head. "She never smiles at me that way anymore."

Darlene recalled all the times Denny wore, what she had dubbed in her mind, his shit-eating grin. It charmed her when they first met; she walked around moonstruck for an entire semester. The smile was for her. Only her. Until it wasn't. She took a deep breath, still unconvinced of her mother's supposed transgressions, but happy that they were finally trying to cut the elephant into bite-sized chunks. She needed to balance reassuring her dad with a healthy amount of realism and respect for his feelings.

"You know, when I'm engrossed in something I love doing, like brewing beer or a project that makes me feel proud, I smile." She patted his hand. "I smile because I'm proud of what I'm doing at that moment. I think Mom is smiling at the screen because she reads a sentence that she's written and feels proud."

"I don't know." He took another bite. "I just don't know." His face reddened. "The things she wrote about in that book." He looked away. "We don't do things like that. I don't know where she came up with that stuff."

Darlene's cell phone buzzed. A text from Rachel: WTF? Yes. I eat bacon.

"Ah, ha!" Darlene showed her father the phone, grateful for a diversion. The last thing she wanted to do was discuss her parents' sex life. "Rachel eats bacon!"

"Whoopee do." He grabbed the phone out of her hand. "What's WTF?"

"You don't want to know."

"Yes, I do."

"Are you sure?" She narrowed her eyes. "Because I can't take it back, once I tell you."

"Tell me."

"It stands for what the fuck."

"That's what I thought."

"No, you didn't." She couldn't help what came out of her mouth next. "Yes, Dad, Rachel uses cuss words." Sid shrugged and gave the phone back. He picked up his sandwich and gnawed at it, putting it down long enough to take a sip of coffee, then picking it back up, repeating this cycle over and over. He finished most of one half, then shoved a fry in his mouth. Darlene resisted the urge to call him out on eating the deadly fries.

"Can you get your mother on the phone?"

"I can try." Darlene pressed the button for her mother and was surprised by the rapidity with which she answered. "Mom...Dad wants to talk to you." She handed her father the phone without waiting for a response.

"What? I can't hear you." He looked at Darlene. "It's too noisy in here."

"Go outside. There's a little patio by the front door."

Darlene watched her father slide his chair out from under the table. He put on his jacket and fedora and shuffled out the door. For a split-second, she worried about him wandering off. She had to remind herself that even at eighty, he was still sharp, still quite physically fit. It was just that during this visit, he seemed so...old. Almost frail. She chalked it up to his emotional state.

She poured a blob of ketchup on her plate and stuck the corner of her sandwich in it, moistening the dry turkey. She was not even sure why she ordered turkey; it wasn't one of her favorite things to eat. Maybe she should start a new tradition this Thanksgiving. Lasagna. Yes. Wouldn't that be nice? Shelly might go for it, but Denny would object. *Why do I even care what he thinks*? She had been tempted to tell her father about Denny leaving her multiple times today. And now she felt tempted to tell Shelly. Seriously, her daughter deserved to know the truth. She wondered why Denny was so hell-bent on keeping up this charade. Stupid. The whole thing was utterly ridiculous.

"Can I get you anything else? Another Diet Coke? Coffee? Dessert?" Darlene gave the server a puzzled look, wondering how anyone could possibly want dessert after eating even a fraction of these massive sandwiches.

She shook her head. "Nope, nope. Just the check. And two boxes." She saw her father come through the front door. "On second thought, let me at least see the dessert menu. My father has a sweet tooth." The server reached into his pocket and pulled out a small menu. Darlene scanned it and asked him to bring a brownie sundae with two spoons.

Sid shuffled in and sat back down, taking off his fedora first, then slipping out of his jacket. "Your mother is letting me come home."

"Did you apologize?"

"No." He smoothed his shirt. "I don't have anything to apologize for."

"You falsely accused her of having an affair."

"She's the one who kicked me out. She owes me an apology."

Darlene could not believe she was sitting in a deli, on the verge of her own divorce, counseling her father on whom should apologize to whom. The server arrived with their ice cream.

"I just divided it into two bowls. More sanitary than sharing." He set a small container of rainbow-colored sprinkles in the middle of the table. "Just in case."

"What's all this?" Sid gestured at the items.

"What does it look like?"

"Calories you don't need."

"Speak for yourself." She shook some sprinkles over the whipped cream on her sundae. "So, Mom's letting you come home. That's good, right?" It was welcome news for Darlene. She hadn't yet begun to consider how she would deal with a long-term visitor.

"I guess so." He stabbed his ice cream with his spoon and took a large mouthful. "Your mother doesn't let me have ice cream." He shoveled more into his mouth. "This is good."

"When are you heading back?" She looked down at her bowl and realized she had eaten half of it and didn't remember doing so. Mindless eating. She pushed it away. "You know, you really should get a cell phone." She wagged her finger at him. "I don't like you driving without one. Especially such a long drive."

"What are you talking about, long drive? It's less than three hours."

"I don't want you driving in the dark."

"It's only," he looked at his watch, "one o'clock." He put his fedora on and grabbed his jacket. "I'm ready. Let's go."

"Dad, we have to pay." She waved at the server. "What do you want to do with your sandwich?"

"I'll take it home. Your mother might like to try it." He tapped the bread. "The turkey was a little dry, though."

The server delivered the check and their boxes. Darlene handed him her credit card, then turned to look at her father. "I'm glad you're going home." She patted his hand. "You and Mom will get through this." She shook her head. "Mom wrote a book! I can't believe it." Her father was already away from the table by the time she signed the check and stood. She watched him turn left toward the restrooms instead of heading out the door.

∼

A WALL of photos in the vestibule near the restrooms caught Darlene's eye. Family photos, some old, some recent, some color, some black and white. Photos of customers. Customers with...Fran? She took a step toward the wall to get a closer look. That was Fran, alright. And his late wife—the woman in his Facebook profile picture. Wait a minute. His late wife. Sadie? She read and reread the inscription under the centermost photo. *In Loving Memory of Sadie Wilkins*. His wife was Sadie. Of Sadie's. So, this is Fran's place. She studied the photo, the easiness between Fran and Sadie unmistakable. Sadie's head tilted back, obviously laughing at something Fran had just said, bits of loose hair from her ponytail dangling around her neck. His eyes were crinkled in laughter, just like they had been the other day. She wished she could span the boundaries of time and space, jump into the photo, and be privy to their joy. Maybe even steal the recipe and sprinkle the secret ingredient onto her own marriage. If only.

Her father emerged from the men's room. She took his arm and led him outside and into the car, thinking about the complexities of life and how bits and pieces of a person reveal themselves in odd ways.

17

F ran took his time driving to the deli. He needed to make his weekly appearance but did not want to risk running into Darlene and her father eating lunch. He didn't need her thinking he was a lunatic stalker. He winced, certain she at least thought he was a bit off-beat, or, dare he say, strange. Maybe not a lunatic, but something. Something unusual.

He rolled into the parking lot and scanned for her car. Crap. He had no idea what she drove. He thought he remembered seeing her in a blue Honda Civic the other day. Or was it an SUV of some sort? Silver. Right. He saw a silver SUV in her carport at the condo. He sighed, his eyes darting from one car to the next. Several SUVs, one silver, two black. No blue Civics.

Wow, the place was busy. Pulling into a spot several rows back from the door, he marveled at how unpredictable a given day could be. It wasn't the weekend and wasn't the high season. Sadie would have loved this. She thrived in the chaos and loved flitting from table to table, chatting with the regulars, the weekenders, and the random one-offs. She knew no strangers, that was a fact. Staffing had been so difficult to pin down in the early days. For the first six months, they danced between having too many staff and having too few. The winter months had been the hardest to predict, especially with the summer hires heading back to school. But Sadie always seemed to work it out, sometimes doubling down as a server. Fran even made sandwiches a few times. He liked to think he mastered the Rueben, and suddenly was hungry for one.

Reaching for the door handle, he saw Darlene's father step out of the deli. Darlene followed, then took his arm and led him to the silver SUV. His stomach rumbled for a sandwich. He patted it, then waited until he saw Darlene pull out into the street and disappear around the corner before getting out of his Jeep and making a beeline for the front door.

SADIE DID RIGHT EARLY on to insist on a focused menu and very conservative hours. Eleven until four. Thursday through Sunday to start. They eventually opened daily but kept the hours. Fran thought they should open earlier and offer a limited breakfast menu in addition to their lunch items. Sadie didn't want to hear it. *You stick to what you're good at, let me do what I'm good at.* She had said it so often that the phrase was burned into his brain. He was sure glad he listened.

"Hey, Paul, mind if I make myself a sandwich?" Fran washed his hands and put on a pair of plastic gloves.

"Have at it, my friend." Paul, the kitchen manager, tossed him an apron. "Or you can wait for about ten minutes, and I'll make you one."

"Thanks, but no thanks." He tied the apron around his waist. "I'm craving a Reuben. My Reuben." He collected his supplies and got to work, putting extra butter on the bread and an extra-large glob of Russian dressing on each slice. He topped one slice of bread with cheese, corned beef, and sauerkraut. He threw the whole thing on the griddle; the sound and smell of sizzling butter made his stomach growl in happy anticipation.

"Looks yummy," Paul said as he set three plates on the counter for the server to pick up.

"The secret is a little bit of extra butter on the rye." Fran laughed. "Or maybe it's the extra slices of corned beef. I'll never tell."

"That thing looks like something Dagwood Bumstead might enjoy," Paul said, licking his lips.

"Ha! You're right!" Fran plated his sandwich and sat at a small table against the wall. Paul handed him a Coke from the fountain and sat down. "You know, Sadie says I should stay away from Coke." Paul raised an eyebrow. "Okay, okay." Fran took a bite of his Reuben and sighed in delight, then shot Paul a serious look. "Yeah, I still talk to her."

"It's okay, man. I'm not here to judge."

"Thank God." Fran laughed. "Place is busy today, huh?" He pinched a bit of loose sauerkraut between his fingers and shoved it into his mouth.

"Don't be fooled." Paul looked him in the eye. "Today's crowd won't make up for yesterday's non-crowd. Or the day before. Or the day before that."

"You're making it sound awful." Fran guzzled his Coke.

"I wouldn't go that far. It's maybe two steps away from being awful."

"Should I stop by more than once a week?" He wiped his mouth. "Would that help?"

"I don't know." Paul took a deep breath. "I really don't know."

"My sister thinks I should sell the place." No longer hungry, Fran pushed his plate away. "I'll tell you what, let's table this discussion until after the holidays. I'll study the reports and run some what-if scenarios. We can set up a meeting for, say, the first week in January?"

"We should be okay until then." Paul jumped up at the sound of the bell, an incoming order. "Duty calls."

"Go forth and make good sandwiches!" Fran tried to keep his tone light. He pulled the plate toward him and picked at what was left of his Reuben. Blech, it was cold already; this type of sandwich begged to be eaten hot.

The thought of selling the deli unnerved him. He wanted to keep Sadie's dream alive but simply didn't have the gumption to spend more than a day or two a week here. He remembered feeling so over-whelmed the first year they opened. Disappearing forks. Yep. That's what he remembered most from that year—disappearing forks, of all things. One of the kids they hired as a server thought the cutlery was disposable. Fran shook his head at the memory. True, the forks were cheap and flimsy. But the missing forks had been just one annoyance in a string of early annoyances. He had known early on that he wasn't cut out for the restaurant business. But it was Sadie's dream, and he was thrilled to support it. He just didn't want to be involved in the daily minutia. The problem was that he and Sadie had been a team, and he got sucked into it. He'd had some fun too. Sadie had made it fun. That was then, though. The truth was, without her, it was no longer fun; he felt out of place here.

18

———————

Darlene stood and stretched. Her back ached from sitting hunched over her laptop for the past hour. She finally read the cannabis article, sent comments to her colleague, and scanned online do-it-yourself divorce kits. That last bit—the online divorce kits—was impulsive. She wasn't sure she wanted to give up on Denny, on their marriage so quickly. But the uncertainty of her future loomed. She felt untethered and in knots. One minute she couldn't keep down her coffee. The next minute, she was trying to decide if her neighbor's brown eyes were more the color of caramel or honey. She reminded herself that Francisco-o-o-o had invaded her space, had annoyed her to no end, and refused to call her by her own name. Still, she felt an unexpected current aligning her with his corny ways, his crooked smile. None of it made any sense.

If she and Denny were headed for divorce, they needed to decide what to do with the family home. And the condo—there seemed no other choice but to sell it. God, she could not believe she was sitting here thinking like this. So what if he was infatuated with this Remi? The minute they combine households, well, he will realize the grass isn't greener. Won't he? He will come to his senses, won't he? Come running back to her, right? She'd lose weight. Yes. That's what she would do. Starting tomorrow. She popped a chocolate into her mouth. Who was she kidding? Denny looked happy for the first time in an exceedingly long time. There was so much more to this than deciding about the family home and selling the condo. So much more. *Dammit, Denny.* She threw an unopened piece of chocolate across the room. Then another. And another. *Fuck you, Denny. Fuck you!*

Darlene stared at her buzzing phone and exhaled. She had been tense about her father on the road and was greatly relieved to know he'd made it safely. She read her mother's text: Dad just got here. Thanks for talking sense into him. Love, Mom.

Darlene: No worries. I'm glad he's home. He really should have a cell phone.

Mom: I know. Love you.

Darlene: Love you too. Congratulations on your book, btw. A book. Holy cow!

Mom: You should read it.

Darlene: I will.

Honestly, she wasn't sure that she would read her mother's book. She didn't think she could get past the steamy scenes knowing her mother—*her mother!*—wrote them.

DARLENE OPENED the sliding glass door and stepped onto the balcony, searching for signs of Fran over the rail. A *hello Rose* or some other corny remark would make her happy right now, and she wasn't exactly sure why. Reassurance maybe? Had she been rude when she refused to allow him to intrude on her lunch? Maybe so. Perhaps she needed to be rude. Her hackles suddenly raised, his annoying behavior drowning out the color of his eyes. Who did he think he was, anyway? All the *Rose this* and *Rose that*. If anyone was rude, it was him. She was married! At least outwardly, for the purpose of the filming. He had no reason to think otherwise. Reality hit. She was delusional, thinking that he had been flirting with her. Men didn't flirt with her. They simply didn't. She had entered the invisible phase of her life.

She picked up the cat's dish and carried it inside; not two seconds later did the sound of claws scratching on the glass and loud meowing lure her back to the door. The cat in all his furry grayness had his nose pressed against the glass like a kid begging his mother to let him come in and watch cartoons instead of playing outside in the hot summer sun. Only it wasn't hot, and whatever sun had been sparkling on the ocean earlier was now shrouded in clouds. Gray tableau, gray mood. Mood and weather congruency; the sky perfectly matched her emotional state. Nothing was worse than blinding, happy sunshine when you wanted darkness and rain.

She filled the dish with milk and started to carry it to the balcony but turned around and went back to the kitchen. She got another bowl out of the cupboard, then pulled the remains of her leftovers out of the refrigerator. No reason to let this dry turkey go to waste. She removed the bread and tore the meat into bite-sized pieces, arranging them into a pile on the plate. She did the same with the bacon, putting one piece in her mouth for every piece she put on the plate. The bacon certainly made up for the turkey. Succulent.

"I'm eating bacon, Dad," she yelled, waving a piece in the air. "Look, I'm enjoying it too!" She made a mental note to call Rachel later and fill her in on what had gone on with their father over the past two days. Nope. She erased that thought, pleased that her father had come to her with his troubles. Sure, proximity helped. But he shared things with her that he had not shared with Rachel. Finally, she had something Rachel didn't. Something intangible. Something special.

She carried both dishes out to the balcony and set them down next to the cat's blanket. He circled her legs, rubbing against them, arching his back, before finally settling in for his feast. A cat version of a happy dance, complete with a purring accompaniment. Darlene smiled, watching him eat. She had no idea what to do with him when she headed home in a few days. She had never been a cat person. But this little guy amused her.

"Rose."

Darlene slowly turned around. Fran stood on his balcony, just over the rail. How long had he been standing there? Any invisibility she felt before fell away like a protective wrapper. She felt naked and exposed.

"Hi, Fran." She scratched the cat's head, then slowly walked toward the rail that separated the two balconies. "Looks like I have a friend for life." She nudged her head toward the cat.

"Not until you name him. Or her?"

"I looked. It's him." She hadn't thought about naming him. "He's going to be pretty unhappy when I head home in a few days."

"Where is home?"

"Northern Virginia. Leesburg."

"Ah, the W&OD bike trail."

"Wow, you're familiar with the area! We're just a few blocks from the trail."

"I used that trail for many years, bike-commuting to work. Do you use it much?"

"I used to love walking on it." She wrinkled her nose. "There are too many bikers now, no offense. I can't begin to tell you how many times I was almost mowed down. The riders act like they're competing in the Tour de France." She grew wistful. "My brother was an avid cyclist. He had just taken a job as a tour guide for some European cycling company. I don't remember the name. Anyway, he was just a few weeks from getting on a plane to start his new job." The tears poured out of her eyes. "He was hit by a car while biking on a country road in Pennsylvania."

"I am so sorry." Fran reached over the rail and took her hands. "God, I'm sorry."

Darlene cleared her throat and gently pulled her hands away. "Denny, my ex, um, my husband, runs on the trail a few times a week." She needed to change the subject away from Liam. And fast. She clasped her hands behind her back in a futile attempt to stop the tingling.

"Your husband never gets mowed down by those horrible

cyclists?" Fran cringed. "I didn't mean it like that. After what you just told me. I guess I'm trying to apologize on behalf of all disrespectful cyclists."

"It's okay." Darlene felt her face turning many shades of red. "Honestly, I'm surprised I even told you about Liam. I was eleven when he was born. I acted like he was my baby. When he got a little older, I took him with me everywhere I went." She searched Fran's eyes. "It was a distracted driver. Eating a burger. The guy apparently dropped a napkin and reached down to get it. By the time he saw Liam, it was too late."

"Was this recent?"

"Almost twelve years ago."

"Rose." He hung his head. "I'm so sorry."

"At least the guy stopped. Stayed with Liam until the paramedics arrived." She shrugged. "That's something, right?"

"I suppose that's one way to look at it."

"The funny thing is, the bike wasn't damaged in the accident. Just some scrapes on the frame. The rear wheel was bent a little but that was all. The bike is in my basement at home. I kept it. I never even offered to let my parents have it. And they never asked." She shrugged.

"God, Rose, I mean, Darlene, I'm so sorry. As a person, of course, but as a biker, hearing about this really hits home." His eyes bore into hers. "I don't ride anymore, but when I did, I always worried about distracted drivers."

"What happened to your wife?" Darlene couldn't talk about Liam anymore. She touched her cheek. Hot. She didn't have to look in a mirror to know that her face was red. She never knew so many reds existed until she wanted to paint her front door red and stood, paralyzed, in front of the swatches at Sherwin Williams. Fireweed. Rustic Red. Heartthrob. Real Red. Stop (yes, they had a paint color called Stop). Rave Red. Tanager. Poinsettia. Bolero. And on and on and on. Only to later learn that there was only one shade of red accepted by the historical society—Rustic Red.

"Cancer." Fran shifted uncomfortably from one foot to the other.

Darlene waited a beat, but it was clear Fran wasn't ready to offer more. She felt the blood draining from her head, wondering in horror if she'd overstepped. "Look, I'm sorry for generalizing the cycling population. There are some very respectful bikers out there. My brother was one of them."

"I was one of them too." He smiled. "Good job backpedaling, by the way."

"Pun intended, right?" She felt the heaviness of the past few minutes begin to lift.

"Of course." He laughed. "Seriously, there's no excuse for bad behavior on the bike trail." He stared at her. "But I must say, some of you walkers are flighty and unpredictable."

"Touché." The topic of Liam set aside, she found herself drawn in and curious. "So, when did you live in the DC area? I'm assuming you live here now, to run your deli."

"Ah, you figured it out."

"Only because I saw the pictures while I waited for my father by the restrooms. I put two and two together. I'm sorry about him, by the way. He was kind of a pain in the ass today."

"I enjoyed him. It made me think of my own father, who is long dead."

"You had a crotchety Jewish father?" She held his eyes.

"No, not exactly." He grew serious. "I almost became a priest."

"What made you rethink that path?"

"It's complicated, but, I think God knew I wouldn't have been suited to that life and he made me restless. I barely lasted a year in seminary."

"Wow." And then: "I'm sorry your dad is gone."

"Me too." He looked at the ground. "We didn't always see eye-to-eye. I regret not trying harder."

This was Darlene's cue to say something warm and encouraging. Her mind was uncharacteristically blank. *Think, Darlene, think.* And the more she tried to think of something to say, the more her brain dug its heels in the sand. "I'm sure he knew you loved him." It was all she could muster.

"Yeah, I guess." He rubbed the back of his neck. "Sadie and I lived in Reston. We sold the big house five years ago and bought this beauty." He gestured at his condo with a flourish.

She knotted her brows. "Why have I never seen you here before?"

"I don't know." He shrugged. "Perfect timing, maybe? Sadie got sick. We spent a lot of time at the Mayo Clinic in Jacksonville, Florida. We almost bought a place down there."

"Fran, I'm so sorry." She hung her head. "I keep saying things that bring up your heartbreaking memories."

"I live with my heartbreaking memories every day. Even when I'm not thinking about them, I'm thinking about them." He pulled up the collar on his turtleneck sweater until it covered his chin. "It's getting cold out here. I'd better be going."

DARLENE WATCHED Fran disappear into his condo. Once again, she felt incompetent. Utterly foolish. She sat down on the chair and didn't object when the cat jumped into her lap, trying to wedge his way into a warm place, making himself quite cozy. She scratched the back of his neck, his soft purrs lulling her into an almost hypnotic state. This was dumb, letting a stray cat climb all over her. He obviously wasn't feral. Possibly abandoned? No collar or other identifying paraphernalia. She hoped he didn't have fleas. Oh well, too late to worry about that now. Rabies? If there was anything she should worry about, it was that. She lifted the cat off her lap and put him down, letting him fend for himself. She got up and went inside.

Her cell phone, still on the breakfast bar next to her laptop, buzzed. Denny. She felt like letting it roll to voicemail but found herself picking it up.

"How did it go today?"

"Okay, I guess. My dad showed up last night, long story, and was your stand-in today."

"No, kidding! How did he do?"

"He was a royal pain in the ass, but we got through it." Her hackles went up, chatting with Denny like this, like he hadn't just left her for another woman, like he was just calling from work, checking in, as he liked to call it. More likely, all those check-in calls were a gauging mechanism—how long did he have to fool around with Remi before he absolutely had to be home? "What's up, Denny? What do you want?"

"Why do you always think I have an agenda?" He sighed loudly. "Can't I call to genuinely see how you're doing?"

"First, you usually do have an agenda. Second, there's nothing genuine about this call."

"Fine. Then I won't tell you that I've had a change of heart and want to be on the show with you tomorrow." He paused. "It is tomorrow, right?"

Darlene's stomach fell. She did not want him around, did not want to share the last day of her filming with him. She wanted the opportunity to tour a house by herself.

"You don't have to do that, Denny. I've got it covered."

"I'd like to."

"What about Remi?"

"There's no more Remi." A quiet sob squeaked out of his mouth.

Darlene stared at the floor. No more Remi. What happened? So soon? The blush was off the apple so soon? Instead of feeling elated, she felt her body stiffen. "Where are you?"

"I'm at that diner from yesterday." His voice was back to normal. A quick recovery if she ever heard one. "Can I come over?"

"No."

"It's my condo too."

"I don't care if it is or isn't. You're not coming over."

"You can't stop me."

"Denny, you're acting like a spoiled brat."

He hung up on her, confirming her assessment.

19

————

Secrets revealed. It had taken Sadie a bit of time to open up to Fran, to let him glimpse the closet containing her skeletons. *We all have skeletons*, he pleaded when she hesitated to let him in. *I went to seminary for crying out loud. I almost became a priest!* When she still hesitated, he threw in the fact that he had chosen money over God. What did that make him? A greedy bastard, that's what. He admitted it freely and early. *I chose money over God, how about that for a skeleton?* Had he made the right choice? Probably not. But then he met Sadie, and his desire to work, work, work diminished. He grew closer to God during her illness and was convinced, finally, that God had forgiven him for not pursuing the priesthood.

Perhaps he had been too pushy with Sadie, early on. Well, if he had been, she never let on, and eventually opened up, bit by bit. Her skeletons were not bad, by skeletons' standards. Not bad at all. The kinds of mistakes one makes when they're young and don't quite know themselves. She had a one-night stand, got pregnant, and gave birth to a girl. Tried to make things work with a guy who refused to be a father. Sadie soldiered on, raising Jackie by herself. By the time Fran entered Sadie's life, Jackie was just starting college. Sadie had been nuts to think any of those skeletons would have scared him away. Certifiably nuts.

Sitting on the floor in the guest room, back pressed against the wall and a photo book in his lap, he thought about the woman next door. The crazy redhead. Darlene. No, Rose. She looked like a Rose to him, what could he say? He marveled at how a seemingly innocuous comment about the bike trail had the power to open the floodgates and reveal something that might not have been shared for a long time, if ever. Was it some deep, dark secret that her brother died in a cycling accident? It shouldn't be. But it was clearly painful for her to talk about. Fran imagined her brother's death was something she kept tied up in a neat little package locked away in the deepest depths of her mind. How in the world had he managed to tug on just the precise string? The one that allowed the brown paper to slide off. He had not meant to do that. It just happened. He cringed, remembering how he had shut her down when she asked how Sadie died. No secret there, either. He simply did not have the emotional strength to discuss it.

He held his hands out and studied them, wondering what it would be like to hold hands that were not Sadie's. Something subtle yet powerful, unnerving yet hopeful shocked him in the seconds he held Rose's hands over the rail. Taking them had been an automatic gesture of sympathy. Something he might have done with anyone standing in front of him, crying.

"I miss your hands, Franny." He turned his head and saw Sadie sitting on the floor next to him. He blushed, feeling guilty for reacting to another woman's touch. He patted his shoulder, but she didn't lay her head there like she usually did. "What are you reading?"

"Oh, this?" He demurred, then decided to not hide the fact that he was beginning to get to know the crazy redhead. *No harm in getting to know a neighbor, right?* He wiggled his fingers, letting the lingering feeling of Rose's hands fall away. "The woman next door told me about her brother's bike accident. He died. It made me think about all the riding we did together, all the bike vacations. Remember this one?" He opened the book—a photo book Sadie had made using pictures from their bike tour through California wine country. A long weekend riding from vineyard to vineyard.

"One of my favorites." She smiled. "I think Italy takes the cake, though."

"Ah, yes. Italy was the best." Fran couldn't recall the name of the tour company they'd used and wondered if it was the one Rose's brother would have worked for. "We were pretty lucky, you know. Those were some crazy conditions." The Italian bike vacation had been touted as extreme, for avid cyclists only. Long climbs, mountain passes, fast downhill legs. Six days of riding. It had been mostly fun, but sometimes harrowing. In the evenings over pasta and wine, Sadie chatted nonstop about how exhilarating it was to fly downhill. Fran, though, silently prayed that they would come out of the vacation alive. And they did. They survived Grand Tour-like conditions, and then she goes and dies from cancer. He wiped a tear and turned to put his arms around her, but she was already gone.

20

Darlene could not sit still. Fran had comforted her, took her hands over the rail. And now, Denny's phone call. She thought she might lose her mind. She paced from one end of the condo to the other, picking up the chocolates she threw across the living room earlier.

Half of her brain tried to make sense of what was happening between her and Fran. He held her hands over the rail. It meant nothing; he was just compassionate. He was still annoying, but less so than before. He was growing on her, she supposed. Dammit. She didn't want to be distracted by him, didn't want to feel drawn to him. Not now. Not while she was desperately trying to figure out her path forward, either with or without Denny.

"He's my neighbor. Nothing more." She tossed the crumbled chocolate wrappers in the air and caught them. "And a short-lived neighbor, at that. I'm definitely selling this place." She stood in front of the sliding glass door and looked for the cat, who was probably out doing whatever cats do when they're not eating or sleeping.

The other half of her brain was on Denny and the surprising news that he was no longer with Remi. He destroyed their life to be with this woman, his words still fresh in Darlene's ears. *I wanted to be in lockstep with her. We made a pact.* Thank goodness it had not been a suicide pact. Denny would probably be dead. Not Remi, though. She would be very much alive.

Feeling like she was about to either suffocate or explode, she opened the door and stepped outside. Yikes! The temperature must have dropped at least ten degrees in the past half-hour. She threw on a thick sweater and shimmied into her purple hoodie for added warmth. She grabbed the bag of leftover fries from her lunch and headed to the dune.

THE ONE-LEGGED seagull showed up within minutes. Darlene sat against the dune and held out a cold, limp fry. Looking at the water as to not intimidate the bird, she sat as still as possible. She watched out of the corner of her eye and couldn't tell if the seagull simply wasn't hungry, or just didn't trust her. Probably the latter because seagulls were always hungry. Weren't they? She dropped the fry several inches in front of her and brought her knees up to her chest, hugging them for warmth. She felt like she had the whole beach to herself. The entire East Coast, even. The beach in summer certainly had its advantages, like sandcastles, good books, and a dip in the ocean. But the beach in late fall, well, that was an entirely different kind of delight. Peaceful. Deserted. Quiet. Ordinarily, she relished the glorious solitude. Here she was, under the clouds and soon to be setting sun. The afternoon seemed to be growing colder by the minute. Instead of joy, she felt punished, like the ocean's moans were warning her about things she couldn't see, only feel.

Denny's call unnerved her. She felt hopeful and yet...and yet... There was a part of her that wanted to deny him the opportunity to come back, on principle. She didn't know what to do. He didn't exactly come out and say he wanted to work on their relationship. But wasn't that why he called? Wasn't that what he wanted? Wasn't that what she wanted?

She let her mind drift back to Fran. Her encounter with him over the rail had been startling; she did not know what to make of him. So annoying, so corny on the one hand, and so compassionate on the other. An avid cyclist. Like Liam. She didn't think she could deal with that, becoming close to a man who would be a constant reminder of how her brother died. Or worse, worrying that he would take up cycling again, then go out on his bike and never return.

The seagull, hopping on his one foot, grabbed the fry and bounced away, positioning himself at reasonable distance, but close enough to quickly return for seconds. She placed another limp fry in the same spot and waited.

Darlene felt herself circling the edge of curiosity about Fran, testing the waters in her heart, grasping at a split-second glimpse into a future that did not exist, a future with a complete stranger. She knew nothing about him. She simply couldn't allow herself to get involved with him. And now Denny might be available to her again; a reality she told herself she needed to explore.

She dumped the rest of the fries in the sand and shuffled up the access path to her condo, glancing back just in time to see her little one-legged friend defending his bounty against a flock of highly agitated birds.

BANGING HER SHOES TOGETHER, a puff of sand shot up, then fell in tiny clumps next to the banister. She turned them upside down and dumped out yet more sand. How in the world could she have walked just a few hundred feet and accumulated so much sand? She carried her shoes up the stairs, then reached for the handle on the sliding glass door. She was about to open it when she stopped abruptly, backing away, unsure what to do next. She ran down the steps, turned right, and ran up the steps onto Fran's balcony. She banged on his slider, hoping he was home, hoping he would hear. Relief washed over her as he approached the door, a dishtowel in one hand, and an open beer in the other. He slid the door open.

"Rose?"

She stood, out of breath, the hairs on the back of her neck standing at attention. "There's someone in my living room." She tried to control her breathing. She crouched down, letting her head fall between her knees, wobbling unsteadily. Fran stepped out and crouched down beside her.

"Rose." He grabbed her by the wrists and pulled her up, then led her to a chair and gently pushed her into a seated position. "Take a deep breath." Darlene tried, but couldn't, sending her into a tailspin of panic. She lowered her head between her knees again. "Did you see the person?"

"Yes." She took several broken breaths. "There's someone passed out on my couch." She took another breath, and the air went all the way in. She felt like she had been rescued from drowning. She took a few hefty gulps. "I was sitting by the dunes."

"Could it be a friend or family member? Your father, maybe? Your husband?"

Darlene suddenly remembered Denny's call. Could it be him on the couch? She did not recognize the contour of the body under the throw blanket. The person's back was toward the door, and stretched out the entire length of the couch. Denny was not that tall. Plus, the form was rounder, more substantial than Denny. And it certainly wasn't her father. "I don't think so. Maybe I should just call the police."

"Let me look." He hoisted one long, athletic leg over the rail, then the other. He stood in front of the door and stared, tilting his head. He moved his face closer to the glass and cupped his eyes. He approached Darlene. "It's kind of dark in there, so I'm not a hundred percent sure, but..." He motioned for her to get up. "Come, take a look. Are you sure this isn't your husband."

Not wanting to make a fool of herself by attempting to climb over the rail like Fran had, she descended his steps and then ascended hers. She joined him in front of the glass. A blue ball cap adorned with a white 'curly W' worked its way out from under the blanket and dangled over the edge of the couch, looking like it was about to fall off a cliff. Her breath caught. She knew that hat. Denny's *Washington*

Nationals hat. His favorite hat. She laughed with relief, but then grew serious. There was no question it was Denny who was sprawled out on the couch, yet she didn't recognize the form, the roundness, the girth.

"That's my husband." She looked at Fran, embarrassed. "I have no idea what he's doing here. I'd better go in and find out." She hesitated. "It's a long story, but he isn't supposed to be here."

"I know." He took a deep breath. "My sister mentioned something to that effect."

"Ah, yes. Your sister." It still confounded her that Laurie had neglected to mention that her brother lived next door. And now, she was more than a little irritated that Laurie had shared her private business with Fran. "Sorry to disturb you." She held out her hand. "Thank you for your help." Fran let his fingers touch hers, then squeezed her hand, cradling it in his a second or two longer than necessary, before finally letting it fall away.

DARLENE OPENED the sliding glass door, careful to be quiet, and stepped inside. She closed the door behind her, then stood and watched Fran ease himself over the rail. He turned and looked back in her direction. She was embarrassed to be caught watching and stepped away from the door, hoping he hadn't seen her.

Sitting in the chair next to the couch, she studied her sleeping husband, wondering what had happened, why he was here. Denny stirred, and she moved in closer. He opened his eyes and held out his hand. She hesitated, then reluctantly reached out toward him. His hand felt foreign in hers. Blindfolded, she didn't think she would have known this was Denny's hand; she would not be able to pick him out of a lineup based on his touch. A tingle shot up her spine, remembering Fran's touch; she would have no trouble picking him out. She had known Denny for almost thirty years and lived with him for twenty-five. She had known Fran for essentially two-seconds.

Stunned by this realization, she opened her hand and let Denny's hand drop.

"Denny, what's going on? Are you okay?"

"Not exactly." He pulled the blanket off and swung his feet to the floor. He sat up straight, several throw pillows tumbling down, taking his ball cap with them. Throw pillows—an explanation of the girth she had perceived.

She stared at him, his eyes revealing emotions that she didn't recognize in him. Sadness, guilt, remorse, humility? Suddenly afraid, she didn't want to know what was hiding deep within him. She pushed thoughts of how much he seemed like a stranger to her out of her mind (she pushed thoughts of Fran out of her mind too). They could go back to the marriage counselor. *Denny had a blip*, she would say. *A mere smudge. What's a tiny little spec of dirt on a twenty-five-year marriage?* She would throw it in the wash, apply some bleach, good as new. Or would it be? She supposed Denny's blip would leave a stain. One she would always be aware of. None of that mattered now. They'd deal with it. Together. She took a deep breath, firm in her resolve to do whatever work was necessary to repair the marriage.

"Listen, Dar." He leaned back into the couch cushions, crossing his arms over his chest. "I'm not ready to talk about any of this." He looked at the ceiling. "Please don't barrage me with questions."

"I think I have a right to—"

"I mean it." He held up his hand, then softened. "I know you have a right to ask me anything. I know. We'll get there, I promise." His eyes filled. "Right now, I'm a raw, jumbled mess."

Raw, jumbled mess. Because he hurt her? Because he put her through several days of hell? Because he was guilt-racked and remorse-filled? Or because Remi hurt him? She sat back and closed her eyes, searching for reality. By the time she looked up, Denny was padding into the kitchen, the blanket around his shoulders like a cape.

"Want anything?" He opened the fridge and pulled out a slice of pizza, waving it in the air. "You mind if I have this?"

Darlene looked at her watch—dinnertime. She wasn't particularly hungry but wanted to do a better job of feeding her distraught husband than she did feeding her elderly father last night. She wanted to be a hero. "Of course, you can have it. But why don't we go out and get some real dinner instead."

"That sounds good." He shoved the end of the pizza in his mouth, tearing off the bottom triangle with his teeth. "This will hold me over until then."

"How about we go now?"

"Can I take a shower first?"

"You don't have to ask." She wondered how a person could go from being a raw, jumbled mess to a person who could eat a slice of pizza as a pre-dinner snack. It was going to be a long night indeed.

"Thanks, hon." He disappeared up the stairs with his pizza, slender from behind. The only indication of his transgression was a somewhat new swagger when he walked.

21

They walked across the street to a hole-in-the-wall Chinese restaurant. Husband and wife—to anyone but a keen observer, they appeared to have not a care in the world. Just the smiling faces in a photo with no consideration for the outtakes— the messy, real-life that happened before shouts of *cheeeeeese* and after the click of the shutter. Darlene had no expectations for how the evening might play out. She promised herself she would not push, would not badger him for answers to hard questions. She promised herself that she would simply listen—something she was not particularly good at.

"Table or booth?" A young woman stepped out from behind a counter, wiping her hands on her jeans. She pulled two menus out of a pouch nailed to the wall, poised and ready to follow whatever instructions were given.

"Booth?" Darlene looked at Denny, who shrugged. "Booth," she confirmed.

They slid into their respective sides, and Darlene ordered a pot of green tea. They stared blankly at the menu, using it as a prop to avoid discussing the real issues at hand. The list of Chinese cuisine provided ready-made topics for supporting light discussion. Should they get the crispy egg rolls, fried won tons, or steak teriyaki on a stick? Pork fried rice or combination fried rice? General Tso's chicken or Hunan beef?

Famished, Darlene wanted to order it all. She was suddenly back in high school, when her mother persuaded her to lose weight. Darlene, wanting to please, had set a goal of losing thirty pounds. She and a friend joined a diet program. While her friend half-heartedly played along, Darlene followed the program's rules and regulations to the letter, limiting herself to 1,500 calories a day. She was constantly hungry. So hungry, in fact, that she fantasized about gorging on a dozen donuts, then following it up with a burger and fries, and washing the whole thing down with a chocolate milkshake. One unfortunate day, she followed through. After two donuts and four bites of the burger, and feeling thoroughly sick to her stomach, she quit the diet and never looked back. And, of course, her mother had expressed disappointment that she did not follow through to her goal. Darlene knows better now; she would have gotten sick and malnourished if she had continued to lose weight. Thirty pounds lighter on her stately five-foot-eight frame would have made her look sickly. Bad memories aside, the savory aroma coming out of the kitchen made her mouth water. She truly felt like she could eat everything on the menu.

"Crispy eggrolls, won ton soup, egg foo young, and combination fried rice." Darlene handed the server her menu, then looked at Denny. "You okay sharing?"

Denny nodded and ran his finger around the rim of the teacup. He didn't look all that upset, at least not to Darlene. What happened to his being a raw, jumbled mess?

Darlene couldn't stand it, she had to ask, had to know what had happened. Determined to play the role of supportive, understanding wife, she reached across the table and put her hand over his. "I'm so sorry you're going through all this, Denny. Can't we please talk about it?"

"No." He pulled his hand away.

Darlene knew she was doing a lousy job of keeping the disappointment and confusion out of her eyes. She wanted to engage, to tell him that verbalizing things sometimes takes all of the weight out of them. Sharing was a good thing. Wasn't it?

"I won't pry. I won't ask for details. I don't want to know." She said these things in a desperate attempt to get him to talk. Of course, she wanted details. Unlike how she felt a few days ago, now she wanted to know everything, wanted to understand. She took a deep breath, holding back tears. "I'm your wife. I want to get past this; I want to help. You left me, and now you're back." The tears sprang out of her eyes. "Please, talk to me."

"I don't know where to start." He looked at the wall, then back at Darlene. "You're just going to find fault with everything I did, every step of the way."

Darlene couldn't say she disagreed, couldn't promise anything. "I will try my best not to be judgmental."

"Okay, I'll say it fast." He took a deep breath. "Remi is pregnant." He covered his eyes with his hand, then wiped them with his napkin.

"How?"

Denny stared blankly at her; his eyes moist. "The usual way."

"But you had a vasectomy." She stared at him. "Years ago."

"Exactly."

Darlene gasped. "Ah. I get it. She was still sleeping with her husband." Darlene shook her head in disbelief. "Imagine that."

"Can we live without the wisecracks?"

"No. No, Denny. We can't." She shook her head again, now incredulous. "How old is she, anyway."

"Thirty-seven."

Darlene thought back to the day she saw them running on the beach. "She looked older from a distance."

"What did you expect? That I'd cheat on you with another you?"

"Someone old and fat?"

"That's not what I meant." He pushed himself out of the booth and slid back in, next to her. "I'm sorry. I didn't mean it like that." He put his arm around her, and she let him.

The food arrived, giving them a much-needed break from the

rawness of their conversation. They made idle chit-chat and bemoaned the amount of food. Darlene braced herself for Denny to provide commentary on everything she put into her mouth. But he didn't. She ordered two beers, and when they arrived, poured them into glasses and handed one to Denny.

"Why are you here?" She let the cold beer slide down her throat. "Seriously. Why are you here?"

"I don't know." He guzzled his beer. "I honestly don't know. Please don't think, for a minute, that I ever stopped loving you."

"You have a strange way of showing it."

"I'll make it up to you."

"How?"

"We'll figure it out."

No longer hungry, Darlene picked at her food. She watched Denny out of the corner of her eye, devouring his dinner, an unfamiliar look on his face. Blank. His face was blank. *This is what a broken heart looks like*, she thought.

THEY WALKED SILENTLY BACK to the condo, this time, not looking so much like a normal husband and wife. Darlene was a brisk three or four strides ahead of Denny, who shuffled like a wounded animal, carrying their bag of leftovers.

"What are you doing here, Denny?" Darlene waited until their coats were hung, and the leftovers put away in the fridge before shooting the very questions at him that she promised she wouldn't ask. "I want to know." She raised her voice. "If Remi hadn't turned up pregnant, would you be here, now, at this very moment?" She glared at him. "I'm guessing she's back with her husband. Is that why you're here? Because she went back to her husband to work things out with him?"

"I was wrong about her. I miss you and me." He reached for Darlene's hand, but she hid it behind your back. "I want to try to fix this."

"You were wrong about what?" All the hope she'd felt, just a few hours ago, had been dashed. Popped like a balloon, the shredded rubber all over the floor. "Try to fix what, exactly?"

"Us. This." He sat down and rested his arms on the breakfast bar, then let his head drop. "It's what you want, isn't it?"

She sat down next to him, unsure what to say. Is it what she wanted? Did she want to try and fix their marriage? Two hours ago, yes, definitely. But now? The answer was a resounding no. "This isn't going to work. You can't stay here tonight. I'm sorry." She sighed. "You need to leave."

"But I said I want to fix this."

Darlene got up and made herself a glass of water. She didn't offer to get one for Denny. "You can't barge in here, after what you put me through, and say you want to fix things. Remi is the love of your life, remember? Do you really think I'll be okay, knowing you'll always be thinking about her?"

"Stop. Just stop. I don't know. I don't know anything." He put his head in his hands. "I love you, Dar. I really do." He looked up. "Can I at least do the show with you tomorrow?"

"I don't know."

"Please."

Darlene took a deep breath. Denny looked pathetic, with his still too dark hair. Like a fifty-two-year-old man trying to look younger. Wow, isn't that what women did? Isn't that what she will do when her hair starts to gray? Didn't she want to look as young as possible for as long as possible? Seeing Denny in this new light—pathetic, feeling sorry for himself, not knowing who he was or what he wanted—strengthened her resolve. She did not want to be married to him anymore.

"You can sleep on the couch. Or in the guest room. Filming starts at ten tomorrow." Screw the water. She dumped it in the sink, grabbed a wine glass, and poured the last few ounces of an open bottle of pinot noir into the glass. Screw this tiny sip of wine. She let it slide down her throat as she pulled a fresh bottle off the rack. She opened the drawer and pulled out her bag of chocolates.

"I'll take a glass of that," Denny said, pointing to the wine bottle under her arm.

"You can get your own damned wine. This is coming with me." She felt Denny's eyes on her as she climbed the stairs; she was angry that he foisted himself on her evening. "And don't touch my beer," she said between clenched teeth.

DARLENE SIPPED her wine in bed, growing more restless by the second, feeling violated by Denny's presence in the house. She could have insisted he leave but felt sorry for him. She decided she needed to call Shelly and let her know about the separation. Tomorrow. With or without Denny's support. She turned on the TV and clicked through the array of channels: news; *Seinfeld*; more news; a cheesy Hallmark movie; an even cheesier Lifetime movie; home reno shows; living in the wilderness shows; cooking shows; baking shows.

She turned off the TV and climbed out of bed. She stood in front of the sliding glass door leading to her balcony, the one she had been on when Fran joined her in song and made that corny reference to *Titanic*. She stepped outside and wondered if she could tolerate the cold. She sat down in the chair. Nope. Not without bundling up. She went inside and traded her flimsy cotton pajamas for her striped fleece ones. She put on her plaid, fuzzy robe, and grabbed the wine bottle, her glass, the chocolates, a green slouchy hat, and a scarf. On her way out, she grabbed the pair of fingerless gloves sitting on a shelf by the door. She stepped outside again and marveled at how the right attire made all the difference. The only things missing were a campfire and s'mores.

She topped off her wine and set the glass and bottle on the floor next to the chair. She plucked a piece of chocolate out of the bag and carefully unwrapped the red foil. Leaning back, she took a dainty bite, savoring the initial hit. She popped the rest of it in her mouth and slowly chewed, following it with a sip of red wine. Why should chocolate and champagne get all the attention? There was definitely something to be said for chocolate and red wine. She took another sip. A winning combination indeed. She placed the empty wrapper under the bag—she would read it later—and thought about Denny. How dare he come waltzing back, begging like a child, all because he couldn't have what he really wanted—Remi. Damn him.

She unwrapped another piece of chocolate and held her wine glass out in front of her. The moonlight illuminated the pinot noir, making it look almost translucent. She took a sip, then closed her eyes and shoved the chocolate into her mouth, nearly choking as it slid down her throat. She sat up in a panic and gulped her wine.

A light flicked on in the condo next door. She craned her neck and saw Fran at his sliding glass door. She plastered herself against her chair, making herself as small as possible to avoid being seen. Her first instinct was to flee, but she feared he would notice the movement. She held her breath. Thank God, the light went out. She exhaled slowly, pouring more wine, and stared at the moon's reflection on the water. The sound of a door opening signaled that her evening was about to be interrupted. Any other time she might have welcomed the company. But not now, not tonight, not like this. She continued staring straight ahead, taking intermittent sips of wine.

"Can't you see I want to be left alone?" She spoke to no one in particular, the moon maybe.

"I won't bother you," Fran said.

Darlene sipped her wine and popped another chocolate in her mouth, this time careful to thoroughly chew it. "You're bothering me."

"But I'm not doing anything." He paused. "You could always go back inside."

She whipped her head around. He was sitting just over the rail—on his own balcony, in his own chair, with his own glass of wine—and was equally bundled against the cold. "I was out here first."

"Congratulations," he said. "I'm sorry if you had a rough evening."

"What makes you think I had a rough evening?" She hated when people thought they knew how you were feeling, when, really, they didn't have a clue. How arrogant. She desperately wanted to go inside.

But she couldn't now, not on principle. She would stay out here all night if she had to. There was no way she was going to let someone named Francisco out-stubborn her.

"Your husband shows up unexpectedly. Scares the dickens out of you. Now you're sitting outside in the dark, in the cold, all by yourself, with a bottle of wine."

"So what?" She unwrapped another chocolate and made a show of eating it in front of him.

"Now, I'm certain you had a bad evening."

"How is that?"

"You have a bag of chocolates out here too."

"Are you saying the only reason a woman would eat chocolate outside, in her PJs, in the cold, in the dark, is because she had a bad day?" She looked away.

"No. I am just stating a fact."

"I happen to like these." She ate another one. "And they go great with red wine." She twisted the bag closed and tossed it over the rail. The bag sailed through the air, then hit him in the chest and slid down into his lap. Unfazed, he pulled a piece of chocolate out and ate it, then nodded, chasing it with his own wine.

"Not so good with white wine," he said.

Darlene shrugged, unhappy that her bag was gone. She didn't want to ask him for it back, because that would lead to further conversation, when what she wanted was silence. Six hours ago, she daydreamed about him; now his presence felt almost as intrusive as Denny's unexpected visit.

"Is everything okay with your husband?"

"The woman he left me for...she's pregnant. You can draw your own conclusion."

He peeled the wrapper off another chocolate and held it between his thumb and forefinger. "Mozel tov?"

"Funny." She felt herself soften. "It's not his baby. It's her husband's." She sipped her wine, feeling warm tears rolling down her cheeks, grateful for the dark. "Denny had a vasectomy about fifteen years ago, so I know he's at least telling the truth about that."

"Ouch."

"Yeah. Ouch. The whole thing is like a soap opera. His girlfriend broke up with him and went back to her own husband. How's that for a story line?"

"I'm sorry, Rose. Not to be blunt, or to minimize what you're going through, but he's an ass."

"He is indeed." She turned away from Fran and looked at the ocean. She poured a little bit more wine in her glass and swirled it around in the moonlight, then raised it toward him. "To the moonlight."

Fran raised his glass. "Cheers to that."

"Do you have kids, Francisco-o-o-o?"

"None of my own." He pressed his lips together. "Sadie did. A daughter." And as if anticipating her next question, he added, "We got married later in life. My first marriage, her second."

"How old?"

"We were both in our mid-forties when we got married."

"You never married before then?"

"Nope. I was always working. Climbing the corporate ladder, building my own consulting business." He looked wistful. "Sure, I had relationships over the years. I just never met anyone I could see myself with forever." He grew quiet. "Until Sadie. I knew it in an instant. Tragic irony that she's gone. Forever, what a concept, huh?"

"How old is your step-daughter?" Darlene veered the topic away from Sadie, fearful that talking about her would plummet Fran into a wistful silence. And right now, contrary to how she felt a few minutes ago, she relished his presence.

"Jackie is thirty-six, I think." He calculated on his fingers. "No. Thirty-three. She went to school in Wyoming, then at some point met a cowboy. A rancher." He paused. "On the ranch he owns. They're getting married next summer."

"It sounds like you two have a good relationship."

"She tolerates me." He grew serious. "Actually, we do have a good relationship. I was lucky. When I came into her life, she was already in college. We didn't have to navigate any of the typical blended family stuff."

"A ranch hand!" Darlene loosened her scarf. "That is seriously cool. My daughter, Shelly, would be jealous. She's studying to be a vet. She's out in Colorado."

"Ah, the great Rocky Mountains." He rubbed his hands together. "I should have brought my gloves out here."

"You want mine?"

"What?" He looked confused. "No, no. You keep yours. I have a perfectly good pair downstairs, but I'm too lazy and too comfy to get up." He cupped his hands over his mouth and blew, then pulled the cuffs of his jacket down over them.

"Please, take them." She pulled them off and draped them over the rail. "I'm in the middle of a hot flash."

Fran pulled the gloves off the rail and slipped a hand through one. "They're a little tight." He laughed. "These things have holes!" He held his hand in front of his face and wiggled his fingers.

"That sounds like a complaint." She laughed and shook her head, enjoying herself for the first time in what seemed like a very, long time. "Hey, do you want to take a walk?"

Fran hesitated, giving Darlene enough time to feel mortified that she had just invited this near stranger to walk with her in the dark. How presumptuous of her. She sat forward, ready to be let down easy. As a matter of fact, hoping to be let down. She didn't want to take a walk with him. Not really. She wasn't even sure how or why the question came out of her mouth.

"Sure. I would like that."

"What the hell is this?" Denny appeared on the balcony, looking from Darlene, to Fran, back to Darlene. "What is this, the corner booth at le petit cafe de romance?"

"Denny, what are you doing out here?" Darlene brought her hands to her head. "Seriously. What are you doing out here?"

"I heard voices and thought I was losing my mind."

"So, you just barged into my room?"

"The door was open."

"I think I'll go now." Fran stood.

"Fran, this is Denny." She hesitated for a split-second, then let the words come tumbling out, a bit louder than she had intended. "My soon to be ex-husband."

Fran leaned over the rail, keeping his voice low. "It was nice chatting with you, Rose." He peeled off the gloves and handed them to her.

"Wait," she said, just as he was about to step inside. "Can I have my chocolates back?" He grabbed the bag and placed it on the rail. Feeling like a fool, she waited until he was gone before taking the bag and shuffling back into the warmth of her condo.

22

———————

Wide awake, buzzing from wine and Rose's chocolates, Fran admonished himself for not climbing into bed and going to sleep hours ago. Because if he had been sound asleep, he wouldn't have heard Rose banging around on her balcony. And if he hadn't heard her, he would have had no reason to look out the window. And if he hadn't looked out the window, he wouldn't have seen her bundled up in the corner with her vices. Rose was undoubtedly one of the more interesting people he had encountered in a while. And, of course, if he hadn't seen her, he never would have stepped outside. Who was he trying to kid? He never slept.

Two-thirty. Early for owls like him. He emptied the wine bottle into his glass and carried it to his desk. He had received several questions on the proposal; now was as good a time as ever to answer them. Firing up his workstation, he had a sudden feeling of foreboding. Rose's husband had seemed agitated, and more than a little inebriated. He stood and paced within his small office area. Maybe he shouldn't have left her out there to fend for herself. What if he beat her? *Oh, my God!*

He flung the sliding glass door open and stepped out onto his balcony, leaning over the rail to ascertain if anything sounded or looked out of sorts. He could see sheaths of light coming from her slider but didn't hear any shouting or other sounds indicating a brouhaha.

"I'm acting silly," he said to the dark sky.

"Yes, you are." Sadie stood in the middle of the balcony. "She's a grown woman.

"Babe." He sighed, relieved, so relieved to see her. His body went limp, and he fell into her arms. He stepped inside and looked around. Where did she go? "Sadie?" Nothing.

Frustrated, he sat back down at his desk. God, he loved when Sadie showed up. It was the randomness of her visits that unsettled him. He wanted to talk to her tonight. Not about anything in particular. He just wanted to talk to her. His best friend. Her presence might help him convince himself that he wasn't disappointed that Denny had crashed the little party. Or persuade himself that he didn't wish he were taking a moonlight walk on the beach with Rose. Sadie was the force that righted his world, the power that kept him from sinking into a deep, black hole of depression.

He opened a blank document and started typing his response to the first question, bracing himself for another long, sleepless night.

23

Embarrassed did not come close to describing how she felt. Darlene sat up slowly and massaged her temples, trying to rub away the pain. How much wine had she consumed? Her head felt like it could explode at any moment, and her entire body felt like it was on fire. She looked down at herself, still clad in her *Nanook of the North* garb. She unwound the scarf, amazed that she hadn't inadvertently strangled herself. She threw her robe on the floor and sighed with relief. She opened the sliding glass door to let the cold air in and sat back down on the bed. Last night's events shot back at her with keen acuity. She was horrified beyond belief for openly flirting with Fran like that. Leave it to Denny to kill the moment—he was remarkably good at it.

She replayed the scene over and over—it jumped and skipped like a broken record, the audio scratchy and piercing. Horrible. Before drifting off to sleep, she sought solace by reminding herself that she had only asked Fran to take a walk. She didn't ask him to sleep with her. It was only a walk. Still, lips loosened from the wine, God knows what she would have said or done had Denny not barged in on the scene.

The sunlight pouring into the room burned bright, hurting her eyes. Not the kind of blinding yellow she wanted to see right now. She didn't need a spotlight illuminating her as the fool in last night's comedy. Not to mention her pounding head. She moaned and rubbed her forehead, then drew the curtains closed, bending down to pick up the discarded bag of chocolates, flattened like roadkill. *God, how many of these things did I eat last night*? She did not remember eating more of them after she'd gone inside. How many had Fran plucked from the bag? Maybe two. That she had seen. She consoled herself by latching onto the idea that he had eaten a handful. Or more. She suddenly felt sweaty. Within seconds her stomach churned, and she felt the pressure of excessive saliva building. She made it into the bathroom just in time. She splashed cold water on her face and brushed her teeth, swearing off chocolate forever. Never again. Never, never again.

"You're not going to say anything to Shelly, are you?" Denny called from just outside the bathroom.

"What is it with you and walking into someone's private quarters?" She needed to learn how to lock doors, apparently.

"Private quarters? This is my condo too."

Darlene felt weary of arguing that point. Technically, they co-owned the condo. "I'm calling her today. I'm tired of all these lies, all this pretending."

"We agreed to get through Thanksgiving."

"No. I'm done pretending. I'm telling her. After that, I'll tell my parents."

"Because you want to be with that guy?"

"What guy?"

"Corner booth guy."

It took Darlene a minute to decipher this. *Corner booth*? *What corner booth*? Oh, yes, the imaginary corner booth that Denny ranted about last night on the balcony. Ranted in a horribly cliché French accent. Her embarrassment about that scene resurfaced anew. "That's none of your business." She crossed her arms. "Why are you acting like this?"

He lowered himself onto the edge of the bed and covered his face with his hands. "I love you, Darlene. I want to try and fix our marriage."

Right now, she felt no sympathy. Maybe it was because her head was pounding, and her mouth felt like she swallowed several hundred cotton balls. Or perhaps it was because, in her heart, she had already moved on, shut him out, closed the door. Bolted it shut. She doubted there was any way to open it back up again. She watched him cry and felt no tenderness toward him. None.

"Denny, there's nothing to fix. Nothing. Anything that could have been fixed went unfixed for too many years, apparently." She sighed. "It's over."

"I made a mistake."

"You hurt me."

"I know I did. And I'm sorry."

"Why don't you save all this groveling for Remi."

He opened his fingers and peeked through them. "You know I can't do that. She went back to her husband. I told you that."

Darlene was furious. "You can't waltz in here and expect me to welcome you with open arms, just because your girlfriend dumped you."

He moved his hands away from his eyes and pleaded. "We'll go back to counseling. I'll make the call today."

Darlene stood. "No way, no way, no way." She grabbed his arm and pulled him off the bed, a feat that was easier than it should have been. "Get out of here!"

"It's my condo too."

"You heard me, Denny. Get the hell out of here!" *It's my condo too, it's my condo too.* She was tired of this refrain. The decision was suddenly easy; she would keep the condo and arrange to have him removed from the deed. Her lawyer would figure out the way. There was only one problem: she didn't have a lawyer. She needed to fix that problem, fast.

"Please don't call Shelly. Please, not today," he pleaded.

"I'm doing it."

"Don't you think we should tell her in person?" Denny stood and shuffled to the doorway. "Wouldn't that be better?"

"I don't want to wait."

Denny shook his head, did a backward wave with his hand, and disappeared down the stairs.

KEEPING her eye on the clock, Darlene let the scalding water from the shower flow over her body, infusing her with life. She washed last night off with soap and watched it flow down the drain. Little molecules of flirtatious thoughts about Fran, well, she washed those away too. Down the drain.

She absolutely hated taking showers. The less time she could spend standing in what was essentially a dunk tank, the better. She never understood the appeal of a luxuriously long shower, something her sister often raved about—the one thing Rachel said she fantasized about. Darlene didn't fantasize about much, but when she did, it wasn't about taking a long shower. Not even the thought of having sex in the shower appealed to her. She and Denny had tried it once. It was a laugh riot; fun, but not very satisfying. Never again. If she spent five minutes showering, it was too long. She even relied on 2-in-1 shampoos; if she could combine the washing and conditioning into one step, the less time she had to spend in the shower. After her night of wine, chocolate, and embarrassment—followed by a healthy dose of puking—she began to see the appeal.

She stepped out of the shower feeling like she might be able to make it through the day. Wrapped in a thick towel, she studied the clothes in her closet. Was today supposed to be the same day as yesterday for filming's sake? She tried to remember Gloria's instructions. Of course, she couldn't remember, because basically she wanted to block the whole TV show out of her mind. Plus, she had been so full of Fran and so full of her father's problems that her external surroundings had barely registered.

She pulled down a lavender Henley—ribbed and fitted—and

held it against her chest. Not very purply, but colorful enough. She let the towel drop to the floor and climbed into her panties and bra, then her jeans, and finally, the shirt. A bit apprehensive about the fitted cut, she held in her gut and examined herself from all angles. She took a deep breath and slouched, letting the flesh of her lower belly loose. She squatted a few times to stretch out her jeans, then stood and regarded herself. A little bit of a muffin top presented itself, but otherwise, she looked okay. She slipped her feet into a pair of boots; just enough of a heel to elongate her already long legs. She took one last look in the mirror, feeling somewhat ready to face the camera.

24

———

The condo that she would see today was only six blocks north. Darlene impulsively decided to walk there. The crisp November air and light wind aided in pushing her hangover into the background and helped to mitigate the throbbing in her head.

"In the spirit of full disclosure," Darlene heard Denny say as she turned the corner and approached the front of the building, "we're splitting up." He was talking to Gloria while the rest of the production crew, including Jesse, stood milling about. So, that was it then. He no longer wanted to try and fix things? A tiny part of her felt rejected.

"Concerning what?" Gloria looked confused. "Splitting up in the house search?" She looked at Darlene. "Or splitting up-splitting up."

Darlene stepped closer to Denny and glared at him, her body language asking *what are you doing*? He looked disheveled like he had slept in the car, which she knew he had not. His skin gave off the faint smell of alcohol, something she'd always noticed the morning after he'd overindulged. Sometimes the scent would still linger—escaping through his pores, she supposed—days later. She had not seen him since he backed out of her bedroom this morning and wondered how recently he had been drinking.

"I thought we agreed we weren't going to mention this."

"You look good. You're glowing." Denny looked her up and down, ignoring her comment, his eyes filled with lust. "You slept with that guy, didn't you?"

"That is none of your business." While she knew she could have just said no, she wanted to make him squirm.

"Ahem." Gloria stood off to the side, looking frustrated.

"It's true," Darlene said, addressing Gloria. "We're separated. As of a few days ago." She looked at the sidewalk, the particles in the concrete glistening in the sun. She felt ridiculous hearing herself say this out loud to the person in charge of this fake-ish reality show. She might as well start tap dancing, right here, right on the sidewalk. In retrospect, it would probably have been easy enough to get out of their contract. Life happens, after all. Someone could have died in the time between when they agreed to do the show and now. She couldn't help herself and did a little soft-shoe dance, then smiled and opened her arms wide. "Yes, I'm tap dancing. We should have told you sooner. Maybe even canceled our obligation." She glanced at Denny, who was sitting on the curb, his head in his hands.

Gloria's pen danced across her clipboard. Darlene could almost visualize what she was writing: *these people are nuts*. When she was finished writing, she motioned for Denny to get up. "We'll work this in. Somehow, we'll work it in." She resumed scribbling. "How about we do this. How about we say that your work obligation ended early, and you're happy to be back." She looked at Denny, then at Darlene. "We'll proceed as if everything is normal. You're a happy couple." She took a deep breath. "Then, during the update segment, we'll have the narrator or one of you say something about the marriage not working out."

"Won't that be a little heavy for your average viewer?" Denny's tone turned sarcastic. "Your viewers want happily ever after, don't they?" He glared at Darlene. "Well, don't they?"

"Denny, calm down." Darlene glared right back at him.

"This isn't a Hallmark Christmas movie," Gloria said. "Sometimes, we like to spice things up a bit." She waved at Jesse, who extracted himself from his gaggle and walked toward them. "We'll make it work. Somehow, we'll make it work." She studied Denny, motioning for him to turn around. "I don't know what to do about your wrinkled clothes."

"She's right, Denny," Darlene fumed. She didn't want him here in the first place, didn't need his input on a fake house that they were not going to buy. "Why don't you just leave, and we'll pretend you're in some distant land." She shook her head. "Like we did yesterday. Nobody missed you."

Jesse appeared, looking weary and ready to be done with the Feldman's, his interruption clamping Denny's mouth shut. A win for Darlene, for sure. He looked at Gloria for direction.

"Start rolling in five minutes." Gloria looked at Denny again. "I just had a brilliant idea." She wrinkled her nose and smiled. "The idea just flew in and landed on my nose." She swiped at it with her hand. "We'll have you say something to the effect of just having gotten off a plane." She rubbed her chin. "Yes, you took the red-eye to be here. Literally got off the plane and came straight here." She pointed toward the street, beyond where they stood, then turned to Jesse. "Let's get a shot of them walking up the beach access toward the building." She turned to Darlene and Denny. "So, start back there, on the beach, then walk up the access. The camera will be rolling, so talk about stuff related to the building." She looked at Denny. "This might be a good time to mention the red-eye. I'll have the narrator reiterate that a few times during the tour just in case a viewer comes in midway and is curious about how you look."

"Oh, for God's sake, I don't look that bad." He ran his hands over his shirt and pants as if doing so would remove the landscape of wrinkles.

"Yes, you do," Darlene and Gloria said in unison.

"Sorry, Dude, but you look like crap," Jesse added.

"I didn't ask you." Denny didn't try to hide his annoyance and flipped Jesse the bird.

"Moving right along," Gloria said, "you'll walk up to this gate." She pointed at a gate with a cipher lock. "Laurie will be waiting here and will open it for you."

Darlene felt her stomach drop. She craned her neck and didn't see Laurie. She tried to suppress the fact that she had been surreptitiously scanning the scene for Laurie since she'd walked up from the beach, and again over the past few minutes. She didn't want to admit that she'd been holding onto a sliver—a hair's width, really—of hope that Fran might be filling in for Laurie again. She put on her best neutral face.

"Ready?" Gloria pointed toward the ocean. "Walk to the beginning of the access path, then turn around and walk this way."

Darlene and Denny walked, side by side, down toward the Atlantic Ocean. She didn't want to stop at the end of the path. She wanted to keep walking, kick off her shoes, and let her feet sink into the wet sand while the frigid water slapped and churned around her ankles.

"So, how long have you been involved with that guy?"

"I'm not involved with him." She emphasized involved. "I only met him a few days ago. Look, Denny, you left me for another woman. What I do from here on out is none of your business." She stopped walking and looked at him. "You never sought my input on your involvement with Remi."

"That was different."

"In what way?" Darlene was incredulous. The nerve of him. "Please, enlighten me."

"It just was."

"I fail to see how it was different."

"It just was." He didn't try to hide the sadness in his voice.

"Camera rolling!" Jesse walked backward.

"Wow, the beach access is great!" Darlene's voice was, perhaps, just a tad too cheery. Fake is how it sounded in her ears. She was acting, though. A missed calling, perhaps. "I'm so glad you were able to catch the red-eye to be here." She put her arm around Denny. "I can't believe how close this place is to the beach!"

"It's not as close as the place we saw the other day."

"Sure, it is." She smiled and pulled him closer. "You're just sleep-deprived." She patted his back. "You've never been able to sleep on airplanes. Oh, look!" She picked up the pace. "There's Laurie!" She waved. "Hi, Laurie!"

"Hi, guys!" Laurie opened the gate. "Denny, I'm so glad you were able to join us today. Long flight?" Denny grumbled a few unintelligible words in response. "Right. Well, I can't wait to show you this unit." Darlene and Denny stepped through the gate. Laurie let it swing shut; the sound of metal crashing against metal was loud and startling. "This is a semi-gated property. Open access from the street, but you can't get onto the grounds from the beach without the gate code."

"Nice pool," Darlene said.

"It's kind of small." Denny stopped and regarded it.

"Well, you have a massive pool just beyond." Laurie pointed at the ocean.

"Yeah, but it's hard to swim laps out there," he argued.

"I see people do it all the time." Laurie waved her arm, pointing from one lifeguard stand to the other. "They wear inflatable swim buoys tied around their waists, and they swim laps."

"Well, good for them," he grunted.

"Let me tell you a little bit about the unit. It's on the fourth floor, and has a fabulous enclosed balcony overlooking the beach. The building was built in 1975 and has an association fee of $423 a month."

"That's high." Denny looked at Darlene. She clenched her teeth and nodded.

"I agree, it's high."

"Yes, but it's gated access from the beach," Laurie reminded them. "And you don't have to lift a finger in maintenance."

"Is there an elevator?" Denny made a show of yawning. "I don't think I could handle walking up four flights of stairs this morning."

"You're in luck." Laurie smiled. "There is an elevator."

"Actually, I'd prefer to take the stairs," Darlene said.

"What? Suddenly you're interested in exercise?" Denny moved an inch toward her; she caught a whiff of his breath and recoiled.

"You smell like a distillery."

"CUT!!!" Jesse lowered his camera and set it down on a chair by the pool. He sat down beside it and shook his head, then looked up at Darlene and Denny. "Everything was going so well. Here I was, thinking, wow, they made it through a whole scene without stopping. I told myself, I said, Jesse, maybe you'll get out of here early. Maybe this day will be smooth and easy." He stood. "I was so hopeful." He hung his head. "Are you ready to continue now?" They nodded. "I'm going to go up ahead of you." Jesse looked at Laurie. "I'll start the camera rolling as you're walking down the hall toward the unit. I'll meet you up there." He looked at Darlene and Denny. "Got it?"

"Yes," Darlene said. "We'll do better. We don't want to be here any longer than necessary." She turned to Denny. "Right?" Denny nodded with what seemed like the last of his strength. She wanted to be far away from him. "I'm taking the stairs. I'll see you both up there."

"I'll go with you," Laurie said.

"No, I will." Denny turned to Laurie. "You go ahead and take the elevator. I'll walk with my lovely wife."

"Forget it, Denny. I don't want to spend any more time with you than necessary." She jogged to catch Laurie. "Wait, I'm taking the elevator." Laurie stopped and waited, and, much to her dismay, Denny boarded it with them. The elevator bucked and sputtered, taking an inordinately long time to go four floors. Darlene wasn't a fan of elevators, and was glad the condo they actually bought didn't have one.

"As expensive as the association cost is, why the hell don't they bring this piece of crap into the twenty-first century?" Denny grumbled as the elevator spit them out. He looked up and down the corridor. "This place reminds me of an assisted living facility."

"You'll never have to live here, so just give it a rest." Darlene spotted Jesse in the distance and quickly got back into character.

Laurie began her spiel. "The unit comes fully furnished, so you could walk right in and start living the beach life." She held the door open. "Look at the ceiling fans. They really help circulate the fresh ocean breeze."

"What ocean breeze?" Denny walked in and went straight to the balcony, bypassing the kitchen, which was just to the right of the front door. "There's no ocean breeze. This balcony is enclosed."

Darlene shrugged and followed him. "We could open the windows to let the fresh air come in." She fiddled with one and raised it. "See? A nice breeze. And wow, what a view, huh? Gorgeous."

"If you're going to have a balcony, then have a balcony." Denny turned around and went into the living room.

"Let's look at the bright side," Laurie chimed in. "You won't have to worry about mosquitos, and, it's another living space, really."

"I hate these beige tiles on the floor," Denny said, apparently moving on from his hatred of the enclosed balcony. "Why do so many beach houses have these ugly beige tiles? What's the matter with a nice, hardwood floor?"

"Denny, the unit is way under budget. We could easily have the floors redone." Darlene hated the tile floors too. It was hard, pretending to be a happy house hunter. She just wanted to go home. Wanted to be as far away from Denny as possible. "The rest of the space looks updated. I like the paint color. It's a nice, warm gray. And I love the wainscoting. They did a nice job."

"What do you think of the furnishings?" Laurie patted the couch cushion. "I think I mentioned before that this unit comes fully furnished."

"It's beachy enough, but not really our taste," Darlene said. Ratan and mauve. Beige and blue. Wicker. Blech.

"Does this fake fireplace convey?" Denny tilted the white box, then let it fall back in place against the wall. "This is the stupidest thing I've ever seen. It doesn't even look real."

"It doesn't even have a mantle to hang stockings." Darlene attempted to form a sort of solidarity with Denny, at least for the camera. She ran her hand over the top of the box, thinking, yes, you could hang stockings and decided to say as much. "I suppose you could, with the right kind of hooks."

"We're Jewish, Darlene." Denny whipped his head around. "Since when do we hang stockings?" He kicked the fireplace. "In all honesty, I don't even envision us using a beach house in winter."

"I love the beach in winter," she said, her voice barely a whisper. "I've always especially loved the beach on cold, gray days." She walked toward the kitchen, deflated. His words stung, not because he was wrong—he was right, they did not celebrate Christmas—but, because he wouldn't play along. "A genuine, wood-burning fireplace would be wonderful, but not in a condo, I suppose."

Darlene worked her way from the living room into the tiny kitchen, making a show of looking around, touching things, considering herself living in this house. The camera was still rolling, and she was surprised that Jesse hadn't yelled 'cut' during Denny's fit about the fireplace. Maybe he would edit it out. Perhaps he wouldn't. It was hard to know what would be considered good fodder for TV. She never saw anyone opening cabinets on these shows. In their real house-hunting days, Darlene always peeked inside the kitchen cabinets. A neat, tidy house with cluttered cabinets suggested heaven and earth had been moved to create an inviting first impression, leaving real-life hidden. She mindlessly opened the cabinet above the dishwasher and glanced at its contents: color-coordinated dishes stacked neatly by type. She closed the door.

"Wow, this is a tiny kitchen." She tapped on the tile countertop. It looked like the one in her condo, but not nearly as new or as nicely done. She ran her fingernail over the grout and tried to scrape off the gray film that it had absorbed. "These things are so hard to keep clean."

"And look at the cheesy backsplash." Denny came up behind her, his breath hot on her neck, the smell of alcohol still evident. Thank God television didn't have a smell feature. He turned to Laurie. "The '80s called. They want their décor back."

Darlene rolled her eyes and stomped out of the kitchen. "You know that line is old and worn out. I can't stand it." She looked at Laurie. "Let's see the bedrooms."

"CUT!!!" Jesse set his camera on the kitchen peninsula. "We're so close, folks. So close." He pointed at Denny. "You!" He motioned for Denny to come closer. "I don't know what's going on here, but you need to lose the attitude."

"What the fuck?" Denny crossed his arms. "Where's the production manager? What's her name?"

"Gloria."

"Where's Gloria?" He trotted to the front door, opened it, then slammed it shut. "Who the hell do you think you are, talking to me like that?"

"Enough, Denny." Darlene pushed him toward the couch and shoved him down. She hadn't stopped to consider the fact that in his agitated state, he might react physically. He had never been physically aggressive. Today, though, she didn't know. "Sit."

"Who are you, my mother?"

"You're drunk." Darlene kneeled on the floor next to the couch, placing her hands firmly on his knees. "You've been trying to hide it all morning, and for that, my hat goes off to you." She stood. "But enough is enough. Suck it up and walk through this house like a normal person or leave." She marched toward the bedrooms, then turned around and went back to the couch and plopped down next to him. "I need you to remember that I'm staying in the condo until Friday. I'd better not find you there."

"Well, I have news for you. I own the place too, so I can do whatever I please."

Darlene couldn't stop the tears, born out of anger—pure, unadulterated anger—that poured out of her eyes. She knew her face was redder than a pomegranate, she could feel the heat. She clenched her fists in an attempt to still her shaking hands. Suddenly aware of eyes on her, she looked up and saw Laurie and Jesse standing by the door, whispering. "I'm telling you, Denny, I'll have you arrested for trespassing."

"Good luck with that."

"Why are you doing this?" She took a deep, shaky breath. "Three days ago, you said you didn't care if you ever saw the condo again."

"I'm rethinking that." He stood up. "I think I'd like to buy you out."

"No. We used my money for the down payment. It's my condo more than it is yours. I'm planning to have you removed from the deed." She fought a fresh wave of tears. "You don't even really like our condo."

"I have a whole new appreciation for it after last night."

"You are being an asshole."

"As are you, fatty."

"ENOUGH!" Jesse took several giant steps forward until he was standing in front of the couch, towering over Denny and Darlene. He tapped on his watch. "I have exactly thirty more minutes, then I need to hightail it to my next gig. I'll give you five minutes to pull yourselves together. You got that?" He looked at the ceiling. "Five minutes."

With four minutes, fifty-nine seconds left, Darlene got off the couch and walked into the first of the two bedrooms. She didn't know if Jesse was following or if the camera was rolling. Again, with the wicker. Why do people think they need to have wicker furniture at the beach? She stood in front of the mirror and adjusted her posture. She sucked in her belly and examined herself from all angles. It was no use. She looked frumpy. She stuck out her chin and smoothed her jowls, trying to think of something, anything positive about herself. Bright eyes, straight teeth, red hair. That was it.

"You okay in there?" Laurie came into the room and put her hand on Darlene's shoulder. "My brother told me that you and your father were quite entertaining yesterday."

Darlene looked at Laurie, suddenly remembering the familial connection to Fran. She really didn't resemble him. Maybe without glasses? But her forehead. Yes. There was a certain similarity there. "I'm horrified by what's been going on out there," she said, nodding toward the door. "I truly regret getting involved with this show." She flashed back to last night, hoping to never see Francisco-o-o-o again. She was mortified. Simply mortified.

"Hey, don't sweat it. Trust me, this isn't the first time a couple broke up or had some other significant life change between the time they signed on and the actual filming. We'll get through this."

"Is Jesse ready?" Darlene stepped out of the bedroom.

"We're just waiting on you." Laurie took a few steps toward the living room. "Jesse, Denny, we're ready." She turned back toward Darlene. "Not sure what your plans are later, but Fran and I were going to find a place to have dinner. Want to join us?"

If Darlene's face turned the color of a pomegranate a few minutes ago, she was sure the hue had gone up a few notches. "I don't know, I'll have to see."

"Think about it. We both know where you live." She laughed.

"Camera rolling!" Jesse followed Darlene and Laurie into the bedroom.

"More wicker," Darlene said, looking around. "But the room is a good size."

"I hate the color of the paint." Denny stood in the center of the room. He looked up. "Popcorn ceilings? They weren't in the living room or kitchen."

"The owners upgraded the ceilings in those rooms, but not in the bedrooms." Laurie walked into the bathroom. "Come look, Denny. A tub."

He stepped into the bathroom and opened the shower door. "A tub and shower combo. I guess it would be okay. Not much ambiance, though."

"Oh, wow, this is nice." Darlene opened a narrow door in the bathroom, revealing a small linen closet. "Not many places have linen closets anymore. I love it."

"A waste of space, if you ask me."

"Well, I have news for you." Darlene glared at him. "I didn't ask you."

"People," Jesse said from behind his camera. "Let's just get through this. Please."

Darlene stepped around Denny and into the narrow hallway. She poked her head into the second bathroom. "Another full bath. Great. No tub, though. But perfect for our guests." Wandering into the second bedroom, she was struck by the paint color. Jesse followed with the camera, and she pretended to study the walls. "I like the color. It's very purply." She smiled into the camera. "Very purply."

"Since when do you like purple?" Denny appeared at her side.

"Two days ago." She sighed. "I decided I like it two days ago."

"Yeah, well, it's hideous." He touched the wall. "The first thing I'd do is repaint this purple throw-up."

Darlene braced herself for a frustrated cry of 'cut', but one did not come. She searched for something positive to say about the bedroom, something she might say had she been really looking for a house.

"Wow, they have a full-over-queen bunk bed! That will be great for when we have grandkids one day." She spun around on her heel. "It would be good for my parents, too."

"Your parents would never sleep on a bunk bed, are you kidding me?" Denny laughed. "Could you imagine Connie climbing this narrow little ladder."

"My mother is quite agile." She didn't want to engage with him but couldn't seem to stop herself. "Why would my parents need to climb up the ladder, anyway? There's a perfectly good, queen-sized bed right here." She bent down and patted the mattress, wondering, maybe for the first time, what had really gone wrong between her and Denny. Perhaps the fault line had been there all along, and only recently the seismic shift began to cause the rumblings that set the marriage's demise in motion. A seismic shift named Remi.

"I can see that you do not love this condo," Laurie said to Denny.

"You're right. I don't love it." He looked at Darlene, then back at Laurie. "But it's got a great view, and it's under budget. Let's keep it on the list."

"Glad to hear it."

"CUT!!!" Jesse put down his camera and wiped his forehead with the back of his hand, sighing loudly, making a statement with his deep breath. "I think I have enough footage inside the house." He looked at Denny. "Mr. Feldman, Mrs. Feldman, we need to get some footage of you two discussing the houses and making a decision."

"Wait, there's more?" Denny paced the living room. "I don't have time for this."

"Where do you have to go?" Darlene didn't want to argue with him, didn't want to beg. "You're the one who wanted to do this today. You had a ready-made excuse to get out of it. So now that you're here, you need to follow through." She shook her head and did not try to conceal her weariness. "Let's just get this over with. Please." Her cell phone buzzed and bounced around on the small entryway table where she had left it. "Excuse me, I need to take this."

"Is it that guy?" Denny gave her the finger.

"It's my father," she snapped, wishing she had said *yes, it is that guy, and he's calling to tell me his bed is lonely without me in it.* She marveled at her father's impeccable timing. It was as though he had telepathic sensitivities. How did he know she'd been talking about him just a few minutes ago defending her mother's ability to climb a ladder? She could see him now, sitting in the sunroom going through the day's mail. Something made him think about his daughter at the beach, inspiring him to pick up the phone and call her instead of his precious Rachel. She pushed the button and heard her father's voice before she even had the chance to say hello.

"Your mother and I are fighting again."

"Dad, I can't do this right now." She whispered. "I'm in the middle of filming."

"Another fake house?"

"Yes."

"She wants to do a book signing at our golf club."

"That's wonderful, but, Dad, can we talk about this later, please?"

"I don't want our friends and, especially, my colleagues in the medical community to know what kind of smut your mother wrote."

"It's not smut." Apparently, her mother's pen name was not meant to obfuscate her identity entirely, at least not at the golf club.

"Can we get out of here, please?" Denny stood in front of her, looking at his watch. "I need to go too." He moved in closer. "Remi wants to talk."

"Denny, not now." So, Remi wanted to talk. She imagined Remi begging him to accept her husband's baby. Two seconds ago, it seemed, Denny wanted counseling. Now he wanted Remi. And possibly a baby. Her eyes filled.

"Denny's there?" Her father's scratchy voice piercing her soul. "Denny!" Darlene winced and held the phone away from her ear.

"Hi, Sid," Denny yelled. "Did you know your daughter is divorcing me?" Darlene pursed her lips and shoved him out of the way.

"What's that?" Sid's voice was so loud Darlene feared he would damage his vocal cords. "What is my daughter doing?"

Darlene covered the phone with her hand and turned to Denny. "I'll meet you downstairs in front of the building."

"Okay but hurry up. I want to get out of here."

"If you hadn't been such an ass in there, we'd be long finished with everything by now." She uncovered the phone. "Dad, I'm back." She sighed as she watched Denny and the crew walk out the door and mouthed *sorry* to Laurie. "I told you this wasn't a good time. Can I please call you later?"

"Your mother insists on doing this book signing. She's already made all the arrangements."

"She has every right to do anything she wants to do."

"She's going to destroy my reputation."

"How?"

"People are going to read that book and picture us engaged in those horrid acts."

Darlene snorted. She couldn't keep the laughter in. She covered the phone, then pretended to cough, not wanting her father to think she was dismissing his concerns or making fun of him. "Dad." Cough, cough, cough. She cleared her throat, the laughter threatening to betray her. "Dad, I'm choking on a sourball. I'll call you back." She hung up.

Darlene squinted in the blinding midday sun, stunned at how warm it had gotten. The production crew was gathered in a semi-circle near Denny's car. She joined them.

"Finally." Denny tapped his foot. "I was beginning to think you'd been abducted by aliens."

"Give it a rest, Denny." She shook her head. "Give it a rest." And then, to Laurie, "What's the plan?"

"Since we all seem to be in a hurry and have other things to do," Jesse chimed in, "I vote for the two of you sitting in the sand, marveling at the balmy weather, discussing the houses. I'll film you walking down the access path."

"It would be great if you could hold hands or something," Laurie said. "Because as far as the viewers know, at this point at least, you're still happily married."

Happily married. Such a loaded phrase. What did that even mean? Was there really the expectation of happiness? As in smiles, sunshine, birds chirping, and butterflies landing on your finger? There were only a few expectations she had brought into the marriage. The expectation of faithfulness was, of course, a huge one. And the expectation that he would share equally in parenting their daughter, especially when she was little. Then there was the expectation that he would make her feel beautiful, even when she wasn't. He was good at making her feel ugly, feeding into her insecurities, fanning that fire until she knew it would only be a matter of time until he cheated. And she had been right.

"Camera rolling!"

Darlene grabbed Denny's hand and swung it light-heartedly as they walked. Having been briefed on what to say, she made the first move. "This is a big decision." They came to the end of the access path and continued walking toward the water. A yellow lab ran by, its only focus was the frisbee flying across the beach. "I can't believe it's this warm in November. Let's sit down and talk about the houses. What did you think about the condo on 57th Street?"

"It was at the top of our budget." Denny looked straight ahead, a breeze blowing his hair around. The smell of alcohol on him was fainter outside. "It was more like a townhouse than a condo. I liked that."

"Yep, it was the biggest and had the best outdoor living space. And the whole third floor was one, big master suite. I loved that the beach was right outside the door."

"Right. With a dedicated balcony." He raised his eyebrow. "But the balcony was right next to the neighbor. Too close, if you ask me."

Darlene felt her face redden but played the part and put her arm around his shoulder. "You didn't see the house on Fenwick Island yesterday, but you saw the pictures."

"I like that house." He turned his head to face her. "I'd never considered the Delaware beaches, and I was pleasantly surprised."

"The area was quiet, and it overlooked a lagoon."

"But no beach access," he said

"You know, the point of this is to get a beach house. To me, that means beach access. I think we should cross the Fenwick Island house off the list."

"I agree." He scooped up some sand, sifted it through his fingers. "How about the unit we saw today?"

"I liked the price. And it was plenty big. But the kitchen was tiny."

"And the bathtub wasn't as nice as the one in the first house."

"It had a great view, but the balcony wasn't really a balcony."

"But we could use it as extra living space, year-round." He rubbed his hands together, flinging sand into the air. "It's practical."

"True, but if I'm going to have a balcony," she said, "I want it to be open. I want to feel and smell the salty ocean air."

"So, what are you thinking?" Denny stood, then took Darlene's hands and helped her up.

"Well, you know me," she said. "It's all about the beach.

"I think we've made our decision."

"The one on 57th Street!" They hugged.

"CUT!!! Bravo! Bravo! Bravissimo!" Jesse smiled wide, exposing several silver fillings. He quickly closed his mouth, his lips forming a severe line. "I thought this day would never end."

Denny extracted himself from her hug. "I'm out." He shook Jesse's hand and gave Laurie a perfunctory little squeeze. Darlene watched him walk up the beach access path and disappear around the corner, a happy little jig in his step.

"We still need to do the update segment." Gloria watched Denny walk up the sidewalk and get in his car. "You are planning to keep the condo, right?"

"I'd like to." Darlene took a deep breath. "It's too good of an investment. I want to have him removed from the deed. We'll see what my lawyer says." She wondered how long it would be before the show aired. How long before the narrator's voice would need to be edited in. They could be dead by then, for all she knew.

"Either way, we need to get a few seconds of you on the balcony with a glass of wine, or in the kitchen chopping vegetables and building a charcuterie board for guests. We'll be in touch in the next few days or a week. Or thereabout. We'll make everything look seamless." Gloria held out a bag of bakery-style sugar cookies. Darlene reached in and took one, breaking a piece off and shoving it in her mouth.

"Hey, can I offer you a ride home?" Laurie asked.

"It's so nice out. I think I'll walk."

"So you'll join Fran and me for dinner tonight?"

"I don't know. I really don't. I'm kind of frazzled." Darlene made a face, indicating her state had everything to do with Denny.

"I get it, I really do." She lowered her voice. "He seems like a handful."

"I hope you won't be offended if I beg off."

"No, of course not." She smiled. "I'll text you anyway. Just in case you change your mind."

25

———————

Darlene was a few hundred yards away from her condo when the urge to sit and talk to the waves hit. She sat down in the sand and tilted her face toward the still-strong November sun. The wind had picked up, blowing mist off the tops of the waves and carrying it through the air to the shoreline. The temperature was rapidly descending. She moved back a few feet to get away from the cold, salty spray. Still chilly, she held her arms close to her chest and rubbed them for warmth.

So much internal chatter clamoring for her attention. So much. Not one pressing issue, but many. Her father had called twice in the time it took her to walk from the condo she and Denny had just toured and where she had stopped to sit. She didn't answer either call; she simply couldn't face hearing her father prattle on about Belinda Moo and *Beach Kiss*.

Her mother was next in the parade of calls, texting to see if Darlene could come to Philly for a few days, to talk to her father. And of course, there was Denny's drunken spectacle today. He was probably with Remi right now, making up, promising to love her husband's baby, Remi promising to leave her husband, and Denny promising no pressure.

She tapped the sand, working her fingers like piano keys, her right hand beating out the staccato melody: Dad, Mom, Denny. Her left hand lazily fleshing out the harmony: Fran, who had been floating in and out of the background noise in her head all day. What had started out as a tight-fisted admonition to stay as far away from him as possible, gradually loosened and morphed into renewed curiosity. Laurie's dinner invitation unnerved her. Part of her wanted to go. With Laurie there as a buffer, things between her and Fran had no place to go. The three of them could eat, drink, laugh, swap stories, laugh more, drink more, and generally have a grand old time. But, wanting a buffer suggested she didn't trust herself with her feelings. She didn't want to admit any of it, not even to the waves. And that didn't even begin to address the scene on the balcony last night. Ugh.

She needed a distraction and needed one fast. She pulled out her phone and started to call Shelly, then thought better of it. She owed Denny nothing. Not even the expectation that they would have Thanksgiving together, lie to their daughter, then drop a bomb on her the next day. Shelly's view of their favorite holiday would be forever marred. Maybe it would be better to hold off until spring or summer. By then, she and Denny would have a clear path forward.

A shadow darting just off to the left caught her attention. The one-legged seagull had found her, far from the dune. She smiled, happy to see him, but disappointed to be empty-handed. Wait a minute! The cookie! She reached in her pocket, pulled it out, broke a piece off, and tossed it to her friend.

"I've been flirting with a man, across the balcony railing, and I like it. I'm pretending not to like it, to myself, that is, but the truth is, I like it. It's been a long time since a man flirted with me." She tossed another piece of cookie to the seagull, then showed him the ring on her left hand. "I can't remember the last time Denny flirted with me." Of course, she knew that flirting within a long marriage was different than the heady kind of flirting that kicks off a new relationship. The seagull swallowed the treat and waited for more. Darlene broke off two more pieces and tossed them in the air.

"The thing is, I don't want a new relationship!" Or did she? No! She didn't. But she was beginning to like Fran. And she feared her overindulgence last night, along with Denny's outburst, put an end to anything that might have developed between them. Unless the flirting was all in her head.

"I'm probably reading in." She looked at the bird and waited to hear his opinion. When he didn't offer one, she put her arms behind her back and let her elbows sink into the sand. "Nope. He wasn't flirting with me at all." She sat up, then slowly stood, brushing the sand off her arms and legs. She held her left hand in front of her, took a deep breath, and pulled her wedding ring off. She held it up to the sky, and for a moment, was tempted to toss it into the ocean; she dropped it into her jeans pocket instead.

She suddenly felt better. Much better. Because the seagull didn't judge her. He didn't look at her like she had lost her mind. He didn't call her a fatty. He just stood there and listened. She took a deep breath. Pause. Yes, that's what she would do. Pausing would prevent her from saying something she might later regret. A dire mistake, as it were. Dire, of course, was relative. Most of the time, what felt urgent one minute made her laugh and shake her head and shout *what was I thinking*, the next minute.

It felt cleansing just admitting to the seagull, and, to herself, the things plaguing her. She walked up the beach access path, determined to put any flirty thoughts out to pasture, and just focus on reality—the here and now. Technically, she was still married. Until such time as she was not, she would keep a level head. She crumbled the remainder of the cookie and let the pieces slip through her fingers.

~

DARLENE LOOKED up and saw Fran standing on his balcony, leaning on the rail, looking out at the ocean. Heat rose from her chest all the way up to the top of her head. Despite the rapidly dipping temperature, she was sweating. She did not want to be seen, did not want to face him. She tiptoed across the balcony.

"Rose!" Darlene froze, unsure what to do next. Stay and say something witty? Or take four giant steps forward and lock herself in the condo. "I thought that was you sitting in the sand." He smiled. "You're one of the most unusual people I've met in a long time."

"I'll try to take that as a compliment."

"You should." He stared at her. "What were you doing out there in the cold?" He hugged his chest and rubbed his arms. "It looked like you were talking to the waves."

Darlene felt the blood draining from her head. How did he know? Did voices carry two hundred yards up the beach? "No, not the waves." She sighed. "I was pouring out my troubles to a bird. A one-legged seagull, to be exact." *Please don't press. Please don't press. Please don't press.* "I owe you an apology, by the way." She shifted on her feet. "I got a little carried away last night."

"A little?" He laughed. "Chocolate anyone?"

"Don't' remind me. It will be a long time before I eat that stuff again." She patted her belly. "If ever."

"No apology necessary." He hesitated. "So, my sister mentioned you might join us for dinner tonight? She said today's film shoot was a three-ring circus, and you might need a drink."

Darlene laughed. "Three-ring circus is putting it mildly." She took a deep breath. "As you can imagine, I didn't sleep very well last night. I'm pretty exhausted. So, I'll probably pass on dinner."

"Right." The disappointment in his eyes was apparent. "If you change your mind, great. If not, well, I enjoyed our late-night chatting."

Darlene felt herself blush as she stepped inside. She leaned against the wall and put her hand on her chest, begging her heart to stop pounding. The cat scratched and clawed on the sliding glass door. She maneuvered her body toward the glass, craning her neck to make sure Fran wasn't still outside, then opened the door just wide enough for her body to fit through, and stepped out. She picked up the empty bowls and carried them to the kitchen, relieved that she had not been seen. She was reaching for the milk when her phone rang. *Oy vey, Mom.* She answered.

"Your father is driving me up the wall. I'm ready to pull the book off Amazon."

"You can do that?"

"Yes, but I don't want to. I want your father to respect my decision to write."

Darlene chose her next words carefully. "Mom, I get where you're coming from. But from Dad's perspective, well, I suspect he feels left out."

"How could he possibly feel left out?"

"You wrote a sexy book, and you gave your male protagonist a name that's hauntingly similar to your neighbor's name."

"That's a big coincidence."

"I'm sure it is." She took a deep breath. "Dad doesn't want his professional colleagues and his friends to know you wrote a book worse than *Fifty Shades*." She laughed. "His words, not mine."

"That's exactly why I used a nom de plume."

"What about your book signing."

"Oh, he told you about that?"

"Kind of defeats the purpose of a pen name."

"But how will I gain publicity?"

"Mom, you can't have it both ways. You already have publicity. You have a few hundred reviews on Amazon." She wanted this conversation to end. "Where is Dad? I'd like to talk to him."

"I sent him to the liquor store for champagne."

"Champagne?"

"That's what I just said."

"But why?"

"I'm going to try romancing him a little."

"Too much information, Mom." She chuckled. "Why didn't you just buy the champagne yourself? That's kind of how it works. The person doing the romancing buys the props." She thought of Fran and tried to flick him out of her mind. "Listen about your text earlier." She took a deep breath. "There's no way I could make it up to Philly between now and, probably January. You and Dad are welcome to come for Thanksgiving. That is if things fall through with Rachel."

"They won't."

"Hey, why don't you see if Rachel could pull strings and set up a book signing for you somewhere out there. Nobody will know who you are. She could just wave around that magic wand of hers." Darlene felt her usual animosity toward her sister rising like bile. She tried to swallow it.

"Now, that's a brilliant idea."

"Mom, I need to go." Darlene sighed with relief that her blatant dig at her sister apparently went over her mother's head. The refrain from her childhood was still fresh in her mind: *You could be just like Rachel if only you worked a little bit harder in school and paid better attention to the things you put in your mouth.* "Go easy on Dad. He loves you. Don't worry. I told him to go easy on you too."

"Okay, Lovey. Bye."

Darlene set her phone down, weary that she had to coach her mother like this. She supposed this is what happens as you get older. Your parents become more childlike as you become more and more parental. She would have to call Rachel after Thanksgiving to hear her perspective on all this. Because if there was one thing she and Rachel could commiserate about without it ending with someone hanging up, it was their parents.

She poured milk into the cat's bowl and carried it outside, momentarily forgetting to check for Fran. She set it down, rethinking Laurie's dinner invitation. If nothing else, it would be a venue to ask Fran if he would be willing to feed the cat until she could get back to the beach in a few weeks.

———

26

Four emails from work—their subject lines increasing in urgency—stared at Darlene, daring her to open them. She sat on the couch, her laptop balanced on her knees, unsure what to do next. Opening them would be a start. Reading them might be helpful too. But she didn't want to.

She closed email and promised herself she would deal with whatever was going on at work later. She opened Amazon, typing *Beach Kiss*, by Belinda Moo into the search bar. The cover image appeared and was a jarring contrast to Darlene's mental image of her mother; an image that didn't include sexuality. Yes, her mother was elegant and beautiful; judging from photos of her as a young woman, she was also sexy. And yet, she simply could not imagine her mother dreaming up the kinds of scenarios that, according to her father, lay between the pages of the book. It was stunning how little she really knew about her mother. It occurred to her that she didn't know a thing about her mother's soul or her deepest dreams and desires. Or what made her heart beat faster. Or how she viewed the world. She was simply Mom. Not Connie Bloom. Not Belinda Moo. Simply Mom.

She tried to approach life differently with her own daughter. She wanted Shelly to view her as a strong woman with her own life and interests apart from her role as a mom. She thinks she succeeded at that. She hopes she did. But did she believe Shelly knew her soul? Her deepest desires? Her innermost vulnerabilities? Probably not. And maybe that was the way it should be. Perhaps it was for the best. But a dream like writing a book? Shelly knew she loved brewing beer, and that someday she might like to explore the possibility of opening a tiny craft brewery. Someday, maybe. She could not imagine hiding that type of dream from her family, her daughter.

Darlene clicked on the *Beach Kiss* reviews—mostly four and five stars—and read a few of them:

Five Stars: Beach Kiss is a riveting romantic novel for the over sixty-five crowd that follows the complicated friends-to-lovers relationship between Julia and Johnny. The widow and widower meet by accident in their senior housing facility. Author Belinda Moo weaves a multi-layered tale of friendship, drama, secrets, and passion.

Five Stars: Belinda Moo succeeded in writing a compelling tale that has a great mixture of steamy romance and drama, but alas, the author teases with a cliffhanger ending that left me wanting more.

Three Stars: I really enjoyed this book. I enjoyed the characters. The storyline wasn't what I expected, it was so much more. But the writing style was strange with a mixture of past and present tenses in the same sentences, which had me scratching my head a few times.

Five Stars: I couldn't put this book down. I wanted to know what happened next. It had me trying to guess what happened next.

Two Stars: This is a poorly written book with a limited vocabulary. I could not read any further than the third chapter. Not sure how I came to choose it in the first place, but I shall avoid this author in the future. I would not recommend it to anyone.

Five Stars: So refreshing to read about senior citizens enjoying an emotional and physical (very physical) romance. You are doing yourself a great disservice by not adding this to your bookshelf, ebook, or however you get your next great reads in your hands. Go, go now, go quickly, and enjoy it.

One Star: I wouldn't recommend this book to anyone. The sex descriptions aren't really much of an enhancement to an otherwise cute story.

One Star: Who in their right mind wants to read about geezers having sex? Gross!

"So then why did you buy the book? Read the blurb next time." Darlene shook her head in utter amazement at how idiotic people could be. The cursor hovered over the little red circle in the upper left-hand corner of her web browser. She watched it flash, almost like it was in slow motion, tempting her to close the window. One more review. She would read just one more.

One Star: I guess I did not read the same book as those giving it 5 stars. It was a struggle to even get as far as I did. Julia kept saying she wanted a beer, hated the foo-foo drink she was drinking, but kept drinking it. How many times does that have to be repeated? The characters and the situations were ludicrous. It seemed to me that everything was repeated and over the top. I skimmed ahead to see if the book got better. It did not.

She stared at the screen, shocked that so many people had read her mother's book. Not only did her mother write a book, but she somehow had learned the ins and outs of independent publishing. She clicked the *Look Inside* link. The book appeared professionally formatted, had an ISBN, copyright, a cover design credit. Damn. How did her mother do this? She felt like an entire world existed within her own family that she was only now becoming aware of. Like when Denny dropped his bomb. He apparently had been seeing Remi for quite some time. An alternate reality he had been living in, a world in which Darlene had not been privy to.

She clicked the *Buy Now* button, and, for the low, low, price of $8.99, will gain insight into her mother's inner world. Taking a deep breath, she closed Amazon and re-opened email. A fifth work message blinked like a neon sign. IMPORTANT—in all caps. And highlighted in red. She opened the email and skimmed it, feeling her face grow hot and her eyes grow wet. She set the laptop on the couch next to her and let her body sink into the cushions.

LIFTING HERSELF OFF THE COUCH, Darlene looked around the room, not entirely sure where she was. One leg dangled over the edge. She winced, trying to sit up and bring her other leg down to the floor. Her lower back ached. She rubbed the back of her neck and tilted her head in both directions, trying to loosen the stiffness. The room had grown dark, the only sound was the waves crashing outside; she could hear them even through the closed door. She slowly stood, noticing her laptop on the coffee table. She didn't remember putting it there. She rolled her fingers through her matted hair, walked over to the door, and peered out at the ocean. Her cell phone buzzed, indicating an incoming text. Probably Laurie. Her desire to be around people tonight had evaporated after she read the email from the pharmacy.

Darlene's mind drifted back to the day after Denny announced he was leaving her for another woman. Reluctantly, she'd gone to work. Looking back, she should have just called in sick. It wouldn't have been a lie. She sunk back into the couch cushions and tried to fend off the beginnings of a full-blown panic attack. *Breathe. Slowly. Breathe.* How could she have been so careless? A woman had been rushed to the hospital with a racing heart with arterial fibrillation. Apparently, Darlene had filled a prescription for thyroid medication. She racked her brain, trying to remember the customer. It wasn't one of her regulars, of that, she was sure. But she did remember filling the prescription. Her mother was on the same medicine, just a lower dose. She studied the photo of the medicine bottle her boss, Bill, had attached to the email. *Breathe. Slowly. Breathe.* She hung her head between her knees, fearful she might pass out. She filled the right medication but got the dosing wrong. Clear as day, right on the bottle: *Take one tablet by mouth twice daily.* Twice daily. It should have been once daily. How could she have been so careless? Darlene was expected back at work for an emergency meeting tomorrow afternoon. She would need to leave before ten if she had any hope of making the meeting on time. *Breathe. Slowly. Breathe.*

She limped to the kitchen and flicked on the light. Her phone buzzed again. She was right, two texts from Laurie with the name and address of the restaurant. She looked at the clock. She still had time to make it, and for a half-second decided to walk out the door and get in the car. Then she saw her reflection in the microwave glass. Matted hair. Puffy eyes. Nope. Not going. She opened the fridge and pulled out one of her IPAs. She popped off the cap and took a swig, sighing in pained delight at how good it tasted.

"Pharmacists hold the ultimate responsibility at a pharmacy," she said to her beer bottle. She pulled a bar stool out from under the breakfast bar and sat down, holding the beer bottle in front of her and twirling it around. "We're responsible for patient safety and education." Panic engulfed her. She would lose her license; she was sure of it. Forgetting the beer, she laid her head down on the counter and quietly sobbed.

27

The loud trill of the alarm cut through Darlene's sleep like a chainsaw. She never bothered to go upstairs last night, and after her second beer, had fallen into a death-like state on the couch. She slept so deeply, in fact, that she momentarily forgot her troubles. Forgot that she needed to be back at work this afternoon for a meeting she feared would mean the end of her career. Forgot how Denny acted like a jackass on camera yesterday. Forgot. Forgot. Forgot

She bolted upright and got tangled up in the blanket—she had apparently rolled herself up like a burrito—and nearly stumbled, trying to free herself. The sun's rays poured into the living room, exposing dust on the coffee table. Individual motes floated through the air, dancing on the streaks of light. She swirled her finger around on the coffee table, tracing a smiley face in the dust. She tipped her head and looked at it, wrinkled her nose, and with an aggressive swipe of her finger, turned the smile into a frown.

She took a deep breath and stood squinting in the sun, wishing for dark. She shuffled to the sliding glass door. The few people out and about on the beach looked like they were dressed for spring, not late fall. Wouldn't it be nice if she had slept the entire winter away?

She opened the slider and stepped outside. Warm. Okay, warm-ish. A balmy November morning. Stranger things have happened. She stepped back inside and closed the curtains. There. Dark. In the dark, she couldn't see the dust. In the dark, she couldn't see the happy people frolicking on the beach. Happy, oh, so happy. She hated those happy people. If she looked hard enough, she might even see Denny and his pregnant sweetie-pie running and laughing and swatting each other's asses. It made her sick.

She reached for the curtains and threw them open—a bit more aggressively than she had intended. The massive curtain rod quivered under the force. She stepped out onto the balcony again, forcing herself to feel happy. If for no other reason, because the sun was shining, she was alive, she was healthy, and she had a good job. Of course, she had a good job. She loved her job. She was passionate about her job. She would not allow herself to entertain the thought that her error would mean the death of her job, her career. She sat down on the chair and let her head hang between her knees. *Fuck, I'm getting fired*. She knew it. Felt it in her bones.

The cat circled Darlene's legs. She tilted her head and met his emerald eyes. Emerald eyes. Emerald City. The cat was gray. Like the hues in the black and white portion of the *Wizard of Oz*, before the tornado. Gray. Ray. Ray Bolger, the farmhand. Ray Bolger, the scarecrow. Ray Bolger.

"Hello Ray," she said, scratching the cat's head. "There. I named you. I'm in trouble now." She knew she couldn't take Ray back to Leesburg with her. Just couldn't. She didn't want to put the house on the market with a cat in it. The realization that she and Denny would put their home on the market startled her. This was real. She was really going to divorce her husband. She felt both heavy and light at the same time, if such a thing were even possible.

She slowly lifted her head, careful to not make herself dizzy. She sat still for a moment to regain her bearings, then stood and smoothed her jeans and shirt—the same outfit she had worn yesterday and slept in last night. She walked out the door, setting aside any thoughts that she looked like a creature from a horror movie, and climbed the steps onto Fran's balcony. She didn't have time to make other arrangements and needed someone to feed Ray for the next few days, or at least until she could figure out what to do. She stood paralyzed, wondering what she was doing there. Any sense of having a carefree spirit and not caring how horrible she looked evaporated when she saw her reflection in Fran's sliding glass door.

"Get a grip," she whispered. "Forget what you look like and just knock on the door." She moved in closer, her knuckles poised to knock. She suddenly became aware of the sound of running water. Fran's slider was partially open, a flimsy screen separating her from the inside of his condo. She stepped away and pressed her back into the shingles, just to the left of the door. She peered inside and saw him standing at the kitchen sink, washing a pot. She moved away and sat down on a wooden side table next to the door, which was thankfully out of Fran's line of sight. She took several deep breaths, willing the courage to just go up to the screen, and somehow get his attention.

"I know, Sadie, I know." Fran's voice traveled from his kitchen, into the living room, and through the screen—right into Darlene's ears. "I just don't understand the issue with the blue shirt. Please explain." Silence. Darlene craned her neck and looked in, wondering if there was indeed another person in there, someone named Sadie—a strange coincidence given that was the name of his late wife. "Yes, I wore the blue shirt last night." Darlene let her eyes scan the room. Fran was most certainly alone. "But it wasn't a date. Babe, she didn't even come. Yep. It was just dear Laurie and me." Darlene's eyes grew big. She rubbed the nape of her neck, unsure what to do, where to go.

"Rose!" Darlene jumped up, causing the tiny table to topple over and bounce across the balcony. The screen door opened, and Fran stepped out, wiping his wet hands on his jeans. "I thought I heard something." He smiled, rubbing his chin. "Laurie and I missed you last night." He looked away.

"Well, I, um." She took a deep breath. "Look, I need to ask a favor."

"Shoot." He picked up the table and set it right side up. He sat down on it, motioning for Darlene to sit on the chair beside him.

"Something came up in the city. Work issue. I'm leaving in a little bit."

"Today?"

"In a half-hour."

"Oh. That's too bad." He smiled, then looked at his feet.

"I named the cat," she said, in an attempt at changing the subject, getting back to the reason she traipsed over to his balcony.

Fran brought his hand to his mouth and feigned an exaggerated gasp, then chuckled. "I knew you'd get attached!"

"Attached?" She laughed. "Hardly." She grew serious. "I have a lot of stuff to sort through at home—emotional stuff, not physical, but maybe some of that too." She shrugged. "So, I'm not sure when I'll be back here."

"Let me guess." Fran closed one eye and looked up at the sky. "You want me to feed—"

"Ray. Ray Bolger."

"You're kidding, right?" He laughed. "I had that cat pegged for Buddy. Or Jovie. Papa Elf, maybe. Mr. Narwhal?"

"Right." She laughed too.

"What's his favorite food?"

"Leftover turkey and bacon." She fixed her gaze on the ocean, then looked at him. "From Sadie's Deli."

"You didn't like the food?"

"Yes, yes, I did. I loved it." She looked away. "Honestly, it was too much food." She chuckled. "That sandwich was huge. Trust me if I have trouble finishing something..." She was backpedaling and decided to slam on the breaks. "Actually, the meat was a bit dry."

"That's not possible."

"It is, and it was." She shrugged. "The turkey was dry. What can I say?"

Fran looked at his hands, then stood, pacing back and forth on the balcony. "I'll need to talk to Sadie about it." He sat back down and put his head in his hands.

"Fran, I didn't mean to upset you." Ugh, did she really have to tell him that she fed the cat half of her meal from his restaurant? She reached into her pocket and pulled out a folded, twenty-dollar bill and held it out to him. "I had planned to buy a bag of cat food today, but I just don't have time. I need to get on the road soon." She shook her head. "I'm not sure when I'll be back."

"You didn't upset me." He took the money. "I was washing dishes and having a conversation with my dead wife. That's what I was doing when I noticed you sitting out here."

"I know."

"Was I that obvious?"

"You were that loud." Darlene pressed her lips together and shook her head. She felt an odd tenderness toward him, exposing a part of himself that she didn't feel she should have insight into. They barely knew each other. There was no basis for anything between them. Neighbors at the beach condo. A burgeoning friendship based on fleeting encounters. A few pleasant exchanges over the rail, some old wounds exposed. Nothing more than that. She felt like she had just seen him naked—something she could not rewind and un-see. Embarrassed, she kicked an oyster shell across the balcony.

"Rose." He let his arms fall to his legs, then propped himself up with his elbows on his knees. He looked up at her. "You probably think I'm off my rocker."

"No, just a man who lost the love of his life and is still hurting." Darlene didn't know where she came up with that. What she really wanted to say was: *you need to talk to someone real, a professional, oh, and why the hell were you talking to your dead wife about...me?* She kept all that to herself and stood, holding out her hand. He took it, shaking it briefly before letting it drop. "Thank you for agreeing to feed Ray, but I really do need to go now."

❧

DARLENE OPENED the door to her SUV and tossed her travel bag onto the front passenger seat. She had one more load to carry out of the condo, plus she needed to take the trash to the dumpster. She let the front door slam behind her and climbed the steps up to the main living area, where she heard a faint tapping on the sliding glass door. She rounded the corner and saw Fran with his nose pressed against the glass, his hands cupping his eyes. She took a deep breath, momentarily happy to see him, then furious for yet another invasion of her privacy.

"Rose?" Tap. Tap. Tap.

She opened the door and stood in front of him, hands on her hips, afraid of what her face might be saying. "What is it? I'm loading my car. I really need to get on the road or I'll miss my meeting."

"Rose, just five minutes, please?"

"Darlene. My name is Darlene." She stood in the doorway, painfully aware of the minutes ticking by. She finally gestured for him to enter. They stood just inside the door, neither making a move toward the couch, a chair, or the bar stools at the kitchen counter. She could smell garlic on his clothes—most likely a remnant from wherever he and Laurie had eaten last night. "What's up?"

"You never did tell me what I'm supposed to feed the cat."

"Um, cat food?" She didn't try to hide her frustration.

"Okay, okay." He plopped down on the chair. "I sense you're unhappy with me?"

"I'm kind of strung out right now." She took a deep breath. "Look, I don't know you well enough to be happy or unhappy with you. You're a stranger. In fact, you might be a lunatic, and I just let you into my house." She crossed her arms and tapped her foot, like a drummer, softly at first, then louder and louder, hoping he would get the hint. When that didn't work, she looked at her watch. "I really need to get out of here."

"We're not exactly strangers, Rose."

"Darlene." Any tenderness she had felt before vanished. "My name is Darlene."

"I'm sorry, Darlene." He narrowed his eyes. "I promise you that I'm no lunatic." He tried to smile, but it wouldn't form. "I may be nuts, but I'm no lunatic."

She looked askance at him. "Fran, why are you here?"

"So, I talk to my wife." He hung his head. "Is that so bad? I consult her like some people consult God." He fidgeted with his hands. "I worshiped her."

"I'm so sorry, Fran." And she was. Very. She never came close to worshiping Denny, and wondered what it would have been like. "I think a lot of people talk to their loved ones who are gone. I sometimes talk to my bubbe."

"Grandma."

"You know Yiddish?"

"I own a Deli."

Darlene felt herself relax. When she exhaled, she realized she had been holding her breath.

"Last night, when you didn't come to dinner." Fran picked a rogue thread from his shirt and twirled it between his fingers. "Let's just say I was disappointed."

"I never said I would come." She looked at her watch. Ten minutes. That's all she could give him, that's all she would give him. "Look, you don't know anything about me." She threw her head back and stretched her arms to the ceiling, then looked at him. "My life is a complicated mess right now. I think I'm about to get fired. And, as you already know, I'm soon to be divorced." She rubbed her forehead. "And now some things have come up with my parents."

"Laurie filled me in on—"

"Of course, she did." Yesterday, she sensed Laurie playing matchmaker. And yesterday, she was flattered. Today she was weary. "The bottom line is I have no room in my life for more drama."

"I'm certainly not trying to create any drama for you."

"You consulted your late wife about me, down to what she thought of your shirt color." She felt her face growing hot and red. "What am I supposed to make of that?"

"I'm sorry, Rose."

"Please stop apologizing." She shook her head and sighed. "And please, please, please stop calling me Rose." She stared into his eyes. She still couldn't decide whether they looked like caramel or honey.

She went into the kitchen and pulled the trash bag out of the can. "I'm running terribly late."

"Fair enough." He winced, rubbing his back. He limped to the kitchen and met her at the breakfast bar. "I'll throw that in the dumpster." He took the bag from her. "It's the least I could do."

"Sit down." She pointed the bar stool. "Are you okay?"

"I'm fine."

"I don't mean emotionally." She crinkled her nose. "That didn't come out right. You looked like you were in pain a second ago."

"I'll be okay." He rested his arms on the counter and laid his head down across them. A few seconds went by before he looked up. "I don't know why I'm telling you this, but I have chronic kidney issues. Sometimes it flares up, like now."

"Are you drinking cranberry juice?"

"I abhor the stuff."

"You should drink it anyway."

"I will not drink it on a boat, I will not drink it with a goat."

Darlene laughed, giving in to it, letting it come in waves and fits. She covered her face in her hands, and when the laughter passed, she noticed that Fran was not laughing with her. She peeked through her fingers and saw him staring at her, pain on his face. "You started it."

"I did indeed," he said, letting a weak chuckle escape his lips.

"Cranberry juice is great for chronic kidney patients." She couldn't leave it alone. The bee in her mouth was about to escape, again. Such a simple addition to his diet could make a big difference. "I sincerely believe that cranberry juice can—"

"Stop." He held up his hands. "Just stop."

"Francisco." She felt like a jerk for being so persistent, for overstepping, for continuing to push cranberry juice after he said no. She grasped for a thread of the playfulness they shared just a day or so ago. "Francisco-o-o-o..." She looked at the floor, then looked up and forced a smile. He didn't smile back. He stood up and carried the trash bag down the front stairs, letting the door bang shut behind him.

28

Fran walked along the beach until he came to the spot where he saw Darlene sitting in the sand yesterday. No. Not Darlene. Rose. She would always be Rose to him. The next time he sees her, if there is a next time, he will make it clear. She is Rose. Like Beth and Manly (Laura and Almonzo) in *Little House on the Prairie*. Rose and Franscisco-o-o-o. Francisco-o-o-o and Rose.

He pulled a quilt, Sadie's quilt, out of a reusable grocery bag. He flipped the quilt with his hands, watching it parachute in front of him, letting it float down and slowly settle on the sand. He kicked off his docksiders and kneeled next to the quilt, smoothing it out with one long, swooshing motion. He closed his eyes, feeling the fine mist blowing off the waves. It was a bit chillier down here by the water than it had been on his balcony, where he sat for a long time after throwing Rose's trash in the dumpster. He had no idea how much time had gone by. But the sun reflecting off his third-floor window and beating down on the balcony drove him to seek cooler temperatures by the water. Sadie had stopped talking to him after this morning's argument over the shirt. She did this sometimes, stomped off in a huff if you could even hear a dead person stomping. This time was different, though. It was like Sadie sensed Rose. Sensed something different. Or sensed something changing in him.

He crawled onto the quilt and sat cross-legged. At sixty-two years old, this was a feat he was proud of. He leaned back on his hands and tilted his head toward the sun. No use. Whatever anomaly had caused the morning to be so warm was gone. Now, he felt downright cold. He reached into the grocery bag and pulled out a sweatshirt. He put it on and sighed with relief at how snuggly warm he suddenly felt.

Last night, Sadie told him to go out and have a good time. He found it odd since she never commented on his weekly dinners with Laurie before. Fran may have forgotten to mention that Rose might be joining; clearly, Sadie knew.

"Just go out and have a good time," she'd said, watching him dress.

"It's just dinner with Laurie. Our usual, boring weekly dinner."

Replaying their conversation, Fran realized he must have sounded like he was justifying, or reassuring Sadie that there wasn't anything special about this particular dinner. The bottom line, of course, was that he hadn't been honest with her. He didn't feel ready to admit that he was falling for Rose. Dripping with shame, he let Sadie's words from last night jostle him.

"Just go out and have a good time." She wouldn't let it go, and Fran finally lost his temper.

"How can I go out and have a good time when I'm supposed to be sad that you died?"

"Supposed to be sad that I died? Supposed to be?" She looked at him, tears streaming down her cheeks. "I thought you are sad."

Fran couldn't think about last night anymore. He tilted the grocery bag on its side and fished for the cardboard box containing his leftover pizza. He had wanted to show Rose his favorite pizza place. He shook his head, embarrassed that he had been so presumptuous to think she would care. Or care to know that his favorite pizza is Hawaiian. Yep. He freely admits it. He loves grilled pineapple, and he especially loves it on pizza. Sadie hated it and never missed an opportunity to make faces every time he ordered it. Maybe that was what had gotten Sadie so upset last night—the fact that he ordered Hawaiian pizza.

He reached into the bag and gently lifted out a cobalt blue ceramic tray. The one Sadie made for him during her short-lived pottery kick. The thing wasn't level, and the two handles were different sizes. Honestly, it looked like a five-year-old made it out of Play-Doh. He thought back to the day she gave it to him. It could have been yesterday, or an hour ago, the memory was still so vivid. She carried it home from the art center in a pizza box and set it on the kitchen counter. He happened to float through the kitchen and saw the box, wondering why she picked up a pizza at such an odd hour (it had been 3:26 pm, how he remembered the exact time, he didn't know).

"Pizza?" He looked at her, puzzled, and went over to the box. "Hawaiian, I hope."

"Hardly." She laughed and lifted the lid.

"Oh." He bent down to examine the contents. "That's the strangest looking pizza I've ever seen."

"Out of my way." Smiling, she gently nudged him to the side, then lifted the tray out of the box and placed it in his hands. "Proof that I didn't miss my calling as a potter." She stood on her tiptoes and kissed him. "Happy birthday."

His fifty-seventh. The tray was the star of the show during the casual get-together with friends later that night; it sat on the coffee table in the living room, its raw beauty covered with bowls of pistachios, cashews, almonds, and dried dates. Later, it took up permanent residence on the breakfast bar, holding napkins, the salt and pepper shakers, and sometimes, when applicable, a jar of red pepper flakes.

Fran set the tray on the quilt and arranged his two leftover slices of pizza on it. Then he placed the whole thing on his lap, to leave room for Sadie in case she decided to join him. He picked up a slice and took a bite, closing his eyes, enjoying the salty-sweet-savory taste, just as good cold the next day. Maybe even better.

He knew it was sneaky, using Sadie's quilt like this to entice her out of hiding. The first time they made love, it was on this quilt, spread out on a porch swing in the back of her house. He drew a deep, shaky breath and pressed his fingers into his eyes. He did not come out here to wallow. He simply came out to think. And to talk to Sadie.

"I am sad," he said. "I'm sad every day. What I said last night, well, that came out all wrong." He rubbed his hand back and forth over her spot. "I'm sad every day."

Laurie had been nudging him to get help—gently at first, then after a year, a bit more aggressively. *Talk to someone*, had been her refrain until recently, when it shifted to *close the deli*. Dammit, how could he close the deli? It had been Sadie's dream. From the moment he met her, it was something she talked about incessantly. One of the driving forces in selling his company was so Sadie could realize her dream. If he sells the deli, though, what the hell will he do? Stay in Ocean City? Go back to Reston? Maybe ride his bike across the country. At sixty-two years old. Right.

"Sadie, what should I do?" He didn't know. He just didn't know. And now he didn't understand why she wouldn't talk to him. "Come on, babe. Please. I need to hear from you, need to feel you." He uncurled his legs, lengthened them out in front of him, leaned forward, and touched his toes, holding the position for ten, twenty, forty-five, sixty seconds. He lowered his head and was pleased when the tip of his nose touched his knee. Sixty-two years old. *Hell, I could bike across the country*. "Sadie, babe. I love you. Only you. Always you. Please don't be fearful of anyone taking your place. Ever."

Fran's shadow elongated in the waning day. He looked at his watch—almost two o'clock. He slid the empty pizza box into the grocery bag and froze when he saw Sadie standing beside the quilt.

"Babe." He moved the grocery bag out of the way and held out his hand. "Please sit with me." Sadie took his hand and sat down, shivering against the cold. Fran pulled off his sweatshirt and draped it around her shoulders.

"You wore the blue shirt last night." She stared out at the ocean.

"Yes, I did."

"The one I always said makes you look like George Clooney."

"I'll never look like George Clooney."

"When was the last time you wore that shirt?"

Fran closed his eyes, his mind drawing a blank. He didn't know when he last wore the blue shirt, the harbinger of all this strife. If only he had grabbed the pink one. Or the yellow one. Or better yet, his ratty, old gray Henley. He racked his brain. When did he last wear that damned blue shirt? After stepping away from the nine-to-five rat race, there were not many reasons to wear a dress shirt. Not that the blue shirt in question was dressy. It wasn't. But it had buttons and a collar; it was Sadie's favorite. She always, always, always told him he looked good in it. Sometimes she threw in the George Clooney bit, sometimes she didn't. He couldn't even remember where or when he acquired that shirt. All he remembered was that Sadie liked it. Of course. How could he be so stupid? That was it. The last time he wore the shirt, it was for her. Just a few weeks before she died. He hung his head.

"I'm sorry I lied." He opened his eyes and searched for Sadie, but she was gone. He tried again. "Laurie invited the crazy redhead to join us for dinner. And I wanted her to come. There. I said it. I wanted her to come. It doesn't mean I'm in love with her. She is a friend, okay? A neighbor. Just a friend." Still no sign of Sadie. "But she didn't come last night. She didn't come."

29

Distracted and worn out, Darlene wasn't aware of how fast she was driving. She didn't see the police car in the median. At least not right away. Instead of songs on the radio, she was listening to her boss's words playing on a continuous loop in her mind. *Administrative leave. Investigation. Career-ender. Distraught family. Almost died. Tsk-tsk.* Like a horror movie, his voice morphing and changing—growing more ominous by the second. She had arrived at the meeting with seconds to spare, only to have her worst fears confirmed. Bill didn't fire her, but he might as well have. Administrative leave, pending a full investigation. And the likely loss of her pharmacy license. On the way out of the pharmacy, she half-heartedly suggested to her tech, Susan, that they grab a glass of wine and talk. But she declined, saying she wanted to go home to her husband. How nice it would be to go home to a loving husband's waiting arms to be comforted and told that everything will be okay. Darlene hadn't been back to the house in Leesburg since her few days at the beach; she dreaded the emptiness of it.

The flashing lights in her rearview mirror jolted her back into the present moment. She pulled onto the shoulder, then partially onto the grass beyond. She lowered the window and put her hands on the steering wheel so the officer could see them. Full of bravado, he approached her car.

"Good afternoon, Ma'am. Do you know how fast you were driving?"

"No, Officer, I'm sorry, I don't know how fast I was driving. I was completely distracted. I lost my job today. I lost track of my speed." *Too much information Darlene, too much information.* She closed her eyes tightly and started over. "No, Officer, I don't know how fast I was going."

"I clocked you at sixty-seven in a fifty zone." He moved closer to the window and looked around. "I'll need to see your license and registration."

"Yes, Officer." She reached into her purse for her license. She pulled it out of her wallet and saw a smiling, vibrant Darlene staring back at her. She almost expected the photo to wink. When was that picture taken? Nearly ten years ago. Wait a minute. Her birthday is tomorrow. How did she get so distracted over the past few days that she forgot her birthday? Her fiftieth birthday. She tried to keep her voice humble as she handed the officer her license. "My registration is in the glove compartment." He nodded as she reached across the passenger seat and popped it open.

She watched the officer disappear into his car to run her information. She could see it now, flashing across his screen: *Old, fat, failure. Couldn't keep her husband happy. Incompetent pharmacist. Jowly, ugly, sorry excuse of a woman.* Or worse: *Invisible.* She put her head on the steering wheel and sobbed.

"Ma'am?"

Darlene sniffed and took a deep breath, her tear-streaked face sure to soften his blow, make him change his mind about giving her a ticket. She looked into his eyes, wondering how old he was. He looked barely twelve.

"Ma'am, I'm sorry about your work predicament, but I'm going to have to give you a ticket for speeding." He handed it to her. "If you'd have run off the road and gotten yourself injured or killed, or hit someone, you'd have paid for it for the rest of your life." He narrowed his eyes. "When you're behind the wheel, you need to be behind the wheel. Fully present."

"Yes, Officer." She stared straight ahead, careful to not look at him.

"Happy birthday, by the way." He gave her back her documents. She nodded and rolled up the window, watching in her rearview mirror as the twelve-year-old cop walked away.

She pushed the button to start the engine and slowly, hesitantly, set her car in motion. As soon as he was out of view, she punched the accelerator, sticking her tongue out and discreetly holding up her middle finger. A hundred bucks and two points on her license. She needed this now like a *lokh in kop* (hole in the head). Her bubbe always said this Yiddish phrase in response to a calamity. She smiled, thinking about her grandmother. She took a deep breath and set the cruise control for fifty. Her birthday. Her age tomorrow.

30

Darlene did not remember leaving a light on in the kitchen. For all she knew, she might very well have. Who knew whether she had left the light on or off? Or if her coffee mug from last Saturday was still in the sink. Who cared?

She let her travel bag fall off her shoulder and winced when it hit the floor with a thud. She had stopped at Total Wine after settling down from the stress and embarrassment of being pulled over. She set the cold bottle of chardonnay on the entryway table, and hung her purse on the hook beside it. The sounds of rustling in the kitchen commanded her attention. She stood erect, eyes scanning, paralyzed, and unable to move. Footsteps growing closer and louder seemed to push her backward toward the door, one hand on her cell phone, the other hand reaching for the door handle.

"Dar."

She pressed her back against the door, and, legs weak from fear, slid down, holding the doorjamb for support until she was crouched on the floor. She let her butt fall the rest of the way down. Thump. "Denny, have you lost your mind?" She started hyperventilating, not sure whether she was angry or relieved. Maybe a little bit of both. "You scared me half to death." She put her head between her knees. "What are you doing here?" The sound of her own voice, echoing off the hardwood floor in the chamber she created between her legs, startled her. She looked up, and this time didn't try to reign in her anger. "What the hell are you doing here?"

"I still live here."

"You left me for another woman. As far as I'm concerned, you could go live under a bridge."

"Enough with the histrionics. Susan called me a little while ago. She was worried about you and wanted to make sure you made it home." He raised his eyebrows. "She said you were a mess walking out of the pharmacy."

"Why didn't she just call me?"

"She said she tried." Denny bent down and offered her his hand. Reluctantly she took it, struggling to stand up under her own weight. He grunted and pulled harder, scrunching up his face, making a show of how heavy she was.

"So then, you know I got fired today?" She grabbed her bottle of wine and limped to the kitchen.

"Administrative leave," he corrected, following her. "Not permanent." He pried the wine bottle out of her hand and set it on the counter. "The woman didn't die. That's really all that matters. Susan laid it all out for me." He opened the drawer where they kept the wine supplies and retrieved a corkscrew.

"I made an egregious error." She sat down at the table and took a deep breath, tears welling in her eyes. "A woman almost died because of my carelessness." She looked sideways at him. "So, that's why you're here? To check up on me?"

"I live here, remember?" Denny shrugged and handed her a glass of wine.

"I don't want this." She handed it back. "I don't want you here." She rested her head in her hands. "Please leave."

He put the wine down on the table and pushed it toward her. "Take a sip. You'll feel better."

"I don't want to feel better." She glared at him. "I want to wallow.

And I want to wallow alone." She grabbed the glass and brought it to her lips. "There. I took a sip. You can go now. Go home to Remi."

Denny sat down across from her. His hair was almost back to being completely gray. She didn't want to admit it to herself, but he looked good. He poured himself a glass of wine and drank half of it in one gulp. "I told you, there's no more Remi." He sighed. "Can't we just talk?"

"There's nothing to talk about. I got fired. I will likely lose my pharmacy license. A woman almost died. And, I got a speeding ticket on the way home. Oh, and let's not forget—my husband left me for another woman."

"Didn't you hear me the other day at the beach? It's over with Remi." He reached across the table and patted her hand, letting it linger a fraction of a second too long. She pulled away. "And don't worry so much about your job. You'll get another one. You can even start a second career if it comes to that."

"At age fifty?" She glared at him. "Hey, who said you could dip into the wine I bought?"

"Holy crap!" He smiled, ignoring her comment about the wine. "Tomorrow's your birthday!" He walked around the table to the back of her chair and began massaging her shoulders and neck.

Darlene bent her head, letting herself get caught up in his fingers, kneading her. She did not realized how tense she was until now. She felt other parts of her body react, too, much to her surprise and dismay. She pushed her chair back with her feet. Denny's hands fell away from her neck.

Feeling bold, reckless, and in need of escape and numbing, she stepped closer to him and reached around his neck, pulling his head close to hers, and kissed him hard on the mouth. His tongue immediately sprang to action. She suddenly didn't care if Denny was or wasn't with Remi. She didn't care about her job or the speeding ticket. Nor did she care that she felt ugly and had not showered since yesterday. She didn't even care that she was wearing a pair of incontinence panties. She pulled her shirt off, then fumbled with the button on Denny's jeans. He took a step backward.

"Are you sure?"

"Yes." She held out her hand and let him lead her up the stairs.

DARLENE AWOKE in a tangle of sheets. Their lovemaking had been part awkward, part tender, part passionate—like their first time had been, so long ago. Feeling hopeful for what might lie ahead, she let her toes feel around for his foot, but all she found was empty cotton, wrinkled, and spent. She half-sat, propping herself up on her elbow, scanning the room. Denny's clothes were draped haphazardly across the back of her reading chair, just where he had tossed them last night. She heard the toilet flush. She sat up, hanging the sheet over her chest, anticipating his return. She envisioned a lazy day together, trying to reclaim what Remi had ripped away. Yes, she would blame Remi.

Denny emerged from the bathroom, face damp from having splashed water on it, red from...a hot shower? Red from...straining on the toilet? Red from...crying? He sat down on the edge of the bed, taking her hands.

"What's wrong?" She could see the moistness pooling in the corner of his eyes. So, he had been crying in the bathroom. Tenderness toward him washed over her, imagining him crying, unable to hold in the emotion bubbling up inside of him, realizing, finally, that he really did love her. That he really did desire her. She smiled.

"I can't do this." He dropped her hands.

Darlene's brain cells could not overlay the passion from last night onto the reality of what he was trying to tell her. Some of her synapses carried visions of sugar plums, others carried images of Denny leaving her for real. Something in his tone told her that *I can't do this* was not just about coming back to bed or spending the day together.

"I can't do this, Dar." He repeated it as if she hadn't heard him the first time. "My head is totally fucked up."

"Remi?"

"Yeah."

"Get out." Darlene's embarrassment, combined with this complete and utter rejection, pierced her in ways that she didn't know were possible.

Denny stood, then sat back down. "I love you; I really do." He put his head in his hands, muffling his voice. "Please, believe me, I never wanted to hurt you."

She pulled the sheet all the way up to her chin. "Are you with Remi or not?"

"I'm confused. She's confused." He hung his head. "Her being pregnant doesn't help."

"So, that's what this is about?" She felt disgusted with herself for falling into his trap. "You're sad and lonely and needed a piece of—"

"You started it last night, in the kitchen."

"I didn't start anything." She shook her head. "You gave me wine, knowing it would lower my defenses. You took advantage of the fact that I'm an emotional wreck. You're the one who massaged my neck."

"Dar. Please."

"Don't 'Dar' me." She stood, taking the sheet with her, and wrapping it around her body like a toga. "Get the fuck out, Denny. I mean it."

"Alright, alright. I'm going." He shuffled to the chair and dressed. "I just want you to know that this isn't easy for me."

Darlene followed him into the hallway and down the stairs, wanting to be sure he did, in fact, leave. He opened the front door and stepped outside, holding the door open and lingering on the stoop. "Happy birthday," he said, before finally shuffling to his car. As soon as he was out of sight, she pulled the door shut.

31

For the next two days, Darlene was in a frenzied state of agitation, fury, and a new sense of purpose. She flitted from room to room with a realtor's eye, or at least the kind of eye she imagined most of them had. Anything and everything to keep her mind occupied, keep her body in motion. Stopping to breathe only invited unpleasant images of a woman stretched out on a gurney, defibrillator paddles being slammed against her chest. At least she didn't have to worry about her lost income. Not yet, anyway. The one smart thing she and Denny did early in their marriage was to save, save, save. He had encouraged her to build her own little nest egg. She could use it for anything she wanted, no questions asked. Only she never used it. And now, twenty-five years later, it was quite substantial. Was she rich? No, not by a long shot. But it was more than enough for her to live on until things got sorted out at the pharmacy, or she found another job.

They needed to sell this house. The house where they raised Shelly. Memories lurked in every corner. Darlene had always thought Denny was happy. How could she have been so blind? Now she was certain she wanted to keep the condo, and wanted Denny removed from the deed—a process she would need to carefully strategize. She met with a lawyer yesterday who said that she could buy Denny out of the condo by giving up some of the proceeds from the sale of the Leesburg house. Sharing the condo with him was something she would not consider. Now that Remi was (supposedly) out of the picture, Denny would be combative and harder to negotiate with. She needed to tread lightly.

She stood in the middle of Denny's home office, contemplating how to stage it. He came by yesterday to pack some of his things—clothes, work files, running shoes—but left the space mostly intact. He was noncommittal when she asked him where he would go, mumbling something about trying to stay with his brother while he sorted things out. The sting of rejection still fresh, she hid in the backyard while he rifled through his belongings.

She ran her fingers along the top of his desk and picked up a coffee-stained mug. She sniffed it, then set it back down. She reached under the desk and picked up the pair flip-flops he kept there. He bought those things, oh, ten years ago maybe, at the beach. She threw them, hard, across the room. They bounced off the wall, one landing on top of his treadmill, the other near her foot. She kicked it.

Hanging on the far wall was a photo of Denny in his 1972 green Plymouth Duster. She lifted it off the wall and studied it. Denny behind the wheel, a high-school student with a fresh driver's license smiling out the window. She sat down on the floor and stared at the photo, suddenly overwhelmed by all of the change beginning to close in and choke her. She stood up and tossed the picture across the room. It hit the wall and crashed on the floor. Suddenly feeling like she was in an inferno, she ran to the window and opened it, letting the cold, November air swirl around her.

She took a deep breath and picked shards of glass off the floor, the big pieces first, as her mother always said to do. When she and Rachel were about six and eight, long before Liam was born, their father had somehow reached a tipping point on how messy the play-room had become. One Saturday morning, when all the neighbor-hood kids were getting ready to go to the swim club, she and Rachel stood in the middle of the room, paralyzed, unsure where to start.

"Pick up the big pieces first." Their mother crouched down and folded a game board. She looked around for the box, found it, and put the board in. "When you're finished with the big pieces, you can concentrate on finding all the little pieces that go with the big pieces."

Pick up the big pieces first. Darlene placed large, jagged pieces of glass into a trash bag, then used the cardboard backing of the frame to sweep up the smaller ones. Luckily, the photo wasn't damaged. She wished she could give it to Liam. He loved Denny's old Duster.

She carried the bag of broken glass outside to the trash bin, and for the first time since she had left the beach, thought of Fran. The image of him carrying her beach trash down the stairs and slamming the door behind him was still so vivid. How could she have forgotten it until just now? When had that been, anyway? Yesterday? Two days ago? Three? She could not remember.

The front stoop needed a good sweeping. And the ivy growing around the railing needed a proper pruning. Or better yet, she should just rip it out. She hated the vine. The only reason it was still there was that Denny liked it. Well, no more. He simply did not have a say. She touched one of the brown leaves; it crumbled in her fingers, a fine powder swirling as it floated to the ground. She tugged the vine; it gave up without a fight, like it wanted to be put out of its misery.

An hour later, she stood across the street and regarded the house. Better. The front stoop looked naked but better. A few pots of flowers in spring would fill the gap. If she was even still here by then. She wanted to put the house on the market soon. Sooner than soon. Yes. Sooner than soon.

She looked at her watch. If she was going to get to Philly before dark, she needed to get packing. Two days with her parents was going to be brutal; she was not looking forward to it. But her mother had called last night, pleading. And now that she was unemployed, well, she couldn't think of an excuse not to. Her mother promised a mini Thanksgiving. *No thanks*, Darlene said to that. She took a deep breath, wishing she had never agreed to go.

32

———

Darlene's mother outdid herself. She had taken to heart her daughter's objections to having a mini-Thanksgiving and made lasagna instead; she was famous for it. Three different kinds of cheese on the inside. Homemade meat sauce. Mozzarella and a good, aged parmesan sprinkled generously on top.

It had been an uneventful visit so far, pleasant the way that visits often were when a respectable amount of time and distance separated one visit from the next. Although she had just seen her father last week, this was the first time Darlene had been home in over a year.

The dining room table was littered with the remnants of a pleasant dinner. Surface topics only. Safe territory. The conversation bordered on the polite, everyone being careful to avoid known triggers. The issue of *Beach Kiss* had only come up once. Her mother had decided to forgo a book signing at the golf club, or, translated: her father won that battle. Case closed. Nothing more to say. Her father, somehow between last week and now, had accepted that his wife was not involved in a steamy romance with their greasy neighbor. And had come to terms with her new hobby. *My second career*, her mother corrected. He also seemed more relaxed that her pseudonym might provide a least a modicum of anonymity.

"Good dinner, huh?" Sid fiddled with remnants of mixed greens at the bottom of his salad bowl. "I'm stuffed."

Darlene leaned back in her chair and patted her belly, bracing herself for a snide comment about her weight, which, she smiled to herself, had come down a pound since the beach. She tried to get up and help clear the table, but her mother instructed her to stay put. She straightened her chair and pushed her plate away.

"Dad, you do know it's not good to store your medications in the bathroom, right?" Last night, she opened the medicine cabinet in the upstairs bathroom in search of Tylenol PM. She noted the shelf containing her father's medication, vulnerable to the heat of the small bathroom from his long, hot showers. The vent fan never did work properly, and stepping out of that shower was like stepping into a thick fog. "The heat and dampness from the bathroom can make them less potent or ineffective even." She blinked slowly. "You're a doctor. You should know this."

"Forever, I've been keeping my medicine in the bathroom." He pursed his lips. "Why do you think they put medicine cabinets in bathrooms?" He swiped at a crumb stuck to the corner of his mouth.

She took a deep breath and tried to keep her voice calm. "Just because something has always been done a certain way doesn't mean it's the best way." Frustration was mounting. She had overeaten and felt like she might soon explode. Not a good feeling. She was downright tired and cranky and just wanted to crawl into bed.

"Let's call your sister and see what she says." He pulled his new cell phone out of his pocket. "Your mother made me get this. I have no idea what I'm doing. She put Rachel's number in, so all I have to do is tap a button."

"Give me that phone." Darlene reached across the table and snatched it, maybe a little too aggressively. She scrolled to 'favorites', and sure enough, there was Rachel, in all her glory. Number two on the list, second only to his wife, who was number one. Number three? His doctor. That was it. No number four. No Darlene. She would have gladly settled for being last if it meant being on the list. "If Rachel tells you to move your drugs out of the bathroom, you'll do it?" He ignored her and held out his hand for the phone.

"No. You're not calling her." She felt herself beginning to hyperventilate. A teenager again, juggling flaming bowling pins to get her father's attention. "Rachel tells you to eat tofu, you eat tofu, even though you hate tofu." She glared at him. "I'm tired of it. She tells Mom that hair dye causes cancer." Her arms shot up in the air, and she waved them around, to accomplish what, she wasn't quite sure. "Mom, who always said she'd go to her grave with dyed hair, decides to stop dying her hair." She took a deep breath. "Why? Because Rachel said so." She shook her head. "But, when I tell Mom to drink cranberry juice to help prevent UTIs. She balks and doesn't do it." She cringed, thinking of Fran and their last conversation. *I will not drink it on a boat, I will not drink it with a goat.* She shuddered —*someone walking over my grave*—as Bubbe sometimes said. Her face felt hot, but she was determined not to cry. Not in front of her father. Not now. She closed her eyes and let her chin fall to her chest. Her father sneezed.

"Ah-ha! Now you're sneezing into your elbow! Wow, you have finally taken something I've said seriously." Darlene felt weary. "We're making progress, I see."

Sid tried to grab a tissue, but the box was out of reach. Darlene leaned over and plucked one out and handed it to him. He held the tissue to his nose and blew, like the sound of the shofar, loud and long. He finished and wiped the residue from under his nose.

"Dad, remember the shofar?" Darlene tried to suppress a laugh but couldn't.

"I remember that day like it was yesterday," he said, a smile forming on his lips. He crumbled the tissue and stuck it in the pocket of his cardigan. "How old were you then? Four? Five?"

"Something like that." She smiled at the memory. It had been the first time she got to go to synagogue with her father on Rosh Hashanah. Just the two of them. Rachel had a stomach bug, and their mother stayed home to take care of her. Rare time alone with Daddy.

He had been chosen to blow the shofar that year—quite an honor. He was well versed in the Torah, and the congregation loved him. It certainly didn't hurt that most of the congregants were also his patients. She sat on the bench next to her Aunt Dora. When her father blew the shofar, Darlene bolted from her seat, dodging stocking-clad legs, announcing: *Daddy needs a tissue! Daddy needs a tissue!* She proudly handed him a crumpled tissue that she pulled out of the little purse dangling from her arm. Later that morning, during the kiddush repast, the little old ladies swarmed around Darlene and her father. *What a girl you've got there. So funny. We were in hysterics. Connie should have been here, she would have died.* And on and on and on. Darlene ate up the attention, ate up the fact that she was Daddy's girl. She remembers wishing her mother could have been there but feeling happy that she wasn't. Because if her mother had been there, Rachel would have been there too.

"I know it seems like I always dismiss you."

"No, it doesn't seem like you do. You just do."

"You're a good pharmacist." He looked at her. "And I'm proud of you." He reached behind his head and rubbed the back of his neck.

"But Rachel has more credibility, because she's a doctor, like you."

"Don't be like that." He folded his hands in front of him on the table.

"Truth is, I'm a lousy pharmacist." She tried to suck in her gut, to gauge, on a scale of one to ten, how full she really was. Her stomach was so bloated and distended that she could not suck it in. She discreetly unbuttoned her jeans, feeling like she had just been freed from a boa constrictor's grip. She felt a swarm of bees buzzing around in her mouth. Without her knowledge or consent, they escaped; her lips started moving, spilling the entirety of what had happened at work. She felt a strange, unexpected relief, staring at her words, now all over the table.

Sid took off his glasses, sticking one end of the frame in his mouth. He held it there as the glasses dangled like a rag doll. They moved up and down as his teeth worked the plastic. He massaged his forehead, then extracted the end of the frame from his mouth, wiping it on his sleeve, before positioning his glasses back on his face.

"My doctor put me on a new medicine last month. I won't go into what it is, because that's not important." He took his glasses off again, but this time set them down on the table. He looked deep into her eyes. "When I went to pick it up, the pharmacist came out from behind the counter and said the new drug will interact with my blood pressure medicine. He said it could cause a severe reaction." He put his glasses back on. "I had the pharmacist call my doctor right then and there. I could not believe he would prescribe something that might interact badly with something else. But he did." He pinched the bridge of his nose to suppress a sneeze. It worked. He took a deep breath and looked at the ceiling. "My point is that the pharmacist knew better than the doctor. Even I made mistakes in my practice. Not many, but I made them."

"Dad, don't you think I feel bad enough about this?" Darlene grabbed a tissue and held it to her eyes. She couldn't stop the tears from coming. She saturated the tissue and grabbed another. And then it hit her—her father just admitted that sometimes doctors are not the all-knowing oracles he makes them out to be. Just because one has more formal education than the other, doesn't mean the other's opinion should be dismissed. About where to store his pills, the reality was simple: he simply chose to trust Rachel. Period. If it was cloudy outside, but Rachel said it was sunny, as far as Sid Bloom was concerned, it was sunny. Period.

"What will you do if you lose your license?"

"I don't know." And she didn't. She had absolutely no idea. "I just don't know."

"Connie?" Sid pushed his chair away from the table. "Connie, get in here," he yelled. "Your daughter has something she wants to tell you."

"Dad." Darlene shook her head. She looked at the doorway, relieved that her mother apparently had not heard him calling. "Please don't do this. I'm not ready for this to be public knowledge."

"Public, my foot." He walked to the doorway. "She's your mother."

"Right, and within two minutes of telling her, she'll be on the phone with Rachel."

"Connie!"

"Dad!" Darlene startled herself by yelling. "Stop. I'm not ready to tell Mom about this."

"Not ready to tell me what?" Her mother appeared in the doorway covered in flour and cocoa powder. She turned toward her husband. "What are you yelling about? Can't you see I'm busy."

"Well, whatever you're doing, it can wait." Sid nodded at the empty chair beside him. "Sit down, would you?"

"No, I won't." She looked at Darlene and smiled. "I'm making our daughter her favorite brownies. Birthday brownies."

Darlene cringed at the thought of yet more food. "Aw, you didn't have to go through all that trouble. I should have known that's what you've been up to in there." She stood up—anything to get away from her father. "Let me help you."

"No way." She took Darlene by the hand and led her back to the table. "Sit. Enjoy this time with your father." She ambled over to the sideboard and opened the bottle of red wine Darlene had brought, filling three glasses.

"Have some with us, Connie."

"I'll have mine in a little while, with the brownies."

33

―――――

"I'm not wearing the George Clooney shirt!" Fran wandered from room to room, shouting to the walls, shouting to Sadie. "Look, I'm not wearing it." He opened the closet, hoping to find her in there. With Sadie, he never knew where she would turn up. Sometimes, she appeared on top of the refrigerator, sitting in the lotus position, watching him cook. Other times he'd walk into the living room and find her stretched out on the couch. Or sitting in her favorite chair on the balcony. "Come on, babe. I'm not wearing the George Clooney shirt. And I'm not going out on a date. I'm not even going out with my sister." He poked his head into the guest bathroom. "I'm just going to the pet store."

Two days ago, after his failed picnic with Sadie on the beach, he drove to the pet store with the money Rose gave him and bought a bag of cat food. He was not a cat person—he much preferred dogs— and had no idea how much or how often to feed one. Ray Bolger. What a silly name. And now, the cat seemed to want toys. How did Fran know this? He didn't.

Walking down the stairs from the bedroom to the living room, he glanced at the wall of photos—the stairway to heaven, Sadie had dubbed it. Pictures of her great-grandparents. Photos of distant relatives she had never met. Her aunt in a cotton dress leaning against the hood of a car. A photo of Fran's grandfather and great-uncle as teenagers at the beach, right here in Ocean City, showing off their abs, his grandfather posing like a flamingo. A smattering of childhood photos: birthdays, holidays, random scenes of familial bliss.

Then there were the more recent photos: Sadie and Jackie on horses. Jackie's first day of school. Sadie and Fran at Jackie's college graduation.

Finally, the bicycle pictures: Sadie and Fran on a bridge overlooking a ravine in Pennsylvania. Sadie and Fran surrounded by red rock formations in Utah. Sadie and Fran laughing as they shoved grapes in their mouth at a California vineyard. Sadie never wanted to take her helmet off for pictures, hated what it did to her hair. So, Fran started leaving his helmet on too. Cycling had been such a big part of their life; he couldn't face riding without her. Their bikes were collecting dust in a little-used room on the first floor. He really did need to get off his butt and sell them. Maybe he should list them on eBay.

He sat down on the landing and fished his cell phone out of his back pocket. He pressed the speed-dial number for his stepdaughter. She had sent him a save-the-date for her wedding, which he'd promptly hung on the fridge and just as quickly forgot about. Until he noticed it this morning and realized the RSVP date had come and gone, two times over.

"Jackie." He was surprised that she picked up. He looked at his watch, noon in Wyoming.

"Hey, Fran!" She paused. "Hold on, just a sec."

He heard muffled voices, the sound of footsteps, dishes clanking, and the unmistakable swish of a swinging door. When she returned, he launched right in.

"I'm a complete idiot. I hung your beautiful save-the-date thingy on the fridge, and it blended in with the background, and I just noticed it this morning, and I realize I'm terribly late." He took a long, slow breath. "I hope you'll still let me come."

She laughed—Sadie's laugh. "You'd better come." And then: "Bring someone."

How could he bring someone to Sadie's daughter's wedding? He could not imagine it. Such an intimate thing, a wedding. He never understood people bringing casual dates to weddings. Mostly, he couldn't imagine Sadie's daughter seeing him with anyone other than, well, Sadie.

"Seriously," she said. "Please. I mean it. You have between now and August to find someone. That's not too lofty a goal, is it?"

"It's beyond lofty."

"It's been two years."

"And it feels like two seconds." Fran felt the familiar ache in his chest, the one that never seemed to go away. And during the brief respites, well, he felt like a part of his core was missing. Without the ache, he didn't know what to do with himself. The night he found Rose on the balcony drinking wine and eating chocolate, he had forgotten. Almost. And when the spell was broken, the ache came back with a vengeance. And the feeling that he had cheated on Sadie.

"I know." She sighed. "I'm sorry. I'm overstepping."

"It's all good." Fran suspected it was easier to move on at Jackie's age than it was at his. The young seemed to be pliable in every way. Or perhaps that was unfair. Fran knew it had been a rough road for Jackie, watching her mother get sicker and sicker. She had her whole life ahead of her, though. And Fran? Well, his life was more than half over.

"She's still talking to you, isn't she."

"Let's just say she's as opinionated as ever." Fran smiled, then slumped on the landing. He knew Jackie humored him. It was a bit embarrassing, though, how enmeshed his and Sadie's life still was. At Laurie's urging, he talked briefly to a therapist but couldn't seem to form the words, couldn't find a way to share his feelings. And he didn't know how to explain the visits from Sadie. After the third session, he realized that he didn't want Sadie's visits to end, so he stopped going. "The restaurant is doing great." He lied. The restaurant was in trouble. So much trouble that he was seriously considering selling it. Something he couldn't get Sadie to talk with him about. And he wouldn't sell it without her blessing.

Then there was the matter of Rose and the mixed message Sadie was sending. On the one hand, pushing, ever so subtly, encouraging him to go ahead. Go ahead with what he didn't know. And on the other, a bit of jealousy, a sort of peeing on the bushes. He needed more than subtle. He wanted Sadie's explicit blessing. Blessing for what, though. Dating? Feeling the flash of a spark that he hadn't felt in a very long time? He took a deep breath, wondering if he would ever be able to sort his life out. At age sixty-two. Pathetic.

"It will be alright, Fran. I promise." The same muffled voices from the beginning of their conversation were back. The swinging door again. Another plate clinking against a metal sink. It was time to end the call.

"I'll take your word for it." He smiled; glad Jackie wanted to keep him in her life. "Over and out." He stood up and rubbed the small of his back, trying to muster the gumption to go out and buy the damned cat a toy.

34

Fran pulled into the carport and stepped out of his Jeep. On the way to his front door, he nodded to a man standing in the shared driveway, just in front of Rose's condo. He stuck the key in the door and turned the knob, setting one foot inside the door, and tossing the bag containing not one, but three cat toys onto the entry table. He went back to his Jeep and grabbed the cat house that the pet store clerk had talked him into buying. He set it on the ground.

"You're Rose's." He cleared his throat. "Your Darlene's husband." He cleared his throat again as he approached Denny and held out his hand. "Or ex-husband? I don't remember. It was late that night." He smiled.

"Late it was." Denny's hand remained at his side. "We're still married."

"Technically?"

"What difference does it make?"

"Well, we are neighbors, aren't we?" Fran looked around. "Is she here?"

Denny shifted from one foot to another, a puzzled look in his eyes. "Is who here?"

"Your wife." Fran noticed a package in a precarious place between the two condos. He didn't remember ordering anything and stepped away from Denny to have a look. Amazon. Addressed to Darlene Feldman. He went back to Denny and handed him the box.

"Ah. Yes. I mean, no. Darlene isn't here. She's home, licking her wounds. She lost her job." Denny examined the box, turning it over once, then tossing it in the air and catching it. "Probably a book. She always orders a book for her birthday. I'm not sure why she sent it here, though."

Rose's birthday. Fran smiled to himself, wondering how old she was. Just then, a woman emerged from the condo, the storm door slamming behind her. *I put sparkling cider in the freezer*, the woman said as she approached Denny and hugged him, whispering something in his ear. Denny nodded his head toward Fran, the woman's head following. Fran deliberately stood still, not wanting to pretend he didn't see this, not wanting to pretend it was okay. Even though Denny and Rose were getting divorced, it seemed somehow wrong that he would bring his girlfriend to the condo. He tried to imagine Rose with this asshole and couldn't picture it. Denny opened his car's passenger door and held it as the woman slid in.

"When, exactly, is your wife's birthday," Fran yelled before Denny closed the car door. He felt like a high school kid yelling like that, emphasizing *your wife*. On the other hand, doing it gave him perverse satisfaction. He smiled, waiting for an answer, but all Denny gave him was the finger.

Fran turned toward his condo and glanced up at the third-floor window. A familiar face, watching. Sadie. He smiled and gave her a little half-wave. He glanced back at Rose's carport and watched Denny backing out. But by the time his eyes searched for Sadie again, she was gone. He opened the front door and lifted the cat house into the foyer, leaving it there. He climbed the stairs, carrying the bag of cat toys with one hand and holding the banister tightly with the other, the weight of needing Sadie too heavy. Too, too heavy.

"Yoo-hoo! Are you decent?" Fran heard his sister's voice first, then the slam of the front door. *Yoo-hoo*, their mother's favorite way of getting someone's attention. Personally, Fran hated the expression.

"Up here," he called from the kitchen, where he stood at the counter opening the cat toys. He had already put away the bag of chocolates—an impulsive decision on his way home from the pet store. He justified it by telling himself he needed bananas, even though he had enough bananas to last the next few days. When that excuse didn't pass muster, Fran thought it might be fun to put a bowl of chocolates atop the hostess station at the deli. Customers could grab a few on their way out. That was, of course, before he saw the price—almost eighteen dollars, for a bag of chocolates! He stood in the candy aisle and held the bag in the palm of his hand, weighing it, thinking it felt awfully light for that much money. A hundred and fifty pieces. He quickly did the math in his head: a little over ten cents per chocolate. He stood in front of the shelf, comparing the mega-bag against the normal-sized bag. Okay, he was getting a bargain buying in bulk. He wondered how many bags of these things Rose bought each week. Or maybe the other night on the balcony had been unusual. For some reason, he didn't think so. He purchased the mega-bag, smiling to himself at the prospect of one day holding out the bag and offering her one, or two, or however many she wanted.

Laurie clomped up the stairs in her heavy clogs and set two grocery store bags on the counter. She lifted out four bottles of cranberry juice, setting three on the floor next to the trash can and one on the breakfast bar. She opened the cupboard above the sink and pulled out the biggest plastic drinking cup she could find.

"Our little pharmacist is spot on about drinking this stuff," she said, holding the cup against the ice maker, letting cubes fall and crash like a hailstorm. She opened the cranberry juice and poured some in, then stuck the bottle in the refrigerator. "Drink up." She pushed the cup toward Fran, who promptly pushed it away.

"You wouldn't happen to have her phone number, would you?" Fran wished he never told Laurie about what Rose said about the cranberry juice. But he had been distraught after his failed picnic on the beach, his failed attempt to get Sadie to talk to him. He suddenly realized, with a thud, just how troubled he had been since his last encounter with Rose. He acted petulantly toward her and really didn't understand why. Laurie just happened to pop over, to check on him—an annoying little (almost weekly, sometimes more often) habit that started shortly after Sadie's death. As if he couldn't take care of himself. For crying out loud, he took care of himself just fine for nearly forty-five years. Why do people think men are incompetent fools without a woman?

He glanced at Laurie, who was busily scrolling through her phone. She handed it to him, and he wrote Rose's number on the back of the first piece of junk mail in the large pile that was accumulating on the counter. He was fairly good at promptly dealing with the critical items. Still, he couldn't seem to motivate himself to deal with the rest of it until the pile threatened to topple over. Any strife in his marriage was due to his inability to process his mail as it came in. And when you marry later in life, there is a lot of mail to combine. He sometimes wondered if he kept the piles now so that he could hear Sadie complain. She didn't so much anymore, but during her first visits after she died, she groused—or teased him, as she liked to say—about it a lot. Laurie raised an eyebrow, breaking into a grin. "Are you going to ask her out? Why don't you just march your ass over there and knock on her door?"

"What is this, high school?" The cup of cranberry juice magically found its way back to his side of the counter. Now it was his turn to raise an eyebrow at Laurie. He brought the cup to his lips and sipped, the tartness sending unpleasant shudders through his body. "No, I'm not going to ask her out." He thought about Sadie, the blue shirt, and her comment to just go out and have a good time. "She's not here, she's back in Leesburg."

"Are you sure? Her car is out there."

Fran's heart raced, wondering if perhaps, just perhaps she was. What a scene that would be—Rose walking in and finding her dear, soon to be ex-husband snuggled on the couch with his girlfriend, sparkling cider chilling in a silver ice bucket. Wow, would he love to be a fly on the wall—just to see Rose's expression, not the other stuff. "Is it a blue Honda Civic?"

"Yes, I think so."

"That's not Rose's, excuse me, Darlene's car." He looked at his hands. "Her ex-husband is here." He took another small sip of cranberry juice, shuddering just as violently as he had the first time. "He's here with his girlfriend."

"Yikes."

"Yeah, yikes." He sighed. "At least that."

"Why do you call her Rose?"

Fran didn't quite know how to respond. Sure, the easy answer would be to just tell her about how they met, or rather, how he pissed her off out on the balcony. She really did remind him of Kate Winslet in *Titanic*. Okay, his Rose had shorter hair. He sighed. His Rose. How stupid. She wasn't *his* Rose—she wasn't even Rose.

"I don't know." He shrugged. "I called her that the first day we met, and it stuck." He saw movement out of the corner of his eye and turned to catch it, but it was too late. He knew it was Sadie by the wisp of her brown ponytail trailing behind her. He remembered the first time they met. A friend had invited him on a group bike ride. They stopped for coffee and scones at the halfway point. Sadie, not part of Fran's group, sat drinking coffee and laughing with three women. He just happened to look in her direction as she was removing her helmet—a brown ponytail came tumbling out. If she had helmet hair, he hadn't noticed.

He turned back to Laurie, who was, thankfully, paying him no attention. She was digging through his pile of mail, pulling out ads for Walmart and Acme, flipping through coupon leaflets. He never confided in her that he sees and talks to Sadie. He didn't want his sister to worry about him any more than she already did. It was comforting to be open with Jackie about it, especially in the beginning. He didn't even remember how the topic came up, exactly. Still, he recalled saying something and Jackie's eyes getting big, then filling with tears, then telling him that Sadie visited her too. It has mostly stopped for Jackie. They talked about it last summer when he flew to

Wyoming and met her fiancé. He hated the thought of Sadie's visits ever ending.

"So, I'm sitting here getting all excited about these coupons." Laurie waved the Walmart flyer in his face. "I'm thinking, maybe there's something in here I can buy for my baby brother, my pathetic baby brother. Oh wow, cranberry juice! Then I notice the expiration date. Two weeks ago." She pressed her lips together and knitted her eyebrows, opening her fingers and letting the flyer float down into Fran's lap. She shook her head.

"You sound just like my wife."

"Late wife," she corrected.

Fran glared at her. He stood up, walked around the counter and into the kitchen, and promptly—with a flourish—dumped his cranberry juice in the sink.

"I'm sorry," Laurie said, following him.

Fran stood at the sink, not wanting to turn around, not wanting his sister to see him cry, although God knows it wouldn't be the first time. He took a deep breath, dragging his sleeve across his eyes, and turned around. "No, I'm sorry." He wrapped his arms around her. "Thanks for looking out for me." He pulled away. "I don't know what I'd do without you."

"Drink your damned cranberry juice." She smiled and backed out of the kitchen, waving her fingers as she disappeared down the stairs. He waited until he heard the front door close before he fell into the couch and allowed himself a good, old fashioned cry.

Fran opened the sliding glass door in his living room; the late-afternoon November breeze was just as balmy as it had been two days ago. He stood at the screen listening to the waves, inhaling the brine deep into his nostrils. Brine. The smell of the ocean had always been Sadie's favorite smell. He remembered teasing her about it, back during the playful phase of getting-to-know-you. *That's everyone's favorite smell,* he'd said, before disclosing that his own favorite scent happened to be the smell of brand-new tires. It didn't matter what kind—bike, car, truck, wagon. All that mattered was that they were made of rubber. Walking into a Goodyear tire store sent him into an almost embarrassing ecstasy—his mouth would water. He would stand in front of a display, playing the part of a wise consumer, studying the specs, hiding the fact that he was inhaling the rubber. Sadie had no response to that, except to say that she would take the smell of the ocean over the scent of a tire any day.

He took a deep breath, unable to move away from the window. He closed his eyes and fought hard to conjure Sadie's image. He hadn't seen her all afternoon, not since he caught her peeking out the window during his encounter with Rose's ex. Brine. Sadie. He held onto her like that, trying to remember her subtleties, the millions of little things that made her uniquely Sadie, the fingerprints she left wherever she went. Time was dulling his memories of the 'alive' Sadie. Like how she always threw her head back when she laughed or scrunched her nose whenever she was about to make an important point. The sound of her voice on the phone. Her love of old music and the way she knew most of Frank Sinatra's songs by heart. It seemed that with each passing month, more memories fell by the wayside. Except, of course, his memory of the last few weeks of her life. Those he remembers vividly—a sort of *Groundhog Day* loop. When Sadie ran out of treatment options, she wanted to return home to the condo, to her ocean, to her brine.

The memory loop always started with Fran waking to the sound of the doorbell. He had fallen asleep on the couch, next to the hospital bed they had brought in. He tried sleeping in it with her the first few nights, but she insisted he sleep in their bed upstairs—she simply tossed and turned too much, her pain barely manageable. There was no way he was going to be on a different floor. No way. He compromised and slept on the couch, his arm draped across the bed, touching a leg, a foot, her hand—whatever body part just happened to be within his range—for as long as she could stand it. The doorbell rang again, a bit more urgent, several ding-dongs in rapid succession. He ran down the stairs to open the door, half asleep, finding himself face-to-face with a seasonal couple who lived in the building across the parking lot. Apparently, the wife had noticed lights on at all hours in Fran and Sadie's condo and wanted to make sure everything was okay. While Fran didn't consider this couple close friends, they had gone to dinner as a foursome many times. *The cancer came back...Nothing more they could do...Hospice...A week to ten days...No, we're good, we don't need anything...Up all night...She doesn't have the energy for visitors...Her daughter is flying in tomorrow...Yes, I'll tell her...Sure, you can drop off a casserole...The deli is doing fine...My sister is helping me out.* After the couple left, Fran closed the door and pressed his back against it, sliding down to the floor, where he sat, catatonic until he heard Sadie stirring upstairs.

"A week to ten days," Fran whispered to the wind. Remembering those days sent a sudden chill through him. He took several deep breaths of the briny air and was about to close the slider when he heard voices coming from Rose's balcony. He adjusted his position so he could see without being seen. Denny and his girlfriend were sitting on two chairs pushed beside each other, a blanket wrapped around them, each holding a champagne flute. The cat circled the two chairs. He saw the woman reach down and scratch the cat's head, Denny brushing her hand away, saying *fucking cat, don't touch it.* Fran shook his head, feeling suddenly protective of Ray Bolger. He opened the screen and stepped outside.

"Excuse me," Fran yelled. Two heads whipped around to look at him. He hoisted himself over the rail in one graceful motion. *I'll pay for this later*, he thought, trying to ignore the searing pain in his hamstring. "Your wife asked me to look after the cat, so I'm going to do that." He walked across the balcony, to the corner where Rose had set up the makeshift cat palace, picked up the bowl and blanket, and carried them back to his balcony, the cat trailing behind. He stood at the rail, contemplating a similar show of his athletic prowess, imagining falling on his face this time. He chose the sane and cautious option, and walked down Rose's steps, onto the sand, then up his steps onto his balcony, with Ray Bolger trailing closely behind.

FRAN PACED the length of his living room. Then into the kitchen and back again, over, and over, reeling with disgust over Denny, feeling sorry for Rose. He opened the refrigerator and stuck his hand inside. He was about to grab a beer, but saw the bottle of cranberry juice looking up at him with big, red eyes. He tried to ignore its stare and closed his fingers around the neck of a beer bottle. Dammit. He uncurled his fingers and left the beer sitting on the shelf; he pulled out the cranberry juice and poured it into a glass. He set the glass and the bottle on the counter and snapped a picture with his cell phone, then sent it to Laurie, complete with a green, nauseated face emoji.

"Sadie." He set his phone down and went to the couch, leaving the untouched glass of cranberry juice right where he had left it. He sat down beside her. She stared straight ahead as if watching TV. He picked up the remote and clicked it on, then scrolled to the Food Network, her go-to comfort channel, an unfortunate rerun of *The Pioneer Woman* filling the screen. "I'm sorry, babe. I know this isn't your favorite show." He left it on anyway and watched as she stared at the TV, or more accurately, stared past it. He leaned back and waited, knowing it could be a long time before she said anything. He was okay with these long silences. Her presence was what mattered. Sometimes words were overrated.

Sitting beside her, the *Groundhog Day* loop began again. He couldn't let it overtake him. Not now. Not with her sitting so close. He did not want to relive those horrific last few days of Sadie's life. He stood, surprised by how much his hamstring hurt. He massaged it, then stretched, wincing in pain. He hobbled to the kitchen and put the bottle of cranberry juice and his glass, in the fridge. He was about to close the door when he thought, *what the hell*, and rescued the beer. He grabbed the mega-bag of chocolates and carried everything back to the couch. He opened the bag and held it upside down, a cascade of individually wrapped candies bouncing and scattering across the coffee table. He regarded them, strewn all about, the pattern they made looking very much like a cat. He opened one and popped it into his mouth. *Why the hell not.* Chocolate and beer. Yum.

A week to ten days. More or less. That was how the hospice nurse had quantified it—*more or less.* Sadie was still lucid at that point. It had been a hard conversation, both of them in denial for the next three days. With the right amount of pain medication, she couldn't sit still; she wanted to be productive, go on walks, sit in the sand with her feet in the ocean. She felt invincible during the last of the good days, talking about the future, forgetting that her time on earth was rapidly ending. Final boarding call. The vacation would soon end, like it or not.

A week to ten days. More or less. Six days went by before the plane threatened to take off, launching them into the final countdown as it taxied slowly toward the departure runway. *Maybe I imagined it,* Fran would think when Sadie became agitated. Soon she couldn't seem to find a comfortable position during the day. Before the first string of bad days, her discomfort seemed to only plague her at night. Her inability to stay content became exhausting, not only for Sadie but for Fran and her other caregivers. Visits from friends became too taxing, too depressing, and she withdrew from wanting to see anyone, including, at times, Fran. He tried not to take it personally, but he couldn't help it. He didn't remember any time in his life when he'd felt so useless.

A week to ten days. More or less. He blinked, and Sadie's interest in eating or drinking took a nosedive. He couldn't even entice her with a strawberry milkshake from Chick-fil-A, her all-time favorite. Even now, Fran couldn't walk into a Chick-fil-A and see that damned milkshake on the menu without getting teary-eyed. She started sleeping more during the period of the plane leaving the gate; when she wasn't sleeping, she was lethargic, in a fog. During one of Sadie's decreasing moments of lucidity, she demanded a family meeting to tie up loose ends. *There are no loose ends,* he had assured her, reminding her that Jackie would be there the next day. And as if on cue, Jackie arrived, and Sadie relaxed.

A week to ten days. More or less. Well past the halfway point with

Sadie still hanging on, the plane prepared to take off. Her hands and feet began swelling, and there were longer and longer periods of pausing between breaths. As the plane sped down the runway, her agitation became challenging to manage. She hallucinated, her personality rapidly fading, being replaced by someone Fran (and Jackie) didn't recognize.

A week to ten days. More or less. How could a nurse have looked at Sadie three weeks ago and predicted, so accurately, the beginning of the end? The plane lifted and was airborne, wheels up, no way out. Fran and Jackie couldn't seem to rouse her. Soon came dramatic changes in her breathing pattern. He sat, helpless, as her lovely skin started to take on a bluish hue, and her beautiful hands grew colder and colder.

Finally, but way too soon, she was gone. *A week to ten days, more or less.* Sadie lasted exactly eight days, two hours, and seventeen minutes from the day she came home to die.

Fran popped another chocolate in his mouth, peering at Sadie sitting beside him on the couch. He didn't turn toward her, didn't want to do anything that might cause her to go away. He watched her out of the corner of his eye as he opened yet another chocolate. She still stared straight ahead, wearing the faraway look she wore when she wanted to tell him something but hadn't yet found the words. He reached out to touch her—just to let her know he was there and would wait until she was ready to say whatever she needed to say. He set his hand, ever so gently, on her thigh. The day she died, her leg became ice cold, hours before she took her last breath. He had been wearing shorts that day, and at one point, crawled onto the hospital bed and held her, astonished at how icy her thigh felt against his, despite the three blankets.

The sea of chocolates (and empty wrappers) scattered about the coffee table made him think of Rose. He glanced at Sadie, ashamed that he could think of another woman in the presence of the love of his life. He shook his head and took a swig of his beer. How could he so vividly remember the temperature of Sadie's thigh on her deathbed, yet not remember her favorite candy? What was it? Heath bars? M&Ms? Snickers? Skittles?

"Charlie Chewies," Sadie whispered, still staring straight ahead.

Of course! Charleston Chews. Charlie Chewies. He teased her about it the first time she mentioned it. Such a specific candy. And of course, their first Valentine's Day together, he gave her six bars, in a vase, tied with red ribbon. He smiled at the memory and turned toward her, relieved to hear her voice. Happy to have her pierce his wallowing in the memories of her death. He knew it was only temporary, that there would be another trigger, the memories never really fading. The tragic irony was that while the death memories stayed colorful and vivid, the living Sadie—the essence of her—grew dimmer and father out of reach.

"Your friend likes those?" Sadie nodded toward the chocolates on the coffee table.

Fran took a deep breath. Not wanting to respond too hastily, he wondered, what, exactly, Rose was to him. A friend? He didn't think so. Not after the other day. Not after she badgered him about drinking cranberry juice. Not after he stormed out of her condo with the trash. He had acted like an imbecile and regretted it. Perhaps Rose was his friend, after all. Wasn't that what he wanted? A friend? Because he certainly was not looking for a girlfriend. He shuddered. *Girlfriend*. At his age. Nope.

"I know what you're thinking," Sadie continued. "You want to downplay the way you're beginning to feel about her." She searched his eyes. "Please don't downplay that you're beginning to have hope." A single tear trickled down her cheek. "Just say the word, and I'll leave you alone." She took his hands. "I'll go."

"Please don't." Fran's heart broke anew. Before the plane took off, before Sadie had lost lucidity, she held his hands and told him she would go, that she would leave him, and that he should start a new life. *Just look in on Jackie every now and then. Go to her wedding someday. Let her kids call you Grandpa.* "I can't bear the thought of never seeing you again." Fran leaned back on the couch and closed his eyes, thinking about Charlie Chewies, using all his willpower to try to control his emotions.

FRAN LIFTED his head and rubbed his eyes. Darkness had descended on his condo. He looked at his watch, squinting to see it in the dark before remembering that it lit up with the push of a button. Holy smokes! How did it get to be seven o'clock? He rubbed the back of his head and slowly became aware of his surroundings, vaguely remembering sitting down with a beer and the bag of chocolates. He brought the beer bottle up to his eye and peered down the hole, then gently shook it. Empty. He stood up, stretched, and wandered into the kitchen for another. The light from the fridge illuminated the kitchen, and there sat the bottle of cranberry juice, right in the center on the top shelf, not letting him catch a break. It was all coming back to him—the first trip to the fridge a few hours ago, choosing the beer over the healthy stuff, sitting down with the chocolates, and...Sadie. Yeah. She had been here too. He grabbed a beer, promising himself that he would drink a big glass of the red poison before bed. He wanted to be able to tell Rose that he'd taken her advice. His backhanded way of apologizing.

He picked up an empty chocolate wrapper and turned it over, examining the message written there: *Leave your phone behind*. Brilliant. "Be proud of your age," he read the next one out loud, laughing. "Yeah, right." He picked up several more wrappers—had he really eaten so many? *Be someone you look up to; Kiss and tell; Be the sculptor of your dreams; Your vibe attracts our tribe; It's your call; Be with people who make you laugh; Be fearlessly authentic*. He let that last one sink in: *Be fearlessly authentic*. He was fearlessly authentic in his dislike of cranberry juice. He was also fearlessly authentic in his desire to mitigate his chronic kidney issues, sort of. His doctor warned he was heading toward dialysis if his numbers didn't improve, urging him to limit his intake of red meat and increase his overall fluid intake. But never once did his doctor utter a single word about cranberry juice. Or was Fran fearlessly authentic in his selective hearing?

He looked at the chocolates and thought of Rose, remembering that it was her birthday. Today? Yesterday? Three days ago? Tomorrow? He didn't know and suddenly didn't care. He leaped off the couch and found the envelope where he had written her phone number. *Be fearlessly authentic.* He authentically liked Rose. He didn't exactly know what that meant, but he liked her. And he authentically wanted to show her that there were no hard feelings between them, at least none on his end. He typed her number into his phone and created a new contact: Rose.

35

Darlene sat up straight, dreading what was about to happen. She turned her head toward the kitchen. Yep. Just what she thought. The telltale swoosh of Reddi-wip shooting out of the can—a harbinger of her mother emerging with a tray of brownies. Her mother's footsteps drew closer. The click of the light switch. A suddenly dark dining room. The distant glow of a candle, the North Star. Her parents, in unison and off-key. *Happy Birthday to you. Happy Birthday to you. Happy Birthday dear Darlene* (trying to make the syllables fit—dear Dar-le-ene). *Happy Birthday to you.*

"And many more." Her father tried to sound like Bing Crosby and failed miserably.

She closed her eyes and pretended to make a wish, then blew out the North Star amid applause and cheering. Her mother turned the light back on and stood at the table, transferring brownies from the tray to individual plates. Darlene looked down at the two brownies her mother had piled—one atop the other—on her plate.

"Why do you make digs about my weight, then give me two brownies?" She picked up the offending extra brownie and dropped it back onto the tray.

"I didn't say a word about your weight, honey."

Sid pounded his fist on the table. "Your mother worked very hard to make a nice birthday for you."

"I'm not five!" Darlene took a large sip of her wine. "You could have just put out the truffles I brought." She hung her head, feeling like a certified bitch for lashing out at her mother. "I'm sorry, Mom." She picked up her remaining brownie and took a large bite. "Delicious. Thank you."

They ate in silence. The clanks of forks against plates were deafening. Darlene's cell phone buzzed. A text. From a number she didn't recognize. Probably spam. Or meant for someone else. She clicked on it anyway. Photos. A bag of cat food. A dish filled with cat food. And a cat eating cat food. Ray eating cat food. She smiled. The arrival of a second text made her jump.

Fran: I just wanted to assure you that The Scarecrow (a.k.a. Ray) won't starve. By the way, I bought him a little house. And, horror, toys!

Darlene felt heat rising from her toes all the way to the top of her head. She already felt flush from the wine; she was certain her face was redder than what was in her glass. She started to type, then stopped. What could she say? Something witty? Something cute? A heartfelt apology for being pushy about cranberry juice? How did he even get her number?

Fran: Happy Birthday, Rose.

Darlene's heart stopped. How did he know? Had he been Facebook stalking her? Even if he had been, she kept her profile locked down. Only friends could see her birthday. She took another sip of wine, suddenly feeling bold, no longer irritated by his insistence on calling her Rose.

Darlene: Thanks. Feeling old. Fifty.

Fran: Don't talk to me about feeling old. Sixty-two. And then: a photo of a bottle of cranberry juice. Followed by a picture of a glass half full, or was it half empty? She wished she knew.

Darlene: I thought you said you would not drink it on a boat.

Fran: I'm not on a boat, and I'm not with a goat.

"Everything okay, bubbeleh?"

Darlene looked up and saw that her father was staring at her. Her mother seemed lost in thought, eating her brownie, dipping it in a blob of whipped cream. She looked at her father and nodded. *Sixty-two.* She would have never taken Fran for sixty-two. Fifty-five is what she thought.

Darlene: How did you know?

Fran: About what?

Darlene: My birthday.

Fran: Your ex mentioned it...He's here.

Darlene: What???!!!

Fran: At your place.

Darlene: Is he alone?

Fran: No.

Darlene couldn't breathe. The nerve of him, bringing Remi to the condo. She did not care that Denny's name was on the deed. She did not care that he had every right to use the condo. She did not care about any of that. Because in her heart, is was her condo and hers alone. The thought of him there with another woman was infuriating. They were probably having sex in her bed. Darlene wished she leaked on the sheets the last night she was there. Wished she had left a lovely yellow pee stain that would make Remi throw up a little in her mouth. *Damn you, Denny.* How dare he defile her sanctuary. Her mind raced back to making love with Denny a few days ago, how hopeful she had felt. She tried to swallow her ball of grief.

"I'll send the rest of the brownies home with you for Denny," her mother said, brushing the remnants of Darlene's earlier outburst under the rug. Her mother had no way of knowing she was about to incite another.

Darlene slowly returned to the present, the image of Denny and Remi intruding on her space, and Denny interacting with Fran, sharing that it was her birthday. She shot out of her chair, slamming her hands down on the table in the process. Her parents (and the dishes) jumped. She rescued her wine glass just as it was about to topple over. "Denny and I are getting a divorce," she yelled, standing motionless, pressing her palms into the table to stop her hands from shaking.

"Easy, bubbeleh, please sit back down," her father said. At the same time, her mother stared blankly into space, fork mid-air, a chunk of brownie coming dangerously close to falling off the tine.

"I don't want to sit down."

"What is all this?" Her mother's frozen spell broken, she brought the fork to her mouth and sucked in the dangling brownie. She took a sip of wine. "Whatever is going on, the two of you will work through it. Your father and I worked through our recent meshugas." She smiled one of those sly smiles that had meaning beyond what a parent would ever share with a child, even an adult child. "We worked through a lot of meshugas over the years." She looked at Sid. "God knows, there have been times when I wanted to send him to Siberia."

Darlene sat down and looked at her hands under the table. They were still shaking. Work through it? She wondered what, other than Belinda Moo and *Beach Kiss*, her parents had worked through over the years. To say that her father was difficult at times was an understatement. He had mellowed some since Shelly was born, but he could still be a pain in the ass. Her mother had always been the peacemaker. They were still together, though. More than fifty years. What transgressions, other than assuming the role of old-world patriarch, had her father committed? Could there have been a Remi in his life? A beautiful colleague? Someone from the golf club? Or, perhaps it was her mother who had strayed, predisposing her father to assume preposterous, imagined scenarios like her mother and Jimmy Finch. Or maybe it was none of the above. Maybe her father was just too absent, working long hours, getting called in for medical emergencies at all hours of the night.

A memory surfaced that Darlene had not recalled in ages. She was a young child and had snuck out of bed, drawn to the light in her parents' bedroom and the loud noises that sounded like a party. Peering in through the door, open just a crack but wide enough for her little eyes, she saw her mother throwing shoes all around the room. At first, she didn't see her father ducking between the dresser and the bed. Then she saw his head pop up, and she ran into the room, wanting to play, grabbing a red ballet flat, laughing, and yelling *catch, Daddy, catch*. She doesn't remember what happened next.

"There's nothing to work through." She glanced at her phone. No new texts. Just as well, she didn't have anything else to say.

"Nonsense." Her father's voice was stern. "You'll work it out. You don't throw away a quarter of a century."

"Denny fell in love with another woman." *In love*. This was not a fling. Denny was *in love*. She fought tears.

"Your father and I will pay for counseling."

"Mom, are you not listening?" She leaned across the table and looked into her mother's eyes, her voice strangely calm, her hands no longer shaking. "Denny is in love with another woman. He doesn't want me."

"What about the beach house?" Her father looked confused. "The fake house show? The one you dragged me to?"

"The show was a sham, Dad. Denny showed up on the set the last day, and we came clean with the production team. They're going to try to write the break-up into the story. What about the beach house? I'm going have his name removed from the deed." She didn't mention that she had no idea how she was going to deal with paying the mortgage on her own.

"Denny will snap out of it." Her mother patted her hand.

"He won't snap out of anything." Darlene yanked her hand away. "He doesn't want me."

"Your mother kept herself fit. Maybe if you—"

"No!" Darlene held her hand up. "We're not going there." She raised her eyebrows. "I mean it. We're not." She picked up her half-eaten brownie and shoved it into her mouth, her eyes never leaving her father's. She sat back down and folded her arms on the table, resting her head in her makeshift nest. Her parents made her feel like a five-year-old; she might as well act like one. She felt her mother's hand caressing her arm. She couldn't stop the tears. They came against her will, but the warning lights had been flashing bright red

—she wasn't surprised. She let her mother comfort her. When she lifted her head, she saw that a box of tissues had been set beside her. She pulled one out and pressed it into her eyes.

"Sweetie, I'm so sorry." Her mother's words soothed.

"Where's Dad?" She hadn't noticed that he'd left, or how long she'd been sitting like this. A pile of crumpled tissues made a semi-circle around her place at the table.

"Oh, I don't know. Bathroom? He'll be back."

"So, yeah, I'm kind of a mess at the moment."

"Your father told me about your job."

Darlene exhaled slowly, angry that her father would go against her wishes. "I wanted to tell you myself."

"No, you didn't." Her mother's face hardened. "He said you didn't want me to know."

"I'm feeling kind of like a failure right now." She decided to be truthful. "I know you'd tell Rachel, and I don't want her to know about this. Or about what's going on between Denny and me. I don't want to have to deal with her judgment."

"Rachel loves you."

"She tolerates me." Darlene picked up one of the tissue balls and quietly chewed around its edge.

"Rachel loves you," Connie repeated.

Darlene was beginning to see that this was not just about Rachel's passive-aggressive bullying. It was about a mother who looked the other way when Rachel climbed onto Darlene's bed and ripped the eyes off her stuffed animals. A mother who believed Rachel when she said she didn't do it. A mother who dismissed the crying younger daughter and scolded her for not taking care of her toys. Her mother simply never believed in her as a person. Was she neglected? No. She wasn't. Her parents provided a warm, comfortable home. Plenty of food (more than enough food). Nice clothes. Toys and games galore. Looking back, none of that mattered as much as Darlene's craving to be loved just as she was. Instead, her mother picked her apart, item-izing every blemish, every flaw. Rachel, conversely, had always been fawned on and praised.

"Mom, it's complicated with Rachel." She raked her hair with her fingers, her curls a matted mess.

"I really wish you would consider flying out with us for Thanks-giving. Rachel has a new beau."

"No, thank you."

"What did Rachel ever do that was so terrible?"

"Let me count the ways."

"You know, it wasn't always a bed of roses for your sister." Her mother's tone was different, more serious, less judgmental. "She had some problems in medical school."

"What? She got an A-minus on an exam?"

"Watch your tone."

"Come on, Mom." Darlene laughed. "What problems could Rachel possibly have had that bear bringing up now. She's smart, beautiful, accomplished, fit, and fabulous." Darlene rolled her eyes. She knew, of course, that nobody's life was as simple as what you see on the surface. She lived under the same roof as Rachel for the first sixteen years of her life but barely knew her.

"She has problems, just like the rest of us."

"At this point in my life, I'd gladly trade my problems for hers." The clock on the sideboard—a '70s flip digital clock radio, complete with a faux wood veneer—suddenly came into focus. Darlene had looked at that clock during family dinners for most of her childhood —looked at it but never really saw it. Her mother often had the clas-sical music station playing in the background, many times jumping up from the table to adjust the antenna. The radio was long defunct but the white on black digits continued to flip. Twenty-four hours a day, seven days a week, three hundred and sixty-five days a year. Rachel hated that clock. When they were little, they made a game of staring at the clock and trying not to wince or jump when the digit flipped. Darlene never winced—a feat that, even now, made her proud. Rachel always jumped. She'd try again. And jump again. Frustrated, she would cry, then try (and fail) again. Finally, Rachel would stomp off. Darlene stared at the clock; the digits flipped and she didn't jump.

"If you bothered to have a relationship with your sister, you'd know that she was taken advantage of, sexually, during her first year in medical school."

Darlene felt her body go numb, feeling hurt that Rachel never told her this. True, they had never been especially close, but they talked on the phone every few weeks or so during that period in their lives.

"It was an older student," Connie continued. "One she had a crush on. She never pressed charges."

"Why don't you just call it by its name. Rachel was not 'taken advantage of.' If what you are saying is true, then she was raped." Darlene dipped her finger in a pool of wax floating in the candle. She pulled her finger out and examined the wax, peeling it like sunburned skin. She noted her fingerprint, then rolled the wax into a ball.

"She downplayed the incident. She liked the boy. She didn't want him to get in trouble."

"That's bullshit." Darlene squirmed in her chair. "I can't believe Rachel wouldn't have wanted revenge." She balanced the tiny wax ball on her forefinger, then set it down on the table. "Rachel is no shrinking violet." She picked up the wax and worried it between her thumb and middle finger. "How could I have not known about any of this?" She looked at her mother. "We're not mortal enemies. We talked a lot back then." Mortal enemies. A strong phrase for her to choose right now. Maybe on some level, they were.

"I don't know. I don't know. I don't know." Connie picked up a napkin and dabbed at her eyes. "She never told your father or me either."

"How did you find out?"

"My cousin Edith." Connie drew in a shaky breath, then dabbed at her eyes again.

"Edith? Why?"

"She lived a mile or so from Rachel's apartment. Apparently, they spent a lot of time together that semester."

"When did Edith tell you?"

"About ten years ago."

Darlene's eyes grew big. "Does Rachel know that you know?"

"No." Connie blew her nose. "Neither does your father."

Darlene sat, unmoving, staring at her mother, feeling like a space alien who had been dropped into this dining room—into this family. Rachel was raped in medical school and didn't tell her Mom and Dad, but instead sought comfort from a somewhat distant cousin. Her mother's cousin. Not even a peer but an elder. Why couldn't Rachel have just picked up the phone and called? Darlene would have been right there. Typical Rachel, shutting her out. Always. Darlene couldn't fathom that all these years later, her mother had never talked with Rachel about this. Her mother could have come clean a million times over. *What kind of dysfunctional family is this?* She was about to open her mouth and go into a tirade when it hit her: she repeated this pattern daily. *Ignore it, and it will go away. Brush it under the rug.* How long had she ignored the subtleties of Denny slipping away? She followed the sounds of her father's footsteps as he rejoined them in the dining room. He pulled out his chair and sat down.

"Why are you crying?" Sid looked quizzically at his wife, who was sitting with a napkin pressed into her eyes.

"I'm not crying," Connie said. *Ignore it, and it will go away.* If she pretends she's not crying, then she's not crying.

"She sniffed the pepper." Darlene picked up the pepper shaker and unscrewed the lid. "We were chatting, and she mindlessly picked it up, took off the top, and sniffed." Why she wanted to protect her mother, she couldn't say. She simply did not know. "See, like this." Darlene made a show of sniffing the pepper and immediately regretted it. Grabbing for the tissue box, her eyes welled. She grabbed a tissue and pressed it into her eyes just as her mother had done. And then, a rapid succession of sneezes. Her father, counting out loud, stopped when she sneezed for the eighth time. Darlene had never been caught in the throes of laughter during a sneezing fit before. This was a first, and she felt like she would choke on spit and snot. She imagined a line from her obituary: *Loving daughter trying to protect her mother's fantasy that her kids are not fucked up aspirates and dies laughing.*

"Why in God's name did you sniff the pepper, Connie?" Sid was the only one at the table, not laughing. "Why?"

"I wanted to make myself sneeze." She looked at Darlene and winked. "I felt like I had a sneeze coming, and it wouldn't dislodge."

"But you always look into the light of the sun when that happens?"

"Dad, it's pitch black outside. I shoved the pepper at her." Another lie. At least her mother was in on it. "I did it. You know me, always shoving a remedy up someone's nose." She didn't mean to be so blunt and covered her mouth with her hand.

"Ach. The two of you are nuts."

Darlene looked around the dining room—the room where they ate dinner most nights during her childhood. The place where they celebrated all the holidays. The room where her parents and their friends played bridge twice a month. And the cackling Mahjong ladies. Too dark, too dingy, a clock that should have been thrown in the trash years ago, a wood floor in desperate need of repair, a Persian rug under the table, faded and nearly threadbare. The set of Russian nesting dolls on the opposite end of the sideboard from the clock. The room where every morsel of food Darlene put in her mouth was scrutinized. Tonight, this room would become the room where she would finally attempt to break the destructive cycle that she had carried from her childhood into her adult life. No more ignoring and hoping big problems would resolve themselves. No more secrets to avoid losing face. There was nothing more to lose.

Darlene locked eyes with her father. "Dad, about the pepper, it wasn't really—"

"Don't you dare," her mother interrupted through clenched teeth.

Darlene glanced at the small, framed picture on the sideboard, next to the clock. Liam, posing with the new bicycle he bought shortly before...

"What?" Sid looked at her, confused. "What about the pepper."

"Nothing, Dad. Nothing about the pepper."

DARLENE CIRCLED THE TABLE, picking up plates and stacking them in the crook of her arm like a server in a fancy restaurant might do. It was late when they finally went to bed last night and ended up leaving the dining room untouched, the kitchen in similar disarray. She grabbed the three empty wine glasses, carefully squeezing their stems between her fingers, and carried them to the kitchen, depositing them as gently as possible into the sink. She repeated this process, grabbing silverware, gathering the used napkins—crumbled and discarded, the table's tumbleweeds—and brushing brownie crumbs into her palm. She found herself wiping the same spot on the table, over and over, as she replayed the evening. Slowing regaining a sense of the present moment, she walked around to the other side, dousing it with lemon-scented furniture polish, wiping it in stripes rather than circles.

"Bubbeleh, what are you doing?" Darlene looked up and saw her father standing in the kitchen, leaning against the doorway. "Your mother and I will clean up. You go get ready, you're leaving soon, no?"

"Pretty soon." She heard the coffee maker gurgling in the kitchen. "I'll have a cup of coffee, then I need to hit the road." She finished polishing the table. "Where's Mom?"

"Still sleeping. I think she had a little too much wine last night." He winked, then pivoted on his foot and disappeared into the kitchen.

Darlene stood and stared at the empty doorway where her father had been. She imagined her mother sprawled out on the bed, lightly covered with just the top sheet, mouth dry from the wine, head tilted back on the pillow, snoring loudly. She smiled, thinking about her mother embarking on a new adventure so late in life, still filled with passion and vitality in her mid-seventies. It gave Darlene hope, a glimmer, really. A barely perceptible flicker. Maybe fifty was not so old after all.

Sid returned to the dining room with two mugs of steaming coffee. Darlene gasped when he set them down on the bare wood. She grabbed a couple of coasters from the sideboard. The flip digits on clock turned, startling her. She jumped.

"What is it, bubbeleh?"

"Nothing." Darlene didn't turn to look at him. Still, she continued staring at the clock, remembering Rachel never being able to anticipate the flip, always being taken by surprise. Darlene's trick had been simple. Just count. One. Two. Three. Four. Just count. She knew that the closer she got to sixty, the more likely the digits were to flip. Darlene figured Rachel counted the seconds too. It seemed so simple, and Rachel was older, so clearly, she should have known to count the seconds. But now, the clock caught Darlene off guard, and it unnerved her. A harbinger of things to come, perhaps. A new way of looking at life, now that she knew divorce was imminent, now that she had lost her job and potentially her license—the key to a career she loved. She wondered what Rachel had lost in the rape. What part of her soul had been taken? She took a deep breath and sat down with her father, the hot coffee a temporary distraction. The digits flipped, and Darlene jumped again. "Don't you think it's time you and Mom replaced that clock?"

"A new clock?" He waved his arm. "Your mother would have a conniption. Bubbe gave that to her, oh, I don't know, you were little. Kindergarten, maybe." He blew on his coffee, then took a tiny sip. "She tried to write a book back then, you know."

Darlene's eyes grew big. "So, her writing a book now, it's something she's always wanted to do?" She shook her head. "Why didn't she ever talk about it? Why didn't you ever talk about it?" She knit her eyebrows and looked askance at him. "Why did you act so shocked when she finally did sit down and write a book?"

"You don't need to attack me! You asked me about the clock." He picked up his mug then set it back down, missing the coaster.

Darlene reached over and fixed it. "She was going to try to work on it, the one back then, when you and Rachel were in school. I bought her a pack of legal pads, but she wanted to type it, so we went to Sears together and picked out a typewriter."

Darlene cradled the mug between her hands. She mined the deep well of her memory for anything resembling a typewriter and came up blank. "I honestly don't recall there ever being a typewriter in this house."

"Ah, that's because she used it once and decided it wasn't for her. We returned it a few days later."

"She wrote on the legal pads, then?"

"For about two weeks." He looked at the clock. "Bubbe bought her the clock so she could keep track of time while she worked, so she wouldn't forget to pick you girls up from school."

"An alarm clock might have made more sense."

"It has an alarm."

Darlene wondered if a portion of her childhood had been wiped away—a *Men in Black* neuralyzer—when she least expected it. She thought she knew that old clock inside and out. She had played with the radio. She had stared at the digits. How could she have not known it had an alarm?

"Rachel, God bless her, was deathly afraid of the alarm on that clock." He looked at the table, then back at Darlene. "She stayed home sick one day. Your mother was at the dining room table writing. The alarm went off." He mimicked the sound. "It sounded like those Emergency Broadcast System tests. Rachel was a mess." He scratched his head. "What your mother went through." He shook his head, then scratched it again.

"How come I don't remember any of this?" She was incredulous. She had a good memory, dammit. An excellent memory. How, in the name of God, did she not remember a typewriter coming into the house. Or her mother camped out at the dining room table with legal pads and old coffee can full of pens and pencils. If her mother *went through* something with Rachel and the alarm clock, why had it been lost on Darlene?

Sid shrugged. "You were a little girl." It was the only thing he could offer. "Bubbeleh, you were just a little girl."

So, that was it. That was what had been so troubling to Rachel with the clock. She was afraid the alarm would go off. Darlene stood up and carried her coffee mug to the kitchen, setting it in the sink with last night's dishes. Her father followed her in and set his mug in the sink too.

"Thanks for the coffee, Dad." She wanted to thank him for the insight, but she didn't quite know why she wanted to or how to do it. "I'm going to hop in the shower, then I need to get on the road." She looked toward the dining room, then back at her father. "Should I wake Mom before I leave."

"She'll have a fit if you don't." He put his arm around her shoulders. "Call me when you find out about your license. I know people. I can pull strings if need be." He removed his arm and retrieved his mug from the sink, filling it with more coffee. "I also know of a good marriage counselor. I can ask him for recommendations in your area."

"Dad." She pressed her lips together and turned toward the doorway, then turned back to face him. "I don't want you to pull strings. If I lose my license, I lose my license. I'll deal with it."

"What about the marriage counselor?"

"No. The marriage is over. Do you hear me? It's over." The trails of moisture under her eyes, tracking down her cheeks, surprised her. As did her tone and volume.

Sid took a step toward her and opened his arms for a hug. Reluctantly she let herself fall into his arms. This was the daddy who waltzed with her at her wedding. In that one shining moment, she was in the limelight of his gaze, while Rachel stood in the background. She gently pulled away.

"If you lose your license, you could do like your mother and write a book." He smiled, then reached out and grabbed her hand. "You'll be okay, bubbeleh." He patted her hand, then released it before letting both of his hands slide back into his sweater pockets. "You're a smart girl. You'll figure it out."

36

———

Darlene worked her way through each room in the condo, like a forensics expert combing a crime scene, searching for evidence of Remi. By the time she got to the laundry room, she realized what a futile waste of time it was to look for something she knew to be true—something that was out in the open. It wasn't as if she were looking for evidence to prove Denny was having an affair. Honestly, she should have done that months ago. What evidence could she have possibly needed, even then? A woman knows. Plain and simple. How had she missed it? How had she allowed herself to be blind to it?

She opened the washer and pulled out the tangled blob of bedding and towels, tossing the whole mess into the dryer and slamming the door shut. The first thing she did when she arrived, even before unloading her car, was to march straight up to the master bedroom and strip the beds. She didn't trust that Denny would have taken the time to wash his and Remi's soiled bedding before heading home.

"Crap! My wort!" Darlene pushed the button to start the dryer and ran up the steps, taking them two at a time. She reached the stockpot on the stove just as the rolling boil reached its tipping point.

She turned down the flame, allowing the agitated liquid to exhale. Out of breath, she brushed the back of her sleeve across her forehead and leaned against the counter. She had been so distracted combing the condo for remnants of Remi, that she'd completely forgotten about her pot on the stove. A malty, syrupy boil-over would have been more than she could bear.

With the pot safely back to a rolling boil, she took a chance and stepped onto the balcony to check the cat's status. She noticed the dish and blanket were no longer in her corner. She glanced over the rail and saw the cat house—a blue country cottage—and smiled at the thought of Fran buying it. She scanned for signs of him, wondering where he was and what he was doing. When she pulled into the carport earlier this morning, she felt a pang of disappointment that his Jeep wasn't there.

She spent the bulk of the drive to the beach seething over the fact that Denny had brought Remi to the condo. The closer she got to the shore, the more she let her mind drift to Fran and the texts he sent her when she was in Philly. Then she would think about Denny and Remi romping around the condo, and her blood would boil anew. She knew, legally anyway, that Denny had every right to use the condo. At least for now. She was so upset and angry that she pulled over and left a pointed message on Denny's voicemail. *On my way to the beach. I will be there for a couple of weeks. Do not even think about showing up!* He called her back within minutes, assuring her that he was traveling for work. Bullshit. He was with Remi; she just knew it. Not that it mattered. Because it didn't. She needed to take a deep breath and let it go—all of it.

"Rose?"

Darlene turned and saw Fran, over the rail, standing in his doorway. She sighed audibly, embarrassed by the unjustified relief she felt at hearing her 'new' name. Her entire countenance lifted, and she couldn't help thinking that if this were a movie, the clouds would part, the sun would come out, and the gray sky would turn blue. She looked up, just to check. Still cloudy. She took a deep breath. "Hey, Fran."

"Do you smell that?" Fran tilted his head and sniffed.

Darlene shook her head, wondering what she was missing. She shrugged. "What does it smell like?"

Fran scratched his head, then tilted it again and sniffed, waving his hand around in front of his face. "I would say it smells like toast." He smiled. "Warm, buttery toast."

Darlene moved closer to the rail and tilted her head up, just as Fran had done. She didn't smell anything. At least whatever it was, it wasn't an offensive smell. She shook her head. "Nope. I still can't smell it, but I wish I could. Warm, buttery toast is a lovely smell." She looked at her feet. "And an even lovelier taste."

He came out of his doorway, climbed over the rail, and stood beside her. She subtly moved a half-step away from him, not wanting her personal bubble penetrated. He moved closer to her sliding glass door, which was wide open, sniffing into the air. "It's coming from your place. Are you making toast?"

Darlene broke into a grin, amazed that she couldn't smell it before. Of course, her beer. "Buttery toast? I've had my homebrew called many things, but never buttery toast." She laughed. "At least you didn't stand here and tell me you smelled chicken shit!" They both laughed.

"Homebrew! I should have known!" His eyes danced. "Sadie and I used to frequent a brewery just off the bike trail." His eyes abruptly stopped dancing, as if the mention of Sadie had caused the music to come to a screeching halt, and he froze. He took a deep breath and continued. "We'd be riding our bikes, and if the wind blew from a certain direction, you could smell the beer for miles." He nodded toward the open door. "It smelled just like this."

"The technical term for what you smell is wort."

"I knew that." He smiled, the light in his eyes beginning to return. "Actually, I had no idea." He looked at her. "How long have you been a brewmaster?"

"Not sure. Five years, maybe?" She stepped around him and into the house. "Come in for a minute, and I'll show you what I'm doing."

She looked at her watch. "It's about time for the next step, and timing is important."

～

DARLENE TURNED OFF THE BURNER, and with a pair of long tongs, lifted the mesh bag containing her spent grain—a pound each of Munich and Victory malts—out of the pot and set it in the sink. She felt Fran's presence behind her and tried to keep her nerves from announcing themselves through her voice. She took a deep breath. *Steady.* "I found a recipe for making dog biscuits out of this stuff. I'm going to try it."

"You have a dog?"

"No, but I have friends who do." She turned around and rolled her eyes. "One lives in Manhattan and has a small, yappy, toy something or other." She laughed, the nervousness gone. "I have no idea. She carries the damned thing around New York City in a purse. If the biscuits turn out okay, I'll send her some for the holidays."

"I'm picturing Elle in *Legally Blonde*." Fran scrunched his nose. "Believe it or not, my wife loved that movie." He rolled his eyes, and a wistful look washed over his face. He smiled as if to somehow dull the memory.

"I like that movie too!" Darlene wanted to hang onto the moment, sharing something she and Sadie might have had in common. "Underneath all that fluff, Elle is a strong, smart woman. I love watching her grow."

Instead of commenting, instead of taking that breadcrumb and following it toward a more in-depth conversation about movies, or life, Fran pointed to a bottle of vodka sitting on the counter next to the stove, six charred habanero pepper halves floating inside like dead bodies.

"I'm going to add those peppers! I enjoy a beer with some heat. But until I started brewing myself, I had no idea how many options there are for how and when to use peppers." She moved from one end of the counter to the other, not quite sure where to put herself.

Standing in her kitchen with him, chatting as if they had known each other for more than a week felt strange. She silently thanked God for the ready-made topic at hand. "The first time I tried it, I left the peppers whole. I wanted to minimize the heat."

"Sounds like you took a conservative approach."

"Right. I didn't want to potentially ruin the beer."

"Because it's all about the beer."

"No, treble."

Fran knitted his eyebrows and cocked his head, a blank look on his face, as if not wanting to admit he had no idea what she was talking about.

"It's all about the bass, 'bout the bass, no treble..." Darlene sang a portion of the Meghan Trainor song. She looked at the floor, then at Fran. "Never mind." She chuckled. "My daughter, Shelly, well, it's one of her all-time favorite songs." She took a deep breath, wondering what it would be like to date a man so much older. Five years was one thing. But twelve? Enough of a difference to have more moments like this, when cross-generational pop culture references clashed. She tossed the thought away, not because of any real or perceived age conundrum, but because she had no interest in dating. Not now. Probably not for a very long time. "Anyway, putting the peppers in whole was a complete waste of time."

"Not enough heat?" Fran seemed to have recovered.

"Try no heat. The next time I brewed, I cut the peppers in half and threw them in, seeds, pith, everything." She waved her hand in front of her mouth. "Made all the difference."

"So why do it this way?" He picked up the bottle and held it to the light. "It looks pretty, though." He locked eyes with her, setting the bottle down on the counter without regard for where it landed. Luckily, it didn't topple over.

Darlene held his gaze until she began to feel lightheaded. She blinked and ran her hand through her hair, taking her eyes off him and looking at the floor. She mindlessly poked the spent grain bag a few times with her finger, then sat down on one of the bar stools. Fran stood frozen in the middle of the kitchen. Darlene tried to quietly push the other stool away with her foot, but the screech of the legs on the wood floor scolded her ears. She cringed, then gestured for Fran to sit down. She took a deep breath, determined to remain calm and laid back. Beachy. Casual. Uncaring of any particular outcome, again, grateful for the topic at hand.

"There's a lot more to infusing beer with peppers than the way they're cut," she explained. Fran sat on the stool and turned toward her, crossing one long leg over the other. He folded his hands in his lap as if settling in to absorb everything that she had to say. "You can add them late in the boil. If I were going to do the peppers like I've done them in the past, I'd have added them right to the wort." She gestured with her head toward the stove. "For this batch, I'm going to add them to the carboy for fermentation."

"Carboy?"

"It's a big, glass jug." She lifted her feet and pointed under the counter to where she put it this morning. "Most homebrewers use five-gallon carboys. Mine is only three gallons." She suddenly felt playful. "Can you guess why I use the smaller version?"

"Because that's all they had at the brewing supply store when you bought it?"

She made the sound of a game show buzzer. "No, but if I could give you points for a good guess, I would."

"Why can't you?"

"Because that would go against the rules."

"What rules?"

"Come on, just guess."

"Guess the rules? Or guess the reason for the tiny carboy?" He laughed. "Okay. How about this: it has something to do with the particular recipe you use?"

Game show buzzer again. "Another good guess. One more."

Fran shrugged. "I give up. I have absolutely no idea."

Darlene threw her head back and laughed. "Because three-gallons of liquid is all I can manage to carry up and down the stairs." She couldn't help herself, she snorted, inciting more laughter. She finally regained her composure but noticed that Fran was not laughing with her. He sat staring at her, hands still folded in his lap, legs still crossed. She cleared her throat, hoping he didn't notice how red her face was. She would blame it on her laughing fit if she had to. "Anyway, I've read that adding peppers during fermentation offers heat, pepper flavor, and aroma. Doing it the other way just adds heat, no flavor or smell."

"So that's what those are for?" His trance apparently broken, he pointed at the bottle on the counter.

"Yep. You have to sterilize the peppers for at least forty-eight hours, hence the vodka." She smiled. "The recipe calls for one habanero. I'm using three."

"Holy smokes!" It was his turn to laugh. And laugh, he did. He finally came up for air. "Save one for me." He shuddered. "The brewery on the bike trail back home makes a jalapeño beer I love. It's not too hot. Mostly, I love the smell of the peppers." He looked like a lightbulb just went off. "Now, I get it. You don't want to add peppers to the boil because you won't get the nice smell."

"Ding-ding-ding!" She cocked her head, leaning in on something he had just said. She didn't want to pry but was curious. "Back home, as in Reston?"

"Yeah, Reston."

"So, you don't consider this home?"

"No." He looked at his hands. "I don't."

They sat in silence. Darlene suspected it had something to do with Sadie. The fact, maybe, that they bought the beach house together to fulfill a dream. A dream that turned into a nightmare before they even had the chance to fall asleep. Fran uncrossed his leg and rubbed his thighs, then slowly stood up.

"Thank you for the homebrewing lesson, Rose." He smiled a small, closed-lip smile, then blinked slowly. "Do you want me to move the cat stuff over the rail to your side?"

Darlene stood too, feeling paralyzed, wondering what she said wrong. She chided herself for getting too playful. God, she hoped she hadn't come across as flirty. That was the last thing she needed.

"I'm not sure how long I'll be here. At least two weeks, for my beer to ferment." She looked at the floor. "Beyond that, well, I don't have any plans." Thanksgiving flashed before her like a neon sign. She didn't feel up to it this year and was close to telling Denny that he was on his own and that she would have a casual mother-daughter Thanksgiving with Shelly. "You might as well keep the stuff on your side, that is, if you're okay with that." They walked to the sliding glass door. Darlene opened it and waited for Fran to say something, anything.

"Sure, I'll keep feeding Mr. Bolger."

She stood at the door and watched him climb over the rail and disappear into his condo.

37

———

The days seemed to be growing shorter by the second. Less than two weeks out from Thanksgiving and wow, barely five in the afternoon, almost dark. The low, thick clouds precluded any hint of a colorful sunset. Darlene climbed the steps to Fran's balcony, a cold beer in each hand. No way was she about to climb over the rail like he did. A few yoga poses were about it, in terms of stretching her limbs in unnatural ways.

She had not encountered Fran since he walked out of her house two days ago, full of the smell of buttery toast and whatever memories had gotten to him. She wanted to follow up, to ask about it, to see if she could understand. Not that it was any of her business; it certainly wasn't. But she was tired of always playing it safe. She stewed in it as she transferred the buttery toast wort into the carboy for fermenting. Stewed about it when she added the peppers. Stewed about it when she carried the whole thing down the stairs to the first-floor bathroom, where it would sit in the tub and ferment for the next two weeks. Stewed about it when she attached the airlock and fed a rubber hose into the waiting mouth of an empty milk jug to catch any spillover.

Give him space, the safe part of her brain commanded. *Let him come to you.* She wasn't even sure that she wanted him to come to her. All she knew was that she had said something to upset him, although she had no idea what it could have been. At least it wasn't blatantly obvious, like shoving cranberry juice at him.

Yesterday, she knocked on both his front and back doors, to no avail; the fact that his Jeep was not in its parking spot should have been a clue. It was there now, though, and without overthinking it, she employed a tactic from one of her favorite TV shows: *Seinfeld.* She remembered an episode where George did the opposite of what he would ordinarily do. She Googled *opposite George* and YouTube video clips by the dozen popped up. In the episode, George decided that going with his gut instinct was the reason for all his woes. George: *My life is the complete opposite of everything I want it to be. Every instinct I have in every aspect of life, be it something to wear, something to eat... It's often wrong.* Jerry: *If every instinct you have is wrong, then the opposite would have to be right.*

Darlene took a deep breath as she prepared to do the opposite of her gut instinct, which was to leave Fran alone. Nope. Not this time. She was determined not to let her fears overtake her desire to...well... she wasn't quite sure what she wanted to happen. Despite their corny meet-cute out on the balcony, she kind of liked him. Enjoyed chatting with him in the middle of the night, over the rail, sharing her chocolates and gloves. She enjoyed his company the other day—enjoyed talking to him about her homebrewing hobby. Appreciated his willingness to feed a stray cat. Whatever her fear was—rejection, exposure, discovering spinach lodged between her teeth—she would do the exact opposite of her gut response.

She was about to knock when she noticed that the sliding glass door was open a crack—she could hear running water and the sound of clanking dishes. She listened to his voice, muffled, but unmistakably his. The running water stopped, as did the music of dishes hitting granite (or Formica, or quartz, or whatever his countertops were made of).

"I told you already, she's my neighbor." Fran's words were laced with frustration. "I didn't stay long." Frustration gave way to defeat. "I would never do that. You know you're the love of my life."

So that was it. It was why, twice, Fran had abruptly left. Not because of her pushiness and unsolicited advice about drinking cranberry juice. And not because of anything she said when he was in her kitchen the other day. It seemed simple: he promised his wife—probably while she was on her deathbed—that he would never move on.

She heard footsteps and quickly moved away from the door. She pressed her back against the house. She wanted to run, escape, flee— her gut instinct. She was finished with opposite George. Maybe she should flee—she would lose nothing and still be a fifty-year-old, unemployed woman getting a divorce. She didn't need to enhance her life by making a new friend. She stood, paralyzed, afraid if she retraced her steps down the stairs, the way she had come, Fran would see her. She set the beers down on his chair and inched her way toward her condo—slowly, quietly—suppressing a grunt as she lifted her leg onto the rail the way Fran had done the other day. She held onto the rail while she scooted her butt closer, but when she tried to hoist her leg over the rail to the other side, well, it refused to budge.

The sliding glass door opened. She imagined dry, worn rubber seals creating the excess noise (Denny had fixed theirs shortly after buying the condo). She heard Fran step out onto the balcony. *Oy vey. Caught.* She twisted her torso to turn around, leg still on the rail, and met Fran's eyes. She shrugged. He walked toward her, holding both beers, by their necks, in one hand. He set them down on top of the rail.

"What on earth are you doing?" He stood in front of her, head cocked, trying, unsuccessfully, to hold his laughter in.

"Can't you see, I'm stretching." She looked at him as if to say, *what else would I be doing with my leg dangling over the rail*?

"Going out for a run, are you?" He raised an eyebrow. He looked at her clogs. "Funny shoes to run in."

"I don't run." She gave up and smiled, her own laughter escaping. "It's a new yoga pose I'm trying." She hopped on the foot that was planted on the balcony and attempted to adjust her other leg. Nope.

Not moving. "It's called 'the burning thigh of hell, and I'm stuck' pose." She burst out laughing.

Fran held out his hand. "Hold onto my wrist." She did, trying not to think about how warm his skin felt. The light on her balcony flicked on, prompted by the dark. When had the color of the sky turned to charcoal? He gently lifted her ankle off the rail, freeing her leg. She yelped as her foot hit the balcony, and she noted, with dismay, that she was still on his side. She bent down at the waist and rubbed her thigh—the burning thigh of hell, aptly named, for sure.

"Rose, what are you doing?"

"My leg hurts. I'm rubbing it."

"I can see that." He picked up the beers and waved them around. "I'm sure these didn't just magically appear by my door."

"Be careful with those!" She grabbed them out of his hands. "Homebrews tend to be a bit more carbonated than commercial beer." She limped toward the stairs.

"Where are you going?"

She stopped, turned around, and handed the beers back to him. "Home. I'm going home."

"Home-home? Or back to your condo?"

"Condo."

"So, the beers are for me?"

"Yes." She took a deep breath. "Yes, they are."

"I thought you said it would take two weeks for your beer to ferment."

"It will." She relaxed a little. "The ones in your hand are from an older batch. No peppers." She continued toward the steps.

"Beer tastes better when it's shared." His words came out rushed, nervous. "Won't you come in and share one with me?" He shrugged. "You can tell me about how you made it. I'd really like to learn."

She didn't know what to say, didn't know what to do. She wasn't sure she wanted to compete with a dead woman. Wait a minute. Compete with a dead woman? No. She did not want to compete with anyone because this wasn't a competition. After all, dammit, she didn't think of Fran in that way. No. He was her neighbor. One day he might become her friend. But that was all. Nothing more. Ever. That was precisely what she told herself as she slowly turned around and followed him through his squeaky, sliding glass door.

GRANITE. Darlene stood in Fran's kitchen; it was the same layout as hers, a carbon copy, really, except for his granite countertops and white shaker style cabinets. She ran her hand across the cold stone, admiring the subtle red swirls and gray veining. The entire main living space looked like a picture right out of a magazine.

"This was all Sadie's doing." He put two beer glasses into the freezer to chill.

"It's beautiful." She gestured around the room with her arm. "The whole thing." Neither of them had mentioned anything about her overhearing his conversation with Sadie. She supposed he didn't think she'd heard.

"We gutted the place. Well, just this level." He opened a bag of sea salt and cracked pepper flavored potato chips and poured them into a bowl. Denny would have just eaten them out of the bag. "Sadie wanted to turn the entire first floor into a bike room." He looked wistful. "We both had multiple bikes. She was going to use one wall to hang them artfully. She wanted to set up a training room, so we could spin in the winter." He avoided her eyes and turned away, lifting the glasses out of the freezer. He placed them on a ceramic tray. A bright, blue, hideously ugly ceramic tray. She wanted to crack a joke, make light of a heavy topic, but something told her not to. He opened the beers and put them on the tray too.

"I'm sorry, Fran." Darlene didn't know what to say, didn't have words of comfort or empathy. She just didn't. "I'm sorry you lost her."

"Me too." He cleared his throat and carried the tray into the living room, setting it down on the coffee table.

Darlene didn't know what to do with herself. There was no way she was going to sit on the couch with him. She eyed a club-style chair on the other end of the coffee table, then glanced back at the couch. She took a deep breath and chose the chair, the safer bet for sure, and sat down before Fran could claim it for himself. If she chose the couch, he might have plopped down beside her, and, if he didn't, who's to say he wouldn't have changed his mind at some point and… plopped down beside her. Nope. She could not let that happen. She sighed. She probably didn't need to worry. Not with Sadie lurking. She wondered if Sadie would join them. Or if she would watch from afar like Darlene had done when Rachel's first boyfriend stood awkwardly in the foyer enduring the obligatory *Mom, Dad, this is Scott. Scott, these are my parents.*

"Nice coloring," Fran said, pouring the two beers into their respective, frosty glasses. He raised his glass and lightly tapped it against hers. They both took a sip. He held his glass to the light and examined the liquid gold. There it was, right in front of her, as plain as day. The color of his eyes. Liquid gold. He took another sip and smacked his lips. "It's nicely hoppy. Let me guess. About 74 IBUs?"

Darlene nodded, still staring at the liquid gold in his eyes, a perfect match to what was in his glass. "You know what an International Bitterness Unit is! I'm surprised! Here I am, ready to school you, and you already know about IBUs!"

"I'll admit, I know nothing about homebrewing, but I do know a lot about beer."

"What do you like?"

"I'm partial to IPAs."

"Phew. If you said Budweiser, I'd have to leave." She laughed. "Just kidding. Sort of." She put her beer down and looked at her hands. When she lifted her eyes, she noticed that Fran was staring at her. She reached into the potato chip bowl and pulled one out, daintily inserting it into her mouth, chewing imperceptibly. She didn't realize how hungry she was. She stuck her hand in the bowl again, her eyes never leaving Fran's, and ate five chips, one by one, making a show of chomping. Chomp. Chomp. Chomp. She chased the chips with an impressive guzzle of beer, then set her glass on the coffee table with a thud. "I know what you're thinking. You're thinking my husband left me because I'm a fat pig."

"Whoa." Fran held up his hands. "First of all, you have no idea what I'm thinking." He narrowed his eyes and leaned forward, resting his elbows on his knees. He moved the potato chip bowl closer and started popping chips in his mouth in rapid succession, just like she had done. "Here's what I'm thinking," he said between chomps. "I'm thinking Denny is a fool." He looked into her eyes, but she turned away. "Rose. Look at me, Rose." She did. "He's a fool."

"Yeah, well…" She looked away and shoved another chip into her mouth. "I don't know how I missed the signs." She nursed the little bit of beer that remained in her glass.

"You probably wanted to make it work."

"It's why we bought the condo, or so I thought."

"It didn't fix anything?"

"Apparently not."

"I'm so sorry, Rose." He traced the rim of his glass with his finger.

"You know what they say about hindsight." She looked at the ceiling. "It's the subtle things that only someone sharing life or a household would notice. A tiny change in the atmospheric pressure. A small nudge in the earth's orbit. I can't even explain it. All I know is that I should have known." She drained the rest of her beer. She looked down at her belly and squeezed, pumping the roll up and down with her hand. "This is what it was about for him." She drew in a shaky breath, determined not to cry, wondering how they landed on this joy-killing topic. She sighed, avoiding eye contact.

"Like I said before. He's a fool." Fran stood up and carried the empty glasses into the kitchen. Darlene wondered if this was about to become Fran shut-down number three. She sat motionless, waiting for him to show her to the door. Instead, he returned to the couch with two fresh beers, but no glasses. And as if reading her mind: "I didn't want to wait for the glasses to chill." He handed one to her. "I hope you don't mind." He smiled. "And, I hope you don't mind that the beer I'm offering you is far inferior to your IPA."

"Thank God, it's not Budweiser." They clinked their bottles together, sipped, and both, at the same time, reached for the potato chip bowl. Darlene reflexively moved her hand out of the way. She didn't want this encounter to turn into a Hallmark movie where they brush hands reaching for a chip, and suddenly cupid is hovering overhead, wearing a self-satisfied grin.

"Never. I would never."

"Like you would never drink cranberry juice?" She laughed, suddenly worried that she had upset him. Screw it. She was going to be herself. And maybe throw in a little opposite.

"In the spirit of full disclosure, I told my sister about your suggestion, and, well, she took it upon herself to load me up." He tilted his head toward the kitchen. "My pantry is full of that nasty stuff." He smiled. "But I've been drinking a full glass every night before bed."

So, he talked to Laurie about me. What did that mean? Darlene flicked the thought aside, grateful for a less emotionally charged topic. *Keep it light.* "You'll have to come over on bottle day. You might find the process interesting." She tilted back her beer, attempting enthusiasm, but really, her pallet had been compromised by her IPA and the chips.

"I'd like that." He leaned back on the couch, then, as if unable to find a comfortable position, sat up straight. "The fact that you're in Ocean City long enough to brew, ferment, and bottle a batch of beer tells me that the work meeting you rushed out of here for didn't go too well."

Darlene cocked her head and scrunched her eyes. How could he be that perceptive? She barely even remembered telling him about it. "You got that right." The sobs came without her will or consent. In fits and starts, she told him the whole story, culminating with the woman almost dying, the administrative leave, and the potential (likely) loss of her pharmacy license. Fran eventually handed her a box of tissues (she had no memory of him getting up to get it). She plucked one out and blew her nose, right in front of him. Opposite. She never blew her nose in front of people. Not even Denny.

"I could use some help at the deli, if you're interested, that is."

"Oh, no." Did she hear him correctly? The deli? "No way. I waitressed in college for two days. Yeah, I was that lousy at it."

Fran burst out laughing. "I have enough wait staff." He grew serious. "Truth is, the place is struggling. Has been ever since Sadie got sick." He gestured toward the bowl, offering her the last chip. She shook her head, giving him the go-ahead to pop it in his mouth. He chewed it slowly. "I need a pair of fresh eyes to spend a few days there, observe things, help me decide what to do."

"I don't know." If there was anything Darlene hated, it was ambiguity. She imagined hanging out at the deli, standing around, being in the way, carrying a clipboard, jotting notes. Not her cup of tea. "I need to think about it." Opposite. "Actually, Francisco-o-o-o, I'm going to decline your kind offer." She shrugged. "What are your options?"

"Sell the place. Or sell the place."

"It's that bad?"

"Pretty much."

"Would dry turkey have anything to do with it?"

"Watch it." He wagged a finger at her. "The turkey was never dry."

"Okay, if you say so, Francisco-o-o-o."

Fran crumbled his napkin and tossed it, hitting her in the chin. She raised an eyebrow and threw it back, wondering what was happening between them, feeling her defenses lowering, yet trying hard to maintain a sense of propriety. Laughing, he caught it and dropped it on the coffee table.

"Honestly, I don't know what to do. The deli was Sadie's dream, not mine. Selling it feels like a betrayal."

Darlene searched for something to say. Something laced with compassion and sprinkled with wisdom. "You said you consult her." She gingerly glanced at him. "Have you talked to her about it?"

Fran rubbed his legs, then crossed one over the other, just like he did sitting on her bar stool the other day. "She doesn't always answer." He looked at the floor. "Lately, she's been strangely quiet."

"Maybe it's her way of nudging you to make your own decision."

"I don't know." He massaged his temples as if to ward off an impending headache, or the tension seeping into the room. "I just don't know." He stood, the period on the sentence, the transition to a new topic. "I'm starved. I was going to order a pizza before I found you doing yoga on the balcony." He enclosed the word yoga in air quotes. "Interested?"

～

DARLENE SAT at the breakfast bar, watching Fran dig around for the pizza menu. She insisted that she would like to try his favorite Hawaiian pizza. He countered that it was an acquired taste. *Pick whatever you want. Everything is good at this place*, he assured her. He acted like he didn't want to disappoint her and didn't want her to regret staying for dinner. He moved around the kitchen awkwardly, opening this drawer, closing that. She wondered if he was feeling as off-kilter and unsettled as she was. He stood, staring into a cabinet, then turned around and smiled his crooked smile.

"I know I have a menu here somewhere."

"Francisco-o-o-o." She laughed. "Let's just order the Hawaiian. I know I'll like it. It's pizza. What's not to like?" A split-second flash shot through her brain: Fran standing on the beach in a Hawaiian shirt, bare feet, khaki pants rolled up at the ankle, hair blowing in the wind, slipping a ring on her finger. Startled by what she was capable of thinking, she looked at the floor, feeling her face get hot, certain it was the color of cranberry juice.

"Let me just look in one more place. I'll be right back."

Darlene watched him disappear down the hall; the fantasy of him standing on the beach, took on a life of its own: Fran standing under a canopy, beaming as she walks toward him in a sundress, flowers in her hair. Her most prominent memory of Denny on their wedding day was of him fidgeting. Walking down the aisle on her father's arm, all she could focus on was Denny picking at his nails, looking at the floor. It wasn't until the last minute, when she was practically on top of him, that he looked up. She spent most of the day crying, getting more worked up with every perceived disaster: dinner being served almost a half-hour late; Denny's Aunt Esther complaining about where she was seated; her band of cousins bemoaning the fact that there wasn't an open bar.

"Found it!" Fran emerged, waving the pizza menu above his head like a flag. He set it in front of her, then sat down on the stool beside her. "They make their own crust." He stared at her. "Fresh." He leaned in a little closer. "Baked daily, on the premises." Fran's face was so close now, their noses almost touched. She could smell beer and chips on his breath, not at all a bad combination. He took her hands. "A little while ago, you complained about how you look." He took a deep breath. "All I see is a fun, vibrant, healthy woman."

Tears filling her eyes, she squeezed his hands. "Hawaiian." She threw her head back and laughed. "I want to try the Hawaiian pizza."

"Hawaiian, it is." He squeezed back, holding her hands tightly in his, then let them go.

Not knowing what to do next, Darlene got up and ambled to the coffee table, placing the empty beer bottles and potato chip bowl on the blue tray.

"It's okay, I got it," Fran said, gently nudging her out of the way.

"No, I insist." She grabbed the tray by its handles.

"Rose, I got it."

Just as Darlene let go of the handles, Fran banged his shin on the coffee table. He winced and swallowed a yelp, and as if a scene in a slow-motion video, the tray slipped, sending the beer bottles and chip bowl to the floor, where they bounced but did not break. The tray toppled over itself and landed, face down on the coffee table, sliding toward the edge. Wanting to be a hero, she threw her hand down to stop the tray from plummeting to the floor. The tray had other plans; it catapulted in the opposite direction, flying a few feet in the air and hitting the floor before shattering into what seemed like a million pieces. A quick glance over her shoulder at Fran's face revealed more than anything he could have said. Darlene might as well have murdered someone.

The slow-motion suddenly back to regular speed, Darlene flailed her way to the mess, and, on her hands and knees, began picking up the pieces, muttering, more to herself than to Fran. "Start with the big pieces. Let's pick up the big pieces first."

Fran bent down and put his hands under her arms, lifting her up to a standing position. For a split second, she wondered if he was going to kiss her. "I think you should go." His harsh reaction to this calamity cut her to the core. "Please. I beg you."

Ordinarily, she would argue, defend herself, remind him that it was an accident, fight for her innocence. But, tonight was the night of the opposite. She slipped out the sliding glass door without a word.

38

The song *Bicycle Race* pierced Fran's reverie. He was still sitting on the floor with the broken pieces of Sadie's tray; getting up to see who was calling felt like too much work. He decided that the phone could ring all it wanted—he simply didn't care. He stretched his legs out in front of him, stiff from sitting in the same position for so long. Several piles of blue ceramic pieces formed an arc around him. After Rose left, he got down on all fours to start picking up the remnants. Only he couldn't move, couldn't seem to lift his hands off the floor to move toward the mess. He had no idea how long he had been paralyzed like that. His body eventually found itself, and, as Rose had suggested, he started with the big pieces, arranging them by size until a mound had formed. The smaller pieces were harder to deal with; he pricked himself on one, derailing his efforts for more long minutes while he sucked blood out of his fingertip.

Bicycle, bicycle, I want to ride my bicycle, bicycle. Fran's phone rang again, and instead of getting up, he leaned forward to touch his fingers to his toes, wincing in pain as his hamstrings screamed four-letter words. He scooted across the floor on his butt toward the couch and leaned against it, letting his legs splay haphazardly in front of him. He looked around the room that Sadie had decorated and wondered if he should move back to Reston. He could rent out this place, sell the deli, and go back to being bicycle Fran, or better yet, go back to working full time.

The urge to pee hit him like a bolt out of the blue. His doctor had warned him about holding his bladder for long periods. Bad for his already compromised kidneys. He took his time standing, and when he was finally upright, made a beeline to the bathroom. A minute later and feeling twenty pounds lighter, he found himself dropping pieces of blue ceramic into a plastic bag. He didn't know what he intended to do with it, he simply knew that he couldn't throw it away. Throwing Sadie's tray in the garbage, no matter how little it resembled the original, made him feel like he was throwing away a part of her. If she touched it, he couldn't bring himself to get rid of it. Jackie had asked if she could have her mother's favorite scarf; he felt sorry for her and let her take it, immediately regretting it. After that, he vowed never purge Sadie's closet, her dresser drawers, or any of the nooks and crannies that contained proof of her life.

He swept the pieces that were too small to save into a dustpan and carried it out onto the balcony. The cold made him shudder as he walked down the steps and shook the dust from Sadie's tray into the sand. He couldn't even bring himself to throw that in the garbage.

The light was on in Rose's living room—he could see it through the slats in the vertical blinds—and for half a second, he had the urge to talk to her. He stood at the top of the steps, staring at her sliding glass door, wondering what she was doing. He looked at his watch— almost eleven. If she were sane, she would be sleeping.

He sat at the breakfast bar, starving. He was too tired to eat and too weary to climb the stairs to the bedroom. His legs were too leaden to even shuffle to the couch. He listened over and over to Rose's voice-mail. *I am so sorry about the accident. I take full responsibility and will*

pay you whatever it's worth. Please tell me, and I'll drop the money off tomorrow. How could he put a price tag on such a thing? How could he assign value to something priceless? How? He didn't want Rose's money. Right now, he just wanted her to leave him alone.

He opened the plastic bag and extracted a small piece of the tray. He studied it, spinning it and viewing it from various angles. If he tilted it a little bit to the left, it looked like a bluebird. He pulled out a small piece of sandpaper from his junk drawer and carried it back to the counter, eyeing the bag of chocolates. He slammed the cabinet door shut so he wouldn't have to look at it; he didn't want anything reminding him of Rose tonight. Dammit. He put his head in his hands, releasing the sandpaper and letting it flutter to the floor. How many times tonight had he wanted to kiss her? How many? He had been hopelessly caught up in her laughter—it had taken every ounce of his strength not to kiss her. Sadie's tray crash-landing on the floor might as well have been a bucket of ice tossed over his head. It instantly brought him back to reality, preventing him from doing something he knew he would later regret. He took a deep breath, picked up the sandpaper, and rubbed it back and forth over the rough edges of the bird. Sanding, sanding, sanding. He stopped only when his fingers were raw.

"What are you doing, you big bonehead?" Fran opened his hand, finally at ease, and allowed himself to exhale. He wondered if Sadie had witnessed the fiasco.

"I'm so sorry, babe. I broke your tray." He could not stop the tears. He set the bird, which now looked more like a blob than a bird—his frantic sanding reduced what would have been the beak to a nub— on the counter. It was no use. A bird or a turtle or a frog. None of it would replace the tray that Sadie had so lovingly and playfully made. Her love for him had been visible in the tray. He could look at the tray and see the story of their life written on it, without words. A sign- post in time. An anchor in a rough sea. He would never forgive himself for his carelessness, his utter disregard for his vow to love only Sadie.

"You didn't break it." She stood in front of him, hands on her hips.

"I know." He wiped his eyes with the back of his hand. "I know. I'm sorry. I shouldn't have invited over."

"What would you have done instead, just taken the two beers she gave you and enjoyed them by yourself?" Sadie's eyes seemed changed, different. Vacant and hollow.

"I don't know." Fran panicked. "I'm so sorry, babe."

"You really are a big bonehead." Her eyes suddenly filled with light and mischief; she looked like she might laugh. "You didn't see me. That's how I knew. You didn't see me."

"That's how you knew what?" Fran didn't understand. *What are you talking about*, he was about to say, when it became clear, like a dimmer switch gradually turning up the brightness of an overhead light. "You were here." Not a question, but a statement. For the two years since she died, he lived for her visits. Anticipated them. Relished them. Tonight, when Rose was here, he didn't look for Sadie. He had long moments when he didn't even think about her. He felt flushed, like he could pass out, and hung his head between his knees. When he regained composure and looked back up, his eyes were wet.

"Ding. Ding. Ding." Sadie clapped.

Fran took a deep breath, thinking of Rose and her silly guessing game. "You were here." He felt like he had been caught cheating. But that was just it, he would never cheat on Sadie. Never. "I haven't done anything with Rose."

"But you want to."

Fran held out his hands—stop sign style.

"Hear me out," Sadie said. "I know you. I know all your little looks, all your silly facial expressions, the way your tone changes when you're trying to impress."

"I'm not trying to impress anyone, and I can't—"

"I'm not finished." Sadie raised an eyebrow. "I broke the tray."

Fran covered his ears. He didn't want to hear this. Wasn't ready to listen. Sadie gently took his hands in her own and removed them from his ears. "Why?" It was the only word Fran could get his lips to form. "Why?"

"Because you're a bonehead." She narrowed her eyes. "I tried to trip her, but she was too quick, so when she picked up the tray, and then you butted in to take it from her, well, I got in the middle and shoved it."

"You're joking."

She jutted her chin toward him. "This is no joke." She sighed. "I've been trying to get your attention for a while now. Breaking that damned tray was an opportunity I couldn't pass up." She smiled but looked like she might cry. "I'm leaving you, Franny." She looked into his eyes. "Do you hear me? I'm leaving you."

Fran could barely hear her through his sobbing. He shook his head and tried to take her hands, but his fingers slipped right through them. "I don't know how to live without you."

"You lived without me for forty-five years before we met." She looked around the room. "You'll be okay. It's time."

"I promised to always love you."

"Till death," she reminded him.

"I wasn't expecting death."

"Neither was I."

"What about the other day?" Fran pleaded with his eyes. "You didn't want me wearing the George Clooney shirt for anyone but you."

"Burn the damned thing." She laughed. "Or donate it." She grew serious. "That shirt could be ours and ours alone." She sighed. "Apart from that, you have a lot of life to live, a lot of love in you. I haven't seen you look at anyone the way you looked at her tonight." She looked up at the ceiling, then looked at him, smiling. "Except me. You looked at me that way."

"I'll always look at you that way.

"Promise me you won't try to glue that silly tray back together." Sadie seemed intent on changing the subject, lightening the mood. "If you must, just keep one piece. Keep that blob you were sanding. It kind of looks like a heart. Keep it in a drawer or on a shelf or wherever. Think of me when you look at it. Just remember, it isn't me. Keep my memory in your heart, but for God's sake, Franny, move on already. Be with people who make you laugh. She makes you laugh. Don't be a bonehead."

Be with people who make you laugh. Fran remembered that from the chocolate wrapper. Sadie took his hand and led him to the couch where they curled up in each other arms, and Fran rested for the first time in what seemed like a very long time.

Darlene stared at the coffee maker, trying to forget last night's fiasco. She couldn't shake the look of pure devastation on Fran's face when she broke his tray. The mishap had implications beyond anything she could comprehend. Like her father swatting her butt (hard!) when she carelessly broke her mother's favorite teacup. As if a three-year-old could be held accountable, could possibly understand the value—both monetary and sentimental—of an object. As if she could have understood the concept of an heirloom—a big word thrown around for days after the incident—and that it didn't have anything to do with an ear.

The slow drip of the coffee finally increased; a sound as distinct as raindrops on a metal roof. She closed her eyes and took in the smoky smell of the coffee, her mind drifting to Fran's description of her wort smelling like buttery toast. She wished she knew what she did wrong, why the visceral reaction to what looked like someone's half-baked ceramics project. She drew in a sudden breath. Of course. The tray was more than a tray to Fran. Had to be. Why else would someone display and use something so ugly? He never answered his phone last night, never responded to her voicemail offering to pay. The item she broke may not have been an ear-loom, but, like her mother's teacup, it held intangible value.

Darlene bolted to the sliding glass door and stepped out. Leaning over the rail, she noted with disappointment that Fran's blinds were closed. It was still early, barely past sunrise. She would knock on his door later and apologize for being such a klutz. She slipped back into the house and stood frozen at the precipice between the living room and kitchen.

"What the hell are you doing here?" She narrowed her eyes, rubbed them, then, determining that she wasn't hallucinating, raised her voice. "What are you doing here?"

Denny stood in the kitchen, stirring his coffee, making a show of clanking the spoon against the mug, something that grated on her like fingernails on a chalkboard. He teased her about it when they were dating, and later, did it only to annoy her. She bit her tongue and struggled to keep her face neutral—any hint of annoyance on her face or in her tone would simply egg him on. She did not want to give him the satisfaction.

"I heard that the show is doing the update shoot today." He set the spoon down directly on the counter—another habit that drove her crazy—and brought the mug up to his lips. "I was in town. Wouldn't miss it for the world."

Gloria, from the show, had called yesterday to say they wanted to come by and shoot the update segment tomorrow; Darlene had said *sure, why not*? She intended to mention it to Fran last night, thinking it might be fun to have him drop by the 'new house' for a glass of wine or a beer. But she got lost in the moment, feeling that something was developing between them, and it slipped her mind. And then the fiasco with the tray. And now Denny in her kitchen. She wanted to scream.

"By the way," he said, walking toward her. "I noticed you pulled out all the ivy at home." He glared at her. Darlene took a step backward, determined not to let him see how upset she was. "You can't just do things like that. I'm a co-owner of that house." He stepped into the living room, leaving his coffee mug on the counter, and waved his arms around, twirling on his heel. "I own this one too."

"Your name is on the deed." she corrected.

"Semantics, Dar, semantics. Plus, you'll never be able to pay the mortgage on your own, without my help."

"I'll make it work. Even if I have to take a second job. Look, Denny, the money from my grandmother's estate paid the down payment. You know that. Essentially, I bought this condo. If it weren't for Bubbe's money, there would be no beach condo." She took a deep breath. "I told you I'd be here for the next couple of weeks."

He held up his hands in the act of surrender. "I know, I know. I'm not here to infringe."

"You infringed last weekend when you brought your girlfriend here, and you're infringing now." She raised her eyebrow. "By the way, my lawyer said he wants to help me sue my cheating husband."

"Mea culpa." He made a peace sign with his fingers—like Richard Nixon—as if to say *I am not a crook.*

"What were you thinking?" All resolve to hold in her anger and upset exploded, shrapnel flying in every direction. His apology, acknowledgment, or whatever it was opened the floodgates of her rage. "How could you bring her here? How could you defile our bed?"

He opened his mouth to speak but didn't say anything. Darlene shook her head and sunk down into the couch cushions, weary. Denny disappeared into the kitchen, then returned and handed her a cup of coffee. He made it the way he knew she liked it—just enough cream to lighten it to the color of sand. She sipped it, infuriated that he could be such an ass, and yet, hand her a cup of coffee the way he had handed her one almost every morning for nearly twenty-five years. She thought of her sister, then, unsure exactly why Rachel popped into her mind. Was it true, what her mother had said? That Rachel had been raped? That Rachel has scars she never shared?

"I know we're supposed to have Thanksgiving with Shelly," Darlene said, looking at her watch. It was barely dawn in San Francisco; she would have to wait a few hours to call. "I'm considering flying to San Francisco. I'm going to ask Shelly to change her flight and meet me there."

Denny slumped in the chair, kitty-corner to the couch. She couldn't help remembering that the furniture in Fran's living room was similarly configured. "To see Rachel? You hate her." He shook his head. "What about me? I want to spend time with Shelly too. We agreed we'd tell her, you know, about us."

"We can do that later." She counted on her fingers. How about the three of us get together when Shelly comes home for winter break."

"Remi left her husband, for good this time," he said, ignoring her suggestion and looking at his feet.

"Am I supposed to congratulate you?"

He took a deep breath and shrugged. "New beginnings?"

"What about the baby?"

"We'll share custody with the dad."

Darlene couldn't believe it. Her anger surged to the surface anew. He was replacing her with not just Remi, but with a whole new family. "Denny, you're fifty-two! Do you really want to be a seventy-year-old father at this kid's high school graduation?"

"Stepfather."

"Dammit, Denny. You know what I mean." She stared at him, unbelieving. How had this happened? Where had she been for the past six months? "Where will you live?" She felt herself calming down, becoming businesslike.

"We're looking at houses, believe it or not."

"Before we're even divorced?"

"I'll buy it first, then add her name later."

"Speaking of houses. I've contacted a realtor about ours." She waited for a response. Or for him to get angry. But he just sat there, looking at his shoes. "We agreed to do it, but never sat down to put together a timeline." She touched his arm. "Denny, it's time."

"I know." He finally looked up, moving his arm out from under her hand.

"We need to talk about the condo, too." She looked at him, hard. "I want you to think, seriously think, about not fighting me on this."

She feared she wasn't doing a stellar job of keeping the desperation out of her voice. "This is my happy place. This is a place I could come to heal. Start over. I don't know what's going to happen to me career-wise. It would mean a lot to me if you'd just let me have your name removed from the deed."

"I might want to use it once or twice over Christmas break. I'm considering spending a few days out here with Remi, but after that, we'll talk."

"Denny, look, there's nothing to talk about. It was my money that enabled us to buy this place." She hardened. "I don't want her in here. Ever."

"Look, Dar, I'm telling you that I might want to use the condo." He stood up, then sat back down.

She crossed her arms over her chest. "No! I will not agree to that." She glared at him. "If that bitch wants to come to the beach, you two can just rent a place." She took a deep breath in an attempt to reign in her emotions.

Apparently finished with this conversation, Denny got up, did the Richard Nixon peace sign impersonation again, and got himself another cup of coffee. "What time are they coming, anyway?"

"They should be here any minute." She opened the refrigerator and pulled out a tray of cut fruit and pastries. "I guess we could pretend to be eating breakfast in our new beach house."

"Got any OJ?" He reached around her and opened the cupboard.

"Wait, what?" She laughed. "Mimosas?"

"Fake ones," he said, pulling out two champagne flutes.

"How will we explain a divorcing couple sharing breakfast and drinking mimosas?" She laughed harder, shaking her head, then looked at her watch. Still too early to call her sister, so she texted her instead: Change of plans. I'm coming your way for Thanksgiving. Maybe Shelly, too, but probably just me. That is, if you'll have me.

40

Fran's foot hit the floor with a thud. He lifted his head, confused, slowing coming to, wondering how long he had been asleep. He untangled his gangly limbs until he was sitting upright on the couch, carefully stomping the floor with the fallen foot, bracing himself for the pain of it coming back to life. Sure enough, within seconds, his foot felt ten times its size. The pins and needles would be next. Damn. Here they are. He stood up and stomped with more fervor, thankful that he didn't have a neighbor below him. Neighbor. Rose. He took a deep breath and sank backward into the couch, replaying the night's events.

"Sadie?" He quickly scanned the room. "Babe?" He remembered snuggling with her on the couch. Or was it a dream he remembered? No. It could not have been a dream. Sadie had been there, her head nestled in the crook of his arm—her favorite position when they used to watch movies together. It always left his shoulder either sore or numb, depending on the precise location of her head. He rubbed his left shoulder, then his right. No pain, no tenderness. Did that mean he imagined her visit last night? Not necessarily. He supposed the weight of her head was different in the state she was in. Weightless. She was here, he just knew it. He could still feel her in the air.

More alert and awake by the second, Fran's stomach demanded to be fed now. It was pitch-black outside; the clock on the microwave told him that dawn was still a few hours away. His stomach threatened war if he dared walk out of the kitchen without eating. He patted his belly. *Okay, okay, calm down.* He pulled a bowl of grapes out of the fridge and leaned against the counter, popping them into his mouth like candy. After a few handfuls, he pushed the bowl away, knowing that he would likely have the runs later if he kept this up. He pulled out a carton of eggs. Might as well have bacon too. He grabbed an unopened package and checked the date: excellent, four days left before it turns into a pumpkin. He opted for a large glass of cranberry juice instead of coffee.

The condo was soon filled with one of the most primal smells in the world—bacon sizzling in its own fat. His mouth watered as he stood at the stove and scrambled eggs, alternately flipping bacon and shoving bread into the toaster. He inhaled the aroma, momentarily forgetting Rose, Sadie, the tray, and everything else. He laid the bacon on paper towels and ate a slice in two big bites. A tornado could blow the house away, as long as it didn't interfere with his bacon.

He sat at the breakfast bar and ate with reckless abandon, pausing just long enough between bites to force cranberry juice down his throat. Finally sated, he leaned back in his chair, wanting, more than anything, to knock on Rose's door and apologize for how poorly he behaved last night. He closed his eyes and tried to will Sadie into the room, but he knew it was no use. He felt her, but this time, it wasn't her presence, but more like a whisper in his ear, her words from last night a refrain he couldn't shake. *I'm leaving you, Franny. Keep my memory in your heart, but for God's sake, Franny, move on already. Be with people who make you laugh. She makes you laugh. Don't be a bonehead.*

"Be with people who make you laugh," Fran repeated, out loud. Rose makes him laugh. He got up and fished the chocolates out of the cupboard and carried them to the living room, shaking the bag like a cup of dice before letting the foil-wrapped squares tumble out and slide across the coffee table. He counted thirty-four, then shook out another few, not stopping until he got to fifty. Fifty chocolates for Rose's fiftieth birthday. He had an idea. He got up and rummaged through the junk drawer until he found what he was looking for—a pad of tiny Post-It notes. He fanned them with his thumb, hoping there were at least fifty, then grabbed a pen and an envelope from his mail pile.

First, he numbered one through fifty on the back of the envelope. Then, he jotted down ideas for activities that he and Rose could do together—some corny things, some serious things, some quirky things, some fun things. Number 9: Find a playground and swing on the swings. Number 14: Binge watch the Netflix show of Rose's choice. Number 15: Binge watch the Netflix show of Fran's choice. Number 20: Create a new beer recipe together. Number 27: Discuss our favorite books. Number 32: Share a bucket of Thrasher's Boardwalk Fries. Number 38: Teach Rose about the Tour de France. Number 40: Watch a foreign film. Number 47: Walk on the beach. Number 48: Talk about our childhoods. Fifty things. It could take a lifetime to do them all. He then transcribed them—one on each Post-It note—and folded the Post-It notes in half.

Fran stretched and wiggled his fingers, numb after unwrapping fifty pieces of chocolate. One-by-one, he pressed a single note into each wrapper, placing a piece of chocolate on top, then rewrapping. Finally finished, he took a deep breath and stood, satisfied with his creativity.

HE DIDN'T CARE what he looked like. He didn't care that he hadn't showered or that his clothes were a wrinkled mess from having slept twisted like a pretzel on the couch. He didn't care that the smell of bacon—thanks to the lousy vent system in the condo—would be on his skin and in his hair for the next three days. Nor did he care that he hadn't brushed his teeth after breakfast. And he especially didn't care that he had hair like a mad scientist. None of it mattered.

He screwed the lid onto a large mason jar and held it out in front of him. All fifty pieces of chocolate inside like a complicated puzzle. Something was missing, though. Ah yes, a ribbon. He couldn't present Rose with a birthday gift without some sort of bow. He scoured the condo until he found something suitable—a random shoelace from an old pair of running shoes—and held it against the jar. The green and blue stripes clashed with the red chocolate wrappers. He shrugged. So, what? He tied it around the top of the jar, satisfied.

The jar tucked under his arm, Fran opened the sliding glass door and stepped out onto his balcony. The sun had risen and was announcing full-blown morning. He wasn't sure if Rose would be up yet and would use her blinds being either open or closed as his permission to knock. Not wanting to risk dropping the jar, he took the safe route, down his steps, left turn at the bottom, and up Rose's steps. He couldn't stop smiling, feeling a school-boy giddiness that he hadn't felt in years.

He took two long strides toward her sliding glass door, happy to see that the blinds were, indeed, open. He took a deep breath and extended his hand, stopping it mid-air, thanking God that he had seen what was unfolding in the condo before his knuckles hit the glass. He skirted sideways and peered inside to get a better look. Rose and Denny on the couch, Rose's hand on Denny's arm.

Fran quietly turned away, then bolted back down the steps, taking them two at a time, wondering how he could have been so stupid. He tripped on the bottom step, stumbling in the sand. In his scramble to pick himself up, he let the jar slip out from under his arm. It bounced, then landed on its side. He looked at it, half-buried in the sand, and crouched down to retrieve it. If he could bring himself to be angry with Sadie, he would. This was her idea, she pushed him in this direction. *Oh, Sadie.* It was so much easier to live an uncomplicated life, holding onto her, living for her visits, relishing their conversations, never letting go.

He took a deep breath and left the jar lying in the sand, then reconsidered and flipped it into the beach grass with his foot. He climbed his steps and slumped down in his chair, hugging his chest against the cold, staring blankly at the ocean. It was only then that he realized he forgot to bring Sadie her coffee, forgot to sit with her to watch the sun come up.

41

The heart-shaped blob rattled around the cup holder in Fran's Jeep. He rolled up to a red light and picked the remnant of Sadie's tray up and held it toward the sun. A blue heart. How fitting. He dropped it back into the cup holder and a minute later, found himself holding it between his fingers as he drove.

Seeing Rose and Denny together, sitting so cozily close to each other, had set off a rush of adrenaline that made it difficult for him to sit still. His pity party on the balcony reminded him that he needed to keep moving. He needed to propel himself into some sort of action; mundane tasks to occupy his mind. He never finished cleaning up the residue from the broken tray and figured he would start there. He revved up his Shop-Vac, then sucked up every square inch of debris from the living room floor. He ended up sucking up a lot of dust that he never noticed before. Might as well hit the stairs too, all the little dust bunnies in the corners, doomed. Up the stairs to the master bedroom, down the stairs to the first floor. And when he put the Shop-Vac away, he stood in the center of the first floor and stared at his and Sadie's bikes, dusty from years of dormancy.

"What do you say, Sadie?" He looked around the room as if to find her dancing a jig. "Should I take Mertz out for a spin?" He ran his finger over the bike's tire, then spun it like a boardwalk prize wheel. He squeezed one tire, then the other, amazed that they weren't completely flat. "McGillicuddy will have a hissy fit if I leave her behind." He turned over a Lowe's five-gallon bucket and sat down and gazed at the two bikes, named after characters from *I Love Lucy*, Sadie's favorite show. One Christmas, he bought her an *I Love Lucy* DVD box set. All one hundred and eighty-one episodes, plus the thirteen *Lucy-Desi Comedy Hour* episodes. "Sadie?" He looked around the room, then stood. Of course, she wouldn't answer. *I'm leaving you, Franny. Do you hear me? I'm leaving you.* Sadie's words from last night, spoken harshly but from a place of love. Logically, he knew this, but his heart didn't want to absorb it. Sadie had been wrong about Rose. Of that much, he was sure.

FRAN PULLED into the parking lot at Assateague Island National Seashore, suddenly questioning his impulsive decision to get on his bike after all these years. The weather app on his phone reminded him it was only forty-seven degrees outside. Damn cold even when he was cycling almost daily, commuting to work on two wheels instead of four, and was able to gradually acclimate. Today was more like plunging into the ocean in winter. He was going to freeze his ass off.

He lifted Mertz off the bike rack and rolled him over to the bathroom facility, leaning him against the wall. He slipped off his docksiders and slipped on his bike shoes, then wiggled his way into a lightweight wool turtleneck that had somehow shrunk over the years. He put on his heaviest bike jacket, zipping it all the way up to his chin. Then the balaclava that had taken him almost a half hour to locate. Finally, his helmet and gloves.

He straddled the bike, clipped his left foot into the pedal, then pushed off and clipped in his right foot. His legs moved. The wheels turned. The pavement grew blurry. The trees whooshed by and the icy sea breeze reached its tentacles under his sunglasses, making his eyes water. He blinked and saw Sadie riding next to him, looking peaceful and content despite the cold.

THE ODOMETER BATTERY died after three hours; Fran had no concept of how far he had ridden. He never intended to ride that long, but didn't want to go home, didn't want to potentially face Rose and Denny. In a way, it was like losing Sadie all over again. As long as he was on his bike—the cold air keeping him on high alert, the landscape stretching out before him—he didn't have to think about anything else.

By the time he dragged his ass back to the parking lot, he couldn't feel his feet. He pedaled up to his Jeep; holding onto the door handle for leverage, he carefully unclipped. Once his right foot was safely planted on the ground, he unclipped his left. He rubbed his hands together, cold despite the fleece-lined biking gloves, a Christmas gift from Sadie, oh, maybe ten years ago. Wearing them was like holding her hands. He sat down on the curb and released his feet from the confining bike shoes. He massaged his toes, scolding himself for not wearing heavier socks. He took a few sips of water, then started his Jeep, which was, thankfully, toasty warm from sitting in the sun. He slipped in, curling up in his seat like a cat maximizing a tiny patch of light.

"Oh, no! Ray!" He pulled his gloves off and wiggled his fingers, still somewhat numb from the cold. He reached into his jacket pocket and pulled out his phone and half of a peanut butter and jelly sandwich. He pressed the button for Laurie but got her voicemail.

"It's me. I need a favor, please. Could you pop over today and feed the cat? I'll try you again later." He put the phone down and devoured the sandwich, chasing it with the little bit of water left in his water bottle. He had thrown an overnight bag in the Jeep, just in case—in case of what, he wasn't sure. He had enough insight to realize he wouldn't want to go back to the condo. And he was right. For the past few months he had been toying with the idea of moving back to

Reston, maybe buying a condo near the Town Center. Laurie wasn't thrilled about the prospect of him moving, but grudgingly sent him real estate listings.

He dug through the glove compartment in search of more snacks —an emergency bag of pretzels, perhaps? No such luck. The only thing he came up with was a candy cane from last Christmas. He tore the wrapper off and bit into the sticky, minty delight. As he sat enjoying this long-forgotten treat, he tapped the realtor app on his phone and scrolled through some of the listings Laurie had earmarked for him. Okay, then. He would drive to Reston this afternoon. No need to go home first. He reached behind him and grabbed his bag, then went into the bathroom facility to change.

42

———

Darlene kept her eye on Denny, who was out on the balcony on his phone—probably talking to Remi—while Gloria and Jesse stood in the living room. They were discussing what kinds of scenes to shoot for the update segment. She considered asking Fran to pop over, vacillating between wanting to get past the awkwardness of last night and wanting to hide from it forever. An hour ago, in a moment of boldness, she went over and knocked on his sliding glass door. A futile attempt. The minute she got close enough to see inside, it was clear Fran wasn't home. A half-hour after that, she walked downstairs and out the front door. His Jeep was gone, confirming what she already knew. And now, with the filming about to begin, she called Laurie. She wasn't sure what she wanted from her; a body in the house so she didn't look destitute and friendless, or a link to Fran. The call rolled straight to voicemail. She hung up without leaving a message.

"*Beach Kiss*, by Belinda Moo." Jesse's voice rang through the condo. Darlene looked up and saw him flipping through her mother's book. "Sounds steamy." He put the book down and gave Darlene a little wink.

"It's funny you should pick that book up." She joined him in the living room. "My mother wrote it."

"No!" Jesse covered his mouth. "Really?"

"Really."

"The wife of your father, the hater of everything in House Two?" He laughed.

"The one and only."

"Belinda Moo." He picked the book up and flipped it over to the back cover. "No author picture."

"It's a pen name. Apparently, it was the only way my father would allow her to publish it. No picture."

"Fascinating." He stood up straight and clapped his hands, his interest in the book suddenly gone. "Let's get this show on the road." He looked at Darlene. "I have a brilliant idea. I'm a genius, really." He paced in front of the couch. "Gloria, come listen to this." He stood in the middle of the living room, holding out his cell phone, tapping the screen. "FaceTime. Darlene, I'd like to FaceTime with your father. You can give him a virtual tour of the house you picked out."

Darlene shrugged and placed the call. "Hello?" Sid yelled into the phone, the top corner of his forehead taking up the entire screen. "Hello? Who is this?"

"Dad, look at your phone."

"Rachel?"

"No, it's your other daughter." Darlene looked at Jesse, imagining him wishing he never suggested a FaceTime session with Sid. "Dad, this is a video call."

"A what?"

"A video call." She emphasized the word video. "You know, so we could see each other." Her father's forehead grew bigger. "Take the phone away from your ear."

"What do you mean?"

"Just look at the phone." His face came into view, then shot back to his forehead. "Where's Mom? Maybe she can help you."

"Connie!" Sid put the phone down, indicated by the ceiling

Darlene was now looking at. She noticed a cobweb. "I think she's in the shower." The top corner of his forehead again.

"Dad, listen to me." She took a deep breath. "Do exactly as I say." She rolled her eyes.

"Did I tell you that your mother saw a shooting star last night?"

"Dad!" Darlene watched Jesse twirl his finger, mouthing *let's go*. "You can tell me about the shooting star later. For now, please take the phone away from your ear."

"If I do that, how will I hear you."

"Trust me, it won't be a problem."

"Huh?"

"Dad. Please take the phone away from your ear. Hold it out in front of you." Finally, Sid's face. He was sitting in the kitchen, a cup of coffee in one hand, a bagel bag and a block of cream cheese on the counter behind him. "There you are!"

"I see you!" He smiled big, revealing several poppy seeds wedged between his two front teeth. "I see you! I wish your mother were here. She'd get a kick out of this." He put his coffee down. "I'll get her."

"No! Dad, let her enjoy her shower." She walked the phone over to Jesse and pointed it toward him. "The film crew is here doing the update segment for the show. Remember Jesse?"

Jesse waved at the phone. "I want to get a few shots of you talking to your daughter."

"I'm already talking to her."

"I know you are, Dr. Bloom, but I want to film you and your daughter talking about the house."

"What house?"

"The beach house your daughter selected."

"But she didn't select a house, she already has a house."

"Dad, we're pretending, remember?" She forced a smile and tilted the phone away from Jesse. "We just need to pretend I'm showing you the house, now that we've moved in."

"You moved in last year, bubbeleh."

"Ugh. Dad, when I say something about the house, just ooh and aah, okay? Can you do that?"

"Here's your mother." Darlene watched as he turned away from the phone. "Connie! Your daughter is on the phone."

"Rachel?"

Of course, Rachel. Always the default position. Darlene, still an afterthought. "No, Mom," she yelled into the phone. "It's your other daughter."

"Darlene! I saw a shooting star last night."

"Mom, can you see me?" She held the phone in front of her face.

"Yes, yes."

"We're filming the segment when they show the people in the new house having a drink or hanging curtains or some other such thing."

"Did you get new curtains?"

"No, Mom. I did not get new curtains." Darlene's patience was wearing thin. How could her mother write and publish a book, yet be so dense about certain things? So dense. She closed her eyes and counted to ten, then handed the phone to Jesse.

"Mrs. Bloom? I'm Jesse, the cameraman. We need to wrap this up." He fingered the book that was on the end table next to him. "Congratulations on your book, by the way. Your daughter is immensely proud of you."

"You told me nobody would know it's you," Sid interrupted, looking pointedly at his wife. Darlene walked away, utterly frustrated, then turned and came back.

"Dad, stop. Just stop. You should be proud."

"I'm going upstairs." He handed the phone to his wife. "Connie, you talk to them."

"Dad, no." She softened her tone. "It would be great to have you and mom see the house with me. Remember, we're just pretending. Pretend I just moved in, and you're seeing it for the first time." She handed the phone back to Jesse.

"Dr. Bloom, Mrs. Bloom." He took a deep breath. "Just follow your daughter's lead. If she asks you a question, just answer it. I'll give you a minute or two to get in character. Pretend you're actors in a movie.

Your daughter just bought a beach house. You're seeing it for the first time. Got it?"

"Got it," they both said.

Jesse handed the phone back to Darlene, then opened the sliding glass door and yelled to Gloria and Denny. "I'm doing a quick shoot with Darlene's parents on FaceTime. I'm going to have her walk out onto the balcony. I'll need the two of you to give me space. I don't want you in this shot. Give me ten minutes tops." He came back in, hoisted his camera onto his shoulder, and nodded at Darlene. "Camera rolling!"

Darlene walked around the house with her phone, her parents making enthusiastic remarks. "And this is where you'll stay when you come to visit." She panned her phone around the guest suite. "See, it's plenty big, and you'll have your own bathroom."

"When are you going to show us the beach?"

"I'll take you there now." Darlene walked down the stairs, Jesse trailing behind her, getting a front-row view of her parents on the screen. She opened the sliding glass door, just as Denny and Gloria were walking in.

"Denny?" Sid looked at his wife, who shrugged. "What are you doing here? I thought you were—"

"Getting divorced?" Denny made a face into the phone. "Yes, we're getting divorced."

"Is that your girlfriend?" Sid pointed at Gloria. "She looks too old for you."

"Dad!" Darlene looked at Gloria. "I'm sorry. His vision is impaired. You're not too old for Denny." She turned back to the phone. "Gloria is the production manager. She's not Denny's girlfriend."

"So, you told them about Remi?"

"It's none of your business what I told them." Whatever goodwill she felt toward Denny vanished. "What's the matter with you? Why are you acting like this?"

"Acting like what?"

"Cut!" Jesse let the camera drop off his shoulder and set it down on the couch, glaring at Denny. "Mr. Feldman go sit in the kitchen, please. I don't want to hear a peep out of you until I'm ready for you."

"How will I know when you're—"

"Not a peep!" He held a finger to his lips and slowly backed out of the kitchen.

"Why is Denny there, bubbeleh?"

"Dad, he just showed up, out of the blue." Darlene lowered her voice. "We talked earlier. I think he's going to let me remove him from the condo deed. I want to keep it."

"What about the big house?"

"We're selling that."

"Where will you live?"

"Here." She felt clarity that she had not felt since she lost her job. "I'll live here." She threw her head back and laughed. "Yes, I'll live here."

"What about work?"

"What about it?" She shook her head. "I'm probably looking at changing careers anyway."

"Can we please save the career counseling and life goals discussion for another time?" Jesse tapped on his watch. "Please?" He stood, hands on his hips, glaring at Darlene.

"This was your idea." She glared right back at him.

"Touché. Let's get a shot out on the balcony, then we'll say goodbye to your lovely parents."

Darlene walked outside, carrying her parents like some sort of shrunken action figures. *Pain in the Ass Parents Play Set. For kids age fifty and above.*

"And this is why we chose this condo." She held the phone in front of her and panned the horizon, big waves crashing in the November wind.

"It looks cold," her mother said.

"It's freezing. But I love it. The beach is my happy place."

"We know, bubbeleh. It always has been."

"Can't wait for you to see it."

"Wait a minute, my phone is ringing," her mother said, pulling her phone out of the pocket on her cardigan.

"Don't answer it," her father scolded.

"It's Rachel." Her mother held her phone to the camera as if Darlene didn't believe her that it was Rachel. She opened the phone. "Rachel, we're on FaceTime with your sister. We're filming the beach house show they went on...What? She is? Wonderful!" She turned back to the camera. "Darlene, why didn't you tell us you're coming for Thanksgiving?"

"Because I made the decision, oh, an hour ago?" She couldn't believe she was having this conversation yet felt powerless to make it stop.

"I saw a shooting star last night," her mother said into the phone that held Rachel. "You know, that's a good sign, a good omen. Maybe your new beau will be the one."

"Don't listen to her, Rachel," Darlene yelled into the phone. She didn't care whether or not her voice could be heard, twice removed. "She saw a shooting star two days before my wedding. And look at me now!"

On the small screen, Darlene watched her parents talk to Rachel, utterly oblivious to the fact that she was still standing on the balcony, Jesse's camera still rolling. She signaled for him to cut. "Bye Mom, bye, Dad." They looked up and waved, then went right back to Rachel. She stabbed at the phone, missing the target several times before the screen finally went blank, her parents disappearing back into their little corner of the world. She jammed the phone in her back pocket and stomped into the house.

DARLENE SAT down at the breakfast bar, while Jesse conferred with Gloria outside. Denny was sitting on the arm of the couch, scrolling through his phone. He was so focused on whatever happened to be on the screen that he didn't see her walk in. Or if he did, he simply ignored her. She stared at the plate she made earlier and mindlessly picked up a cinnamon scone and held it to her nose. The spicy-sweet smell of the cinnamon produced an instantaneous reaction—her mouth filled with saliva. She couldn't help herself, and took a large bite, oblivious to the healthier options within reach. Plump, red strawberries, blueberries the size of marbles, and chunks of fresh pineapple. Beautiful to look at, scrumptious to eat, yet none of it compared to the soft scone that was melting in her mouth. She poured herself a cup of coffee and enjoyed the pure bliss of the bitter coffee paired with the sweet scone.

"Denny?" She ran her hand across the blue tiles that made up the countertop. She liked them, found them fun, bright, and quirky. But now she noticed the dinge in some parts of the grout. She bent her head toward the grout to get a closer look. Black and dark gray cells, tiny on their own, but combined made the grout appear dirty. Maybe down the road, she would replace the tiles with something sleek and neutral, something like the countertops in Fran's house. She lifted her head and looked at Denny; he was still fixated on his phone. She finished the rest of the scone, chased it with a mouthful of coffee, wiped the crumbs and coffee residue off her lips with a napkin, then crumbled the napkin and tossed it at her soon to be ex-husband. To her surprise, she hit him square in the middle of his forehead. He looked up, startled.

"What the hell?" He threw the napkin back at her, but she ducked, and it hit the floor instead of its intended target.

"I'm trying to talk to you, and you're scrolling through that phone like it's a life force."

"Stop nagging." He sighed and shook his head. "You're not the boss of me anymore."

"Was I ever?"

"Sometimes, I think you wanted to be."

"I wanted you to love me." A lump of emotion threatened to pop out of her mouth. She swallowed it, surprised at how raw this still felt. She had moments when she thought her heart was as hard as it could possibly be toward him. Maybe it was as simple as too much change. Her job loss, the prospect of selling their home—the one they raised their daughter in. She picked up another scone—this one cranberry-orange—and held it up to her mouth to take a bite. *Nope. Not doing it. Not letting Denny start me on an emotional eating binge.* She put the scone back on the plate and picked up a strawberry instead. She popped it in her mouth. Blech. Dry. Sour. Oh well, what did she expect in November?

Denny put his phone down and came over to the counter, plopping himself down on the other stool. He reached over and tried to lift her face with his finger, but she tensed her neck and pressed down with her chin. She didn't want to be patronized by him and swatted his hand away. She shook her head, exasperated. "What are you doing here, Denny?"

He closed his eyes, then opened them, running his hand through his hair. "You don't think I feel guilty and remorseful?"

"I meant here." She waved her arm in front of her. "Here. Now. At the beach." She took a deep breath. "Not here, on this stool." She stared at him, wishing he would disappear. Poof. Gone.

"You do know I feel guilty and remorseful, right?"

"Guilty that you're replacing me? Remorseful that you and you alone destroyed our marriage?"

"I, alone, didn't destroy our marriage."

"You know what I'm talking about, Denny." She drew in a shaky breath, unhappy to be crying in front of him. She picked up a fresh napkin and dabbed at her tears. "It would have been so much easier if it had been a string of one-night-stands." She blew her nose. "The thought of you 'in love' with someone else, while pretending to still love me..." Her voice trailed off, and the tears started anew. "What are you doing here, Denny?"

"I don't know." He shifted on the stool. "I really don't know. The show called about the update, Remi wanted to go to the beach, and I—"

"In November? Really? Remi wanted to go to the beach in November?"

"It doesn't matter. If the condo was in the mountains she would want to go to the mountains. What can I say?"

"Why do you want to have anything to do with the update?" She wiped her tears with the back of her sleeve. "You didn't even want to do the filming in the first place."

"I don't know. I just want closure, I guess." He exhaled through his nose. "I guess I want the world to know I'm not an ass. That I can be friends with my ex-wife. That we can share the condo."

"You are an ass, we'll never be friends, and I don't want to share the condo." She stood, bending at the waist to stretch her hamstrings, one of which was still sore from her rail-yoga. She felt a flash of sadness wash over her, remembering how things ended at Fran's house last night. She wanted to curl up in a ball and pull a blanket over her head. She wanted to hide from the world.

"The truth is," he said, plucking his phone from the arm of the couch where he'd left it, "I wanted to be here to make sure you didn't lambast me on camera."

"You really and truly are an ass, Denny." She opened the sliding glass door and saw that Jesse and Gloria were sitting, waiting, enduring the cold. "God, I'm so sorry. Please come in. I had no intention of making you wait outside." They walked silently into the house. "My ex-husband and I were arguing." She looked pointedly at Denny.

"No big deal. It's not bad out there in the sun, out of the wind." Gloria smiled. "It was quite pleasant." Her smile disappeared. "But we do need to wrap this up. Hopefully, you two are on the same page about the update. During editing, our narrator will improvise, saying something like the condo was an attempt to try and fix an ailing marriage, the couple tried but realized they couldn't make it work. Something like that." She searched Darlene's eyes. "The only thing missing is what you're going to do about the condo. Sell it? Keep it? Share it?"

Darlene did not want to fight any longer. Yes, she would make every attempt to remove his name from the deed. She would even beg if she had to. But for now, her pathetic husband just wanted to save face. He didn't deserve her help with that, not by a long shot. But she suddenly felt sorry for him. "You can say we're still friends, and we've come up with a schedule for sharing the condo." She looked at Denny out of the corner of her eye, just as he was mouthing, *thank you.*

⁓

"Too bad it's so cold out," Denny talked into the camera, a fake smile plastered across his face. "It would have been nice to sit out on the balcony."

Jesse turned the camera toward Darlene, who was standing at the kitchen counter, rearranging the fruit and pastries, setting out napkins, silverware, and champagne flutes.

"Yeah, the drawback of buying a beach house in the fall. I hope our guests don't mind sitting in the living room." Jesse followed her with the camera as she carried the tray of goodies to the coffee table. "I wish Shelly could have come today."

"We'll have this house in the family for a long time, so she'll get her chance." Denny picked a scone off the tray, and Darlene swatted him with a napkin. "Wait until our guests arrive, please."

"It's like we're still married," he said, chuckling.

"Well, we were married for a long time." She shrugged. "Old habits die hard, I guess."

"Cut!" Jesse put his camera down. "Nice job. Was that the doorbell?"

"I'm on it." The doorbell rang again as Gloria ran down the stairs to answer it.

Jesse pointed at Denny. "I think I'll need one more shot of you doing—"

"Laurie?" Darlene's heart leaped at the sight of Fran's sister. A link to him, however obscure. She smiled. "You're just in time!"

"Looks like you're having a party."

"A fake party," Denny chimed in.

"We're filming the update segment." Gloria looked Laurie up and down, assessing her attire, nodding in approval. "This is perfect. You could be one of their guests."

Laurie leaned in closer to Darlene and whispered, "I thought you and your husband split up."

"We did. It's all good. They're writing it into the narration." She walked over to the coffee table. "We already filmed Denny and me talking about it." She shifted from one leg to the other, then looked at the floor. "Is Fran around? He could come over too." She tried to keep the hopeful anticipation out of her voice. She took a deep breath and forced herself to look neutral.

"I haven't seen him in a few days," Laurie said. "In fact, he sent me a somewhat cryptic voicemail, asking if I would feed the cat, saying he'd fill me in later. I saw a missed call from you, so since I was here feeding the cat anyway, I thought I'd drop by."

If Darlene's heart leaped a minute ago, it plummeted to the floor now. Why hadn't Fran simply asked her to feed the cat? It would have been a perfect excuse to stick a toe in the water after last night's fiasco. A risk-free way to ascertain mood. All except it had been Fran who went berserk when the tray broke. There was no water for him to test. Whatever that tray represented, Darlene having broken it was apparently unforgivable. A crime punishable by death of a budding friendship. She took Laurie's coat and draped it over a chair in the corner of the room. She sucked in her emotions, allaying her fears that she couldn't undo what she'd done, and put on a jovial air.

"So, Jesse," Darlene said, back in character. "Should we show Laurie coming up the stairs?"

"Um, let me do my job." He looked around, fluffing the couch pillows. "Okay, Laurie, why don't I film you coming up the stairs. Here's the drill. They invited you over to toast the new house since you were the realtor and all that."

"More than a realtor," Darlene said. "Laurie is a friend." She needed an ally and needed one fast.

"Should I put my coat back on?"

"Sure." Jesse picked up his camera and hoisted it onto his shoulder. "Makes it more realistic."

Gloria grabbed the coat and tossed it to Laurie. "Hey, why don't I pretend to be a guest too."

"Do you think that's a good idea?" Jesse put the camera down and scratched his head. "What if people associated with the show watch this?"

"Then, they already know about the fake bits."

He nodded, looking at his watch. "Hurry up, then. Maybe put your hair up, so you look different."

"Who am I?" Gloria looked at Darlene as she piled her hair high on her head, tying it with a hair tie that she pulled from her purse.

"How about a neighbor?" Darlene offered.

"No, I don't think so. There needs to be some realism, and your immediate neighbors will know I'm not one of them."

Darlene thought about Fran, her real neighbor, and felt an ache in her heart—an ache for the friendship that could have been. After having spent those few hours with him, chatting, drinking beer, slowly peeling back layers of the onion, she had gotten the feeling that he would be in her life for a long time. It was a fleeting feeling, lasting no longer than a soap bubble. She had forgotten all about it until just now. "How about you're my friend from home, from the city."

Gloria shook her head. "I don't think so. Too many variables, too many opportunities for questions."

"Oh, for God's sake." Jesse rolled his eyes. "Then don't be an extra. Or be one. I don't care. Let's just get on with it already."

"How about this." Darlene raised her eyebrows. "It's brilliant in its simplicity."

"Out with it already," Jesse said, tapping his foot. "Let's go, people, let's go."

"You're in my all-female homebrewing club."

"You're in a homebrewing club?" Denny, who had been quietly scrolling on his phone, suddenly sprang to life.

"I just made that up." She looked around the room. "We could go downstairs and get a shot of my beer fermenting." She tried to contain the sadness that was seeping out of her; the memory of teaching Fran about homebrewing, bittersweet. "Viewers might resonate with that."

"And suppose a viewer resonates and then writes to us enquiring as to how to join said all-female homebrewing club." Jesse pointed to his watch. "I'm running late."

"I don't know," Darlene said. "I don't know."

Gloria put her arm around Darlene. "You met me out walking on the beach. We became friends. I live in a condo a few blocks away, bayside. It's random enough. I could be anyone."

"Brilliant." Jesse raised his camera. "Realtor, you go on downstairs. Gloria, you're already here." He looked at the ceiling. "On second thought, we don't need to show anyone coming up the stairs. Let's just get a few seconds of footage standing around on the balcony. Then we'll come in. Gloria, you can pick up something off the tray and put it in your mouth. Laurie, you can say you want to see the beer." He took a deep breath. "Camera rolling!"

43

At five in the afternoon—darkness descending and waves crashing—Darlene felt drained. The update segment with Denny had gone surprisingly smooth. He seemed relieved that she toned down her hostility toward him. He didn't deserve her cooperation, and he knew it. He was on his best behavior, lamenting into the camera the sadness of the breakup and getting teary-eyed when he said they would always be friends. She went along with it, but the whole thing screwed with her emotions. Laurie and Gloria joining the pretend party had offered comic relief.

She closed the magazine she was reading—tired of all the articles on how to have a simpler holiday season—wishing that she never agreed to meet Laurie for dinner. Darlene had suggested a sports bar, two blocks north on this side of the street, hoping beyond hope that the Ravens weren't playing tonight. Who goes to a sports bar on a Thursday night during football season? Football fans, of course. And she was the biggest non-fan in the world, or at least it felt that way. She sighed, amazed at her own stupidity. All she wanted to do was keep it simple. Easy food, smooth beer, and walkable. She typed *Thursday Night Football* into her phone. Thank God, Colts versus Texans. No one in Ocean City would care.

On any given evening, people were waiting. Waiting for their pasta water to boil. Waiting in line at the grocery store. Waiting for a loved one to walk through the door at the end of a long day. Waiting for a traffic light to turn green.

Darlene stared at the clock, waiting for the right time to start walking to the restaurant. They agreed to meet at six-thirty. It would take her three to five minutes to walk the two blocks. Which meant she needed to be out the door by six-twenty, to give herself a little wiggle room. She would need to layer up for the cold, which meant throwing her purple hoodie over her already layered shirt and sweater ensemble, grabbing a pair of gloves, and maybe a scarf. No need for a coat. At least she didn't think so.

She pushed the magazine away and stood to stretch. Laurie was practically a stranger, a superficial friend at best. What would they talk about? They didn't have much in common. Laurie's eyes had glazed over when Jesse filmed her rambling about the beer fermenting in the downstairs bathroom. Conversely, Fran's eyes had danced and seemed to hang on Darlene's every word about home-brewing. Plainly, he seemed fascinated by it.

The big hand on the clock barely moved. Waiting. Always waiting. Waiting for paint to dry. Waiting for hair to grow. Waiting for fat cells to shrink. Waiting for babies to be born. Waiting for a child to grow up. Waiting for a college acceptance letter. Waiting to hear whether your brother would live or die. Waiting for your perfect sister to screw up. Waiting for your husband to love you. Darlene had waited for all of these things at one time or another. What was she waiting for now? To know whether or not she could continue to practice pharmacy? For clarity about Fran? A do-over, perhaps? A replacement blue tray? An epiphany? A friendship? A potential new love? A *Ghostbusters* proton pack and Neutrona Wand? Yes. That was it. Her epiphany: Sadie. Fran simply was not finished grieving his wife. And as long as he was still grieving, Sadie would be immune to anything the *Ghostbusters* could pull out of their bag of tricks.

44

———

The bar was comfortably crowded; plenty of people just kicking back, festive in their anticipation of Thanksgiving lurking just around the corner. Darlene noted, with a hint of panic, that if she really planned to hop on a plane and visit her sister across the country, she needed to book a flight soon. Sooner than soon. In fact, it was what she should be doing now, instead of sitting at a bar, waiting for a woman she didn't particularly feel like spending time with. The pre-game shows filled two TV screens, a third was tuned to The Weather Channel. According to the meteorologist, San Francisco would enjoy a slightly higher than average temperature on Thanksgiving Day. The downside: wind. Lots of wind.

Darlene found two free stools at the corner of the bar, kitty-corner to each other, perfect for chatting. She liked the idea of sitting at the bar. Much less intimate than a table. She pulled off her hoodie and draped it across the seat of the empty stool, reserving it for Laurie. She eyed the bartender, who was lounging against the far end of the bar, drying a glass with a hand towel. His head was tilted toward the TV; he seemed mesmerized by the pre-game show. Too bad she didn't have a handful of peanuts to throw at him. She studied the beer taps behind the bar, all ten of them, none of them inspiring. She considered ordering a glass of wine, but for some reason, the thought of wine and burgers turned her stomach. A craggy voice at the other end of the bar broke the bartender out of his trance. She watched an elderly man in a yellow ball cap point to his whiskey glass, and within a flash, it was no longer empty.

"How about one of those?" Darlene said, taking advantage of the bartender's reentry into the real world. She had never tried the local IPA she was eyeing.

"Menu?" A man of few words.

"Two, please."

He returned a minute later with two menus. Darlene watched as he filled a frosty pint glass, then set it down in front of her, a bit harder than necessary, thin streams of amber trickling down the glass. She folded up her napkin and placed it under the glass, like a diaper. She took a sip.

"What do you think?" The bartender stood in front of her, expectantly, as if he, himself, had brewed it.

Unhappy about the intrusion into her beer moment, she held the glass up to the light. "Interesting slight orange hue." She turned the glass around. "One finger white head, fair retention." She held the glass to her nose and sniffed. "Smells of toasted malt, toffee, caramel. And a tiny bit of citrus and pine." She took a sip. "Good hoppy background. Good carbonation."

"You're either a good improv actor, or you know what you're talking about."

"She knows what she's talking about," Laurie said as she approached the bar. She gave Darlene a superficial hug, took off her coat, and sat down. "I'll have the same thing."

Laurie settled herself in her little corner of the bar as Darlene nursed her beer and discreetly studied this woman who shared DNA with Fran. She had been surprised to learn that Fran was sixty-two. If she didn't know Laurie was the older sibling, she would have thought her to be the baby. Sure, she had crinkles under her eyes and two vertical lines between her brows. Her skin, though, was otherwise smooth and natural-looking. Darlene had a keen eye for hair dye and could usually pick out chemically treated hair a mile away. She squinted, trying to decide if Laurie's short blondish hair was natural. Yes. Most definitely.

"Full disclosure," Laurie said after the bartender set her glass down. "I hate beer." She took a sip, scrunching her nose.

"That's a pretty big glass of beer to hate." Darlene took a large sip of hers. "Just order something else. I'll drink yours." She shook her head. "Actually, that would be a lot of beer, even for me. Life is too short. Leave it. Order what you want."

"I hate to say this, but you're right. I'd really rather have wine." She waved the bartender over and ordered a glass of pinot noir.

Darlene wondered if Laurie was one of those people who had an emotional need to please others, even at the expense of their own wants. She knew many people who operated like that and vowed a long time ago to edge away from it. If she wanted a beer, she had a beer. If she wanted a hot dog, she had a hot dog. Even if her dinner companions might be having champagne and caviar. Before meeting Denny, she briefly dated a guy who mirrored everything she did. Everything. Drove her crazy. One night they had dinner at a restaurant known for its ribs. The guy had been drooling over having ribs at this place for days. She saw ostrich steak on the menu; intrigued, she decided to try it. One look at her date's crestfallen face, and she knew. Sure enough, he ordered the ostrich steak. They fought about it at the table, on the walk home, and between classes the next day. She didn't want to be with someone who couldn't think for himself. And then she ended up with Denny—a mind of his own to a fault. Two opposite ends of the continuum. There was no happy medium. Oh well, at least Laurie caught herself and adjusted. For that, Darlene gave her points.

"Much better," Laurie said as she took a sip of wine. "Maybe someday you could teach me to appreciate beer."

Darlene nodded, hanging on the word someday, wanting to assign meaning to it, a Freudian slip of the tongue, an insight that might have to do with Fran. Or might not have anything to do with

Fran. Probably just a polite way of acknowledging different tastes, different preferences.

The bartender paced up and down the length of the bar. He looked bored, and a little bit annoyed that Darlene and Laurie hadn't yet ordered food. She didn't understand his annoyance—it was a bar. If eating had been their focus, she would have chosen a table. Still, she didn't like his hovering and ordered a burger and fries, curious to see if Laurie would follow suit. She ordered a salmon sandwich, minus the bread, sautéed asparagus on the side.

"Are you gluten-free?"

"No, but I do try to avoid bread." Laurie patted her stomach. "Seems to go straight to my gut."

"I love bread, but my biggest downfalls seem to be beer, wine, and chocolate. And chips. And fries." It felt strangely good to make fun of herself. "My sister is gluten-free. She thinks it helps keep her skinny." Darlene rolled her eyes and made a gagging gesture with her finger.

"She doesn't have issues with gluten?"

"Her only issues are between her ears." Darlene shook her head. "Other than that, she's perfect, can do no wrong, blah, blah, blah."

Laurie laughed. "You sound like my brother, describing me!" She grew serious. "That's only partially true. He's two years younger and worlds smarter. Actually, galaxies smarter." She grew wistful. "I'm going to miss him."

"Miss him?" Darlene knew her face had turned bright red. She didn't try to hide it but was careful not to draw attention to it, grateful for the dim lights. Maybe Laurie was referring to another brother. That was it! Had to be. Yes. Another brother.

Laurie picked up her wineglass by the stem and twirled it a few times before finally taking a sip. "He wants to move back to Northern Virginia." She locked eyes with Darlene. "I don't get it, really. He was happy here, or at least I thought he was." She took a deep breath. "Too many reminders of his wife, I guess."

So that was it then. Darlene had spooked him. One way or another, either because of the tray or some other catalyst, he fled. He could have asked her to feed the cat. If only he had knocked on her door, she would have apologized—profusely—and they could have moved on from there. Even if he never forgave her, they could have moved on and still been friendly. She would have gladly fed the cat. Gladly. Dammit. She should never have invited him into her house and been so chummy. Should never have gone over there with the two bottles of beer—again, way too chummy. Her face grew hot, remembering the split-second after the tray fell when he grabbed her under the arms and lifted her off the floor. She thought he was about to kiss her. Cringeworthy.

"Sadie."

"You know about Sadie?"

"Only that they moved here, opened the deli, and she died."

"He told you all that?"

"I pieced some of it together. He told me some of it. I took my father to lunch at the deli, the day we filmed the second house, the day Fran filled in for you." She looked at the floor. "I saw her picture on the wall."

"So, the two of you actually spent time together?"

Darlene sat up straight. Thank God, the food arrived, offering a reprieve from this probing conversation. She took her time prepping her burger, peeling off the lettuce, tomato, and onion, and setting them to the side. She squeezed a circle of ketchup onto the bun, then a mound next to her fries. She made eyes and a mouth with the mustard, squirted a glob of mayo in the center for a nose, then picked up her knife and smeared the face until it no longer resembled a face. In essence, it was merely a hamburger bun spread with condiments. She replaced the lettuce, tomato, onion, and bun, then carefully cut the burger in half. She glanced at Laurie out of the corner of her eye —she was taking dainty bites of her salmon. Darlene sprinkled salt and pepper on her fries, taking one and dipping it in the ketchup before biting it in half.

"We chatted some, mostly outside on our respective balconies, over the rail." She decided to go further. "I was brewing beer the other day, boiling the wort on the stove. It has a strong, distinct smell. It apparently wafted into his condo. He came outside and asked about it." She smiled. "He came over to see." She shoved another fry into her mouth. "I went over there a few days later with some of my previous brews for him to try."

Laurie stopped eating and sat up straight, her fork midair, a piece of salmon speared between two asparagus heads. She raised her eyebrows, then smiled like she had been let in on a secret.

"No. No!" Darlene shook her head. "Nothing like that." She laughed, then grew serious. "We talked. We snacked. We drank beer. It was casual and friendly." She put her head in her hands, peeking out through her fingers.

Laurie didn't ask any questions. For that, Darlene was grateful. They sat silently eating their meals, sipping their drinks. Darlene didn't know what she was doing here, why she'd felt compelled to say yes to Laurie's invitation. She didn't want to believe it had anything to do with Fran. She took too big a bite of her burger and swallowed it, barely chewed, and felt it lodge halfway down her esophagus. In a fit of panic, she guzzled what was left of her beer and swallowed hard, but the stubborn piece of meat would not budge. She picked up Laurie's beer glass and chugged. The rush of liquid proved too strong for the burger and bun, hanging on for dear life. It put up a fight but finally ceded defeat and surrendered, sliding the rest of the way down, waving a white flag. Great. This was the second time recently that she almost choked. She admonished herself to slow down and chew thoroughly when she eats.

Eyes bulging, she took a deep breath, awash in relief. She glanced at Laurie, who was making slow progress on her salmon. She didn't seem to notice Darlene's frantic beer-guzzling or the look of panic on her face. Heart still pounding from the near-choking episode, she acknowledged to herself, finally, that she viewed Laurie, not as a potential new bestie, but as a conduit to Fran. She hung her head, ashamed, and vowed to get to know this woman sitting beside her, for her own sake, and not because of Fran.

"How long have you been a realtor?"

"Not very long." Laurie looked at the ceiling and counted on her fingers. "Five years, if that." She finished her wine and motioned for the bartender to bring her another. "I helped Fran and Sadie find their condo."

"What did you do before that?"

"I kind of drifted for a while."

"I'm having a hard time picturing you drifting." Darlene regarded Laurie's smart black slacks, white cashmere turtleneck, and the pink blazer draped over the back of the stool. "I mean, when I hear someone describe themselves as a drifter, I picture an old hippie." She covered her mouth. "Not that you're old. You're not that old." She laughed. "I have terrible filters. No, scratch that. I have no filters."

"Hey, I am old." Laurie joined in on the laughter. Darlene noted, with a bit of sadness, that Laurie's eyes crinkled when she laughed, just like Fran's. *Francisco-o-o-o*. "I graced turning forty, then fifty, no problem at all. For some reason, sixty freaked me out." She grew serious. "I'm accepting it, though. As they say, it's better than the alternative. Fran's wife never made it there."

No matter how hard she tried, Darlene couldn't seem to veer the conversation away from Fran, at least not for very long. Okay. One more attempt. "My mother is seventy-five and still vibrant, active, and a royal pain in the ass." She pushed her plate aside and motioned for the waiter to bring her a fresh beer. "She recently wrote her first novel."

"I'm impressed." Laurie's eyes grew wet, but she recovered quickly. "In my drifting days, my non-hippie drifting days, I might add, I wanted to write."

"Why didn't you?"

"I never got focused enough. Plus, I didn't have anything particular that I wanted to write about, you know, didn't have the proverbial story inside of me. What's your mother's book about."

"Don't get me started." Darlene rolled her eyes. "This book caused a huge rift between my parents. She wrote a steamy romance. My father was convinced that my mother was really writing about their neighbor." She burst out laughing. "You should see this guy. He is a caricature of an old, greasy Mafioso.

"Complete with gold chains?"

Darlene nodded, then snorted, almost spewing beer all over the bar. As she tried to compose herself, she realized that she was having a good time. "And after your drifter phase?"

"I met my knight in shining armor." She sat up straight and pushed her shoulders against the back of the stool. "My husband was in the Air Force. We saw the world. I raised our son and taught English at quite a few military bases. Now I have a beautiful grandbaby, Jordan. She's almost one."

"I love that name for a girl." The tears flowed freely, and Darlene wasn't sure why. Why had talking about Laurie's grandchild triggered this flash flood? Laurie handed her a napkin. "I'm sorry." She blew her nose. "I have a lot of shit going on in my life right now, I never know when this is going to happen." Her cell phone buzzed. She wiped her eyes and peered at it. Her boss. Probably calling to deliver the news that she had lost her pharmacy license. No need to answer. No need. She blew her nose again, then turned to Laurie. "Thank you for this." She gestured around the bar. "I didn't realize it, but I needed an evening like this." Suddenly feeling bold and needing to talk about Fran, she decided to just let it out. "Last night, at Fran's, I broke something that must have had a ton of sentimental meaning. He went berserk. When I tried to help him pick up the pieces, he asked me to leave." Fresh tears streamed down her cheeks.

"A blue ceramic tray?"

"Yes!"

"Oh, my." Laurie shook her head and put her face in her hands. Several seconds went by before she lifted her head to look at Darlene. She took a sip of wine. "Oh, my."

45

Darlene half sat, half laid in bed, her head propped up on a stack of pillows. She dragged her tongue over her front teeth, scraping the chalky paste left by the antacids she had taken before bed, shuddering at how foul her mouth tasted. She rubbed her chest, still on fire after the burger, fries, and two beers. Not to mention the handful of chocolates she mindlessly ate when she got home.

Reaching for the Tums on her nightstand, her wrist caught the edge of her water glass. She watched as it toppled over and landed on its side on the carpet, water pooling around its mouth like a flood from a bursting dam. In too much gastrointestinal discomfort to care, she reached for the Tums and popped four more in her mouth.

My brother is a sentimental fool. Laurie's words at the bar were the lullaby Darlene had fallen asleep to. Fran had been apparently holding onto the cobalt blue tray as the last vestige of Sadie. *But there are memories of her everywhere*, Darlene protested, pointing out that everything in Fran's condo had Sadie's stamp all over it. Laurie explained that Sadie had made the ugly tray for Fran—it had been a source of humor between them. It wasn't the tray necessarily, but that it represented the intangible fragments of their life together. After she died, the tray signified the day-to-day subtleties that might fade over time without something Fran could see, touch, or hold. A physical reminder of one of their last carefree periods before Sadie's diagnosis.

Darlene leaned back on the pillows, frantically scratching at her head, messing up her already messy hair, trying to will the acid in her gut to dry up. Did Denny ever give her anything she would have held so tightly, had he died during a time when she thought he loved her? She couldn't come up with a single item.

Laurie also described a time when she and her husband went on a sightseeing bike ride with Fran and Sadie; it was very casual, light riding. Sadie's bike skidded on some gravel, and she fell. They hadn't been riding fast, maybe ten miles an hour, if that. As Fran helped Sadie stand up, several pieces of gravel tumbled out of her bike jersey. He stuck them in his pocket. When they got home, he put them on the windowsill in the kitchen, where they stayed until Sadie got sick, and Laurie hired a maid service to deep-clean the condo. Fran was distraught that the maids discarded the gravel; Laurie never heard the end of it.

Darlene supposed she simply was not a sentimental fool. At least not when it came to Denny. They never had the kind of love that Fran and Sadie seemed to share. Darlene knew she couldn't compete with a woman whose husband saved gravel that fell out of her bike jersey. She wondered if she could be happy with a man who goes off the deep end every time something breaks or is inadvertently thrown away. She cringed, remembering Fran's expression in the seconds after the tray shattered, standing among the pieces, shards, and fragments. Suspended in time between the crash and his words. *I think you should go. Please, I beg you.*

Her cell phone buzzed, startling her. Who would be texting her at this hour? She picked up her phone and noted that it was just after midnight, not almost dawn like she thought. Still, she found it odd that her pharmacy tech would text this late. She read the text: Did you hear from Bill?

Darlene suddenly remembered her phone vibrating on the bar

during dinner with Laurie. She flung her legs over the side of the bed and got up. She wasn't sure why, but it seemed like the bed was the last place she wanted to be when she learned that her beloved career was ending. She returned Susan's text, then, holding tightly to the banister, slowly made her way down the stairs.

Sitting down at the breakfast bar, she pressed the button for voicemail. As she listened, her heart seemed to stop. Then it kicked back in, pounding wildly. She didn't know whether to laugh or cry, so she did a little of both. The family of the woman who almost died decided not to pursue legal action, and was prepared to forgive the error. An error that never should have been made; because it had, Darlene would have a black mark in her file, forever. Still, she was offered her job back.

Darlene's grandmother believed in signs. To a fault. Bubbe would not make a move without first looking for a sign, sometimes even creating signs where none existed. Darlene remembered slamming on her breaks to avoid rear-ending a light blue van two days after Denny proposed. She had said 'yes' without hesitation, but the sight of the van unnerved her; a few weeks earlier, she had dreamed of being run over by a light blue van. Perhaps it had been a warning to not marry Denny.

She thought about Fran, the tray, and getting her job back as a sign. A big, bright sign. A neon sign. The tallest, widest billboard imaginable. A plane towing an aerial banner across the sky, words in bold. A flashing marquee on Broadway. She saw no real reason to stay at the beach. Not now. Laurie was taking care of the cat, and the beer still needed another week of fermentation. The answer was simple— she would go home to Leesburg and return to the beach next week to bottle the beer. Figuring out the rest of her life could wait.

46

———

For years, Fran had fantasized about living in one of the high-rise buildings in the heart of Reston, where he could walk out the door, hop on his bike, and ride in either direction on the W&OD bike trail. Or in the evening, walk out the door and eat dinner in a different restaurant every night. He came pretty darn close to buying a one-bedroom, one-bath unit in a brand-new building, just steps away from his work, around the same time he met Sadie. He quickly forgot his life plans, and together they bought a quirky single-family house on a cul-de-sac—still close to the bike trail and walkable to all the action.

Standing in front of the building on Market Street, he scrolled through the listing on his phone. With only five stories, this certainly wasn't the high-rise of his dreams, but the location was ideal, and the price was a little bit below his max budget. He fiddled with the heart-shaped piece of broken ceramic in his pocket as he approached the door. The realtor, a bald man who resembled Telly Savalas in *Kojak*, greeted him with an extended hand. Fran shook it, unimpressed by the guy's pseudo strength.

"Fran, right?"

"That's me." Fran suddenly wondered why he was here, and

wished he had opted for a bike ride instead. His impulsive journey around Assateague yesterday awoke a long-dormant yearning to get on his bike and just pedal. Perhaps a bike ride across the country wasn't such a crazy idea after all. He made a mental note to start researching routes.

"Lon. Lon Shepherd, here." The realtor ushered Fran into the building and started spewing off one amenity after another. "Here, let me show you the gym."

"It's okay, I'm not a much of a gym person."

"I would never know by looking at you."

"I'm a biker."

"Harley?"

"Cannondale." Fran could almost hear Lon's brain processing— Yamaha, Kawasaki, Suzuki...Cannondale? Fran suppressed a laugh and decided to give the guy a break. "It's a bicycle."

"Ah. Right. Of course. Right." Lon regrouped. "There's a fifty-mile bike trail just a few hundred yards—"

"I know," Fran interrupted. "I used to live not too far from here. So, yes, I know."

"Anyway, if you ever decide to become a gym person, this building offers one comparable to any commercial gym. Wouldn't you just like to take a quick peek?"

"I would not."

"You're sure?"

"One more mention of the gym and I'm out of here." Fran didn't try to hide his irritation. He hoped his sister wasn't like this with her clients.

Lon raised his hands in surrender and led Fran to the bank of elevators. "There's also a community center, business office, and concierge service in the main lobby." He nodded a greeting at the woman behind the desk.

"Seems too much like a hotel for me."

"Do you still want to see the unit?" Lon's finger was poised and ready to press the button for the elevator. "I also have a brand-new listing in the building across the street. If you want, you can be the first to see it."

"I'll look at this one." He softened. The guy was just trying to do his job. Fran admonished himself for the lousy attitude. "And yes, you can show me the unit in the other building too." He forced a semblance of a smile. "If you have time."

Lon sounded like a narrator on those house hunting shows, giving new meaning to the term 'elevator speech.' As he listened, Fran's heart tumbled, thinking about Rose, wondering when the show she and Denny filmed would air. His heart plunged further, remembering Rose's hand on Denny's arm the other day. Convinced they had reconciled, he pushed thoughts of her away and willed his heart to forget. Lon's voice, merely a mumble in Fran's ears, became clear again.

"...wall of windows and balcony overlooking the pool. Units in this building rarely come available."

Fran didn't remember stepping off the elevator or even walking through the door to the unit. Suddenly inside, and face-to-face with an entryway table adorned with Hummel figurines, he burst out laughing. "I'm sorry, but I hate these damned things." Early in their relationship, he and Sadie both reacted to the doe-eyed ceramic characters at a flea market. Almost in unison, they both said that their grandmothers collected them. He sighed, suddenly no longer in the mood to laugh.

"Gleaming hardwood floors." Lon ignored Fran and the figurines. "Oh, and granite countertops."

Fran furrowed his brows at the busy granite; the rust-colored veins made the countertops look dirty. "The kitchen is kind of small."

"You'll rarely need to cook, with all of the restaurants practically right outside your door."

Fran shrugged. He enjoyed drinking beer and eating chips with Rose the other night. He winced, remembering the broken tray, but took comfort in Sadie's words the next morning. Still, this new life without Sadie would take a lot of getting used to. He imagined cooking something for Rose in this kitchen. It seemed wrong. So wrong. Not cooking for Rose in general but cooking for Rose here. Not that he would ever get the opportunity to prepare a meal for her. He wouldn't. He opened the door leading out to the balcony and stepped outside.

"Nice view, huh?" Lon followed him.

Fran looked at the pool, covered for winter, picturing himself sitting in a lounge chair with a book. Making small talk, trying to move on. No. Hell no.

"I have a view of the ocean in my current condo." What was he doing here? He couldn't move back to Reston. Just couldn't. "I'm sorry for wasting your time."

FRAN ZIPPED his jacket and sat down on the ledge of the fountain, the gurgling water replaced by a Christmas display—a tower of festively wrapped boxes with a massive Christmas tree behind it. He looked up at the building he had just been in, confident that his days of wanting to live here were over. If there were constant reminders of Sadie at the beach, this place was worse. He looked over his shoulder and saw the outdoor ice rink, dotted with people, where he and Sadie tried to outdo each other ice skating their first winter together. She won, for sure. All he ended up with was a bruised hip and a bruised ego. They had eaten at every restaurant here, at least once. He was certain new ones have cropped up since then, but just being here, sitting on the fountain's ledge, looking up at the Christmas tree was almost more than he could bear. He stuck his hand in his pocket and grasped the piece of ceramic.

He felt like he wanted to flee but instead forced himself to sit on the cold concrete. Maybe, if he sat here long enough, Sadie would appear by his side. He desperately wanted to talk to her—needed to tell her that she had been wrong about Rose. He closed his eyes and ran through all the Saturday nights in summer when he and Sadie set up their lawn chairs and watched local bands play right in front of this fountain.

"You really are a bonehead," a familiar voice whispered. Fran sat up straight and looked around. He didn't see anyone, but instantly knew who it was. "What are you doing here, sitting in the cold, like a lump?"

"I'm waiting for you."

"I promised myself I'd leave you alone."

"I'm glad you couldn't keep your promise." He smiled.

"Stop it, Franny." She locked eyes with him. "Go back to the beach. Close the deli. Tell Rose how you feel."

"She's back with her husband," he said, sensing Sadie's skepticism. "I saw them together."

"Having sex?"

Fran cringed. "No!"

"Kissing? Hugging?"

"I saw her pat his arm."

"What does that mean?" Sadie raised an eyebrow and didn't wait for an answer. "It could mean anything. It could mean nothing."

"I know what I saw." He looked away, focusing his eyes on the building across the street.

"Go back to the beach, Franny."

"Only if you promise to visit me there, like before."

She looked at the ground. "That's not possible."

"Why not?"

"Franny, I'm dead."

"I know."

"Do you?" She shifted on the fountain's edge, crossing her legs. "I should never have come to you on the eve of my funeral, but you were so pathetic, I couldn't stand it."

He remembered. Vividly. After all the guests had left, convinced that he was losing his mind, he heard Sadie's voice. Swatting away the notion of a post-death visit, he continued stacking plates and carrying them into the kitchen. But the voice, a salve to his soul, persisted.

"I'm so glad you came to me that night," he said, trying to reach for her. Sadie moved, causing him to stumble, his elbow landing on the hard concrete. "Ouch!" He rubbed his arm, making a face, pretending to be annoyed. Finally, he smiled. "For the last two years, you saved me from me." He reached for her again; this time, she let him.

"Somebody had to do it," she said, chuckling. She grew serious. "But I can't anymore."

"Then, why are you here now?"

"To say goodbye."

"Please don't go." Fran pulled his jacket cuff down over his hand and swiped at the free-flowing tears. He looked up and saw a group of teenagers walk by, staring at him as if he had lost his mind. Perhaps he had. He turned to Sadie; there was so much more to say. But it was too late. She was gone. This time, he feared it was for good.

47

———

Darlene had been standing at the counter dispensing medication for the past few hours, plastering on a smile and telling people how to take their pills and what side effects to expect. Susan had started her Thanksgiving vacation a week early, so it was just Darlene—pharmacist and tech all wrapped into one.

"When you get home, if you are at all confused, please call us." She handed a bag to her customer. "And remember to take it on an empty stomach." The customer nodded and turned to walk away. "Oh, and no grapefruit," Darlene called after him.

Her stomach growled, and she glanced at her watch. Could it already be two o'clock? The idle hour, the hour before closing on Sundays. The people who had their act together had picked up their medications long ago; the adrenaline rush seekers would wait until five minutes before closing.

Taking advantage of the lull, she slipped behind the partition separating the drug dispense area from the customer service counter and into her tiny cubicle. An hour ago, she pulled her peanut butter and jelly sandwich out of her lunch bag. But every time she sat down to eat it, she got called to the counter, mostly to give flu shots. It seemed like everyone wanted their inoculations before heading off for their Thanksgiving festivities. Didn't they know it would take at least two weeks for the flu shot to take effect? She gave more than a dozen flu shots today. She hated, hated, hated giving shots. Hated it.

Starved, she picked up the sandwich—the bread was already beginning to harden—and took a bite. Blech. She tossed the stale sandwich in the trash, shoving pretzel sticks in her mouth, stopping only long enough to gulp down the Diet Coke she'd pulled from the mini-fridge under her desk. She eyed the bag of chocolates on the shelf above her desk. *No dessert until you finish your lunch.* She hurried with the pretzels—the best option for lunch currently available to her—and pulled down the chocolates.

"You have customers up front." Bill popped his head into her cubicle.

"Coming." *Go deal with them yourself,* was what she wanted to say. The chocolates would have to wait. Bill had been a pill (she giggled at the pun, and the rhyme) these past few days, acting like he had done her a favor by taking her back. *Each and every prescription we fill has the potential to either help or harm the patient,* he'd lectured. As if she didn't already know that. As if she would ever be able to put the incident behind her. The pharmaceutical community was relatively small. Good reputations travel fast. But bad ones travel even faster. She took a deep breath. "On my way."

Darlene stepped up to the counter, shaking her legs while the first customer in line dug for his prescription. Most of the doctors in the area sent in their orders electronically. Still, there were a few who liked to scribble them on paper. She shifted from one foot to the other, lifting the heel of her left foot off the floor to stretch it, then repeating it with her right. It was as if her feet had forgotten what it was like to stand for hours and hours. *I'd give anything for one of Denny's foot rubs.* It had been their post-dinner ritual—her feet in his lap, watching the news while Shelly did her homework. A habit of marriage that lasted up until the bitter end. Just a few days before he dropped his bomb, she automatically put her feet in his lap, and he massaged them, just like always. She shuddered, wondering what he must have been thinking. She didn't often admit it to herself, but there were some things about Denny that she would miss. Like having a sounding board at the end of a frustrating day. And the foot rubs—long minutes of pure heaven, often, better than sex.

Darlene cringed when she saw how fast her line was growing. She entered the information from the paper prescription into the computer and turned to her customer. "I'll have this ready for you in about twenty minutes." She usually had prescriptions filled in less than ten minutes, but with the number of customers in line for drop-off, she knew she would need more time.

"I could use some help," she said to Bill. He was standing off to the side, chatting with Helen, from the flower shop next door. Yesterday, Darlene mentioned that she would be out all Thanksgiving weekend, starting Wednesday, just like she had planned before she was put on administrative leave. *Yeah, well, it's our busiest time, and now with Susan on vacation, I just don't know.* Bill didn't exactly say she couldn't have time off, but he certainly implied it. The impulsive act of courage that enabled her to invite herself to San Francisco to spend Thanksgiving with her sister would probably never come again. She needed to seize it. She didn't believe Bill would fire her (again) if she took time off but knew he would make her pay in a thousand little ways. "Bill!" He turned from his conversation as if she were yanking him away from brain surgery. "Could you please take the customers while I fill the scripts?"

With a showy harumph, Bill situated himself in front of the second terminal and motioned for customers to enter his line. He turned toward Darlene. "I'll help you clear the line, then you can work on filling the prescriptions."

Ignoring him, she took the next customer—a drop-off and pickup. She entered the information into the computer then turned to get the medication out of the 'recently filled' bin. She looked at the label and brought it to the customer. "Three drops in each ear, three times a day." She pantomimed, pretending to hold a medicine dropper between her fingers. "One, two, three, just like that." She waited for the customer to sign for the ear drops, then handed him the bag. "If you have someone to put them in for you, all the better."

Darlene was about to sign out of her computer when she saw a couple turn the corner. *Oy vey. Denny and Remi.* She ducked behind the counter, praying they didn't see her. She slowly lifted her head so that just her eyes peeked over the edge of the counter. She watched them standing side by side in front of the greeting card rack, hip touching hip, Remi swaying slightly from side to side. She lifted one card after another off the shelf, rejecting them almost as soon as she pulled them out.

Sadness gripped the pit of Darlene's stomach. It felt worse than when Denny had first told her about Remi, or when she saw the two of them frolicking on the beach. She tried to remember a time when she and Denny stood side by side, looking at cards. Never. They never looked at cards together. Darlene was always the one to buy them, write a cute little message in them, and either give or send them. If she had not, his parents and siblings would never have gotten birthday cards.

She grabbed the counter with both hands and slowly stood, stopping midway and rubbing at a new twinge in her left knee. She straightened herself up and turned to go behind the partition when she saw Denny look in her direction. He nuzzled Remi and nudged his chin toward the pharmacy, kissed her on the forehead, and got in line.

"Bill, can you take this one, please?" Darlene could not guarantee that she wouldn't deliberately screw up Denny's medication. Or better yet, Remi's. She simply did not trust herself.

"Denny, how are you doing, man?" Bill smiled and shook Denny's hand, then looked at Darlene. "You get this. I need to start closing."

"But it's not even two-thirty," she protested. They usually didn't start closing until it was actually closing time. They still had thirty minutes. "I have four prescriptions I need to fill."

"So, now you have five." He closed his terminal and disappeared around the corner.

"I didn't think you still worked here." Denny smiled, his eyes sparkling. He turned his head to look at Remi, still scanning the greeting cards. He handed Darlene a paper prescription.

"Prenatal vitamins. Of course." Her breath caught. "What did I do wrong, Denny?" Tears pooled in her eyes. She blinked, and they streamed down her cheeks. "Tell me, what does she have that I don't?"

"I can't do this right now." He nudged his head toward the left. "Hey, babe." He put his arm around Remi. "Find a card?" She shook her head. "Remi, this is Darlene." He paused. "My ex."

Darlene turned away and wiped her eyes as she tried, unsuccessfully, to compose herself. She did not want to look Remi in the eye. Did not want to acknowledge Remi's face, her soft features. Fresh. Fit. Fabulous. Everything that she, Darlene, was not. "I'll have this for you in about ten minutes."

She left the two of them standing there and disappeared behind the partition. Reaching for the bottle of vitamins to fill Remi's prescription, she didn't think she could trust herself not to make a mistake. She didn't realize, until just then, how tense she had been, checking and rechecking medications and dosages, not trusting herself. But now, staring at the bottle of prenatal vitamins, knowing how easy it would be to poison Remi, well, maybe she did not deserve a pharmacy license after all. She approached Bill, who was sitting in his cubicle, feet on his desk, yakking away on his cell phone. "I need to talk to you."

"I'll call you back, Mom. Yep. See you next week." He put the phone down and glared at Darlene. "What?"

"I'm sorry, but I can't do this anymore."

"What do you mean."

She held her hands out in front of her. "Look at my hands. They're shaking."

"What point are you making?"

"I don't trust myself not to make another mistake."

"I can't afford to give you any more time off. Thanksgiving, okay, you can have the long weekend."

Darlene clenched her fists, hoping it would quell her tremors. "Bill, you're not listening."

"I hear you. I just don't know what you want me to do. My hands are tied. I can't give you any more time off."

She walked away, taking great care to fill Remi's prescription correctly and the four others in the queue. When she was finished, she placed the medications in the bin and slammed it on Bill's desk.

"I quit." Grabbing her coat and chocolates, she ran out the back door without a second glance.

SITTING IN HER CAR, her heart pounding, flushed in the face and feeling emboldened, she threw her hands in the air and shouted at the top of her lungs. She imagined herself as Catherine Zeta-Jones in *No Reservations*, carrying a raw steak through the restaurant like a weapon. It did not matter that Darlene's weapon had been a medication bin and not a steak. It simply did not matter.

48

Darlene sat at the kitchen table, laptop open, flipping between multiple web browser windows. Still riding the wave of adrenaline after quitting her job, she alternated between searching for jobs and sending emails to realtors asking to schedule an appointment for the week after Thanksgiving. She didn't want to waste any time putting the Leesburg house on the market—she was thinking before Christmas. The house was in excellent condition, and she was confident they would quickly find a buyer. She also sent an email to Denny, letting him know of her plans, not asking him, but telling him. She told him she would let him know when an appointment with a realtor was scheduled. She owed him at least that, but not much else.

She opened a beer—one from an old homebrew batch—pleased that it had not gone flat. She took a sip and typed *steak scene, No Reservations* into Google. She watched the short clip over and over, feeling the same empowerment Katherine Zeta-Jones' character must have felt after reaching her tipping point. Images of Denny and Remi standing at the greeting card rack flashed through her mind. It had been a little over two hours since then, and she couldn't shake the image. Was seeing them together her tipping point? If they hadn't walked into the pharmacy, how much longer would she have put up with Bill? A week, a month, a year, a few hours, a few days? She didn't know. He left several voicemails offering to meet with her, promising she could have Thanksgiving weekend off, begging her to reconsider. She deleted all of them and had no intention of responding. Truth was, it wasn't just about Bill or wanting to take time off. The mistake she had made with the woman's medication rattled her to the core. She didn't know if she could ever practice pharmacy again.

Could it be possible that she misread the signs? A few days ago, she was confident that getting her job back was a sign. A warning to stay away from the beach, a reminder that she initially didn't want to keep the condo. An arrow pointing her back to where she felt the most comfortable in her skin, in her community, behind the pharmacy counter. Now she wondered if the sign had been Denny and Remi—a sign pointing her back to the beach, away from here.

Taking a sip of beer, she closed her laptop, no longer able to concentrate. She shuffled around the kitchen, not hungry but feeling like she should eat something. She opened the snack cabinet and pulled down a bag of potato chips. Ha! They were the same kind of sea salt and cracked pepper chips that Fran had shared with her the night of the broken tray. She didn't remember buying them. She looked at the expiration date. Of course. She didn't remember buying them because she bought them ages ago. She tossed the bag in the trash, then quickly pulled it out. A sign? She guzzled the rest of her beer and started typing a text to Fran, fast, before she could change her mind: How are you? She searched for an appropriate emoji but couldn't come up with one. She continued texting: I am so sorry about the tray. Genuinely sorry. Can we talk? Her finger hovered over the text, about to send it. And as if her finger knew better than her heart, it backtracked and deleted each word, one by one.

She reopened her laptop and resumed searching for jobs. Silly jobs like a circus clown or professional mourner. Weird, obscure jobs like pet food taster or snake milker. Finally, after having a bit of fun, she typed *pharmacist* into the search bar and included Ocean City in her search radius. Maybe she could do something pharmaceutical that didn't involve filling prescriptions. Several opportunities in hospitals popped up, as well as a smattering of remote positions. She clicked on one and studied the details for Pain Management Pharmacy Specialist: *Lead a team on the development of an opioid stewardship program.* She would need to get licensed in Maryland. And have two years in pain management or equivalent experience. Scratch that. Too bad, because that sounded like it could have been an interesting job. She scrolled back to the remote opportunities. Senior Biostatistician. Probably not qualified. She clicked the link anyway. *Work with a team of highly competent statisticians and programmers on the delivery of clinical development projects.* She didn't need to read further to know that she wasn't qualified. A statistician, she was not.

She yawned and stretched. Way past dinnertime, she was more tired than hungry. She left her laptop behind and trudged upstairs. She didn't have to figure anything out right away. Tomorrow she would head back to the beach to bottle her beer. Then she would either come home first before flying to San Francisco, or she would drive to the airport straight from Ocean City. Better be prepared for either. She felt a bit heady, thinking about seeing her sister, wondering how Thanksgiving might play out. Maybe she would gently bring up the topic of the rape—without throwing their mother under the bus for telling. Or perhaps she would simply be there, and with her new set of eyes, see things differently.

49

Darlene opened the door to the condo and let her backpack fall off her shoulder. She stood in the small, dark foyer and breathed in the smell of her homebrew. The aroma had permeated the entire first floor. It was a good thing Fran wasn't around—he would probably complain. She moved thoughts of him into the far recesses of her brain. In the nearly three hours it took her to drive here, he barely crossed her mind. It felt good to not be haunted by him, and it felt good to be back at the beach. So good, in fact, that she wished she hadn't bought a plane ticket to San Francisco. She stood, smiling, breathing deeply, feeling the air go into her lungs in a way it hadn't in a long time.

She approached the bathroom, fully expecting to see her carboy lying on its side, empty; a sticky, fermented mess in the tub. She had checked on it before she left—the fermentation had slowed considerably. Still, there had been times when a batch of beer she was brewing seemed to slow, then pick right back up again, building up enough pressure to blow the airlock off like a champagne cork on New Year's Eve. She held her breath and pushed the door open. *Phew*. Everything was just as she had left it.

~

IIF THE FOYER was dark and dingy, the second floor was flooded with light, as if the sun saved its best rays just for her. She set her equipment on the floor next to the breakfast bar, then rolled up her sleeves and lined the bottles on the counter by the sink. Her process down to a science, she squirted sanitizer in each bottle, then filled them with scalding hot water. When she was finished, there were bottles all over the kitchen. Forty-eight of them. Soldiers lined up and ready for battle.

She couldn't face the prospect of rinsing, which was a long and arduous process to make certain she got all the sanitizer out. Denny used to help her in Leesburg, taking turns at the sink, one rinsing while the other set the clean bottles to dry. She imagined Denny and Remi, standing side by side at the sink, washing and drying dishes together, hip touching hip. Turning on the hot water, she let the image fade, picked up a bottle, and started rinsing. She let the water flow in and out of the bottle until it ran clear of soapy bubbles, then filled it, dumped it out, and filled it again—ten times—before she was satisfied. She set up the drying rack on the breakfast bar and slid the mouth of the now sanitized bottle onto one of its outstretched arms.

She grabbed a second bottle and held it under the hot water. Two bottles turned into three. Forty-five to go. She turned off the water and wiped her hands on her jeans, the sun beckoning through the sliding glass door. She left the remaining bottles untouched and stood in front of the door, opening it a crack, then stepping out. A bit chillier than it seemed. She glanced over the rail at Fran's place and noticed the cat happily lapping away at his bowl. Laurie must have just fed him. She started to climb over the rail to see if she could catch Laurie, then backtracked, feeling happier to just be by herself today. The cat lifted his head and looked at her.

"Hi, Ray." The cat trotted toward her. "Hi!" She bent down and scratched his neck. "I know. He up and left you, didn't he?" Ray purred then trotted back to his dish. Darlene figured a stray cat didn't care much who fed him. All that mattered was that the food showed up, day after day. She shivered. If she wanted to sit on the beach, she would need to put something else on.

50

Fran stood in the corner of the living room, back pressed against the wall, head tilted slightly so that he could see, yet not be seen. Rose's hair sparkled in the sun. She looked radiant. He caught his breath, his eyes filling with tears. He blinked, letting them run down his cheeks, and took a deep breath, standing as still as his body would allow. His heart raced—was she coming over here? She lifted her leg over the rail, paused for a split second, then, apparently, thought better of it. He exhaled his relief, grateful that she didn't come over and knock on his door. He simply didn't know what he would say. He had behaved horribly and wondered if he could ever recover and get back in her good graces.

He talked to his sister yesterday and told her that he had given up the idea of moving back to Reston. He didn't ask her if she had seen Rose, didn't even mention her name. Laurie, though, found a way to weave her into the discussion. He didn't know how to interpret the two of them having dinner together; he wondered how much of his baggage Laurie had shared.

Through the glass, he watched Rose bend down and pet the cat. Laurie managed to work into their conversation that Rose and Denny are, indeed, getting divorced. Fran had no idea what to think about that, what to believe. He saw what he saw. A split-second image of two people with a history that he would never be able to compete with. A gentle hand resting on an arm. A sign of reassurance. A symbol of love. His gut had told him to back away, to leave Rose to work on her marriage. His gut had never failed him in the past.

He slid down the wall until he was on the floor, feeling like an idiot. By the time he turned his head to resume watching, Rose was gone. He stood up and opened the door, sticking his head out just long enough to look around. He sighed and closed the door, then plopped down on the couch.

A change in color—a shadow, perhaps—something subtle out of the corner of his eye grabbed him. By the time he made it to the sliding glass door, he could see Rose in her purple hoodie and bare feet, walking toward the water.

51

___

Darlene slipped her purple hoodie over her head and stepped outside. The wind—nonexistent five minutes ago, stung her face and made her eyes water. She lifted the hood onto her head and tied it tight, tucking loose strands of hair—too short to gather into a ponytail, but long enough to be a nuisance blowing around her face—under it. She didn't know how long she'd last on the beach but felt compelled to sit in the sand and watch the waves. Trotting quickly down the steps, her foot landed the wrong way and she tumbled, face first, landing in a not so graceful belly flop.

She sat up, spitting sand out of her mouth, rubbing the bottom of her foot, hoping she didn't sprain something. She noticed an object laying in the beach grass, near the air conditioning unit under her balcony. She took a deep breath and lowered herself onto her hands and knees and crawled toward what looked like an old, glass jar. She brushed the sand off her face and out of her eyes. When she stood, she was still covered in sand; she swiped at her hoodie and jeans, getting as much of it off as possible.

Wait a minute. She bent down to get a closer look. A shoelace? Tied around the top of the jar? A shoelace from someone's dirty old sneaker? She lifted the jar, suddenly feeling like a kid on a treasure hunt. A treasure indeed. Fran. But why? Why would he leave a jar of chocolates in the beach grass, under her balcony? She held it close to her heart and walked toward the water.

SHE CONSIDERED CALLING HIM. Or texting him. Or running back up to his condo and banging on the door. How long had the jar been there? A while, she suspected, based on the cement-like crust of salty sand that was plastered to the glass, just below the lid. She scraped it with her fingernail, wondering what to make of the jar. The whole thing mystified her. Now, she just wanted to talk to him. But Laurie's words from dinner the other night were like cold water thrown on her face: *He wants to move back to Northern Virginia.* Darlene couldn't compete with that. She felt unjustifiably upset that Fran had not mentioned this to her the evening they spent together, before the tray fiasco. He owed her nothing. Perhaps he left because of the tray fiasco. No matter when he had decided he wanted to move, the result was the same. Darlene could not compete.

Afraid to open the jar, she set it in her lap as Fran worked his way back into the forefront of her brain. Her hand hovered over the lid, ready to unscrew it, but something kept stopping her. Maybe she was afraid of disturbing something sacred. This jar of chocolates represented the last link to Fran, perhaps something he had planned to give her before she broke the tray. She promised herself that she would not eat them, because if the chocolates were gone, Fran would be gone too. Never mind that he was already gone. Her heart knew no logic.

She watched the waves as she tugged at the shoelace. Out of the corner of her eye, she saw the one-legged seagull hopping toward her. She pulled the shoelace again, and it finally gave way, coming easily undone. She let the sandy string slip through her fingers and into her lap. She held it up to the sun, stretching it between her hands, as far as it would go. An incredibly long shoelace, clearly from a running shoe. Fran's running shoe. She twirled it around her wrist like a bracelet, tucking the ends in to secure it. Why a shoelace? A subtle hint that Fran thinks she needs to exercise? Lose weight? Run? And as if she had a superpower that made her thoughts materialize, a slightly overweight woman with red hair jogged by. A glimpse into her future, perhaps? Only one with long, straight hair. She patted the top of her head. Even if she decided to let her hair grow, her curls would sprout outward and never hang down elegantly. If Fran wanted her, it had to be on her terms, just the way she was. She refused to be anyone's project.

She lifted her hoodie and grabbed a fistful of flesh. Yep. The shoelace was surely meant to be a clue into Fran's mindset, his bicycle riding, athletic mindset. She opened her hand and released her roll, unaware that she had been holding it so tightly until she almost heard it sigh in relief. Fran could not possibly find her attractive, despite what he said to her the other night. Words she would not soon forget. *All I see is a fun, vibrant, healthy woman.*

She threw the jar, watching it thump onto the wet sand, gain momentum, and roll toward the water. The seagull hobbled away. She watched him make his way back, then think better of it, flying off to someplace safe. She continued watching until her little friend became indistinguishable from all the other seagulls on the beach.

The waves lapped against the sand, and she imagined them swallowing the jar, carrying it out to sea. Years from now, someone on a boat would see it bobbing along. A message in a bottle! Oh, wait! No, not a message! Chocolates in a bottle! Mana from heaven! An answer to someone's prayer. *Chocolates in a bottle, yeah. Chocolates in a bottle, yeah.* Darlene stood up, singing out loud, The Police, and their iconic sound. *Walked out this morning, don't believe what I saw, a hundred billion chocolates washed up on the shore.* Molly Ringwald in The Breakfast Club had nothing on Darlene's '80s dance moves. *I hope that someone gets my, I hope that someone gets my chocolates in a bottle, yeah.*

The tide came in, and a wave came dangerously close to the jar. If nothing else, she could give the damned thing to Rachel, as a hostess gift. She ran toward the jar, wincing as her bare feet hit the cold foamy water. She rescued it just in time—like a lifeguard scooping up a toddler—just before it was about to go under.

52

Fran felt rudderless. Helpless and directionless in a way that was new to him. Even in the throes of grief right after Sadie died, he had a purpose. The purpose of logistics—putting one foot in front of the other, breathing, eating enough to function, managing Jackie's grief, managing his own, barely keeping the deli afloat. The ache of her death never really receded. Not even now, two years later. Yet, even with the pain—his constant companion—he always felt like he knew what he was doing, where he was going. Until Rose upended his role as a grieving spouse. He felt like one of those sad-faced clowns in a comedy routine, shuffling in circles, each hand pointing in a different direction, covering a lot of ground but getting nowhere. He didn't like it. Not at all.

"Sadie, come on." He pivoted on one foot, scanning the living room. "Can't we just talk?" He let himself fall onto the couch. "I'm not ready to say goodbye." He pulled the heart-shaped ceramic fragment out of his pocket and twirled it between his thumb and forefinger. The side he hadn't sanded enough felt rough. He flipped it over, and closed his eyes, letting the smooth side soothe him like a kid with a lovey. Or an old man with a worry stone. He sat up. "What am I worried about?" He held the stone in front of his face, waiting for an answer. "Tell me." He shoved it back in his pocket, frustrated that Sadie wouldn't talk to him.

He stood and stretched, making his way back to the sliding glass door. He watched Rose sitting in the sand, talking to the waves, no doubt. He opened the door to see if he could hear her, but the wind was too strong, the waves too loud. He closed the door and paced the room. *Just go out there.* He felt frozen, like a deer in headlights. *Since when did I become...shy?* Compulsively sticking his hand in his pocket and worrying the piece of ceramic, he wondered if he was afraid of rejection. He didn't know Rose. Not really. He had sensed a connection, but maybe that had been wishful thinking. And then the tray breaking just seconds before he tried to muster the courage to kiss her was like a blaring horn warning him to back off. He had to back off. After all, he had broken his promise to Sadie by even thinking about kissing Rose. Breaking promises unnerved him. He was a man of his word and kept his word in the big things and small. If there was one thing he felt good about, it was that. He promised he would love Sadie and only Sadie. Even as she lay dying, he vowed to love her— only and always.

He went back to the door, took a deep breath, and shook his head. He couldn't do it. He answered his own question. *What am I worried about? I'm worried about leaving my wife. I can't do it. I can't betray Sadie.*

He closed the blinds and went upstairs to his bedroom and plopped down on the bed. He came dangerously close to breaking his promise. Dangerously close. He thought back to that night, how close he had come to kissing Rose, and how the tray broke almost immediately, symbolizing him breaking his promise. *How stupid am I?* He couldn't believe it had taken him this long to figure it out. He shuddered and cringed, remembering the jar of chocolates. Thank God he never got the chance to give it to her. Thank God. Seeing Rose and Denny together on the couch slapped him in the face with reality. Sure, he lamented. Sure, he let his fragile ego be hurt. Thank God. Another mistake was overtaken by the blast of a loud horn. Another decision he didn't need to make.

Fran held the sacred piece of ceramic above his head, tossing it from one hand to the other. After three catches, he missed; it flew across the bedroom, hitting the sliding glass door and landing on the hardwood floor in a pulverized mess.

He slowly became aware of his knees on the hardwood floor. He scooped the mess into his hand and stood, the door a gateway to his future. He stepped onto the balcony—the balcony where he first encountered Rose. He could see her on the beach, tossing a fairly large object into the water. He inched his way closer to the rail, watching her from above. His heart, working independently of his brain, guided him back into the condo, straight to the small urn on his dresser. He stuck his hand inside and pinched a tiny amount of dust between his fingers, mixing it with the ceramic fragments in his hand.

Back on the balcony, he opened his hand and let the wind carry Sadie away. He turned to go inside, then stopped when he saw her in the doorway tilting her head and pointing at the ocean. He reached out to hold her, but when he blinked, she was gone. This time he knew it was forever. He removed his wedding ring, kissed it, and dropped it into the urn.

53

Out of breath and panting, Darlene clutched the wet jar against her chest. Her feet, no longer shocked by the cold, sunk in the sand as the water came up around her ankles, then receded in a rush, leaving her jeans wet and plastered to her legs. She took a few steps in, shocked anew as a wave crashed against her knees.

"Cold! Freezing!" She jumped and shuddered, and when the next wave came, she jumped again. When the shock of cold water, now to her waist, wore off, she stared at a ship on the horizon. She closed her eyes and counted to one hundred, then opened them. The ship looked like it had not moved at all. Okay, maybe an inch or two. From that distance, probably a mile or more. The wind picked up, sending a bone-curdling chill through her body.

"I don't blame you. I would have thrown it away too." The waves broke around Fran's ankles as he stood, hands in his pockets, fleece jacket zipped all the way up to the bottom of his chin, hair blowing in every different direction.

Darlene walked toward him, the bottom of her hoodie wet, the shirt underneath it wet, everything soaking wet. She didn't know how she could stand the cold another minute. Yet something kept her from running up the sand and into her warm condo. "How long have you been standing here?"

"Long enough so that I can't feel my feet anymore." He crossed his arms over his chest and rubbed. "And long enough to know you shouldn't quit your day job to become a dancer. Or singer for that matter."

Darlene's face flushed at the thought of him seeing her crazed display. On second thought, no, she wouldn't allow herself to be embarrassed. She derived great satisfaction, tossing the jar at the water. She walked up the beach to the dry sand and plopped down facing the waves. "I did quit my day job."

Fran raised an eyebrow. "Please tell me it wasn't to try out for *Dancing with the Stars*." He looked down. "May I join you?"

Darlene nodded but didn't offer an explanation about her job. Instead, she sought an answer from him. He lowered himself down into the sand until he was next to her, close enough that their legs almost touched. She moved her leg an inch in the opposite direction and crossed it over her other leg, the jar balancing in the sand between her thigh and Fran's. She picked it up and looked at him, raising an eyebrow. The ship was no longer visible.

"I see you found it," he said.

"Yeah. Just a little while ago." She tried to read him, but he was still staring at the ocean. She couldn't see his eyes.

"You didn't open it?"

"No."

He finally turned to look at her, then gently lifted the jar out of her hands. "You should have just let it go out to sea."

"Give me back my jar." She reached out to take it from him, but he twisted his arms out of the way, making the jar impossible to grab.

"Who says it's your jar?"

"Isn't it?" Could this all have been a big misunderstanding? Her face flushed as heat radiated from her toes all the way to the top of her head. She was sweating, despite the cold. How stupid of her to assume he had left the jar for her to find.

"Why were you throwing it away?" Fran gently placed the jar in her lap.

"Why did you leave it under the balcony, in the sand?"

"It's a long story," he said.

"I didn't throw it away."

"You did throw it away."

"Maybe so, but it's here now." She looked sideways at him; she didn't mention that she'd rescued the jar because she didn't want to see good chocolates go to waste. She tried to open the lid, but it would not budge.

"Please don't open it." Fran took it from her, with a little too much force.

"Hey!" She grabbed it back. "I'm hungry."

"Don't open it."

Darlene suddenly wondered if Fran had wanted to poison her. She eyed the chocolates in the jar, individually wrapped in red foil. They looked like her favorite chocolates at first glance, but upon closer examination, the shapes were somehow off; they looked bulky and haphazardly wrapped. *How did I not notice this before*? She struggled with the lid until it finally loosened, watching Fran out of the corner of her eye as she lifted the lid off the jar. He was looking straight ahead, his eyes tightly closed.

She lowered her fingers into the jar and plucked out three chocolates. The wrappers, ordinarily smooth and flush, looked like they had been unwrapped and rewrapped. Clearly tampered with. *He is trying to poison me*! With a pounding heart, she started on the first piece, and before she had it completely unwrapped, a tiny sliver of paper fell out and floated down, landing in her lap. She unfolded it. Number 37: Have a picnic with McDonald's Happy Meals. She burst out laughing, picking up the jar, and examining its contents. Fran looked at her, then looked away. She popped the chocolate into her mouth without reservation. If Fran wanted to poison her, there were much simpler ways to do it. She folded the note and placed it in the jar, then unwrapped another chocolate. Number 12: Visit a bug zoo. She laughed, wondering what these were all about.

"Francisco-o-o-o." He turned to look at her, his eyes holding something she had not seen in them before, something she could not quite identify. Hope? Reservation? Fear? "These sound like date ideas." She continued searching his eyes. "Which makes no sense, since you're moving back to Reston." He didn't respond, and she tap-danced, desperate to fill the space, suddenly worried that she was making a fool of herself. "A bug zoo! Is that even a thing?"

"Rose." He took the jar and put the lid back on. "That night, the night you were at my house, the night the tray broke." He hesitated. "After you left, Sadie came and said—"

"No!" Darlene stood. "I can't do this. I can't be in a relationship with a man and his dead wife. I just can't." She was suddenly cold again. Very, very cold.

"Rose, wait." He held the jar out to her. "Please don't go."

Reluctantly, she sat back down but didn't take the jar. The least she could do was let him say what he needed to say. Then she would be done with him—finally.

"I made these for you," he said. "The idea came to me, and once I started, I couldn't stop until I reached fifty. Fifty chocolates for your fiftieth birthday." He stared at her. "And yes, they are date ideas, fifty of them." He held the jar out to her, and this time, she took it. "I came over the next morning to give it to you." He shifted, burrowing his feet into the sand. "And to apologize for my appalling behavior when the tray broke." He looked at her. "The thing is, Rose, the tray, well, Sadie broke the tray."

She put the jar down and covered her hears. "No! No, no, no, no, no!" She looked straight ahead. "Dead people don't arbitrarily show up and break things." What would her grandmother think of this? A sign? Of course. "It's obvious that Sadie doesn't want you to have anything to do with me."

"That's just it. She did it to get my attention. I was holding too tightly to everything that had anything to do with her. Including the tray." He looked at the water. "She got tired of it, I guess." He turned toward Darlene. "Look, Rose, I came over that morning to give you the jar. I was about to knock on your slider, and I guess I hesitated too long. I saw you and Denny on the couch. I made an assumption, felt like a fool, and left. I dropped the jar in the sand, then kicked it into the grass under the balcony. I never went back for it." He searched her eyes. "I'm not moving to Reston, by the way."

Darlene opened the jar and pulled out a chocolate, taking her time unwrapping it; she gently pushed it into Fran's mouth. She unfolded the little piece of paper and read it out loud. "Number 4: Karaoke." She laughed. "You already know how badly I sing." She reached for another chocolate.

"Whoa. Let's take this slow," Fran said, laughing.

"The chocolates, or this?" She locked eyes with him.

"Yes? Both? I don't know."

She ignored him and read another message. "Number 21: Create a new beer recipe." She smiled. "Now, that's something I could get behind." She moved an inch closer, letting her leg rest against his. They sat in the sand, legs touching, Darlene not knowing what to do next. They sat and stared at the water until the cold overtook them. He put his arms around her and pulled her close.

AFTERWORD

I'm delighted that you decided to pick up *Over the Rail*. These days, an author's success depends quite a bit on reviews: the good, the bad, and the ugly. I would be hugely grateful if you could take a few minutes and post a review. Whether you liked the book, felt lukewarm about it, or absolutely hated it, potential readers want to know what you think. Feel free to post a review on Goodreads, the retailer of your choice, your own blog, wherever you desire.

JOIN MY ONLINE FAMILY

One of the things I enjoy most about writing is building a relationship with my readers. I occasionally send newsletters with details on new releases, special offers, and other surprises.

I would love to stay in touch. Join my online family to receive updates on Book 2 in the *Over the Rail* contemporary romance series. You can sign up at https://mailchi.mp/lynnstewart/subscribers and receive Book 1 in my *Stay Back!* Trilogy for free.

ACKNOWLEDGMENTS

The experience writing this book differed wildly from writing my previous three novels.

On November 1, 2019, I stared at a blank screen, intending to write the first 50,000 words during National Novel Writing Month (NANOW-RIMO). With no outline or any real sense of the story, I tippity-tapped away on my keyboard and met my word-count goal by the end of the month. Alas, the end result was a piece of s**t. I stepped away from the story to enjoy the holidays in December; in early January, I sat back down to re-work the first half and write the second. I was barely hitting my stride when the coronavirus happened with all of its associated lockdowns and restrictions.

For the most part, living in lockdown-land wasn't much different from my regular day-to-day life. Okay, maybe a little. If I'm truthful a lot. As a writer and an introvert, spending time alone at my laptop and in my own head is normal. Still, I missed the daily interactions with people outside of my household.

Despite all the extra time on my hands, I struggled to make significant progress on the book. I spent the first few weeks of the pandemic wringing my hands. I was huddled over my keyboard as usual. Instead of writing, though, I spent countless hours online, reading about the virus. I drove myself (and my poor husband) crazy. So, I stopped, allowing myself only a half-hour of surfing during each "work" day. Sometimes I failed at that—miserably. But I tried, and it helped. Praying helped too—a lot.

I sincerely hope you enjoyed meeting Darlene and Fran as much as I enjoyed creating them. Their story doesn't stop at the end of this book, so stay tuned for updates on Books 2 and 3 in the series.

I give my heartfelt thanks to the following people: Jim Takajy (aka Cujo) for his "Red Team" review and asking the kinds of questions that made me revisit a few key story elements. He even chiseled away at my opposition to semicolons. Lisa Ray for reading through the physical proof and catching the "gotchas" that everyone else missed. Maiden Maryland owners Tammy and Tracy Lynndee for carrying my books in their shop. And finally, my husband, Mike (aka Sweet Petunia), for his unconditional love, support, plot discussions over wine, many read-throughs of my manuscript, and making me laugh.

As restrictions lift and you begin to venture out, please stay cautious, safe, and healthy!

*P.S. I would be remiss if I didn't mention the fact that Darlene's favorite chocolates are my favorite chocolates too. As you may have already guessed, Darlene enjoys Dove® Promises (dark). My obsession with them involves eating three squares every day after lunch, sitting at my laptop. Remember the blank screen I told you about? I ate my three chocolates while I stared at that screen, wondering where to begin the story. Let me say that even with a fairly detailed outline, the first few sentences are the hardest. As I enjoyed my treat, I envisioned my protagonist standing in front of a mirror, unwrapping a Dove® chocolate. Voilà! My sentence practically wrote itself. Through many revisions, that sentence ended up not being the first sentence. But my character now had an obsession that made her a bit more lovable (to me). In the story, where I quote the sayings on the inside of the wrappers, well, those are real, taken straight from the Dove® chocolates that I unwrapped (and ate).

*I have no affiliation with Dove® or Mars, Inc. and I am not receiving compensation, or profiting in any, way by modeling Darlene's chocolates after Dove® or mentioning the brand in my postscript above.

BOOK GROUP QUESTIONS

Cozy up with a glass wine or beer, a Hawaiian pizza, and, of course, a bag of chocolates!

1. The story is told from the perspectives of Darlene and Fran. In the beginning, we find each one at a crossroads of sorts. How did each character evolve through the book?

2. Darlene has a complicated relationship with her parents and sister, something she, at age fifty, is just beginning to understand. Did you ever have an epiphany regarding your family dynamics? If so, how old were you? How did the relationship change as you changed?

3. Fran couldn't seem to move on after his wife's death. His grieving process involved very "real" visits from Sadie. The grieving process is complicated and differs for everyone. If you feel safe doing so, discuss how you grieved the loss of a loved one.

4. Fran comes up with fifty "date" ideas to do with Rose. What was one of your most creative dates? Who came up with the idea, you or your date?

5. What do you think was the defining motivation for Darlene to leave behind the hope of reconciling with Denny?

6. Have you ever felt an instant attraction to someone? What was it about the person that attracted you?

7. Darlene's poor self-image was born out of years of being body-shamed by her parents and constant comparisons to her sister. Yet, when she looks at photos taken during various points in her life, she sees herself in a very different light. Was there ever a period in your life when you felt ugly, only to look at a photo, years later, and see yourself differently?

8. How would you describe the relationship between Darlene and Denny? Do you think they could have saved their marriage? If so, how and why?

9. There is a scene in the book where Darlene flashes back to her father, making her give back a Christmas coloring book. She was in second grade and felt embarrassed and different. As a child, did you ever feel different? How did you cope? How do you think about it now, as an adult?

10. Darlene is obsessed with Dove chocolates. Do you have any food obsessions? What are they? Do they bring you joy or make you feel guilty?

11. How would you have reacted to Fran when he stepped onto the balcony and started sining with *Titanic* Rose?

12. Discuss Darlene and Fran's 12-year age difference. Do you think this age difference will become an issue as they both continue to grow older?

13. How did you feel with each decade milestone birthday? Did one decade hold more significance for you than the others? What were the best and worst aspects of those ages?

14. There were hints of other characters in the story—mentions, but no real development (Remi, Shelly, Jackie, Rachel). Which minor character would you have liked to learn more about? Why?

15. Is your house (or apartment) in close proximity to your neighbors? If so, how do you feel about it? Do you like your neighbors? Did the relationship with your neighbors grow over time, or become fraught over time?

16. Do you enjoy watching house hunting reality shows, home remodeling shows, etc. Which ones do you love? Which ones do you hate?

17. Darlene and Denny followed through with being on the house hunting how, even as their marriage crumbled. Why do you think they made that decision? What would you have done differently in their place?

18. Fran, at age 62, muses about riding his bicycle across the country. Darlene's mother, in her mid-70's, wrote a book. Have you ever dreamed of doing something (athletic or otherwise) but feel you are too old? Explore the concept of being "too old" to do certain things and what that means to you.

19. Fran freely admits that he loves Hawaiian pizza and that Sadie chided him for it. Do you have a favorite food that garners laughter and snickers from your family and friends?

20. When does Darlene begin to see Fran in a positive light? Why do you think her perspective changed?

21. Other people's truths about you are not the real or only truths about you (particularly the negative). How do you silence the untrue voices and see yourself the way you really are, the way you were meant to be?

22. There is a Robert Fulghum quote in the beginning of the book: "We're all a little weird. And life is a little weird. And when we find someone whose weirdness is compatible with ours, we join up with them and fall into mutually satisfying weirdness—and call it love—true love." Do you have someone in your life that you can be "weird" with. Describe that relationship.

ABOUT THE AUTHOR

Lynn Stewart lives in Cambridge, Maryland with her husband and their four bicycles (Rocky, Red, Whitey, and Streak). This is her fourth novel.

For updates visit:
lynnstewart.ink

ALSO BY LYNN STEWART

Stay Back! Trilogy

Book 1: Stay Back!

Book 2: Back And Forth

Book 3: Stay Here

Follow retired cop John Butterfield's story as he navigates the aftermath of his wife's brutal rape in *Stay Back!*, is thrown into an unconventional mission during the 9/11 attacks in *Back And Forth* and finds himself face-to-face with the kid he walked away from six years before in *Stay Here*.